Risen

A novel of death, resurrection, and life everlasting

Parable Publications

by
Susan Brooks Smith

Risen, A Novel of Death Resurrection and Life Everlasting

Parable Publications is a division of McDougal Publishing, Hagerstown, Maryland.

Published by:

Parable Publications

P.O. Box 3595
Hagerstown, MD 21742-3595

Library of Congress Catalog Card Number: 97-71093

ISBN 1-884369-54-5

Printed in the United States of America
For Worldwide Distribution

Dedicated to the memory of
Katherine Costello "Katie" Valentine,
My Grandmother, my Nannie,
the one who first introduced me to
Messiah Yeshua

Also dedicated to
Irving Brooks
My Jewish Papa
who just by being himself
taught me how to love God's chosen people

Jesus, when he had cried again with a loud voice, yielded up the ghost. And, behold, the veil of the temple was rent in twain from the top to the bottom; and the earth did quake, and the rocks rent; And the graves were opened; and many bodies of the saints which slept arose, And came out of the graves after his resurrection, and went into the holy city, and appeared unto many.

Matthew 27:50-53

HANNAH knelt beside the body of her father, the slope of her shoulders revealing the deep despair of her soul. She tried to memorize this last view she would ever have of her precious *abba*, every small detail, every tiny aspect of his being. Still the muted brown and red stripes of his garment, the soft reddish-brown of his beard, the sun-sprinkled freckles of his gentle face kept dissolving before her in her own tears. Finally she took his big calloused hand in her own small ones and let her head drop to his shoulder, the same shoulder on which he had carried her when she was a small child.

"Oh, Abba, I'm so sorry. Please forgive me."

She said the words over and over again as if by repeating them she might find some small measure of peace for her tormented heart. But a single scene kept replaying itself in her mind, another scene, the scene which had taken place only the day before ... .

✡   ✡   ✡

Itzak had come from the boats early that afternoon. Over his sinewy arm he had carried a small handnet which had torn against the sharp rocks along the coast of the sea and would have to be mended that very night. Yet even with this task ahead of him, he had seemed unusually happy, smiling, even whistling as he curled his way through the small streets of Capernaum, the little town that sloped upward from the sea as though it were reaching out to touch the snow-capped peaks of Mount Hermon above. It lay just north of the Sea of Galilee, which was in reality not a sea at all but a wide fresh-water lake. He, like all who lived in Capernaum, took great pride in the belief that the prophet, Nahum, had once resided there and their city had been named in his honor. Itzak strode from the tiny inlet of blue water around which Capernaum had grown up, past the shining white limestone synagogue, through the market streets lined with small shops and canopied stalls, to the little house he occupied with his wife of fifteen years, Dinah, and their seven children. Hannah was the eldest and the only girl; it was to her he had come as he slipped through the small door in the larger entry gate and stepped into the courtyard surrounded on three sides by the home they all shared.

The packed earth beneath his feet had been paved with small stones set in a random arrangement. Around the perimeter of the court, small shrubs and bushes added a touch of green and hid the cistern which held the rainwater that cascaded from the roof in winter. On one side of the house, a stone staircase led from the court to the balustraded roof where the family often took their rest on hot summer evenings. It was there in the courtyard that Hannah and her mother were just beginning the supper preparations around an open fire.

"My daughter," he had begun hopefully as he lifted Hannah to her feet with one work-worn hand grasping each of her delicate shoulders. "I have news, my daughter, news I trust will please you." Itzak's excitement was bubbling over, contagious, infectious.

"Oh, Abba, what is it? Tell me!" Hannah had danced about him as his deep laughter echoed through the small courtyard, her heart pounding, her face flushing.

Itzak had turned toward her, placed his hands on his hips, and allowed his barrel chest to puff as he gazed at the lovely young woman his daughter had become. She was slim as a reed but with womanly curves that promised many strong children. Her features were as beautifully sculpted as any of the chiseled statues around the fancy villas the hated Romans had built in Tiberias, her smile revealing even white teeth. Her thick flaxen hair fell in gentle waves and came to rest below the wide white sash that held her pale blue tunic at the waist. But it was her eyes, so like her mother's, long-lashed eyes as blue as the sea on which he sailed, eyes that expressed every feeling of her soul and won the hearts of all who knew her. She was a prize, a gem, a jewel, and he had found exactly the right setting for her.

"Aha, Daughter. You would know my news even before supper, would you? So *Ammah*, shall I tell her?"

Dinah had barely looked up from the cooking pot she was stirring with a heavy wooden paddle. As the fire beneath the pot had licked its sides, its glow had also lit Dinah's face revealing a woman of great beauty and few wrinkles whose many pregnancies had not spoiled her soft feminine figure. Only a barely discernible nod which shifted her long hair just slightly had registered her acquiescence.

Hannah did not notice that her mother did not seem to share her father's bursting enthusiasm at the news she was about to be given. "Abba, don't tease me. I can't bear it. Please tell me," Hannah had pleaded, dropping her chin demurely and casting those liquid blue eyes upward with just the slightest flutter of the fringe of lashes. It worked every time.

"I am helpless before you, Child." Abba had conceded. "So then, what would you say if I were to tell you that this very day, on your behalf, I entered into a contract, a very special contract, a contract of marriage?"

Hannah hadn't been able to stand still then. She had twirled around him. She was to be espoused and next year this time she would be a bride and maybe the year after that, if the Holy One was gracious, she might even be a mother. It was the ultimate fulfillment of all of her dreams.

It was the ultimate fulfillment of every young girl's dreams, to be a wife, a mother. And it was the highest goal the Holy One had set for every woman to achieve. Now Hannah's life would really begin.

In an instant of time the faces of every comely young unmarried man in the village had flashed before her. There was Hasrah. He was so handsome but his name meant poor and so he was. No, Hannah knew Abba would never place her in the ramshackle home of such a one. There was Nathan, too, the youngest of Rabbi Tikvah's nine sons and the one who always came to the well to draw water when his mother was unable. They had not spoken since childhood, not since she had become a woman and begun wearing her veil in public signaling that talk between them had ceased to be appropriate. But his strong hand had touched hers every so lightly one day as he helped her lift the heavy stone cover from the well's mouth and his dark eyes had sought out Hannah's as both drew from the cool clear water. Hannah would always drop her gaze just a moment after their eyes met, yet the unspoken message was clear.

But, Hannah had reasoned within herself, Abba had not been particularly fond of Rabbi Tikvah since the Rabbi Yeshua ben Yosef had spoken in the synagogue for the first time some two years before. Something about His gentle voice, His eyes as blue as the Sea of Galilee itself, His wonderful words about the Holy One just as though He knew Him personally, had won her father over. Abba had wanted to hear only Him after that. No, Hannah knew it would not be Nathan.

"Abba, tell me quickly or my heart will surely stop," Hannah begged, her hands flying to her bosom.

Abba had laughed his big booming laugh that filled the courtyard with its resonant tone. "Yes, my daughter. You shall know this very moment. The husband I have chosen for you owns his own fishing boat and with your dowry of another small fishing vessel from my own fleet will become quite the young business man. Last year he earned enough to care for his own needs and those of his father before his recent death and, I might add, enough to put away a tidy sum to purchase for himself the fairest of brides. And he has chosen you, my child. I speak of none other than ..." He had paused creating a drama fit for a Roman amphitheater as Hannah's mind raced. "I speak of none other than David ben Asaph." With the announcement, Abba had held up the golden ring that symbolized the betrothal.

Hannah had frozen in place then. Her face had frozen as well. The happy smile of moments ago had broken into a thousand sharp pieces. The expectant eyes of seconds before had filled with tears and terror. Her hands remained at her sides refusing to receive the ring her newly-espoused husband had sent to her.

"Abba, no! I cannot! The man is an unbeliever! No girl who truly loves the Holy One and truly wishes to obey Him could marry this man. Before the Holy One, I will not do this thing. Please do not ask it of me," Hannah had pleaded and insisted all at the same time.

Dinah had turned her head only slightly, just enough so that her deep blue eyes could peer from beneath the curtain of light brown hair to view both father and daughter. She had known it would be thus but she had been unable to dissuade Itzak from the course he had set just as she had been unable to dissuade him from many of the things he wanted to do since he had heard Rabbi Yeshua speak. Now the tithe of the fish he caught went to feed the Rabbi's disciples or the tithe of the *shekels* he got for them went into the little leather bag carried by the one they called Yehuda. Now, as if all of that were not bad enough, her husband wished to give his own daughter in marriage to another of the Rabbi's followers. She could only wonder, wonder and pray that no such terrible thing would ever come upon her only daughter.

Father and daughter had stared at each other then, both heartbroken, both disbelieving. Their silence hung in the air as heavily as the veil hung in the Temple at Yerushalayim. Itzak had spoken first, his voice soothing and tender.

"David is no more an unbeliever than I am, my child. He loves our blessed Holy One in a way I hope you, too, will someday know. Like I myself, he has met Messiah, the One promised of old. To meet Him does not mean that one loves the Holy One less; it means that one is able to love our blessed Holy One even more."

"Oh, Abba, I love you more than you can know," Hannah had countered. "But I do not understand what has happened to you since you met that Rabbi. How can He be Messiah when He looks so ... so ... so ordinary. When Messiah comes, He will be a glorious King, a magnificent General. He will set us free. You taught me this yourself from the time I was a small child. Now here is this Rabbi you claim to be Messiah. Yet still we suffer under the heel of Rome. How can this be? How can you believe this? How can you want to give me in marriage to a man who believes this?"

"I not only believe this, Child; I know this. David knows it, too. I can only pray that someday soon you and your mother and your brothers will know it as well."

Hannah's heart fell. So did her eyes. She shook her head knowing it was hopeless.

"Oh, Hannah, my dear Hannah," Itzak began again. "Have I not told you how it happened for me? That day in the synagogue, He taught as no man has ever taught before. My heart was on fire within me. I even saw a man freed from an evil spirit that day, a man I know had been in torment for years. Still I was not certain.

"Then there was that day when He taught a great throng of people out on the hillside on the other side of the sea where I had put in during the heat of the day. Somehow He spoke to every man there. Somehow He knew the concern of every heart, even my own, and He met it. I saw people healed that day. And still I wavered.

"But then He fed us, fed thousands of us with nothing more than a small child's lunch. Somehow He made it enough. When I received a fish from His follower's hand, I looked at it carefully. Now, Hannah, if there is one thing I know it is fish, and this fish was like no other I have ever seen, more perfect, more beautiful, more delicious, more satisfying. Only the Holy One Himself could make a fish like those that once swam in the four rivers of Eden. It was then that I knew and I believed. I've never doubted since, not even for a single moment. He is Messiah, Hannah, and I want nothing more for my precious daughter than to know that she dwells with one who knows Him, too. My daughter, you must trust me in this; you must obey me in this."

Hannah's voice was small and sad. "Abba, I cannot believe and I cannot be wife to one who does. Always you taught me that I must love the Holy One with all my heart and all my mind and all my strength. You said nothing of this ... Messiah. I have never before disobeyed you, Abba, but I must disobey you in this. I cannot marry David ben Asaph."

Itzak's face had grown hard then but in his eyes it had been plain that Hannah had broken his heart. "The contract has been signed, Daughter." Again he held up the ring that sealed the bargain and again Hannah refused it, folding her arms and turning away. "You will not disgrace your family in such a manner," Itzak went on. "You will obey me and you will marry David next spring. I will say no more." Neither Itzak nor Hannah had known how prophetic those words would be.

Hannah's face had grown hard, too. "Abba, I will never forgive you if you sell me in marriage to such a man. I will hate you until the day I die ... childless ... for I shall never let him touch me."

With that, Hannah had fled to her sleeping mat. She ate nothing that evening. She had cried herself to sleep and dreamt of some terrible monster who meant to steal away her virtue as he stole away her heart from her Lord. She woke to the sun's first rays but lay with her face to the wall until her father had said his morning prayers, eaten one small barley cake, and taken the eldest of her brothers, Micah, to the boats.

✿   ✿   ✿

Everyone said the sudden spring storm had come out of nowhere just as storms often did over the usually calm Sea of Galilee. Azure blue water had turned deathly black as thunder crashed and lightning split the angry skies. Calm ripples had become raging torrents which tossed tiny fishing boats to and fro with abandon. Abba had struggled to bring his small craft to harbor before it was too late but the harder he worked, the more strongly the tide seemed to be dragging him irrevocably out into the deep. When his boat was finally torn apart to the sound of timbers cracking and crashing all around him, Abba had managed to save Micah by lashing him to the largest piece of wreckage and pushing him toward the distant shore but he had had no strength left to save himself. His last conscious thought had been a prayer to the Holy One for his wife, his sons, and for his precious Hannah. Later that day, after the restless waves had finally subsided, other fishermen, friends of Abba's, had found him and carried him home for the last time.

✿   ✿   ✿

In the distance, Hannah could now hear the death wails of the mourners, her mother's above them all, and her own tears seemed to know no end. She had broken her father's heart and she knew it as surely as she knew it had killed him. He must have had his thoughts on their quarrel instead of on the darkening skies. There could be no forgiveness for her, not now, not ever.

Soon people would come and prepare Abba's body for

burial. They would wash him, as if the sea had not done that well enough already, and wrap him in lengths of clean white cloth laced with fragrant spices to take away the stench of death. Then, before the sun went down, he would be placed on a cold stone slab in a temporary tomb. There he would lay until he could be taken to the family crypt outside Yerushalayim, the city in which he had been born and where he had lived until he had come north to take over the small fishing business of an uncle who had died leaving no sons. In Yerushalayim, he would be laid beside Grandfather Eban and all of Hannah's other ancestors. Hannah would have to turn her back then just as she had done on that last morning and leave her father behind forever. Hannah would never again see his familiar face, never again hear his resounding laughter, never again find peace and safety in the circle of his embrace.

"Oh, my Lord, what have I done?" Hannah screamed in an agony like none she had ever known. "Even You can't forgive me now." She buried her head in her father's shoulder and found in his tunic the salty taste of her own tears.

Suddenly Hannah came bolt upright and stared at the ceiling as if she had gone mad. "You, You Messiah, if that's what You are," she raged. "My abba said You could even raise the dead. So raise the dead now! Raise him! Do You hear me, Messiah Yeshua or whoever You are? Raise my abba now!" One clenched fist challenged a silent Heaven for just a moment before Hannah collapsed on her father's chest one last time.

❧ 2 ❧

LOST in his thoughts, Yakov heard the cry of the child as though it pierced the night from some distant place rather than in his own house. He knew the wetnurse would tend to her needs so, as he had done many times before, he simply refused to hear his daughter's small voice. Instead he comforted himself with vivid images from another time played out against a pale ceiling illuminated in the flickering shadows of a bronze lampstand, each little bowl atop its seven branches casting its own particular pattern across the wall.

But there was one awful problem with Yakov's reverie and he knew it all too well. He always began with the happy halcyon days he had once known only to be carried inexorably by a current of memory toward the terrible climax. The happy halcyon days insisted on his attention and he gave it freely even though he knew the awful ending that waited just out of sight to torment him yet again.

✿   ✿   ✿

Shoshana had been so very beautiful. She was the daughter of a wealthy importer in Yafo: he, the son of an equally wealthy tradesman in the Holy City of Yerushalayim. He hadn't even known her when his father had arranged their marriage and she had lived so far away and the press of his business had been so great that he hadn't even gotten to see her during the year of their

14

betrothal. While that was not unusual, it had filled him with the torment of the unknown that could only be banished when the knowing came.

Yakov had indeed been excited about his upcoming marriage but he had been apprehensive, too. Would he like her? Would she like him? What if he didn't? What if she didn't? Would it matter? What could be done if they hated each other on sight? And yes, what did she look like? He had hated to admit it but it really had mattered to him.

Yakov had gone to his mother's old lookingglass and grimaced as he studied his own long angular form, his light brown eyes staring back at him, his hair falling about his shoulders in auburn ringlets. What if she thinks I am too tall? What if she thinks I am ugly? The question tormented him for days.

He still found it hard to believe the depths of the delight he had felt when he had first seen her. Her father had spared no expense in arranging her bridal procession. Innumerable servants had proceeded her, the first of them calling bystanders from their everyday pursuits to provide an audience for the bride by tossing shiny coins to the adults and small sweets to the children. They were followed by other servants, each carrying some of the household paraphernalia which formed a part of her dowry. There were piles of linens, enough to outfit the palace of a king, all of the very finest materials. There were great silver serving trays and bowls and the most beautiful glazed ceramic dishes available. There was every cooking utensil known to man and a few new ones that Yakov had never before seen. There were chests of clothing for Shoshana and another smaller cask that held the tiny white garments Shoshana had made with her own hands to someday clothe their firstborn. A small coffer held jewelry and gems. Then at the very end of the procession, perched high atop the most marvelously bedecked camel Yakov had ever seen, came Shoshana herself. She was clad in white silk embroidered with gold, veiled in blue, and sparkling in the sun with a cascade of glittering gold bracelets and necklaces layered one atop another and with her bridal headdress of ten gleaming gold coins resting just above her eyes. When the camel knelt just outside the city wall, Yakov had escorted her the rest of the way to her new home, the one he had had built for her by the most talented craftsmen in Yerushalayim. Once the ceremony was over and her veil had been removed, Yakov had found that Shoshana was the most beautiful creature he had ever seen, the most beautiful the Holy One had ever created. And the Holy One had created her just for him. She was small and delicate like a dove, with a cascade of raven hair, eyes as blue as the sky above her, skin as alabaster white as the Temple itself, and lips like a small pink bow that parted to reveal a dazzling smile. He hadn't been able to take his eyes off of her, not then, not ever.

As soon as they had left the festivities on that first night of their week-long wedding feast, she had melted into his arms and become his own in a wonderful haze of gentle love that had left them both dizzy with happiness. When she had come to him only a few months later to tell him that she was with child, their joy had been complete. He had known then that life could not be any better than it was that day and indeed he had been more right than even he guessed.

It seemed Shoshana was just as enchanted with the husband she had never met as he was with his beautiful bride. She would come to his stall on the Temple Mount each day before the sixth hour. There, amidst the bleating of the sheep, the bellowing of the calves, and the cooing of the caged doves, she would pull back the cloth from the small basket she carried to reveal the delicacies she had prepared for their early meal. Together, oblivious to the sounds and smells of the animals and the dust they stirred up, they would gaze into each other's eyes and exchange the encrypted language of lovers while they ate their fill. Then, in the summer, she would return home to remain sheltered from a searing sun from the sixth hour until the ninth. Even the teasing of Yakov's fellow tradesman couldn't cool their ardor. Nothing could tear their attention from each other. Well, almost nothing.

Shoshana had been there just before *Pesach* or Passover when that crazy Rabbi from the north had come, overturning tables, scattering coins in every direction, and shouting something about His Father's house being a house of prayer not a den of thieves. Shoshana had been stunned but according to the custom of women, had said nothing in public. When Yakov had gotten home that evening, however, her questions had tumbled out.

"Who was that wild Man? Why did He do that? What was He saying to you?" Her sapphire eyes had grown wide with fear until Yakov had taken her in his arms and whispered reassurances of his protection.

"He's harmless," Yakov had said at last. "He's just a country rustic from Galilee who thinks the Holy One has personally appointed Him to get us sophisticated city folks straightened out. He came last year, too. Did the same thing. Then after Pesach He was gone just as He had come and everything got back to normal."

It was then that Yakov had explained to his wife how his business, actually his father's business, operated. Those of their faith from all over the world came to the Temple in Yerushalayim, some to make sacrifices for their sins, some to dedicate their infants to the Holy One with the appropriate offerings, most to attend the three high holiest days of the Hebrew calendar as the Holy One had commanded in the Law of Moshe. Then there were those who had determined to come just once before they died to see with their own eyes the magnificent structure that was their Temple. They had heard the proverb that if one did not look upon the Temple in this life, he had lived without ever knowing true beauty.

These people could not bring their sacrificial animals from distant places. After all, who in their right mind would drag a calf or a lamb or a ram or whatever up those winding mountain roads to get to the city of Yerushalayim? And even if one did, it would be inspected by the *mumcheh* who was certain to find something wrong with it. The truth was the animal sellers counted on him to do precisely that. After all, no animal that had endured such a trip could possibly arrive in perfect condition, an absolute requirement if it were to be acceptable to the priests and to the Holy One Himself. That's where the Temple tradesmen came into the picture.

Under the supervision of the priests and Levites, in accord with the prices they set monthly, and under obligation to pay them a handsome percentage of the profit, the tradesmen plied their wares in the outer court of the Temple. Some sold oil; some, incense; some, the finest ground wheat available anywhere; and some, like Yakov and his father, sold animals, each one the right age and in exactly the right condition. A traveler could purchase whatever he needed to make the specific sacrifice his Lord required of him. And if the priests happened to be overwhelmed with sacrifices on a particular day, especially a feast day, and if one animal or a great number of animals found their way back to the stalls to be resold again and again, who was hurt? Everyone including the priests made a pretty penny and the Holy One who looked on the intent of the heart of the penitent, gave him credit for an offering rendered. The animals eventually ended up on the altar anyway. Did it really matter if each atoned for the sins of one or the sins of many? The priests had assured Yakov that it did not.

Naturally, some travelers from foreign nations carried only foreign money and even those from Yerushalayim might carry either the Hebrew shekel or the Roman *denarius*. The money changers provided a great service to them. They would exchange any ordinary money for countercoins which could only be used at the Temple market, thus assuring an endless stream of customers. The money changers were in business to make a profit and the priests also required a percentage of that profit. So the money changers were forced to charge more for this exchange than the actual value of the countercoin they returned, often much more. But again, who was hurt? If it hadn't been for the service they provided, travelers and local citizens alike would have been unable to buy the many commodities the Temple offered, the very commodities that were required to earn the smile of the Holy One.

Shoshana had looked somewhat skeptical at first but after Yakov's careful explanations, she had been content to leave men's business to the men. After all, this was the livelihood that was going to provide for the child she carried, the child whose first move she had felt as the crazy Man at the Temple had spoken.

Once his wife's queries had been satisfied, Yakov had begun to think aloud about the brash Stranger who had threatened to disrupt his comfortable living. "Pesach is our biggest business season and all year we look forward to the money it will bring us. We may sell as many as a quarter of a million animals during that week alone! Then this Madman comes and it takes us half a day to set straight the disorder He leaves behind Him. Who does He think He is? What gives Him the right to sit in judgment on us?" But there was another part of Yakov that quietly pondered different questions, questions he shared with no one, questions he did not even want to admit to himself.

Shoshana had nestled into his shoulder and purred her agreement with him. Just the nearness of her, the warmth of her, the scent of her, the wonder of her had made him forget his anger. Once again, supper would be late that night and neither of them cared.

✡   ✡   ✡

After the Day of First Fruits, it was decided that the old veil of the Temple was to be replaced with a new one to be completed before the New Year, the Day of Atonement, and the Feast of Tabernacles, all of which fell within a fortnight in the fall. Like Aaron of old, the priests let it be known that they required the services of women proficient with needle and thread. When Yakov had mentioned this to Shoshana, she had begged to be permitted to offer her skills. At first Yakov had resisted. He wanted no wife of his to work. What would others think?

"But I only want to do it so I can be close to you all day," she had pleaded, tears engulfing the blueness of her eyes and turning them into vast seas of sadness.

"Oh, I suppose it will be all right," he had finally conceded, "but only until your time to be delivered draws near."

Her smile had returned then and her eyes had brightened. "Done," she had promised.

And so Shoshana had begun to accompany Yakov to the Temple each day shortly after dawn. Together they would make their way down the terraced streets of the Upper City and up to the palace of the Holy One Himself. And it was indeed magnificent. King Herod had meant it to be more grand and glorious than any of the heathen temples anywhere in the world. It was perched upon the highest pinnacle in Yerushalayim so that it could be seen from every quarter of the city. It had already taken more than ten thousand craftsmen more than forty-five years to build it. It was of shining white marble with pure gold covering the Beautiful Gate, the eastern entrance of the Sanctuary, to reflect the morning sunrise. Yet it was still unfinished. It was so wonderful now that Shoshana could only imagine how spectacular it might be when it was completed.

Together with the other women, Shoshana spent her mornings sending her needle flying across the heaviest and purest white linen fabric as they recreated the ancient depiction of the cherubim whose original task had been to guard Eden against sinful man and whose task later became guarding the Holy of Holies, the place where the Holy

One Himself dwelt. Then when the sun was high in the heavens, she would join Yakov for their customary meal before returning to her labors. Often he would see that needle sticks had left her fingers rough and bleeding but she had never complained. And often she spoke of how surprisingly heavy was the segment of the veil that was draped across her lap to be sewn each day.

With many hands to complete the task, the veil was finished long before the holy days and long before the baby was to be born. Shoshana couldn't believe the measure of it, forty cubits high, twenty cubits wide, and a full handsbreadth thick. And it weighed so much that three hundred priests were needed just to hang it in place before the Holy of Holies.

With the New Year festivities over, the fast of the Day of Atonement completed, and *Succoth* or the Feast of Tabernacles about to begin, small booths sprang up on the rooftops of the city, in the courtyards of its houses, and in almost any open space worshippers could find. The booths were built of wood and decorated with the products of the harvest. Each had a small opening in the roof so that prayers could ascend to the Holy One. For a week the devout celebrated successful crops as well as that day when, after forty years of wilderness wandering and living in tents and booths, the Holy One had brought His people into the land He had prepared for them, a land where they could build real homes, a land where they could put down roots and plant and reap and live the good lives He had promised.

On the final day of the observance, Shoshana hadn't been able to resist the temptation to enter the Temple after her early meal with Yakov just to listen to whatever the worshippers might be saying about the new veil. She had worked so hard and so long on it that she felt as if it were merely the first of the babies she would bring forth that autumn. *Did they like it? Did they hate it? Did they even notice it at all?* She had to know.

Forbidden as a woman to enter the main Sanctuary where the men worshipped, Shoshana had waited near the Court of the Women, trying to catch even the most casual remark regarding her handiwork. Even whispered words echoed against the marble and Shoshana had smiled as she overheard several favorable comments concerning the beauty of the new veil uttered by men with covered heads and long beards who were wrapped in robes adorned with long fringes.

As she listened, Shoshana had heard a voice that thundered through the marble passageways. She recognized it instantly though she couldn't remember at first where she had heard it before. Yet somehow she was drawn to it like iron fragments to lodestone.

As Shoshana joined the crowd around Him, she knew Him at once. He was the wild Galilean who had disrupted the animals seller at Pesach. Only this time He wasn't talking about animals and thieves at all. He was talking about water, living water. With His arms outstretched as though He would embrace everyone who heard His voice, with eyes lit by a love that seemed to radiate from deep within and to want no more than to warm every heart before Him, He had promised that all who came to Him would find their thirst quenched forever by this living water. And He said there would be rivers enough left over to flow out to many more.

As He spoke, the child Shoshana carried had turned within her as if it, too, had heard a voice that simply had to be obeyed. Almost reflexively, Shoshana had taken a single step forward, a single step in His direction, a single step to come to Him as He had said, a single step toward this living water that would end her thirst forever.

In the next moment, Shoshana had come to herself and blushed self-consciously. Then she had looked to her right and to her left to assure herself that no one had seen. But He had seen and His eyes had fixed on hers with a gaze that spoke volumes. *It is well,* He had seemed to say. *Even if your feet cannot take that final step just yet, I know your heart did. I saw and I welcome you, Daughter.* He had smiled slightly. But she had seen and she had understood His unspoken message just to her. When His eyes had left hers, she had realized that her cheeks were wet with tears and she hadn't known why she was crying.

As the crowd disbursed around her, Shoshana had found herself listening again. Only this time she wasn't even thinking of the veil; she was thinking only about the Man she had just met. Who was He? Why had He had such a profound impact on her? How had He managed to touch her heart so deeply with just a few words and a glance in her direction?

"I think He must be the Prophet Moshe wrote about in the Law," one postulated.

In another knot of worshippers, an argument was growing intense. "I tell you, He's Messiah. He can be no other," a younger man was saying to the older men around him.

"Messiah!" one of the scribes present had mocked contemptuously. "You know as well as I do the scrolls are clear on this point. Messiah will be of the seed of David and will be born in Bethlehem, the city of David. You can take one look at this Man's clothes and listen for one moment to His speech and you know that He's from Galilee."

"That is truly spoken," another, a Pharisee, had joined in. "He is a Galilean!" the man returned, spitting out the words as though they were an accusation.

To one from Yerushalayim, the Galileans were merely one small step above the Samaritans. While the devout would not trade with the Samaritans or enter their homes or even treat their sick and injured, they did tolerate the Galileans. While a Yudean would walk all the way around the province of Samaria, which lay between Yudea and Galilee, rather than take the shorter route through it, that same Yudean would enter Galilee but only when absolutely necessary. The Galileans were just so far away and so different from their cousins to the south in appearance, in dress, in manner of speech, and in customs. They may as well have come from another country. And most Galileans would have been content never to travel to Yudea if the Temple were not there and if the Law of the Holy One had not commanded them to appear before Him in His Holy Place three times in the year.

So it was no wonder the Pharisee from Yerushalayim ended his diatribe with a sarcastic, "Since when will Messiah come from Galilee?"

The younger man had hung his head in shame. He was in the presence of recognized experts on Scripture. He was no match for them and he knew it. He may as well surrender before they made a complete fool of him, and in public no less. But somewhere deep in his heart, he wondered and he clung tenaciously to some small hope that maybe he was right. Maybe this was Messiah. Maybe he had just met Him. As Shoshana observed the struggle of his soul, she wondered the very same things.

The remainder of the day had been a fog for Shoshana. She had no idea how she had gotten home yet home was exactly where she found herself an hour later. The beat of her own heart had pounded in her ears along with a single word which kept repeating itself to her over and over again. *Messiah. Messiah! MESSIAH!* Her heart said it; it commanded it; it nearly shouted it to her.

Could it really be? Could I have really met Messiah, the One the prophets have been predicting and my people have been awaiting for centuries? In her mind Shoshana did not know the answers to those questions, yet in the depths of her soul, she knew the answers to every one. But how was she going to tell Yakov? How was she going to make him understand?

✡   ✡   ✡

"You seem awfully quiet this night, my dear wife," Yakov had said as she cleared the dishes from the low table after he had eaten a supper she could barely remember preparing. "Tell me what troubles you. Is it the baby?"

"No, not that," she had said as her arms had encircled her ever-expanding abdomen in a protective gesture. She had paused, trying to think of exactly the right words and finding none. "I saw Him again," she had finally ventured softly.

"Him? Whom, my dear? Whom did you see?" Yakov had prompted gently.

"I saw Him, the Madman, the One who knocked over the tables at Pesach. Him."

"The Galilean? You saw the Galilean?" Yakov had been on his feet in an instant, at her side, concerned for her, cradling her in his arms, searching her face for answers to his questions. "When? Where? Did He say anything to you? Did He hurt you?"

"No, no, nothing like that," she had reassured her husband with a smile.

His smile of relief had answered hers. "What did He want of you?" he had asked.

"He was speaking to a huge crowd of people in the corridor of the Temple today, Yakov, after the celebration of the final day of the feast. I just happened to come by. He wanted nothing of anyone. On the contrary, He said He wanted to give us something He called 'living water.' He said that if we would come to Him, He would give us this water and we would never be thirsty again. And some in the crowd said He might be Messiah." Shoshana's eyes had searched her husband's expectantly. She had hoped for some small sign, any sign that he might be open to such a possibility.

"Messiah!" Yakov had snorted. "Does He not know that Messiah won't come from Galilee? Does He not know that Messiah will come from Bethlehem? He had better get His facts straight before He goes about claiming to be Messiah. Do not trouble yourself with Him, Shoshana. He's just a crazy Man. Messiah, indeed! Impossible!"

"Some in the crowd said that very thing, that Messiah must come from Bethlehem."

"Certainly He must. Did your parents not teach you this as a child? I know mine surely did."

"Yes, yes, of course they did," Shoshana had assured her husband. "It is just that ... I suppose you would have had to be there to see Him for yourself in order to understand. What if He was actually born in Bethlehem but then moved to Galilee when He was a small child, just as I was taken to Yafo when I was a little girl. Is that not possible?"

Yakov had looked stricken, shocked. "You do not believe this crazy Man, do you, my dear wife? You do not believe all this talk of Messiah and living water, do you?"

"No ... I mean ... I don't know ... I mean ... oh, I don't know what I mean."

"Shoshana, think about it. If He's Messiah, why do the Roman legions still march in our streets? If He had this living water of which you speak, why did you have to fetch water so that we could bathe, water in which to wash these dishes?" Yakov had questioned as he gestured toward the plates and cups in a small basin nearby.

"I suppose you are right, my husband," Shoshana had whispered before turning to reach for the pitcher so that she could begin that very task. "I suppose you are right."

But Shoshana had continued to wonder. She had wondered if there were not another kind of thirst, a thirst she had first felt as the small child of a father who was always away on business trips to exotic places where he purchased exotic goods but who was always too busy to answer all the questions she had about the Holy One he prayed to, the One he talked about, the One for whom he often grudgingly took days away from his work to observe various holy days. It was a thirst she had brought with her into her marriage to a husband who, while as in love with her as she was with him, also spent much time away from her selling animals for sacrifices he rarely mentioned and never made himself.

Was that the thirst He meant? Shoshana had asked herself. Even as she had pondered the question, she knew that one look into those loving blue eyes of His, one word in His gentle voice, one small step in His direction, and somehow, in some way she could not begin to fathom, that terrible thirst was gone, quenched deep within her heart, replaced by the love she had found in His eyes.

Early in the morning, as soon as Yakov had left for his place in the court of the Temple, Shoshana had felt herself drawn by some power she could not resist, drawn out into the still shadowy streets, drawn back to the Temple. This is silly, she had said to herself on the way. The feast is over. He will be well on His way back to Galilee with all of the other travelers. *Get hold of yourself, Woman! Go back home where you belong,* she told herself again and again. But her feet seemed unable to move in any direction but toward the Temple. *Wait,* she told herself, *at least until the sun is higher, at least until you take Yakov the food you have prepared for him.* But her heart would not wait another moment.

As Shoshana, so near to her time, had struggled to climb the many steps to the Temple, she had listened intently for the voice, the voice that had offered her the living water that had ended the thirst of her soul, His voice. But she had heard nothing apart from the usual activity, the usual morning prayers. As she had come in out of the warm autumn sunshine, her eyes had strained against the cool darkness inside, searching for one face, the face that had offered her that gentle welcoming smile, His face. But she had seen nothing.

Just then several figures had brushed past her. There seemed to be a group of men with a smaller shape, a woman, struggling between two of them. Not knowing what to do or where to go, Shoshana had simply followed along.

As her eyes had adjusted to the dim light, the first face Shoshana had seen clearly was His, shining before her as though illuminated by some heavenly glow that seemed to emanate from deep within. He had been seated in the center of a crowd that separated at the approach of the two men who held the captive woman. The men had angrily thrown the woman to the floor in front of Him as though she presented some devious sort of challenge to Him.

Shoshana had wanted to step forward, to put her veil around the poor woman's shivering shoulders, to comfort her, to do something, anything. But Shoshana had known that this was the business of men, the men of the Sanhedrin, the seventy men who ruled her people in such matters. She knew she must not interfere.

"Master," the men addressed Him, though their tone revealed that He was not their Master at all. "We caught this woman in the very act of committing adultery. According to the Law of Moshe, we must stone her to death. What do You think we should do?"

The air had been suddenly charged as with the lightning that comes just before a summer storm. Even Shoshana had known the reason. It seemed that no matter how He replied, He would be discredited. If He said the Law of Moshe must be obeyed sending the poor woman to her death, those who saw the Holy One as a God of mercy would be forever disillusioned. But if He said the woman should be freed, those who interpreted the Law strictly would be forever offended.

Shoshana had wanted to say something, to do something, but she knew she could not. In any event, there seemed to be no answer that would satisfy everyone. She could think of nothing to help Him; she wondered what would happen if He could think of nothing to help Himself ... Himself and the condemned woman at His feet.

The silence had been so intense that it could nearly be felt as everyone waited for a reply that did not come. Rather He had simply seemed to be ignoring everyone, ignoring the entire issue. Then He had fallen to His knees and had begun to write something in the film of dust that many sandals had left on the polished marble floor.

People had drawn closer, Shoshana among them, to see what He was writing. Was it His reply? Was it the Law relating to the case? Eyes strained to read His words.

WHERE IS THE MAN?

Shoshana had almost chuckled at the brilliance of it. *Where was the man indeed? If the woman was caught in the very act of committing adultery as her accusers claimed, there had to have been a man in her bed, too. Where is he? Why has he not been brought with her? If these men are so knowledgeable in the Law, they must know that in such a circumstance both the man and the woman are equally guilty before the Holy One. Both must be judged and both must be stoned. Where is the man indeed?* As she thought about His response, Shoshana was glad her veil hid the smile that seemed determined to form on her lips.

But His interrogators had only ignored Him, pressing for an answer to their question.

He had stood for only a moment, only long enough to declare, "He who is without sin among you, let him throw the first stone at her." Then He had knelt again and continued to write, His words taking shape in the dust before Him.

WHERE IS THE MAN, AVRAM, AND THE WOMAN, REBEKAH?

An older man who had been standing with arms crossed and a look of self-righteous disdain on his face had suddenly blanched and turned to leave, pushing his way past others who chuckled knowingly. Shoshana would have been willing to bet that his name was Avram. The writing continued.

WHERE IS THE MAN, ASHER, AND THE WOMAN, TABITHA?

Another accuser had drifted away in a hurry to be somewhere else, anywhere else.

And the writing went on.

WHERE IS THE MAN, ESAU, AND THE WOMAN, KEREN?

Another man had nervously cleared his throat as he made his way toward the exit.

The writing had seemed to go on and on, one name after the other, until none of those remained who had dragged the woman into the Temple and accused her. The crowd had stood in stunned silence. Finally He had stopped writing, dusted off His hands, and stood. He made a show of looking around and seeming to be surprised by the number of men no longer present. Suppressed giggles could be heard among those still gathered. With feigned shock that would have done credit to an actor, He queried, "Woman, where are those who accused you? Is there no man to testify against you?"

The woman had sat up looking around for the men who had brought her to this terrible time and place in her life and had seen not one of them. "There is no man, Lord," was all she had been able to say as relief had washed across her frightened face.

Since the Law had no provision for hearsay evidence and since the testimony of two eyewitnesses was required before the death penalty could be imposed, His verdict had been a foregone conclusion. "Neither do I condemn you," He had said with that same gentle voice, that same loving look that had so changed Shoshana's life only the day before.

The woman had scrambled to her feet anxious to be gone before her accusers could return but she had found herself frozen to the spot. She felt compelled to turn, to look at the Man who had somehow saved her life, the Man like no other she had ever known.

He had gazed deeply into her eyes, a look that penetrated to her very soul. Then He had spoken again. "Go and do not sin again," He had said gently.

He knew! He had known all along. And she knew that He knew. She hadn't fooled Him. He had known all about her, about her sin, about her shame. He had known that she was guilty of every charge leveled against her and many more. She felt the weight of her sin, a burden greater than she could possibly bear alone. And for the first time in a long time, she was sorry that she had ever gotten involved in such an empty life. But in His eyes, somewhere in His eyes, she found His forgiveness for it all. Her tears came then, tears that washed away the shame that had clung to her like an indelible stain. In that instant, a terrible weight was lifted from her shoulders. She could have floated from the Temple but she knew she would walk instead, walk straight, walk upright, walk past all of the old temptations, walk into a brand new life. She wondered what kind of a Man could do that for her with a single look, a single word.

The crowd had held its collective breath until He spoke again, spoke of Himself as the Light of the world, a Light so strong that it would banish all the darkness of this world.

Shoshana could only wonder how He had been able to speak to her very heart. *How did He know that I just came in out of the bright sunlight only to wander in the dimness within the Temple until I found Him there before me radiating that heavenly glow that reached out to me from the darkness. How did He know of the darkness inside me that was illuminated by His very being just yesterday? How did He know of the darkness within the poor woman who was hurled at His feet, the darkness He has so easily ended forever?*

There was no longer any doubt. Shoshana knew. This was indeed Messiah. And He had not come to free her people from the oppressive grip of the Romans; no, He had come to free them from the even more oppressive grip of sin, that dreadful darkness of spirit that lurks within the heart of every man ... and woman. She had to tell Yakov the wonderful news.

Her pains had come suddenly and so sharp they nearly took her breath away. By the time she had reached the

Court of the People, she had only been able to gasp that her time had come. Yakov had lifted her into his strong arms, carried her home, and carefully placed her on their bed. She had screamed and doubled over as another contraction came, then another. By the time the midwife was summoned, Shoshana had been wet with perspiration and delirious with pain. The midwife had tried to offer the palliative potion she always carried but Shoshana's teeth were too firmly clenched to permit it to pass her lips.

"It's Him. I know it's Him, Yakov," she had gasped as she clutched Yakov's hand.

"I know. I know," Yakov had replied. "It's our son."

No, she had tried to explain but the blood had come then, more blood than Yakov had ever seen before even from the sacrificed animals. One glance at the midwife told him this was more blood than she had ever seen as well, even in all of her years of experience.

"Do something!" Yakov had demanded. "You have got to save my wife! I cannot lose her!"

"I am trying," the midwife had assured. "She is just so small and the child is so large. It is tearing her apart." She could not know that the placenta had separated from the womb too soon leaving both mother and child in jeopardy of their lives.

As the baby crowned, Shoshana had spoken one last time. "I see You. I see Your light. I'm coming, Father." Her hand reached out past Yakov, past their child, to Someone somewhere above them, above the room, above the pain. She had smiled ever so slightly. Then Shoshana's lovely face had relaxed in death.

"It is a woman child," the midwife had said at last. "I am so sorry that the Holy One did not see fit to give you a son, so sorry He chose to take your wife. I did all I could do, all anyone could have done. When the Holy One summons, what can anyone do?" she said with a shrug of futility.

The midwife's eyes did not meet Yakov's. She could not bear to look at him, feeling somehow she had failed yet knowing she hadn't. She simply kept her attention on the infant as she rubbed her rubbery little body with salt, then bathed her and anointed her with olive oil. Finally the child was wrapped in a swaddling cloth that held her just as tightly and securely as her mother's womb had done. Only her tiny face was visible when the midwife had completed her work. Even as she did all she could do for the child, the midwife knew from experience that nine of the ten babes she helped into the world did not survive to the end of their first month. She wondered what prospect this motherless one had.

Yakov had heard nothing, not the voice of the midwife, not his daughter's first cry. He had not seen his child. He had not wanted to see her. She had killed his precious Shoshana and he would never forgive her for it.

✡　　　✡　　　✡

Yakov's reverie always ended the same way. The beautiful memories of their one wonderful year together always ended right here in this very chamber; they always dissolved into a blur of agony and blood and death. Yakov's nights always ended the same way, too, as he wept into his goat's hair pillow and cried out for his precious Shoshana yet again.

In the distance, as far away from him as possible, he heard the child cry out, too, cry out into the darkness, cry out for a mother who could not come and a father who would not come. He did not care. He had hired a wetnurse to see to that.

Yakov had already decided that his daughter would be called Mara. It meant bitterness and sorrow. It was the only name appropriate for the child who had brought such bitter sorrow into his life. She would bear the brand of it, of what she had done to her mother and to him, for the rest of her life. Yakov didn't care about that either.

❧ 3 ❧

I N a spacious house on a landscaped terrace in the most fashionable section of the Upper City, Naqdimon sat stunned and silent with mute tears slipping from bloodshot brown eyes, cascading down his olive complexion, and becoming lost in his grey beard. Nearby he could hear the sobbing of his wife, Sarah, but he had no comfort to offer her. He still could not believe it had happened. Even worse, he could not believe his own foolishness.

Whatever made me think I had time? he kept asking himself, knowing there was no answer to soothe his aching soul. *How could I have been so blind? Now it is too late ... too late to tell him ... too late for anything but the deepest most agonizing regret and remorse. Oh, why did I wait so long? Why didn't I tell him when I had the opportunity ... so many opportunities? Now he's gone, lost forever, and it's all because of me. What kind of a father was I to the lad?*

Naqdimon made the traditional tear in the soft indigo fabric of his tunic, pounded his chest above his heart with his right hand, and wept loudly and uncontrollably and for a very long time. But his heartbreak was not eased; his torment was not relieved. Perhaps it never would be.

As the night shadows crept silently into the chamber and the lampstands were lit in other houses along the gently curving street, Naqdimon escaped his suffering soul the only way he could, by allowing his mind to wander freely through the memories of other times, other places, other days.

✿   ✿   ✿

From the moment of his birth after years of Sarah's barrenness, Moshe had been a fine strong boy. Naqdimon had never seen a finer. He remembered the slate grey eyes that soon turned dusky brown and black ringlets that grew into long thick tendrils. He remembered the circumcision on the eighth day and the lusty yell that had accompanied the cutting. He recalled the ancient blessing he had spoken, "Blessed be the Lord our God who has sanctified us by His precepts and given us circumcision." The other men present rejoiced with him that another man child had come into the covenant with their Lord while the women in the next room groaned at the baby's cries. Naqdimon had carried the screaming infant high above his head and placed him in his mother's arms to be suckled into a sound sleep that would erase the momentary pain.

Moshe had been all that a father could want. He was sturdy and robust with muscular arms and a powerful body that never shirked from labor. He had a quick smile and laughing eyes that made any chore a delight. He coupled all this with a brilliant mind that could fathom even the most difficult concept in synagogue school. In another year he would have gone on to study with the famous Gamaliel at the school of his grandfather, the even more famous Hillel. Both were gifted teachers who honored the Law of the Moshe for whom the boy had been named. Then he would have joined the sect of the Pharisees and someday would have sat in his father's seat on the Sanhedrin to rule the people of the Holy One as one of the seventy. It had all been planned so carefully. *If only ... if only ... .*

It had never mattered that there had been no more sons in Sarah's womb. Moshe's birth had injured her in ways none but the Holy One could have seen and none but He could have repaired. Naqdimon knew it had been the Holy One's will and with a son like Moshe, he had accepted his Lord's will easily. After all he was not a farmer, a man of the land who would need many sons to help with the sowing and reaping. He was a city dweller, a citizen of Yerusha-layim, a respected member of the community, a revered Pharisee, a member of the Sanhedrin and he had been care-fully grooming his only son to follow in his footsteps. Now all of that was meaningless to him. Even his great wealth was meaningless. Life itself was meaningless. Everything was meaningless. Well, maybe not everything ... .

✿   ✿   ✿

It was a night just like this when I met Him, Naqdimon thought absently. *Well, not quite like this. That night my heart was full of questions not pain. That night my life was changed not destroyed. No, I suppose it wasn't a night like this after all,* he thought sadly.

Naqdimon could revisit the scene in his mind as though it had occurred only yesterday. The Rabbi called Yeshua who made His home in Capernaum had come to Yerushalayim for Pesach. Then He had created quite a stir at the Temple when He had rampaged through the stalls of the money changers and animal sellers accusing them of making His Father's house of prayer into a den of thieves. Others had reviled Him and mocked His fervor but Naqdimon had heard things, things about miracles, things that made him want to find out more. He had sim-ply wanted to meet this Zealot, to explore the strange be-liefs that inspired Him to such exploits.

Naqdimon had come long after the evening prayers were said and the lamps lit. The rented rooms where he found the Rabbi had been small and not lavishly furnished. The Rabbi was just as nondescript, of average build, not at all like the muscular man his Moshe had become. He wore the simple homespun tunic and robe characteristic of the Galileans, not the fine fabrics and embroidered silks in the Greek style so popular among the wealthy in Yerushalayim. Yet there was something about Him, something about those piercing blue eyes that seemed to penetrate to one's deepest soul, something about the tender timbre of His voice, something about the very aura of the Man that had naturally drawn Naqdimon to Him that night.

Only His disciple, Yohanan, was with Him that evening. The others had drifted away to visit family and friends in the city. Yohanan was young but his pale eyes were old, knowing. His hands were rough and calloused, quiet testimony to long days tugging at the ropes and rigging of sailing vessels and their nets. He seemed perfectly at ease with his Master, clearly not the usual relationship one had with one's teacher. Theirs was clearly a connection built without a trace of fear, built upon more than mere respect, built on a firm foundation of love.

Once the three were seated on the couches that clung to the walls of the little room, Naqdimon had begun with a little flattery, calling Yeshua "Teacher," mentioning His reported miracles and generously accepting His presumed association to the Holy One. He knew almost instantly that he had made a mistake. It was clear at once that Rabbi Yeshua cared nothing for idle words. He didn't even acknowledge them. Instead He immediately challenged Naqdimon to be born again.

Naqdimon had blinked involuntarily, his eyes growing wide with wonder. *How had Yeshua known that on that very day, I had been listening to the rabbis at synagogue debate the spiritual consequences of Adam and Woman's sin in the beautiful garden of the Holy One?* Naqdimon remembered the argument well. The rabbis at the synagogue where he served as one of the ten elders were always debating some obscure point or the other. Naqdimon ignored most of them but this one had been particularly interesting.

Rabbi Mordechai had reasoned that the death penalty placed on eating the fruit of the forbidden tree referred to the bodily death all must suffer at the end of their lives. He had sounded cross but then Rabbi Mordechai always sounded cross. He seemed to think the affectation lent a

certain weight to his words even if others did not. He offered as proof of his position the fact that the Holy One
had evicted the sinful pair from His garden so that they
could not eat of the fruit of the Tree of Life and live forever.

"No, no," Rabbi Chaim had interrupted as all eyes
turned toward him. "The Holy One said they would die in
the very day they ate the fruit, did He not? Did their bodies die that day?" he asked rhetorically. Then he answered
his own question before anyone else could assail his logic,
"We know they did not." He continued without pause as
though he had already spent much time considering this
very point, "Did their souls die?" Again he answered his
own query, "No. It is clear they still possessed all of those
aspects of the soul of which our sweet psalmist, David,
wrote ... emotions, will, the ability to think and reason and
make decisions." All around the room heads nodded in
thoughtful agreement encouraging the aged rabbi to go
on. "No, my friends, it was their spirits which died, that
tiny part of them which had the ability to communicate
with the Holy One. And those spirits died that very day
just as the Holy One has said. No longer could they walk
with Him in the cool of the day, commune with Him, receive direction from Him. Only later would their bodies
suffer death. And so it has been with all who have traveled this weary road of life since that day."

Naqdimon had been unable to contain himself. "Rabbi,
if this is so, what hope have we?" he had asked. "Because
of their sin are we forever condemned to carry these dead
spirits of which you speak? May we never commune with
our blessed Holy One again?"

Rabbi Chaim had turned his cumbersome weight
slightly in his seat so that he could face his questioner. "My
son, I fear this may be so," the rabbi had replied sadly.
"This may be the reason the Holy One speaks to us through
others, through His chosen vessels, through the prophets,
through the priests, perhaps through a humble rabbi such

as myself. And of course He still continues to speak to all who have ears to hear through the scrolls of His Word."

Never before had Naqdimon felt it so important to be able to hear from his Lord. In that moment he had longed for it as he had longed for nothing else. He had wealth beyond reason but he didn't have this. He could buy anything he wanted but he couldn't buy this. He had a long list of titles after his name but he knew no title could gain him entrance into the relationship with his Lord that he sought. Yet there must be a way. All of his longings suffused themselves through his final question, "Is there nothing we can do?"

The rabbi had simply turned his palms toward heaven and shrugged his shoulders. Even he did not have a real answer. "Maybe when Messiah comes ... ," was all he could offer.

Naqdimon had felt frustration and a flash of anger. This was the standard diversion used by rabbis when they could not answer a question. *Why could they not simply admit that they did not know everything? They all hid behind the same reply, "Maybe when Messiah comes."* Naqdimon had gone home empty and yearning to be filled, dead and longing to be revived. Then that very evening Rabbi Yeshua had talked to him about some kind of a rebirth.

Naqdimon had blanched at the Rabbi's challenge as cold chills sent involuntary shivers along his spine. He was shocked at the statement, shocked at just how close it had come to the secret desire of his heart. But he couldn't let the Rabbi know how near to the mark He had come, not yet, not when he still knew so little about the Man. So Naqdimon had simply sidestepped the Rabbi's remark with some inane question about the impossibility of returning to his mother's womb to be born one more time as a baby. He had known that wasn't what the Rabbi was talking about, but he just couldn't help himself.

Rabbi Yeshua had simply smiled oh so knowingly, His clear blue eyes searching Naqdimon's hungry soul and laying it bare. Naqdimon had felt such a fool. He had wanted to run, to hide, to be somewhere, anywhere but in that room that had suddenly become so small and stifling. But he knew he couldn't, wouldn't leave. He clung to the desperate hope that maybe this young Rabbi knew the answer that the old rabbi had been unable to give him. Maybe Rabbi Yeshua knew how a man could get in touch with the Holy One once again.

The Rabbi's eyes had melted into a tenderness Naqdimon had never known. His voice became gentle, welcoming, even inviting. "Truly I tell you, unless a man is born of water and of the Spirit of the Lord he cannot enter into His kingdom. You see, that which is born of the flesh is flesh but that which is born of the Spirit of the Lord is spirit. Do not be surprised that I said you must be born again."

As the Rabbi had gone on speaking, the heart of Naqdimon had pounded so strongly that he was certain the Rabbi could hear it from His seat across the room. *He knows! He knows everything! He knows things it is impossible for Him to know! Maybe He knows the answer to the greatest question of all. Maybe He knows what the rabbi does not know.*

"How can these things be?" Naqdimon had finally asked, almost beseeching the Rabbi for the solution to the puzzle, almost begging to be told how his own dead spirit could be revived so that he could know true communion with the Holy One. The air between the two men had seemed alive with excitement. Naqdimon knew he was close, so close to the answer, so close to solving the mystery, so close to knowing the Holy One as he wanted to know Him.

Yeshua had smiled again at the irony of the situation. "Are you a master in Yisrael and you don't know this?" He teased, but only for a moment. Then He had continued, "This is what I know to be true," He had said with assurance. He spoke of the bronze serpent Moshe had lifted up in the wilderness so that all who looked upon it might be saved from the death penalty their own sin had brought upon them. He also spoke of a Son of man who must also be lifted up so that all who looked upon Him might be saved from their sins to live eternally.

Who was this Son of man? Did He speak of Messiah or another? Naqdimon could only wonder.

Rabbi Yeshua had continued, "The Holy One loved everyone in this world so much He willingly gave His only Son that whoever believes in Him will not die in his sin but will live forever. You see, the Holy One did not send His Son into this world to condemn everyone in it but only so that He could save them."

Each time Rabbi Yeshua had mentioned this Son of man, this Son of the Holy One, He had gestured toward Himself. Naqdimon realized that He believed Himself to be the very One of whom He spoke, the very One who had the power to forgive men their sins and give their dead spirits new birth. The words of his rabbi suddenly echoed in his ears, "Maybe when Messiah comes ... . Maybe when Messiah comes." Naqdimon began to believe the old rabbi had been right after all. *Maybe Messiah has come, maybe He sits here before me, and maybe He does have the answers. Maybe He can give my dead spirit life just as He said.* Even as he thought these thoughts he tingled with anticipation at the very prospect.

But could Naqdimon really believe? Could he trust this Man to be all He said, to do all He promised? Still he wanted it so much, ... maybe ... maybe ... . Yes, he did believe! He truly did! *What was it Rabbi Yeshua had said? All I have to do is look upon Him with belief in my heart just as the fathers looked upon a bronze serpent with belief in their hearts. Can it be that simple, that easy?*

Instantly, their eyes had locked in an eternal transaction. Naqdimon had looked upon Yeshua and found in Him everything He had promised. Somehow he had known his life would never be the same. Somehow he had known that his spirit was dead no longer but alive and well and reaching out to the Holy One in a way he had never before known. Naqdimon had been born again and it was glorious!

✡   ✡   ✡

A long agonized moan escaped Naqdimon's lips as tears came once again. *Why did I not tell Moshe I had found Messiah? Why did I not bring him to Yeshua? Why did I think I had all the time in the world? Why did I wait just a day, a moment too long? Now he will never know the joy of the rebirth. Now he will be lost forever and it is all my fault.*

Even as Naqdimon tormented himself with his never-ending questions, in his heart he already knew the answers. He had hesitated to tell his son the good news of Messiah because of Moshe's best friend, Ami, the handsome dark-haired dark-eyed son of Yosef ben Qayafa, the high priest. So many times Naqdimon had wanted to tell Moshe about Messiah. But Naqdimon knew how Ami's father felt about Rabbi Yeshua, knew of his many unsuccessful plots to arrest Him and take His life. He couldn't tell Moshe of Messiah without swearing him to secrecy to safeguard Yeshua's life and he knew such a secret would be impossible for Moshe to keep from Ami.

Moshe and Ami had been friends since attending Temple together as children. It was an impossible friendship from the start, one the son of a powerful Pharisee and the other the son of an even more powerful Sadducee. Yet somehow they had managed to reach beyond the eternal arguments of doctrine so important to their fathers and each found in the other a friend. Thereafter they did everything together, went everywhere together, worked together, played together, grew together into strong beautiful young men. Had it not been for the tragedy, someday they would have sat together as members of the Sanhedrin. They had been together that very morning, laughing and joking, full of life and full of plans to help an old man in the Lower City repair his dilapidated house. Now they had died together in its collapse. Now their bodies lay broken and bloodied and wrapped in white linen in neighboring tombs outside the city wall. Now two fathers' dreams lay crushed as well. Now two fathers grieved alone for sons they had buried together just before the setting of the sun. Now it was too late.

✿   ✿   ✿

In an even more gracious home nearby, Yosef ben Qayafa sat quiet and still, his dark eyes staring at the flickering light of the ornate bronze lampstand as it danced across the wall to frustrate the darkness surrounding him. But he saw nothing. The white hair encircling his balding pate and his neatly-trimmed white beard were disheveled but he made no move to straighten them. His tunic had already been torn to mark his mourning. He had no tears left to cry, no prayers left to pray, no words left to comfort his wife, Leah. He could hear her weeping above the anguished wails of the hired mourners but he made no move to join her.

At sundown *Shabbat*, the Sabbath, had begun. He should have been at the Temple, arrayed in radiant robes befitting the great high priest of Yerushalayim, presiding over the sacrifice, reading the Torah, and leading the assembled worshippers in their prayers to the Holy One. But he had touched the dead this day and according to the Law was unclean and unable to enter into the Temple until the next evening. It was just as well. Yosef ben Qayafa knew words of worship would have died on his lips and he also knew he could not lead others to a place he himself did not really want to go just now.

Why did the Holy One take my precious Ami? he questioned. *Have I not served Him well? Have I not zealously obeyed*

His Law? Have I not stood against the heretics such as that both-ersome Rabbi Yeshua? Why has the Lord rewarded me thus?
The questions came one after another, unbidden, unan-swered because there were no answers. At least there were no answers with which Yosef ben Qayafa could make peace on that dark night. He had known wealth since his earliest days. The family appellation, Qayafa, meant basketmaker and so his people had been for generations, able to make baskets out of almost anything to fit almost anything and amassing a great fortune for their trouble. Rich and re-spected, the family had finally become accepted in politi-cal circles and been welcomed into the Sanhedrin. He had also had the great good fortune to marry the only daugh-ter of Annas, the high priest of those days. He had even been permitted to build a lovely home for himself and his new bride beside the grand and gracious courtyard where Annas and his sons resided.

Qayafa had bided his time, carefully ingratiating him-self with the old man. Finally, after the three eldest of Annas' five sons had served in the office, he, Yosef ben Qayafa, had been found worthy to ascend to the most prominent position in all of Yudaism, the high priesthood and with it the presidency of the Sanhedrin. Now, though he and his wife continued to share the home he had built so long before, his official residence was the palace of the high priest atop the eastern slope of Mount Zion, the old fortress King David himself had conquered. And Qayafa gloried in it just as he gloried in all of the privileges to which his office entitled him.

For years the family had been passing around the plum position of high priest among themselves as if it were a treasured family heirloom. With the offerings and the per-centage demanded from the money changers and the ani-mal sellers, Qayafa's personal wealth had only increased by leaps and bounds. He didn't need to make baskets any longer. In truth, he would not have remembered how to weave a basket if his life had depended on it and it certainly did not.

But now Yisrael was under foreign domination. Now Yosef ben Qayafa remained in office only at the sufferance of Rome. He knew the Roman pigs didn't care who served in his post so long as he was able to maintain order, keep the peasants peaceful, and insure that the required taxes were paid on time and in full. It was shocking to think that the Romans, in their complete obliviousness, would even have named Rabbi Yeshua high priest if He had become more popular among the people and could have better served their purposes!

Yosef ben Qayafa had made sure such a sacrilege would not happen during his tenure; he had made certain he would not be the last of the family to reign. He had hoped Ami might someday follow him. After all, Qayafa had stood against all the self-proclaimed messiahs, systematically discrediting them among the ignorant masses, depriving them of their audiences and thus their revenues, expelling from the Temple any who insisted on following them and, when necessary, taking even harsher steps to rid himself of such petty annoyances. Naturally he consoled himself with the belief that he did all of it for his people and ultimately for the Holy One Himself. He wouldn't, couldn't admit even to his own heart that he actually acted in defense of himself, his office, and his tightly-held grasp on power.

Power ... power. That's really what it is all about, isn't it, he mused. *I thought I possessed the greatest power in all the world but it isn't enough to restore to me my beloved Ami, not even long enough to bid him farewell. What good is it all now? I never even had a chance to say goodbye and now he is gone from me forever.*

Qayafa was recalled from his reverie when his young servant, Malluch, appeared in the doorway. His dark eyes were wet with his tears for he had grown up in this house beside Ami and now mourned his best friend just as David had once mourned Yonathan.

"Yes, what is it?" Qayafa finally asked wearily.

"My lord, the sun has finally set on this day of sadness. Perhaps you would now wish to break your fast," Malluch offered.

Qayafa's eyes took on a faraway look as they stared well beyond Malluch. "I was to have supped with my son this night," Qayafa whispered almost absently. "Now I will sup with him no more." Qayafa focused again on his servant. "No, Malluch, I do not think that I will be wanting to sup at all this night. You may go."

Malluch wanted to say so much more, to offer his condolences, to share his remembrances of the young man who had been like a brother to him. But he had been dismissed and dared not speak again. He disappeared from the doorway as quickly and quietly as he had come.

The air was stirred as Malluch's movement caused the shadows of the lamps to begin again their rhythmic performance along the wall before Yosef ben Qayafa. But he saw nothing. There was much that Yosef ben Qayafa did not see even when it was right in front of him.

⊗ 4 ⊗

RABBI Levi ben Eschol hadn't wanted her. Actually, on the Shabbat day on which she was born, he had considered her something of a curse. He had justified his feelings by telling himself, *Any man, especially a rabbi such as myself, would have preferred a grandson.* The rationalization had worked quite well and whenever his son, Aaron, and daughter-in-law, Naomi, brought little Yael to visit him in his chambers in the house they all shared, he was always able to think of some excuse to depart into his private chamber to console himself among his many scrolls.

When had she stolen his heart? When had she become his heart? Maybe it was that chilly day he had kept the baby so Aaron and Naomi, both strong and slim and swarthy and full of stamina, could attend the Purim festivities near the Pool of Shiloah. That was the day the infant had grasped his finger, refusing to let go, her heavily-lashed deep brown eyes meeting his own. Maybe it had been the first time she had called him *Saba*, grandfather, in her struggling baby talk. It could even have been the day he was studying his scrolls before teaching his small congregation in one of the many synagogues which dotted the city of Yerushalayim and she had crawled into his lap to "help Saba." All he knew was that it had indeed happened and he knew he had never been the same afterward.

One thing he knew of a certainty. He knew without a doubt the very day, the very moment when their special relationship had been forever forged into a bond as strong as iron.

✡   ✡   ✡

It had all begun as he returned from synagogue following morning prayers. He had been thinking of the prophecy he had read that morning, a prophecy of Messiah. *When will He come to us?* Rabbi Levi had wondered. *What will it be like when He arrives riding His white stallion, making war upon the infidels who now trample the Holy City underfoot?* In his mind's eye, he had seen the combat, the flash of swords in the sunlight, blood flowing in little rivulets down the dusty streets. Even though he was bent with age, frail of bone, and grey of hair, he still saw himself wielding one of the long two-edged swords that would slice the heads of the hated Romans from their shoulders and bring his people victory. He could almost hear the shouts of triumph and the Hallel of praise to their Lord which would follow their conquest. As he had strolled the pathway, he even imagined walking past the corpses of the loathsome Roman soldiers who were now so very much alive and so very dominant a presence in the land of his birth.

The day had been one of the first warm ones that spring and Yael had come out to play with the other children. It seemed the rays of the sun and the new life in the air had embraced the rabbi and carried him along as his musing continued.

The call had come quickly, unexpectedly, pulling Rabbi Levi from the sweetness of his daydreams and the magnificence of the Messiah he followed in them.

"Saba, Saba." It had been Yael, a big girl in her ninth year, her smile welcoming him home, her eyes dancing with delight at the sight of him, her dark curls bouncing as she had started across the street to come to her grandfather's side.

It had happened in an instant. There had been the neighing of a horse as his rider pulled him up short to avoid trampling the little girl who had dashed into his path. There had been the coarse call of "Little Yew whore, yield to Rome" from the haughty centurion atop the big black animal. Then the air was cut in two as he brought his riding whip down with all his might across the cheek of the frightened child. "That will teach you to stand in the way of Rome," he had called back over his shoulder as he galloped away, never looking back to see the terrible damage he had done.

Yael had stood stark still in the street, afraid to move, paralyzed by her pain. Her small hand had tried to cover the gaping gash across her face as her own blood had forced its way between her fingers, staining her clothing and the stones under her feet.

As Rabbi Levi had run to his grotesquely wounded granddaughter, he had wanted to shriek, *Roman blood must flow in our streets, not our own. Oh, Messiah, why do You delay when our need is so great?* But a single word of rebellion might be reported and the next time a Roman soldier rode down this street, it could be to arrest him for disturbing the *Pax Romanus*, the so-called peace on which Rome prided herself. He had simply taken the child in his arms, whispered words of comfort, and carried her home to her mother.

The physician had done all he could and a poultice of tonic and honey had been obtained from the nearby apothecary. But even with generous applications of it, Yael's wound had oozed blood and water for many days until at last a scab had formed. When it was gone, it had left behind an angry red scar the thickness of one of his fingers and every bit as long. The once-beautiful child was beautiful no more and he had known that she never would be again. From that day forward she would always be considered spoiled, ruined, maimed.

Once Yael had recovered, she was sent to the well to bring water to bathe her newborn third brother. She had come home quickly, too quickly he had thought, with a full pitcher on her shoulder but with her face downcast and her eyes brimming with tears. After the water had been poured into the pot above the fire to be warmed, Yael had come to him, crawled into his lap, hiding her scarred cheek in the folds of his garment.

"Saba, you still love me, do you not?" she had asked.

"Of course, my dear child," he had responded immediately. "I love you and I always shall. Why on earth would you ask such a question?" he had inquired as he looked into her sad little face. His eyes had smiled down at her and hers had smiled back through her tears.

"The other children at the well said such mean things to me today. One small one even cried because I frightened him so. I just needed to know that you do not feel such things when you see me now."

That was when it had happened! In that instant, Rabbi Levi had opened his heart to a small wounded bird and invited her to find a resting place in the shelter of it. He had held her in his arms until the afternoon shadows had lengthened into evening. He had become her champion, her protector, and he had known that day that he always would be. He would stand with her, beside her, before her if need be, to defend her against the cruelty of a world which could visit such pain upon a child and then rejoice in it.

From that day forward, Yael and Rabbi Levi had been inseparable. She would often accompany him to synagogue morning and evening and to Temple on the Shabbats and new moons and feast days, always observing silently from behind the dark protection of the women's screen. Then she would take his hand, talking animatedly just to him as they made their way home, avoiding the stark stares of children and their parents alike, her eyes fixed only on him and on the unending adoration and acceptance she found in his loving face.

And so it was that Yael had been with him when he had gone to the Temple for the Feast of Dedication. She had always sat wide-eyed when the story was told of the mighty miracle the feast celebrated. It was the story of the heathen Syrian king, Antiochus, who had subjugated her people and then scandalized them by sacrificing an unclean animal, a swine, on the altar of the Holy One in His Temple. It was the story of the Hasmons, a brave family also called the Maccabees, the hammer, because of their exploits in ridding her nation of those who had defiled it. And it was the story of their desire to cleanse and rededicate their Temple. But the Maccabees had found only enough consecrated oil to light the lamps for a single day yet they knew it would require eight days to complete their work and prepare a new supply of oil for the golden lampstands. When they could do nothing else, they simply trusted the Holy One. Miraculously that single vial of oil had continued to flow for the entire eight days, giving out only when their labors were finished and a new supply of oil had been readied. From that time onward, each winter Yael's people had celebrated, lighting lights and retelling the wonderful story of victory and the Lord's mighty miracle of provision.

She had been in her thirteenth year that day. She had become a woman the previous summer and should already have been pledged in marriage. But no man had ever looked on her with love, only pity. No man had desired to make her his bride. Even the poorest, the oldest, the ugliest of men would see her awful pink scar and leave the marriage negotiations, no matter how great the promised dowry, no matter how low the bridal price was set. None ever looked beyond her pain to see the promise of love she held within in her heart.

When the morning sacrifice had concluded that day, Yael had left the Court of the Women only to find that a chilly winter rain was falling. She decided to wait for her Saba on Solomon's Porch, the long covered walkway set on either side with great white columns that lay on the eastern edge of the Temple Mount overlooking a wide chasm called the Kidron Valley. As she waited, she noticed that a crowd had gathered. She pulled her veil across her scarred face just as she always did now and drew closer to the throng.

"What is it? What's happening?" Rabbi Levi had questioned as he searched for Yael.

"It's Him!" a man had responded with a look of total rapture engulfing his youthful glowing face. "Messiah Yeshua is here. Come! See! He's the Man who healed my lame leg." The man spun around as if to prove the soundness of his limb.

Rabbi Levi had heard of this One, of the trouble He caused wherever He went, of His tricks that paraded themselves as miracles, of His teaching that turned the masses from their true leaders in Yerushalayim, of His heresies which mocked Shabbat and the traditions and even the Holy One Himself. No, Rabbi Levi had no desire to see this Charlatan.

As he had turned to go, Rabbi Levi realized he had not yet found Yael. His eyes swept the crowd until he caught a brief glimpse of her dark curls and blue veil. For some reason he couldn't comprehend, Yael had been caught up by the crowd. He could only imagine what might happen if these people saw her face and began to ridicule her as so many had done. Gently and with great civility, Rabbi Levi had begun to propel himself past the people in the crowd. He had searched again for Yael's black curls and brown eyes but had seen only the straight light hair and azure blue eyes beneath a white turban, all so characteristic of Galileans. The Man wore a tunic the color of ivory belted at the waist with knotted fishermen's cord over which a blue mantle fringed at the edges kept out the chill of winter.

That must be Him, he had thought. *Messiah is He? Look at Him! Will this meek Mouse wage war against the Romans for our freedom? He hasn't even got a horse or a sword! Messiah indeed!* Rabbi Levi had spat upon the ground. His contempt had grown into hatred of this Pretender who had deceived so many at the very time Messiah was so desperately needed.

He had seen her then, his Yael. She was to the right of

the so-called Messiah, listening, observing, exactly as she had always done in synagogue and Temple. Yeshua was talking about sheep, comparing Himself to a shepherd and promising to give His life for His sheep. The men around Him began to argue both amongst themselves and with Him.

"If you really are Messiah, just tell us plainly," one had said in obvious frustration.

Yeshua would not be baited. He said the miracles He performed should say all that was necessary. Then He began to talk again of sheep who would hear and answer His voice.

Rabbi Levi had grown even angrier when he saw that Yael was clearly entranced by this Man. She had allowed her veil to fall from her face and the look he found there was of a wounded sheep who longed for a Shepherd who would call to her, a Shepherd to whom she could run for protection, a Shepherd who would see past her scar to the tender heart beneath.

The men around Yeshua had picked up some nearby rocks as though they meant to stone Him where He stood.

"For which of My good works do you wish to stone Me?" Yeshua had asked innocently, too innocently, Rabbi Levi had thought.

The rabbi had continued to press closer to Yael. When those who wished Yeshua harm finally realized they could do nothing in the face of so many enthralled witnesses, they had withdrawn and Yeshua had escaped unharmed. Just as He had started to move away, He had stopped, His attention drawn to a child behind the angry men, to a child too timid, too wounded to come to Him, to Yael. He had reached out to her, one hand resting upon her head, the other cupping her trembling chin. For a long moment no one had moved.

Rabbi Levi had been unable to see Yeshua's face but he had been mystified by Yael's. He had never seen her so happy, especially before this Stranger who looked directly into her scarred face. Yet her eyes were enraptured, her smile wide and welcoming. Rabbi Levi had not been able to hear the words which had been spoken. Then Yeshua had gone on His way.

Yael had stood still, one hand clutching her cheek just as she had when the wicked Roman horseman had so grievously wounded her. But it had not been fear or pain which gripped her; instead she had not wanted to break the enchantment of that moment. She had been oblivious to everything around her. She hadn't even heard her grandfather approach.

"Yael, Yael!" he had exclaimed as he reached her. "What has He done to you, Child? What did that unspeakable Man say to you?"

Yael had blinked back to reality. "Oh, Saba. Did you see Him? Did you see Messiah?"

"I saw Him, Child, but He's not Messiah."

Yael had heard nothing. "He looked at me, Saba. He looked at me, not my scar. And He saw me through eyes filled with such great love. I've never seen love like that except in your eyes alone. Then He touched me and He said, 'My child, you are so beautiful to Me. I love you. May the blessing of the Holy One rest upon you both now and forevermore.'"

Then she was lost in her own little world again. Rabbi Levi had grasped her arm and led her in the direction of the bridge and the city stretching beneath the Temple Mount.

Rabbi Levi had been enraged with the temerity of the Man. How dare He trifle with the emotions of so wounded a child! *How dare He touch so tender a heart and one which belongs to me alone!* Rabbi Levi's frustration had grown into anger which, before they reached their home, had given birth to a terrible loathing of a Man he did not even know.

✡   ✡   ✡

In the days that followed, Yael no longer hid behind her veil or avoided the gaze of strangers or wept at the taunts of the children who played beside the well while their mothers drew water. It no longer mattered to her that no man would ever find her a suitable bride or that no child would ever call her Ammah. She had found Messiah and she was lovely in His eyes. That was all that mattered to her. In the strength of that knowledge, she had confronted whatever the world brought against her and defeated it with a quiet dignity and grace she had never known before. And Yael had told everyone of her Messiah. Some thought her disfigurement had finally driven her into the arms of insanity. Others thought she was possessed by some evil spirit. Even her family wondered what had happened to her but dared not speak of it in her presence.

Rabbi Levi had waited for the sinister spell this so-called Messiah had so callously cast upon his precious granddaughter to lift so that he might be able to reason with her, to reclaim her for himself. Then before he knew it, there had been no more time to wait.

✡   ✡   ✡

The awful fever had struck Yael with a terrible suddenness. Even before her parents had sent for the physician, Rabbi Levi had known it was useless. The physician had tried everything, even the leeches he claimed would draw the fever out of her body along with her blood. But she had vomited repeatedly, then lapsed into delirium, thrashing in her bed, becoming wet with perspiration. Then as the fever had raged on, there was no more perspiration and Rabbi Levi had known that the end was near. As her mother had bathed her hot forehead with a cool damp cloth, he had prayed prayers he knew would not be answered.

Just before the midnight hour, Yael's eyes had fluttered open. She had gazed at some imperceptible presence beyond the sight of the family members gathered at her bedside. She had smiled and tried to speak but her mouth was so dry she had barely been understood. To those nearest her, it had sounded as if she might have said, "I'm ready," and with that she was gone from them forever.

✿   ✿   ✿

Now Rabbi Levi sat amongst his scrolls but they brought him no comfort. Just before sundown, he had watched helplessly as a small figure swathed in white wrappings was laid on a stone bed in the family tomb. His precious Yael was gone from him forever and she had taken his heart with her. In its place, there remained nothing but a rock as cold and hard as the slab upon which they had laid her. The anger rose within him again.

It is His fault. I know that somehow, in some way, it is all His fault. He did something to her that day, cast some sort of an evil spell upon her, and now it has taken her from us, from me, forever. Healer is He? Why did He not heal her face? Why did He not heal her of His spell? Why did He not heal her of this cursed fever? If I ever see that wretched Messiah again, I'll ... I'll ... I'll see Him dead for this!

∽ 5 ∾

DAVID ben Asaph walked purposefully through the narrow streets of Capernaum. The last of the sun's rays were mirrored in his deep blue eyes, the whisper of an early spring breeze gently shifted the soft dark waves of his hair. He strode straight and tall, his skin deeply tanned from so many days at the tiller of his boat, his body rippling with muscles earned pulling so many full nets into his small craft. He was handsome in the same way that Greek statues were handsome, even though he had never permitted his eyes to rest upon such sacrileges and would have cared nothing about such comparisons. More than one feminine eye followed him as he went but he knew nothing of them either. The only eyes he had ever wanted to look his way now seemed closed to him forever and the thought of that tore at his heart as he walked.

It was drawing on toward sunset and the market stalls were crowded with late shoppers negotiating for fish and meat and fruit and vegetables for their suppers. David carried a small scroll rolled carefully and tied with a leather thong. He had business of another kind to conduct this day and he prayed it would go well.

✿　　　✿　　　✿

It had been nearly a year but a year had not been nearly enough. Hannah still smiled very seldom, shared no youthful confidences with the other girls her age, and even had little to say to her mother and brothers. Her sadness enveloped her as if the same waters that had stolen away her father's life had stolen away her soul as well. Hannah helped her mother bake cakes of bread but never smelled their beckoning aroma. Hannah helped her mother cook their simple meals but never tasted what she ate. Hannah helped her mother care for her three smallest fair-haired blue-eyed brothers but never noticed how they had grown. Hannah even stood still and straight as her mother fitted her new tunic to her slender frame but hadn't even noticed the color of the cloth. Something in Hannah had died with her abba out there on the cruel sea and no one who loved her knew if it would ever be revived.

Micah had also never recovered from the loss of his father. While he had crawled up on the shore struggling for breath, his auburn hair tangled by the sea and his brown eyes wide with fear, it sometimes seemed that he had not survived at all. He remained listless, seeing little and comprehending even less. Sometimes when the rabbi tried to teach him some difficult passage from Torah, his mind would wander away. Other times he would sit beneath a tree on the bank of the Sea of Galilee, daring the quiet water to rage and roil and return to take him away with it, too. In his heart he knew he should have died out there instead of his father and he knew he would have, too, if only his abba had not used the last of his strength to save him. Now he wanted nothing more than to join his father in death and so set right what had gone so terribly wrong that day.

Both Hannah and Micah were suffering the same suffocating feelings of guilt and grief. Both blamed themselves for their father's death and neither was strong enough to carry that heavy burden alone. But in their melancholy, they were also unable to reach out to each other to find the coupled strength that might have lessened their burden and saved them both. Instead they went through the motions of living like actors in some doleful drama, while in truth neither was truly living at all.

For Dinah, death had left a gaping hole in her heart where Itzak had once been alive and loving and larger than life. Gone were the strong arms that had cradled her during the long nights and provided for her during the long days. Gone were the pale brown eyes that had looked at her with love and reflected back to her the beauty he always found in her. Gone were the tender words that had sustained her in every crisis and had never failed to hold high the lamp of guidance for the entire family. She now heard only whispers of longing for what she had lost, for what might have been if only they had had a little more time together.

Still, even in her grief, Dinah could only marvel at the grace and goodness of her loving Lord. Micah had been too young and too devastated by his father's death to assume the responsibilities of the eldest son to provide for his widowed mother, his younger brothers and his older sister. Dinah remembered the dark day just after Itzak's death when her mind had careened around the questions that persistently pounded at her. *What will become of Itzak's fishing business? What will become of us now that we are without its support?*

Into the breach, the Holy One had sent David ben Asaph. Though only in his seventeenth year, he had assumed the broken family as his own with a quiet concern and a steadfast strength that spoke security to each grieving heart. Without even being asked, David had gone to the harbor the day following Itzak's burial. He had spoken with the hired men on Itzak's eight remaining vessels, negotiated their wages, much to their relief, and then led them out of the harbor in his own small craft. After the boats had returned with a bountiful catch, he had bargained the sale of the fish, paid each man, and taken the profit to Dinah. When her wondering eyes had asked the silent question, *Why,* he had replied, "Hannah will soon be my wife; you will soon be my mother and I will be your son. I do no more than any son would do." Then he had left before she could even thank him.

So it had been every working day since. David had become a son to Dinah and so much more. Often he brought a few of the finest fish to be prepared for supper. He played with the boys, encouraged them in their studies, and often stepped between flying fists to settle the little ones' disagreements. When Micah had refused to go with him to learn his father's profession, he had simply drafted Manasseh and Manoah, Dinah's twins who were in their tenth year.

"Soon the boats will be yours, one for each of you and the little ones, two for Micah as the eldest son, and one for your sister's dowry," he told them. "You must honor your father's memory by being the best fishermen on the Sea of Galilee and I will teach you how."

The two would smile up into his face, the sun illuminating their bright blue eyes, their ruddy complexions, and their reddish-gold curls so like their father's. Then they would put their young backs into whatever work he assigned them, sometimes laboring until the sun had become a great red ball in the western sky sliding into the waiting sea, learning the trade that would one day sustain them, receiving his praise for even the smallest task performed well. He was their big brother now and even more, he was their friend. They thrived under his caring tutelage.

Each day when he brought the boys home, David tried to reach out to Hannah, the woman he wanted for his wife. Sometimes he carried flowers or a confection from the stalls. She moved, she spoke, she took his gifts from his hand and thanked him while her dead eyes stared into a space he could not enter. But she was still the one that he had chosen to be his own and he knew, no matter what, even if he was never able to rekindle the light of life in her eyes or find so much as a glimmer of love there, he would cherish her until the day he died.

✡   ✡   ✡

Arriving at Dinah's home, David knocked gently on the doorpost beside the open door. He was welcomed immediately. Then he unrolled his small scroll and placed it on the table before Dinah.

"The accounting," he said seriously. "This is the weight of the fish caught by Itzak's boats each day, their price, the men's wages, and the profit I brought to you. As you will see ... ."

Dinah interrupted with a firm hand on his suntanned arm. "David, do you think that I do not trust you, that I must see numbers on a scroll to be convinced of your honesty and integrity? Does a mother not trust her own son? Without you, I would have been forced to sell the boats and we would have had nothing once the money was gone. Now I know that whatever you bring to me is the correct amount exactly. We will speak no more of these numbers. Do you understand?"

"Yes, Ammah," he replied, tears softening his blue eyes. It was only then that he realized what he had said and blushed. "My mother died when I was so small. I remember so little of her," he explained. "Sometimes I try so hard to recall the face above my cradle but I have only the vaguest impressions of her, of a smile tender and caring and of eyes lit with the light of love. I think she must have been very much like you. May I call you my ammah?"

"It would be a blessing from the Holy One Himself to have such a son as you," Dinah answered, her own tears obscuring the tenderness in her eyes. "From this day forward, I am your ammah and you are my ben, my own son."

They embraced for a long moment, their hearts joining together in an eternal bond. Dinah and David had reached out to meet the deepest need of each other and found in the reaching that the deepest need of their own hearts had been met as well.

✡   ✡   ✡

But time moved forward relentlessly and brought with it great obligations. The year of mourning would end just before Micah's twelfth birthday, just before Pesach. This was to have been a very special Pesach, when the family traveled together to Yerushalayim to celebrate, to visit friends and relatives, and to see Micah become a man as he entered into the Sanctuary of the Temple beside his father and worshipped the Holy One. Now they would go alone, carrying the bones of their father and husband as the children of Yisrael had carried Yosef's bones into the Promised Land he had seen through the eye of faith. Now Micah would enter the Sanctuary with David but he would enter it alone, without his dear abba.

And there was also Hannah's wedding. Itzak had wanted it to be held in Yerushalayim during Pesach week so that the entire family might attend. At night, he would whisper to Dinah of his hopes and dreams for their only daughter. Dinah had listened, saying little, knowing Hannah would be reluctant to wed a follower of Yeshua ben Yosef.

It was clear that David still expected to claim his bride in Yerushalayim exactly as he had contracted with her father nearly a year before; it was just as clear that Hannah expected no more than to be left alone with her grief.

Dinah wondered what to do. She loved them both; she wanted both to be happy. But Dinah dared not even hope that they would ever be happy together.

What have you done, Itzak? she would often ask a serene sky. *What do I do now? Do I force our daughter to marry a man she does not love or do I break covenant with a man who has become like a son to me? So Itzak, you who can now behold the face of our father Avraham, tell me the answer to this puzzle.*

The answer was always the same. Complete silence. Dinah only wished her heart would be as silent. Instead it churned out questions faster than she could answer them until she was left exhausted by it all. Too many nights, she would cry softly into her pillow, searching for solutions she did not have, waiting for a deep blue sky to soften into azure, then rising to face another day even more tired than when she had gone to bed. The dark circles beneath her eyes told the story to any who cared to read it. The boys were too young to understand and Hannah was past understanding. So Dinah carried the burden all alone.

It was nearly time to leave Capernaum on the long journey to Yerushalayim for Pesach. It had been arranged that she and the children would stay in the home of her elder sister, Ruth, and that David would stay across the courtyard in the home of Ruth's brother-in-law, Benyamin. This was no more than propriety demanded since David and Hannah were not yet wed. But still Dinah found herself tormented by questions which had no answers. And so one day dissolved all too rapidly into another as Pesach drew ever closer.

ॐ **6** ᘒ

T the sheep market north of the Temple Mount, Meshullam ben Aaron surveyed an endless sea of crates and cartons and carriers, all arranged haphazardly around a collection of makeshift enclosures. In many of the pens, young lambs bleated for mothers they would never see again and in small coops and cages, doves cooed as if they meant to reassure one another. Meshullam bartered with the merchant, his reedy voice rising and falling as terms were discussed and deals made, his hands gesturing wildly, his small brown eyes glinting shrewdly whenever there was some small advantage to be gained, his crinkled face revealing his final satisfaction with the various bargains he made. He was a merciless negotiator and he loved every minute of it.

At his father's right hand, Yakov struggled to keep up with the old man who lived for the dickering more than the deal. Meshullam had two other sons who assisted in the family business, Simeon who kept the books and Helah, a slow-witted youth who could only clean the animal pens. But Meshullam always insisted that only Yakov, his first-born, come along to learn the skills he would someday need when the business became his own. Yakov's body followed obediently, seeing and hearing while not seeing and hearing at all. But Yakov's heart no longer made the trip; it saw nothing and heard even less. Yakov had buried it with Shoshana in a tomb outside the city wall only a few months before. What did he care about the value of a lamb when his own little lamb was gone from his side? What difference did it make to him what a dove was worth when his own dove lay dead and cold and beyond his reach.

The seller at Meshullam's other side grew increasingly annoyed with the sagacious old man who knew precisely what every animal was worth down to the last penny and who allowed very few of those pennies to find their way into his pocket. He was always glad to see the father leave and he lived in anticipation of the day when he would deal with the son who seemed to be learning little about the fine art of business. Yes, his day would come and as he surveyed Meshullam more carefully than usual, he thought that day was not too far off.

On the way home, Meshullam crowed over his prowess as a businessman. "Did you see those first lambs he tried to foist off on us? One look at the eyes and I knew. I always know. They were a diseased lot. We might have lost everything." Meshullam paused and studied his son to be certain he was catching every word. "You must remember, Yakov. Never purchase the first stock you are shown. Be cautious. Let the merchant know that there are other sellers you may wish to visit. Wait until you are shown the good stock. Then before he knows what has happened to him, make your deal just as I did." Meshullam laughed then, the same thin cackle he always used to signal his satisfaction with his marketing skills.

Yakov muttered an occasional, "I see," and "Yes, Abba," as his father rattled on.

"And we shall have the very best animals just as we always do, sacrifices fit for the Holy One, offerings any worshipper will be proud to give," Meshullam finally finished with a great flourish. Satisfied that his son had missed nothing of this latest lesson on livestock trading, Meshullam turned into the little lane in the Upper City where he lived with Helah in the home he had shared with his wife until her death just after Helah's birth. He knew the silent pain that walked with his son but he didn't really understand just as one can never really understand the grief of another. Neither did he speak of it for he was not one to display his emotions even if he might have comforted a son who now struggled with his own grief all by himself.

Yakov continued on alone to the fine house he had built for his bride just across the courtyard from his father's. Once he had loved it, loved building it, loved surprising Shoshana with it, loved living in it, loved loving in it, loved coming home to it every evening. Now he hated it, hated living in it, hated the sounds of the child who cried out for his love within its walls, hated coming to it just as he hated coming to it now. The lengthening shadows of dusk were as nothing when compared to the darkness in Yakov's broken heart.

"My lord, the child is sleeping," Devorah said softly as he entered. "Ephraim and Rachel were very busy this day caring for both your home and your father's so I have made a fine stew of the meat Rachel bought this afternoon. May I set out some for your supper?"

Yakov stared at her for a long moment, not really comprehending what she had said, trying to reconstruct her words in his mind so that he might respond with a coherent answer. She glanced up for only a moment to be certain he had heard. Finally he spoke.

"Yes ... yes. That will be fine, Devorah," he said absently as he seated himself cross-legged on a cushion beside the low table that dominated the room. More from habit than conviction, he bowed his head and mumbled the prayer of thanks for one's provision, "Blessed art thou, our Lord, King of the universe, who brings forth food from the earth."

As he prayed, Devorah returned to the bubbling iron pot and began ladling stew into a small ceramic bowl. She carried it and several small round loaves of freshly baked wheat bread to the table and set the food before him, all the time avoiding his eyes as was the custom. As she served him, Yakov poured himself a goblet of wine from the graceful amphora which stood beside the table in its circular iron rack. Then since it would have been quite unthinkable for a man and a woman or an employee and her employer to share a meal at the same table, Devorah ladled some of the remaining stew into her own plain bowl and returned to her place beside the fire to eat her own supper, just as alone as the man across the room from her.

She almost wished she had not given the servants the evening to rest in their upstairs room. At least then she would have had company. But Ephraim and Rachel were both advanced in years, having worked for Meshullam since youth. Their labors had only increased as dwellings were added around the great courtyard to accommodate grown sons and again after Shoshana had died and Yakov had required their services to tend his home as well.

Devorah remembered other days in another house beside another fire. It seemed a thousand years ago instead of only a few. She remembered Yonah, strong and good and loving Yonah, with hair and eyes the color of coals and teeth the color of a summer cloud. She had never had to avert her eyes from his. His eyes had smiled whenever she came into view and hers had sparkled in response. She had often made the same stew for Yonah but had eaten it as he told stories of his day training horses for the Roman army. Later she would lay beside him just as she had the night he had spoken of some new holy Man he had met at the home of a centurion. But Yonah had fallen asleep before he could finish the story and now she couldn't even remember the new Rabbi's name.

And Devorah remembered carrying Yonah's child until the day a Roman soldier had appeared at her door, his helmet balanced between his hip and the crook of his arm, to tell her that her Yonah had fallen from a horse he was teaching to jump and had broken his neck instantly. Yonah would never again come home to her; he would never again look at her with the fire of love burning in his eyes; he would never again eat the stew she had prepared just for him. And he would never gaze into the face of the son

67

she carried. Her hands had flown to her distended abdomen and in that same moment her pains had come long and hard and far too soon. Their tiny baby boy had been stillborn before the sun went down, before she could even take that one last walk with her beloved Yonah to the place where he would rest eternally from his labors.

Their son was dead, laid beside his father, but Devorah's body still produced milk as though a living breathing child waited to be suckled. When Devorah realized her milk was all she had with which to support herself, she had accepted a position with a wealthy Roman couple and, once their son was weaned, she had come to the home of Yakov ben Meshullam as wetnurse to his newborn daughter whom he called Mara.

At first she had thought this wealthy merchant's wife must be like so many others, women who did not want to be bothered nursing children, women whose husbands hired wetnurses to do it for them. When she learned Shoshana had died in childbirth, she felt guilty for her unkind thoughts. But in her breaking heart, she also felt a painful pang of envy. She wished death had taken her, too. Then she would be with Yonah and their son. They would be together forever and nothing would ever separate them again.

But Devorah lived even when she did not want to live; she breathed even when each breath brought the double misery of her doubled grief. And her pain seemed destined to go on forever. She had now fallen hopelessly in love with the tiny babe with the sapphire eyes and black ringlets who tugged on her breast at each feeding. She hadn't allowed this to happen before and hadn't meant for it happen this time. But it had. She knew just how Mara's little mouth curled into a smile and the very way her deep dimples danced as Devorah entered her chamber. She knew the meaning of each of Mara's cries and her own satisfaction in answering each one. But babies grew relentlessly into children, children who were weaned, children who no longer needed to be nursed. New tears formed in Devorah's translucent blue eyes as she looked ahead to the day she would have to say goodbye to Mara forever.

Yakov scooped up the last of his stew with his bread, took a final gulp of wine, then rose from the table and went to his sleeping chamber alone. He did not inquire about his daughter. But then, he never had. He did not go to her cradle. But then, he had never done that either. He had never played with her or talked to her or even picked her up, never, not once in all the months Devorah had been caring for the infant.

Devorah wondered how a heart could become so hard and so cold against a small child who asked for nothing more than a father's love. Devorah also wondered how she could ever leave that child in the care of such an uncaring man. Alone, Devorah allowed the tears to come, tears for the child she had lost and for the one she was going to lose all too soon.

HE lean stonecutter chiseled away at the clean white limestone on his workbench, oblivious to the flies flitting around his sweaty brow. His sinewy muscles rippled beneath his leather apron as his calloused hands turned this way and that to assure a perfect inscription. It wasn't every day that one was given the honor of creating the little ossuary in which the bones of the son of the high priest himself would soon rest. The Hebrew letters must be formed just so, *AMI BEN QAYAFA*, on the slab that would form the end of the box. Then, when the year of mourning ended and time had done its fearsome work upon the flesh, the boy's bones would be tenderly placed inside. The box, no longer than a cubit and a half, would be slipped into one of the *kokhim* or niches carved into the great burial cave of the Qayafa family. All that would be visible then would be this carefully inscribed name plate and Elihu meant for it to be as beautifully done as the encircled rosettes he had been commissioned to carve into the sides of the box.

Elihu loved his work. He had loved it ever since childhood. He still remembered the day, after he had been weaned and learned his letters at his mother's knee, when he was finally permitted to stand at his father's side to learn the craft that had supported the ben Sefa family for generations. He loved every aspect of the work, from quarrying the soft limestone around the Mount of Olives, to gathering the small smooth stones that could be used for mosaics, to creating the carvings which turned his labors into works of art. His love for his craft flowed through him in his blood just as it had flowed in the blood of his fathers before him. He was never happier than when he sat at his wooden workbench directing his hammer and chisel in their delicate dance across the stone.

Elihu was so intent on his task that he didn't hear the old man enter his shop. After a moment, the man cleared his throat and waited for the absorbed craftsman to turn his way.

"My apologies, my lord." Elihu greeted his guest with a deep bow. "The hammer and the chisel are not quiet in their work and I did not hear you enter." His customer was of the higher class and Elihu had no desire to insult him with even the slightest rudeness.

The man chuckled to put Elihu at ease. "It is nothing ... nothing," he insisted with a wave of a wrinkled hand. "I appreciate an opportunity to observe a gifted craftsman at his work."

"How may I be of service, my lord?" Elihu queried. From the gentleman's sumptuous apparel, it was clear he was rich. Elihu guessed he might be decorating a new seaside villa in the north. "I have some fine mosaics in the back. May I show you something of that sort?"

The old man's eyes filled with tears and his voice became wistful. "No, my son. It is not for adornments that I come. It is for the very kind of thing upon which you were working. In fact I could not help but notice that you are preparing an ossuary for Ami ben Qayafa. He was the best friend of my own son, Moshe. The two were so inseparable that the Holy One in His wisdom chose to take both upon the very same day. So I, too, will soon be requiring an ossuary for all that remains of my only child."

Naqdimon could not continue and Elihu spoke to fill the silence that hung heavy between them.

"My deepest condolences, my lord," Elihu said softly. "I shall be honored to serve you but there may be a problem. Many hours are required for a box such as this. If you will be needing one so soon, I may not have time enough to give it all my skills can offer."

Elihu certainly did not wish to lose such a wealthy customer but a fine artistically-embellished receptacle such as the one he was fashioning for the high priest's son could not be finished in the few months remaining before the year of mourning would end, not with all the other work that Elihu had already promised to do. The Qayafa family had placed their order some time ago to be certain it could be filled in time. This customer may simply have waited too long.

Naqdimon could not speak for a moment. When he did, it was with the halting words that stumble forth from a broken heart. "It is just that ... you must understand ... until today, I could not face ... . The fact that all that remains of the son of my heart may be fitted into such a small box is more than I could bear. I know I have waited too long. It is only that ... . It was only today that I found the courage to do what must be done, what can be put off no longer."

Elihu had dealt with many customers in the past but this one touched his heart in a way no other had. When the representative of the Qayafa family had come some months before, he had been abrupt and demanding, negotiating the price down to the barest minimum and insisting upon the most intricate of engravings in the bargain. But this man was different. He hadn't sent a representative to do his dickering even though he clearly could afford to do so. He had come himself, even though it obviously tore at his heart, to do the last thing he could do for his son in this world. Elihu's heart went out to him. He would work long into the nights if necessary to make for this man whatever he required.

"My lord, I do understand," Elihu responded gently. "It will be my honor to provide all that is needed for your son."

Their eyes met for only an instant but both knew their

hearts had met as well. The tears in Naqdimon's eyes spilled over and disappeared into his beard. He made no attempt to stop them.

"May the Holy One bless you for your kindness to an old man who has tarried too long in his grief," Naqdimon whispered. "I wish for nothing elaborate. My son was a simple boy, simple and good, and so must it be with the receptacle in which he will rest. I wish only that the stone be of the finest quality just as he was in his life and that it be smoothed until it shines just as he shone in the lives of all who knew him. The only engraving I would ask of you is his name, *Moshe ben Naqdimon*. I trust this will create no hardship for you."

Elihu was shocked and it showed on his handsome face. For the first time, he realized that the man before him was none other than Naqdimon, wealthy member of the Sanhedrin and one of the elder statesman of his nation. He had heard of him many times but never hoped to meet such an exalted one personally. Men like Naqdimon had many servants to meet with ordinary tradesmen. Elihu found himself even more impressed with the caring father who stood before him, even more determined to give him the best he had to offer.

"My lord, I promise you before the Holy One that I will spare no effort to create exactly the box you have described and that I will have it ready in time."

"I can ask nothing more," replied Naqdimon. From his wide sash, he withdrew a small leather purse and retrieved a number of silver coins which he placed in the stonecutter's hand. "I will pay any additional cost when I come again," he pledged.

"My lord, you have given me far too much," Elihu protested after he had counted the coins. "I am certain the price will not be nearly so great."

"My son, you have extended great kindness to me at a very difficult moment. The laborer is worthy of his hire, is he not?"

Elihu nodded, unable to speak.

"Then the laborer will be so kind as to allow me to pay according to the value I place upon the service he renders to me, will he not?"

"My lord, you are more than kind."

The transaction completed, Naqdimon bowed slightly and was gone out into the busy street. Elihu was left standing surprised and speechless, thinking of the special present this additional money might purchase for his precious wife, Ruth, or for one of the children, knowing he would work to fashion a box like no other for this most honored of customers.

Naqdimon made his way through the narrow streets and to his home on one of the green plateaus in the northern part of the Upper City. He had been unable to form the words that were really in his heart. He had failed his son, failed to bring him to Messiah, failed to see to his spiritual well-being. One whose soul was not decorated with salvation, the work of the Holy One's hands, could not lie forever in a box decorated with the work of the artisan's hands. The little ossuary Naqdimon had just ordered for Moshe would forever speak of a father's failure to provide the most important necessity of all for his only son.

Naqdimon disappeared into his house and allowed his body to sag into the nearest chair, a Grecian model with curved wood and a tanned leather seat. There, he covered his face with his hands and wept as one who mourned for an only son for indeed he did.

∝ **8** ∾

"**N**OT again. Not so soon." Rabbi Levi whispered the words to himself the moment he heard the news and the request of the high priest which accompanied it.

It had been only a month since he and his family had laid Yael to rest. Now to even consider entering a house of mourning was almost more than he could bear. But he would have to lay aside his own grief to come to the aid of others in their time of bereavement. This, too, was the work of the Holy One and he meant to be His obedient servant in all things.

Young Eleazar ben Shimon had died after a brief illness that was at first not thought to be serious. But death had come with shocking suddenness, leaving his family in stunned sadness. When word was brought to Rabbi Levi, his hand had flown to his breast and his eyes had filled with tears. One so young, so full of life, so like his own Yael, so quickly gone.

But there was much more in Rabbi Levi's heart for Eleazar's father, Shimon, was his lifelong friend. They were as different as night and day, Levi dark from his black hair and brown eyes to his olive skin and Shimon fair with light brown hair and light brown eyes to match. Yet the two had grown up together as best friends on the winding streets of the city of Yerushalayim. Rabbi Levi remembered the chores they had done together, the games they had played together, and the time they had mounted Shimon's father's donkey and careened through the ramshackle booths of the market place scattering people and children and chickens and sheep in all directions. He remembered the stern lecture followed by a firm application of the rod of correction they had received, too. They had cried about it then but they had often laughed about it since.

Shimon and Levi had attended synagogue school together and both had learned their lessons well. Of course they had found time to engage in the usual schoolboy pranks, such as the day Shimon had filled their teacher's inkstand with water and Levi had ever so innocently asked the elderly rabbi to copy for him a particularly difficult passage from Torah. The old man who was almost blind wrote nearly an entire column before he realized the pen in his hand made no mark upon the parchment. Though their teacher had not known who was responsible, there had come the day when both boys had become so convicted in conscience that they had decided to go to him, confess, and accept whatever punishment he saw fit. The old man had sat wrapped in his fringed robe with his turban at a rather rakish angle on his white head and listened patiently to their tearful admission of guilt. Then he enfolded each boy in one of his enormous arms.

"I, too, played the selfsame trick on my old teacher many years ago but I did not have the courage to confess. He died before I could make amends and I have always carried the great sorrow my folly caused me. You have shown much more bravery than I, my sons. You shall have my pardon and the Holy One's. And someday, should the Holy One call you to His service, you will grant this same pardon to others. Yes?"

"Yes, Rabbi," they had answered through tears of forgiveness found and peace restored. The weight of the world had been lifted from their small shoulders; they knew the full release of sins forgiven. That day, it had never been easier for two rambunctious boys to follow the ancient Hebrew maxim directed to all students, "Place thyself in the dust at the feet of the wise," for in their case the wise had been shown to be merciful as well.

Once grown to manhood, Levi had indeed heard the call of the Holy One. Then he had entered the most conservative of Hebrew universities, the School of Shammai, rather than the more liberal School of Hillel, and had studied there to become a rabbi, a teacher of the Holy One's own Word. Shimon had heard a very different call, the call of business, and had become a wealthy producer of dates and figs in the small city of Bethany, only a short walk away on the beautiful Mount of Olives just east of Yerushalayim.

Each had taken a wife, too, and the friendship born in the schoolyard soon expanded to include the two women and the children they bore. Levi's father had chosen for him the girl he had loved since childhood, Hadassah. He still remembered how she had looked on the day he took her to his bosom forever, small and slender with sparkling eyes of brown and flowing long dark hair that clung to her head in waves. Their love, their life together, and the children their love had created were now among his most treasured memories.

Since his parents had died, Shimon had arranged his own marriage to the beautiful Shaloma. She was tiny, her round face lit by black eyes and surrounded by shining black hair. She was also everything her name implied, a woman both peaceful and at peace, quiet, unassuming, content to remain in the shadow of her husband's accomplishments. When his business acumen and the large contributions to the Temple it made possible caused Shimon to be invited to sit as a member of the Sanhedrin, Shaloma had positively glowed.

Then life had taken a few of its many unpredictable turns. Hadassah had died suddenly on a simmering summer day when a white hot sun had hung too long in a pale sky. She had simply raised a tired hand to a sweated brow, sighed deeply, and slumped into the arms of the fathers. Later that same year, Shaloma had died in childbirth with a stillborn infant boy and Shimon's big heart had simply broken as though he himself had placed within her womb the sword that had pierced her fragile heart. Before another winter came, Shimon had contracted the most dreaded of all diseases, leprosy. After that, the friends could no longer be in each other's company for one was a holy rabbi and the other a cursed leper.

Eleazar, though barely a man himself, had risen to the challenge of all that life had done to his family. When his father became ill and had to separate himself, Eleazar, the picture of Shimon at the same age, had assumed the burden of providing for his two older sisters with the maturity of many twice his age. In the early days, Rabbi Levi had made the journey to Bethany many times to offer his counsel and support. He had found young Eleazar more than capable of managing his father's groves and equal to the task of dealing with two women more different than alike.

Miriam was small in size, dark in coloring, quiet and calm and loving just like her dear mother. Martha, on the other hand, was as fair as her father, tall in stature and short in patience, possessing the same forceful qualities that had made her father so successful in his business but which always seemed somewhat disconcerting when cloaked in the contours of a woman. Miriam was always content simply to be while Martha just had to do.

Eleazar took it all in stride, teasing Miriam to bring out her gentle humor and cajoling Martha to deflect her inherent aversion to authority. Somehow he made it all work, much to the amusement, amazement, and general relief of all who knew them. It was often said with a smile that, while only the Holy One could resolve the differences between the schools of Shammai and Hillel, Eleazar ben Shimon always succeeded in resolving the differences between Martha and Miriam. And his sisters adored him for it.

Now Eleazar was gone too soon and too suddenly. *What will become of those girls now?* Rabbi Levi asked himself. *With no man to look after them, they might lose the family business* and with it their income and their home. Without a father or brother to arrange their marriages, they might become prey to a particular kind of men, the too handsome, too charming, oily kind that promised safety and security before marriage and offered only abuse and misuse after. Such might take all that the sisters had and leave them with nothing.

It had been several years since Rabbi Levi had visited Bethany. Once he knew Eleazar was able to care for his sisters, he had not wanted to become like an unwelcome uncle who visited too often and stayed too long. And during those years he had been so concerned with Yael that he had not wanted to leave even for an afternoon. Now he would go once again, this time at the request of the high priest himself.

Knowing of the lifelong friendship between the two families, Yosef ben Qayafa had requested that Rabbi Levi join a delegation that would offer the condolences of the Sanhedrin to the daughters of one of its former members. The rabbi had agreed immediately, dreading the task yet anxious to see old friends once again.

✿   ✿   ✿

The late winter day was surprisingly warm and the small contingent stopped several times to mop brows and to drink from the small wineskins which had been provided for the journey. The Mount of Olives was as beautiful as ever, dotted with small shrubs and old fig trees with twisted trunks and gnarled limbs. The road writhed and snaked through limestone outcroppings until at last the little group crested one of four peaks and approached the tiny town of Bethany. As he neared his friend's home, Rabbi Levi's heart nearly stopped, for at the door greeting each mourner personally was his old friend, Shimon.

Am I drunk? Rabbi Levi thought at first. *No ... no ... I know I am not. Perhaps my old eyes are deceiving me.* But it was indeed Shimon who waited to welcome him! Rabbi Levi immediately felt a stab of anger pierce his soul. *How dare he expose us all to the scourge of leprosy!* he thought. Finally, Rabbi Levi could only stare in wonder for he saw that Shimon's skin was as clear and clean as it had been in those long-ago days they had shared at school. In the next instant, Rabbi Levi found himself enfolded in Shimon's warm embrace complete with repeated kisses on each cheek.

"My brother," Rabbi Levi began, "I am so saddened by the occasion which has brought us to your home today. My heart is with you in your grief."

Tears filled the old man's eyes. "Levi, my friend, my brother, I am especially grateful that you have come. Yes, it is a crushing calamity which has befallen this house." Shimon paused, collecting his thoughts. "I cannot even begin to comprehend my loss."

The two men released their embrace and looked long into each other's eyes.

"You are looking well, my brother," Rabbi Levi pronounced. "The Holy One has surely blessed you with good health once again."

"This is true. I am so much better than the last time you saw me, that day some years ago when we could only call out our greetings to each other from the distance of one hundred paces," recalled Shimon ruefully. "The Holy One has truly done a wonderful thing for me, has He not? I have been longing to tell you about it. Perhaps when there is time."

"Can there be a better time than this?" questioned Rabbi Levi. "Come tell me all the Holy One has done. Tell me how this wonderful cleansing has taken place."

The two walked to a small grove of date palm trees Shimon had planted across the road from his house to honor the occupation that had provided so well for his family. They sat together on a bench built of the stones that had once littered the grove.

"I had never thought to see the day when we could sit together again. I remember when the first lesions developed. I tried to tell myself that it was nothing, a rash, a scrape, nothing more. Then other lesions came and I could deny the truth no longer. For the sake of my children, my friends, my husbandmen, my customers, I went to the priest. When the determination was finally made, when the leprosy was finally pronounced, I thought my life was over and I didn't even care. All through those years, I wanted nothing more than to bid farewell to this old world with all of its sickness and death and pain so that I could join Shaloma. Then He came."

"He?" Rabbi Levi broke in. "Whom do you mean?"

"Yeshua, Yeshua ben Yosef," Shimon replied most excitedly. "Do you know Him?"

"I know of Him," Rabbi Levi answered simply. His mind returned to that day when the wicked Yeshua had cast His spell upon fragile Yael but he said nothing of the incident.

"It seems like only yesterday. I was with others such as myself. One, a Galilean, recognized Him. We dared not approach Him but the Galilean begged Him to have mercy upon us."

"To have mercy upon you?" Rabbi Levi interrupted. "Why? What could He do?"

Shimon's eyes glowed with his remembrance of the event. "Precisely what He did do, my friend," he said quietly. "He simply turned toward us, looked at us with the most loving eyes I have ever seen, and instructed us to go to the priest and show ourselves to him."

"That was all? He did not touch you?" Rabbi Levi interrogated, recalling the day He had touched Yael's face leaving it as scarred as ever but robbing her of her soul in the process.

"That was all," Shimon assured. "Then, we were on our way to the priest, believing against all reason. After all, we were lepers. What business did we have visiting the priest?" Shimon laughed. "We were almost to the priest's house when we suddenly stopped and began to examine ourselves. Each of us was as clean as the day he was born. Lesions had disappeared. Fingers and toes and ears and noses that had been mere stubs were instantly restored. We embraced, we laughed, we cried, we sang, we danced — right there in the middle of the street in front of the priest's door. One of our number, a Samaritan he was, ran off to find Yeshua, to thank Him, I think, but the rest of us did exactly as we had been instructed; we wished to take no chances. We pounded upon the priest's door until he finally appeared and agreed to see us. Shortly after, I was home supping with my precious children, something I thought I would never do again."

Rabbi Levi stared at his old friend as though he had lost his mind. Yet he could not argue with the obvious fact that Shimon had been cleansed; he clearly was a leper no longer.

Shimon continued. "I wanted to tell the whole world what had happened. I especially wanted to tell you but, once the priests knew it was Yeshua who had cleansed us, they forbade it. I did tell the children the whole story. I had to. You understand."

Levi nodded.

"And I showed them proof," Shimon continued as he pulled back the sleeves of his tunic to reveal the perfection of the skin beneath. There was not even a freckle evident on Shimon's arms.

"What I did not know was that they had already met this miracle-Worker. They had even had Him in our home as their Guest for dinner."

"He came to break bread with the young ones?" Rabbi Levi queried.

"Indeed. They said He even came early, while Eleazar was still in the groves and the girls were preparing the feast. And He took the entire afternoon to sit with Miriam and explain to her the love of the Holy One for His children no matter what sins they may have committed."

Shimon shuddered involuntarily and looked down into

his lap. Then in an agonized aside he told his friend, "And I understand that my poor Miriam had committed many in the years that I was gone."

Then Shimon continued. "Later He told her this love often manifests itself in the miraculous touch of the Holy One upon the bodies of those that love Him. Miriam was so thrilled by what she heard that she believed immediately, resolving to receive the Holy One's forgiveness, hoping there might even be such a miracle of healing for me. For Eleazar belief on Him came later. And my own precious Martha ... ." Shimon paused searching for words which did not come easily. "I hope true belief will yet come to her heart."

"And then?" Rabbi Levi encouraged.

"And then He simply went His way," Shimon replied. "But a little seed of faith had been planted in Miriam's heart, a seed she continued to nurture with her prayers. It was only many months later when He came again that this seed came to full growth and bore fruit," Shimon explained, using the metaphor with which he was most familiar.

"Many months? Why many months?" the old rabbi pressed.

"Am I in the place of the Holy One to know such things?" Shimon returned philosophically. "I know not. I know only that Miriam's prayers to the Holy One were answered. I was cleansed. *Cleansed!*"

But Rabbi Levi wasn't listening as Shimon rejoiced. "So it was the Holy One who healed you, not this Yeshua," Rabbi Levi concluded as though he had sprung some sort of a trap on his old friend.

Shimon only chuckled knowingly. "Oh, my brother, do you not see? Do you not understand? He *is* the Holy One, the One whose coming has been foretold to us. He is Messiah," Shimon answered confidently.

"This cannot be," Rabbi Levi replied almost pleading. "This Imposter cannot be the One who healed you and He cannot be Messiah. I know this of a certainty."

Shimon studied the intensity in his friend's eyes. When he spoke, it was quietly, soothingly. "My brother, why do you say such things? Am I not clean? Am I not healed? What then prevents you from receiving our Messiah?"

The barely contained anger in the old rabbi exploded. His words flew from his mouth one after another as though they were birds freed from their cage. "I'll tell you why I know this Man cannot be Messiah. Let me tell you my experience with this Charlatan." The tale of Yael's injury, the terrible scarring of both her soul and her body which resulted, and her encounter with Yeshua spilled out in all its wrenching detail. Then Rabbi Levi covered his anguished face with his gnarled hands and wept as he told the story of her death.

"Why? Why if He can heal, did He not heal my precious Yael? Why if He is Messiah, did He not save her life? Why? Why? Why?"

Shimon's arms were around him then, drawing him close, comforting him as one might comfort a child awakening from some fearful nightmare. "Levi, Levi, my dearest friend, I do not know why the Holy One chooses to heal one and not another. I do not know why He causes one to live and takes another to rest in the bosom of the fathers."

Shimon's voice caught in his throat and for a long moment he could not go on. Then he continued to whisper words of comfort and assurance. "I only know that He loves us and He does only what is best for us. Perhaps in the case of your Yael, it was not her scarred body which required healing but her scarred soul. And, Levi my friend, her soul was healed by His love, by His touch. Was it not?"

"How can you continue to defend Him? What of your own Eleazar? Why does he lie cold and dead in a distant tomb? If He is Messiah, why did He not heal your son?"

Shimon's grey head slumped forward and his eyes filled with tears. When his voice came, it was filled with anguish. "Do you not think I have asked myself these same questions a thousand times during these last four days? All I know is that He was over on the other side of the river when Eleazar fell ill. The girls sent a message to Him immediately but perhaps He could not get here in time. I cannot explain what He has not done; I can only rejoice in what He has done. After all, what am I that the Holy One should take any notice of me at all? Yet look at what He has done for me. How could I even ask for more than this? Once I was dead but now I am alive again and I am alive because of Him and Him alone. Praised be the Holy One of Yisrael."

Suddenly the two men were called from their conversation by some commotion created in the distance as a small knot of people coming from the direction of Yerushalayim turned out of the Yericho Road and into the long upward-angled lane that led to Shimon's house. Shimon blinked his reddened eyes again and again. He stood, looked down the road one last time to be certain, then raced back toward his door leaving a very puzzled Rabbi Levi to follow.

"He's here," Shimon whispered to his daughters. "Yeshua is here."

"I knew He would come," replied the impetuous Martha. She instantly left the gathering of mourners and disappeared through the open door.

Miriam had heard, too, but she knew the anguish of her sister's soul, the questions that could not be asked but had to be answered. As much as she wanted to see Yeshua, to cry out her grief in His loving arms, she knew her sister needed Him more. She also knew that the peace she had felt since her brother's death, the very peace she had first found at Yeshua's feet, would sustain her for another few minutes. Miriam knew Martha must find that same peace. She made no effort to rise from her seat.

Martha did not wait for Yeshua to climb the steep hill to her home. Her anger, her pain, her questions drove her to Him on the road. As she went, her hands formed themselves into tight fists while her eyes dared a single tear to escape their bounds. She wanted to tell Him He should have come sooner, to accuse Him of not caring about Eleazar or her or her family; she wanted to scream, to cry, to bury her fists in His chest. Yet after one look into His gentle blue eyes, she did none of those things. Instead, the love in His eyes met the faith lying dormant in her heart and it was that faith which finally formed her words.

"Lord, if only You had been here, I know my brother would not have died. But I know that even now, whatever You ask of the Holy One He will give it to You."

Yeshua smiled tenderly at a profession of faith worth so much more under such sad circumstances. His eyes held hers in His love and He silently spoke His peace into her soul.

"I promise you, Martha, your brother shall rise again," He assured in a confidence so complete Martha was captured by it. Her own confidence rose up to meet His.

"I know he shall rise again," she began with a certainty that surprised even her. Then realizing the enormity of her own words, she added, "in the resurrection at the last day."

Yeshua smiled again. He knew her struggle, had known of it since the day He had first come to her home for dinner, and He meant to settle it once and for all while there was still time. His eyes locked on hers and drew them into Himself.

"Martha, *I AM* the resurrection and the life. The one that believes in Me, even if he is already dead, yet he shall live. And the one that lives and believes in Me will never die. Do you believe this, Martha?"

His eyes searched hers for her answer. Her heart searched His for the faith to trust in such an impossible possibility. Both found what they were seeking. It was as though some force within Him drew the truth from deep within her soul. She heard herself answer with a quiet conviction she had not known she possessed. But even as she said the words, she knew of a certainty they were true.

"Yes, Lord. I believe You are the anointed One, the Son of the Holy One Himself, the One that had to come into the world." There was nothing else to say. That was all there was and suddenly that was all that mattered.

Martha nearly floated home. Even Eleazar's death no longer held any reality for her. Abba had been right. Miriam, too. And now she knew it as well. She had met Messiah and everything else paled into oblivion. When she entered the house, she was surprised by the great number of people who had come to mourn her brother's death and bring comfort to his family. *Were they all here before?* she wondered. *How is it that I never even noticed them?*

The truth was that Martha had been so consumed by her own grief, she hadn't been aware of the grief of those around her nor of the many who had come to share the burden of it. Now there was no more grief. Somehow Yeshua's words, His voice, His eyes, His very being had banished all grief. Now Martha was able to see the pain of the others, particularly her own sister. Martha went to her side almost furtively. The others didn't know. They wouldn't understand. But Miriam would.

"The Master is here and I think He wants to see you," Martha whispered with a secret smile. She loved the way the word, Master, sounded on her lips. She had said it before, many times in many circumstances. Yet it seemed that just as Yeshua had transformed her mourning into joy, He had somehow transformed this very word into a title fit for a king.

Miriam knew immediately what had happened. There was something about the way her sister's voice caressed the word, Master. Miriam knew that He was now indeed her Master. Martha had found exactly what Miriam had hoped she would find. Now they were sisters, true sisters, in an even deeper way than they had ever before known.

Miriam slid from her seat on one of the couches along the wall and out the door as quickly and quietly as she could but she was not as fortunate as her sister. She had been observed.

The mourners from Yerushalayim assumed she was on her way to the cemetery to grieve alone at her brother's tomb. They could not bear the idea of her shaking with sobs with no one there to comfort her. Without a word, eyes searched other eyes, heads nodded, and one by one they slipped silently out the door and followed Miriam at a discreet distance. They were surprised to find her moving in the direction of a Man on the dusty little dirt road that led to her home.

When Miriam reached Yeshua, it seemed all of the strength left her slender body. It had been there during Eleazar's illness; it had been there the night he died; it had even been there the day he was buried. Now it had deserted her. But she was with Yeshua now. She didn't have to be strong any longer. He was her strength now. She gave in to her grief and collapsed at His feet.

"Lord, if only You had been here, I know my brother would not have died," Miriam said softly. Though she could not know it, these were the very words her sister had spoken. Yet from her lips, the words came as the quiet confession of a strong inner faith that sustained her despite Eleazar's death. In some way even she could not understand, she knew there had to be a reason for all of this, a reason why Eleazar was gone, a reason why Yeshua had not come to prevent it. She knew in her heart Yeshua loved her, loved her brother, loved every member of her family. And in the security of that love, Miriam had found the faith to believe that somehow it would all be for the best.

Still her heart broke every time she thought of her brother, the one who had struggled to sustain his sisters during their father's long illness, the one who had never complained when the harvest days were long and the labor was hard, the one who always found time to place a basket of food or clothes or blankets beneath an ancient fig tree near the deserted spot where the lepers of Bethany lived. He would always bring his sisters the report that Abba looked well or that Abba had waved or that Abba had shouted a message of love for them across the wide chasm that divided him from them. And it was Eleazar who had never forsaken her, not even when her despondency over her mother's death and her father's illness had led her for a time into a life of such abysmal shame that even now she could not recall it without the deepest regret. Eleazar was so good. Miriam couldn't help but wonder why it had to be him. And with the wondering came the tears she couldn't hold back. Now, even though she confidently trusted in the purposes of Yeshua, purposes she did not know and dared not ask, she dampened His dusty feet with tears of grief.

Miriam's weeping coupled as it was with her words of blind belief nearly broke Yeshua's heart. A groan welled up from deep within His spirit and escaped His lips. Everyone had suffered enough, too much. It had to end and He knew He was the only One who could end it. It was time to do what He had come to do. He would wait no longer.

The mourners had reached the place where Miriam lay and recognized with distaste the Man before whom she had fallen. They listened intently to hear what conversation might pass between the two. Shimon and Levi joined them. Yeshua raised His eyes from the sobbing figure at His feet, stood, and caught the eyes of the group that had gathered.

"Where have you lain him?" Yeshua inquired, His voice tired and taut.

With a sweep of his arm in the direction of the cemetery, Shimon spoke. "Lord, come and see." Then as Yeshua approached, Shimon saw that He, too, was weeping.

As the twist of people snaked along the road toward the cemetery, the Yerushalayim mourners whispered to one another behind cupped palms.

"Look how much He loved him," one said almost incredulously, as though an Imposter of Yeshua's sort had no heart with which to love, no soul with which to feel the pain of loss.

"If He was the great miracle-Worker He claimed to be, why didn't He keep His friend from dying in the first place?" Rabbi Levi sneered. Several heads nodded in agreement.

Yeshua didn't hear their comments but He did not need to hear them to know the kind of hearts from which they rose. He had been looking into such stony faces and even stonier hearts for nearly three years now. He knew what they thought, what they believed, what they refused to believe even when it was staring them full in the face. He wept for their blindness even more than He wept for the young man resting peacefully in the tomb.

As the group made its way toward the gravesite, others looked out of their windows and doors, realized who was passing by, and joined in to follow along. They had heard the tantalizing rumors about the miraculous healing of their friend and neighbor. One day Shimon had been among the lepers and the next day Shimon and the lepers had been among them as strong and healthy as any they knew. And they had heard that this Yeshua was the One responsible. They had no inkling of what was about to happen but this time they wanted to see it for themselves so that afterwards, they could tell all the titillating details to others.

Outside Bethany, the cemetery lay bleak and rocky and windswept. It seemed the earth itself mourned those that lay beneath it and the sun itself did not wish to show its face here, as one small outcropping of limestone sheltered another in the cool but eerie darkness. It was as though the psalmist had been thinking of this exact place when he had written for this was the place where the very shadow of death could been seen and touched and even felt.

As Yeshua's eyes adjusted to the gloom, He could see a number of cave tombs carved into the rocky hillside, each with a round flat stone covering its mouth and a family name neatly lettered into the rock beside it. He knew that these were the more expensive tombs, the ones belonging to the wealthy in the community and the ones who merely wanted to appear wealthy. He knew that Shimon had no such pretensions even though his success could have afforded him any tomb he chose. Yeshua's eyes instinctively lifted, searching the stony hilltop. He had indeed been correct. Already local citizens who knew the way were gathering at an elevated site where other less ostentatious tombs had been dug deep into the ground. Each was covered with a round flat stone which bore the family name. He knew that His beloved friend, Eleazar, now rested cold and alone and in the dark in one of those tombs. At the very thought, He knew He did not wish to waste another moment.

"Take up the stone," He ordered.

Martha, always practical and always outspoken, pushed her way through the throng to Yeshua. "Lord, by this time, the stench of death will be unbearable. After all, it has been four days." She thought of the traditional belief that one's spirit remained hovering over the body for three days, after which it departed leaving the body to decay. The three days were over for Eleazar. There was no longer any hope at all that his spirit was nearby and there was every expectation that nature had begun its frightful work upon his body.

Yeshua smiled in spite of Himself and shook His head slightly. His expression seemed to whisper, *Why don't you let Me worry about that?* "Do you not remember what I told you, Martha?" He queried gently. "Do you not remember I said that if you would only believe, you would witness something that would bring great glory to the Holy One?"

Martha jumped back startled. There was something about the intensity of His eyes, something about the fervor in His voice, something about the power which had settled around Him like a cloak. Martha found herself speechless before it.

Those who had moved the heavy stone covering the grave waited, wondering if He would want a ladder so that He could go into the tomb to pay His last respects to His friend. But Yeshua issued no such command. Then the air became charged with an energy they had never before known, alive with a power they had never felt in this place. They stepped back in awe.

Yeshua began to pray softly. Those near enough to hear thought He had lost His senses because He prayed, not for or even about Eleazar; instead He prayed about them.

"Abba, I thank You that You have already heard Me, just as You always hear Me. I only say it because of those standing by Me, so that they might believe You sent Me."

Heads turned. Men stared at each other with quizzical expressions, though not a word was spoken for indeed none could speak. Before they could turn back, they were startled by Yeshua's voice, thunderous now. His tone, authoritative, assured, masterful; His words, commanding, ordering, expecting obedience. The air crackled with a lightning they could not see, touching their hair and standing it on end.

"Eleazar, come forth!" He shouted.

No one breathed! No one moved! No one spoke! No one dared! Birds ceased their singing. Animals halted in their pursuit of forage. A thousand tree limbs hung suspended and silent in space, untouched by even the slightest breeze. A hundred eyes fixed unblinking on the hilltop tomb. Time stood still. It seemed as if the world itself had stopped stationary in its course to bear witness to what was taking place within it.

There was no sound, no clawing, no climbing, no cry. There was only the awful apparition of a shrouded figure rising by some mysterious power from the depths of the earth. For a moment it stood poised just above the opening. Then it settled gently on the ground beside it. Spines tingled, eyes widened, and mouths hung agape. Still there was no sound until Yeshua spoke again.

"Loose him and let him go," He said firmly and with finality.

Men who would never have touched the dead found themselves responding to Yeshua's command. Their hands shook as they fumbled with tightly wound strips of linen. Clumps of spices fell to the earth as cloth was peeled away from pink flesh. Within seconds, Eleazar stood before them all, alive, well, smiling, blinking into the sunlight which had suddenly flooded the hillside, searching the crowd around him for the faces of those he loved best. Someone wrapped a robe about his bare shoulders as his father and sisters reached his side and embraced him. They were weeping again but this time theirs were only tears of joy.

Rabbi Levi had seen it all, heard it all, felt it all. Still he could not, would not believe it all. From somewhere deep within, from a place he did not want to acknowledge even existed, there arose an anger, a bitter envy, a hatred he would have thought impossible. He hated Shimon, Eleazar, everyone involved. And Rabbi Levi especially hated Yeshua.

No, no, it is not fair, Rabbi Levi screamed within himself. *Why would He heal Shimon when He did not heal my Yael? Why would He raise Eleazar from the grave and not my precious Yael? No, no! I will not believe it! I will not! Not now, not ever.*

He turned on his heels and started back toward Yerushalayim alone. He never once looked back. He had a mission to perform now. There were those who would be very interested in what he had just witnessed and he meant to tell them all about it before the day was out.

All eyes were still fixed on Eleazar, all hearts were still pounding with the joy of the miracle they had witnessed, all minds were still trying to comprehend the incomprehensible. But one head turned slightly and one pair of gentle blue eyes settled on the retreating form of the rabbi as if to say, *We shall meet again, you and I. And one day you will believe.*

It would be two months before their next meeting would take place.

✿　　　　✿　　　　✿

Rabbi Levi had made his way down the Mount of Olives, north along the Yericho Road, past the Pillar of Absalom, the Tomb of Zachariah, and the Garden of the Oil Press also known as Gethsemane, then up to the Temple Mount. The afternoon sun had not even begun to abate; neither had his anger.

☙ 9 ❧

YAKOV knew that something was happening. He had been around the Temple long enough that he could sense such things. As he worked, he kept his eyes and ears open. He saw respected Pharisees forming a small restless knot. He heard voices rise from tense whispers to loud crescendos punctuated by angry faces and wildly waving arms.

"I tell you something must be done about Him," an elderly rabbi the others called Levi shouted at a younger man as he crossed his arms and stomped his sandaled feet in obvious disgust.

Another comforted the anxious rabbi.

One turned his palms toward Heaven and shrugged. "What do I know of such things? What do I know of how to stop them?" he questioned.

"The high priest must hear of this," one called Baruch asserted most seriously. "Come, my brothers. Perhaps we still have time to see him before the evening sacrifice begins."

A fourth man chuckled. "It should be interesting to see what a Sadducee such as our esteemed high priest will have to say about this."

Yakov was more than intrigued. His patrons were now merely unwanted intrusions as he sought to learn the cause of the commotion amongst the usually staid and steady members of the Sanhedrin. It had to be something important; they didn't get this stirred up over one more stolen melon or yet another perfidious beggar.

As the time of the evening sacrifice drew near, all of the members of the Sanhedrin disappeared and the atmosphere became deathly still. Yakov knew that some very urgent meeting must be going on in their assembly chamber just outside the stone retaining wall of the Temple Mount. He found himself almost holding his breath as he waited for the outcome when he didn't even know the issue. Time and again, he mentally chastised himself for becoming so involved in their business while badly neglecting his own. *I'm nothing but a gossipy old woman,* he told himself. Still he waited for even the slightest glimmer of information.

"My son, I wish to purchase a young ram for my burnt offering," the elderly man in front of Yakov stated solemnly.

Yakov wanted to tell him to be quick about it and to be on his way. But it was clear to him that the man had reached such an age that he did nothing quickly and that he would be on his way when he was ready and not a moment before. Instead, Yakov smiled a bit too solicitously and directed his customer to the pen which held the nervous young rams.

"Yes, my lord. Here are a fine group of specimens, I'm sure," Yakov bantered.

"Sure, are you," the old man returned with a knowing twinkle in his eye. He pointed to a small ram that had recently been kicked by his penmate leaving a livid bruise to form just under his curly coat. "The Holy One certainly would not accept such a one as he," the old man teased.

Yakov closed his eyes, took a deep breath, and swallowed the churning anger he felt. "My lord, I most humbly apologize for allowing such a one to come before your eyes," Yakov began. "You are most certainly a discerning buyer. For you I will find nothing less than perfection itself."

The customer smiled. He had won his point and he knew it. "Yes you shall, my lad, or there will be no sale today."

When every animal in the pen had been thoroughly examined, the old man stood back, folded his arms across his generous abdomen, and absently fingered his grey beard. He eyed each ram carefully as Yakov clenched his teeth and forced them into a smile.

"This one, I think," the man said finally, pointing to a white creature with gentle eyes and not so much as a thistle caught in his coat. "Yes, this one."

"The Holy One will surely be pleased with such a magnificent offering," Yakov assured.

Finally the old man was willing to part with the little Temple coin he had purchased. As Yakov placed a rope around the animal's neck, the old man spoke.

"So, my friend, what do you think they will do with Him?"

"With whom?" Yakov questioned.

"With that Upstart, Yeshua, of course," the old man replied with some irritation.

"Yeshua? Is that what ... ."

The old man smiled and Yakov realized too late that his customer was taking great delight in the fact that he knew more about what was going on at the Temple than one who worked there every day. But, if Yakov wanted more information, he knew he was going to have to swallow his pride and admit his ignorance. And of a truth, Yakov did indeed want more information.

"What about Yeshua?" Yakov asked, doing his best to feign disinterest.

"You have not heard?" the old man teased, seeing right through Yakov's charade. "It seems He raised one Eleazar ben Shimon from the dead up in Bethany. Do not ask me how He did it, trickery no doubt. Some would now make Him king, others think He is Messiah, and the high priest wants to nail His hide to the nearest Roman tree for His trouble. They're meeting right now to decide what must be done about this Imposter."

So that's it! Yakov thought to himself with more than a little exultation. He remembered both occasions when Yeshua had created more than a little havoc for him. He remembered how He had upset Shoshana so late in her pregnancy and he wondered if that had had anything to do with the final fatal outcome. Now He had finally gone too far. *Yeshua ben Yosef is about to get exactly what He deserves,* Yakov promised himself with a smile.

Night was about to spread her icy fingers across the city of Yerushalayim by the time Malluch led the angry group of Pharisees into the presence of the high priest. Another kind of night was about to darken their icy hearts as well.

᪥ **10** ᪥

NAQDIMON walked with his head down and his beard resting on his broad chest. There was entirely too much sadness in the world and Naqdimon found it unbearable to contemplate on this warm winter afternoon when everything in nature was poised to live again. He had barely recovered from the death of his own son when he had heard of the death of the son of Shimon, a dear friend and fellow member of the Sanhedrin until leprosy had taken him from their midst. When he had received the news that not only had Yeshua healed Shimon of his dreaded disease but had raised his son to life, Naqdimon had been pleased beyond words for his compatriot. And yet there had been that nagging little thought, a thought he didn't even want to admit was his own, that kept asking questions he could not answer. *Why not Moshe? Why wasn't he healed? Why wasn't he raised?* The drumbeat kept on and on in his head.

Naqdimon decided not to stay for the evening sacrifice. He no longer found solace or release in such things. He no longer found solace or release in much of anything. He sleepwalked through his days, going where he had always gone, doing what he had always done. Too many times, he would simply allow himself to slip back into his comforting fog for the short journey home, home to Sarah, home to the only one who really understood his loss for she had suffered it, too, home to the only serenity he now knew.

Yes, that's what I must do, he told himself firmly. I must go home to Sarah.

Naqdimon exited the doors of the Sanhedrin's meeting chamber and walked purposefully to the street, his sandals slapping against the cool white stairs beneath his feet. As he walked, his footsteps created a rhythmic cadence on the neatly arranged paving stones.

✿   ✿   ✿

Not long after Naqdimon's departure, Yosef ben Qayafa stood before the beautifully embroidered curtain of the Temple, his hands raised to the Holy One, his priestly garments draped elegantly around his tall and stately figure, his lips forming the words of the ancient prayers. The evening sacrifice was about to begin and the high priest was feeling more tranquility this night than he had felt in a very long time. He even permitted a small smile to play at the edges of his mouth as he prayed.

It's done, he assured himself. *The Imposter will soon be only an unhappy memory.*

It had been only an hour since a group of Pharisees had brought him the news that Yeshua ben Yosef had claimed to raise Eleazar ben Shimon of Bethany from the dead. Qayafa did not know how He had done it; he didn't care. Perhaps the boy had not died at all; perhaps he had been nothing more than a willing pawn in Yeshua's latest scheme. As a Sadducee, he rested secure in the knowledge that such a thing was quite impossible. But he also knew this claim would serve his purposes very nicely. This time Yeshua had finally gone too far.

Some had practically panicked. One had summed up the situation anxiously, "What can we do? This Man does many miracles. If we let Him alone, everyone will soon believe He is Messiah and the Romans will come and take away our positions and our nation."

It was the very question Qayafa had been awaiting. He had then assumed the demeanor of one in complete control. "You don't know anything," he had chided them. Then he had allowed his voice to take on a conspiratorial tone that took each man into his confidence and made him feel a party to his thinking. "Nor do you consider that it is expedient for us that one Man should die for the people so that the whole nation does not perish." Then he had smiled cunningly.

Once they had understood, once he had explained it to them in terms they could appreciate, most members of the Sanhedrin had realized that they really had no choice. It wasn't personal. It was merely politics. The Romans cared nothing about who ruled the rebellious Yisraelites so long as the peace was kept and the taxes were paid. But now there were those who actually wanted to make Yeshua their king and the Romans just might let them do it. The members of the Sanhedrin did not want to lose their positions of power. Neither did he. Like many of them, his position had been in the family for years and he did not wish to be remembered as the one who lost it. Once everyone had understood the political stakes and the solution he proposed, the answer was obvious and not long in coming.

Naturally there had been some resistance to his plan. Naqdimon had argued for patience and tolerance. *Patience and tolerance indeed!* thought Qayafa coldly. *Sometimes it's all I can do to have patience and tolerance with you, old man,* Yosef ben Qayafa mused to himself.

Qayafa smiled as he thought about it now for he had ultimately prevailed. Naqdimon had finally accepted defeat and hurried from the chamber. The subsequent vote had been unanimous in favor of Qayafa's plan. They had even agreed to put Eleazar ben Shimon to death, too, if that became necessary to stamp out the notion of a resurrection.

There was one more thing that had to be done and Yosef ben Qayafa knew precisely how to do it. The Sanhedrin had issued an order for Yeshua's arrest and trial, a trial that he knew would end in a guilty verdict and a death sentence. But the law now required Roman concurrence.

The Romans might not care in the least about Yeshua's blasphemy against the Holy One of Yisrael nor His transgressions of the Law of Moshe. But the high priest knew exactly what they would care about and he meant to take full advantage of that knowledge.

I'll get their agreement, Yosef ben Qayafa promised himself confidently, *and I'll even let them do the dirty work for us. Stoning is too good for Him anyway. Let Him hang on a Roman cross for a while. Yes, let His followers get a good look at what happens to any who would dare to stand against me. Yes, let Him be crucified!* Right in the middle of the evening sacrifice, Yosef ben Qayafa nearly chuckled aloud at the very thought.

༒ 11 ༒

THE day dawned cool but with a welcome hint of spring warmth bursting forth at its edges. The sun climbed higher in a cloudless sky that seemed to melt into the glassy Sea of Galilee. It promised to be a perfect day to begin the long and arduous trip to Yerushalayim for Pesach.

It seemed that everyone in Capernaum had risen before first light to get an early start. In the crowd, Dinah diligently herded her boys trying to keep all six in sight. Each carried a bundle holding a blanket, parched grain, dried figs and dates, raisins and olives, small loaves of fresh bread, clothes, and such. Micah's also held the robe Dinah had altered for him, one with cascading fringe, reminiscent of the priestly robe once worn by Aaron. Itzak had worn it on their wedding day. Now little Micah would wear it when he took his place among the men of the Temple.

Up ahead, Hannah walked by herself, alone even in this crowd. Atop her head, she balanced her bundle and gracefully made her way along the road, avoiding the ruts of wagon wheels and the rocks and stones released from the compacted earth by the winter rains. Hannah's bundle held something special, too. But Hannah knew nothing of this, not yet.

Beside Dinah, David ben Asaph guided the small donkey cart that carried additional provisions and a simple ossuary containing all that remained of Itzak, her husband and the light of her life. It had been a year since the ghastly storm had snuffed out his life and he would soon rest beside his forefathers in the family crypt outside of the Holy City.

Dinah had made this journey often, the first time shortly after her marriage to Itzak, later to dedicate each of her children. This was to have been a special trip. Itzak had often spoken of it. His firstborn child would be wed and his eldest son would be received into the Temple as a son of the covenant. Now it was a sad journey, for Dinah, too, was alone even in this crowd. She would always be alone since Itzak no longer walked beside her. Without thought, Dinah reached out her hand to touch the little ossuary. Somehow it made her feel less solitary.

As Dinah moved forward, she imagined herself at Itzak's side on that first trip. They had been so young and so much in love. They had made the journey in only four days and the days had seemed as nothing. Neither knew until after they had arrived home that they had taken their first child along with them. Dinah remembered telling little Hannah about it.

"Did you carry me all the way, Ammah," her small daughter had asked innocently.

"Yes, my child," Dinah had responded smiling, "right here under my heart."

Dinah smiled at the memory of Itzak and all they had shared together. The Holy One had been gracious to them, given them many years together and blessed their union with strong sons and a beautiful daughter. Dinah wondered where He had been on that stormy day when Itzak had slipped beneath the angry waves and was taken from her forever?

The road to Yerushalayim was no longer than before and some of it had even been paved with great flat stones, one of the few good things the Romans had done during their tenure. Still Dinah knew traveling with many who were older and many more who had young children, meant the journey would not be made so quickly. They had set out at dawn on the first day of the week and hoped to reach Yerushalayim before the sunset which would begin Shabbat. Dinah thought that only the Holy One Himself would be able to make that miracle happen.

But it was still better than traveling alone. The persistent stories of thieves and bandits, especially along well-traveled roads and especially at feast times, were enough to frighten even the most stalwart traveler. As Dinah remembered some of those stories, she clutched her brown homespun robe close about her as if it might provide her with some protection.

"Are you cold, Ammah," David queried, concern edging his voice.

Dinah smiled into his soft blue eyes. "No, my son. It is not the chill of weather I feel but the chill of fear. I was just thinking about the thieves I have heard wander this road."

David stiffened. "Do not fear, Ammah. The boys and I will be with you. We will allow no harm to come to you ... or to Hannah. I promise."

Dinah felt warmed by the comfort of the presence of her sons, all seven of them now. Her robe slipped carelessly from one shoulder. She made no effort to retrieve it.

The endless road lay before them. The mountains which cradled Yerushalayim were still shrouded in the distant mists.

✡   ✡   ✡

It happened on the fifth night of the journey. At sunset the company had camped along both sides of the Yericho road in a stretch of mountain passes between Yericho and Yerushalayim which many called "the red and bloody way" and not without reason. It was narrow and twisting and offered bandits many locations of opportunity. But before the moon was even high in the cobalt blue heavens above them, the weary travelers had set their fears aside and drifted off to sleep.

Sometime during the night Hannah had risen from her mat and slipped beyond the tree line to the tent that had been erected to provide privacy for the women as they tended to their sanitary needs. She knew she should have awakened Micah or one of the others to go with her but it was so late and everyone was sleeping so soundly, some snoring, some too exhausted to snore.

Still groggy, she was on her way back when she felt a presence behind her in the dark. Before she could turn to run, a muscled arm slid around her slender waist and a rough hand pressed the blade of a knife against her throat.

"Silence, Girl," a deep voice whispered into her ear, "or the blade will do her work before you get the first cry out of your mouth."

Hannah was motionless. Uncertain if she was truly in danger or merely dreaming, Hannah struggled to force her eyes open but saw nothing but the darkness surrounding her, pressing against her, nearly suffocating her. Still, the cold sharpness of the knife at her neck let her know that this was no nightmare. It was all too real.

"Now," the voice continued. "Show us where they keep all their shiny little shekels, Girl, before my hand begins to shake."

Her attacker was joined by another nameless faceless form in the darkness of the night. "Hurry," he pleaded. He sounded nearly as frightened as Hannah herself.

"I have nothing," Hannah whispered, her terror mounting by the moment. "I travel with my mother and brothers from Capernaum to Yerushalayim for Pesach. I carry nothing but food and clothing. I have no money. I know nothing of what the others carry."

A hand explored her sash and found no telltale lump to indicate a purse. "Then maybe I shall have your life for my trouble," the stranger growled. "Or perhaps you have something else to offer," he teased as his hand explored her trembling body.

"No, no, don't!" she begged as she tried to escape his grasp.

The blade pressed deeply into her flesh. Hannah gasped. Her eyes saw the shadowy mountains which surrounded her and she thought of the psalmist who had written of lifting his eyes to the hills from whence came his help. She wondered if there were any help for her there this night or if she would soon find herself with her abba forever. At first Hannah didn't even care which. She so longed to see Abba again, to beg his forgiveness. But in the next moment, she knew she did not really want to die. For the first time in a year, she knew she wanted to live. She froze in fear of what the next minute might hold and she whispered a silent prayer to the Holy One of the hills, the One whose help the psalmist had found.

"Let the girl go," a familiar voice commanded.

The knife stopped still in its path.

"Who speaks?" the bandit cried out, himself afraid now.

"I am David ben Asaph and if you shed one drop of that girl's blood, my sword will sever your head from your body in the next instant."

The sound of a weapon slashing the air echoed through the dark night.

The strong arm released Hannah as the knife left her throat. Suddenly she found herself in David's embrace shivering with fear. As she looked down, she saw he held nothing in his hand but the peeled poplar rod he used to drive the donkey. He had frightened away two armed bandits and saved her life with only a stick and a few brave words. Realizing the enormity of what might have happened to them, Hannah slumped into his arms unconscious.

✿　　　　　✿　　　　　✿

When Hannah opened her eyes, she was lying on the cool grass, her head resting in her mother's lap. Above her, torches blazed and real weapons clattered against the thighs of their owners. A contingent of Roman soldiers assigned to guard the road between Yericho and Yerusha-layim had come upon the scene just in time to capture two rather wretched-looking robbers. With their hands bound and their eyes reflecting their terror in the flickering torch-light, they were not nearly as frightening as they had seemed before.

As soon as David saw that Hannah's eyes were open, he helped her to her feet keeping one arm around her waist to steady her. Dinah hovered nearby, her cheeks stained with mingled tears of both fear and gratitude. The boys stood in a semi-circle, their eyes wide with the wonder-ment of it all. They had never been this close to either ban-dits or Roman soldiers and they couldn't help but be spell-bound by both.

"I think you can all resume your rest now," a tall le-gionnaire calmly assured the frightened travelers. "These two will not bother you or anyone else again. My men will escort them to the city where they will face trial."

"Thank you, my lord," David replied. "May the Holy One bless you all."

"The Holy One?" the puzzled officer repeated. "Yes of course. I see." He seemed to recall talk of the one strange God these strange people worshipped. "Good night then."

The legionnaire, his men, and their miserable prisoners disappeared into the shadows. With the torches gone, the still blackness of the night enveloped the travelers once again. David and the others stood silently for long mo-ments, blinking into the dark, not speaking but not yet wanting to move away from the security of the company.

Finally David, whose bravery had made him their ac-knowledged leader, spoke. "I will keep watch until first light, my brothers. Take your families back now and rest. The Holy One will protect us."

As others drifted away, Dinah looked up to see David and Hannah staring at each other as though they had been struck by some silent lightning. She quietly guided her sons back to the place where they had been sleeping. She said nothing to Hannah. She knew her daughter and her newest son needed time, time to understand what had just happened, time to speak of it, time not to speak of it if they chose. She wisely left them to find that time together.

When they were alone, David reached out and gently brushed Hannah's hair from her face. At his touch, a lonely tear traced a path down a cheek still pale with fear.

"They could have killed me, killed us both," she whispered at last.

"They could have but they did not," David responded tenderly.

Hannah looked into David's eyes, studying them for the very first time, finding in their deep blue depths a love so profound it frightened her nearly as much as her assailants had. She wanted to look away but she was powerless to pull her gaze away from his. His was a love her mind did not want yet her heart reached out hungrily to accept.

"Why?" she asked finally. "Why did you take on two armed men with nothing more than a stick? Were you crazy?"

David chuckled. "No, Hannah, not crazy."

He paused, exploring her eyes, the eyes of a doe staring into the bow of the hunter. When he spoke, he spoke gently. "Do you not know, Hannah? Do you not know that I love you? Do you not know that I would gladly give my life for yours if need be?"

David took a single step toward Hannah. Hannah took a step backward.

"Oh, David, don't say such a thing. I'm not worthy of such a sacrifice."

"Let me be the judge of that," David countered.

"David, I can never love you the way you desire. I can never be the wife you want me to be. Do you not understand? Torah tells me I must love the Holy One with all my being. So how can I love you when you no longer follow Him?"

"Oh, Hannah, I also love the Holy One with all that is

within me." David's voice trailed off as he remembered a time in his life when this had not been so. He started to turn away. No, he thought. She has to know. My wife must know the truth, all of it.

"Hannah," he began slowly, gathering his courage as he went. "My ammah died when I was but a child." He paused as he searched his heart for a truth he did not want to acknowledge and searched his mind for the words to explain it. "I blamed the Holy One for taking her from me. I blamed Him ... " he paused again but he knew he finally had to speak the truth. "I hated Him for what He had done to me and my father."

Hannah gasped. She had never in her life heard such blasphemy. "David, don't say that."

"Hannah, you above all people must understand what Yeshua has done for me."

Hannah's face hardened. "Don't. I want to hear nothing of Him."

"Please, Hannah. Please listen. I've never told anyone else but I want to tell you."

Hannah's silence signaled her reluctant willingness to allow David to continue.

"For years I wanted nothing more to do with the Holy One. Oh, I took my part in all of the formalities, the sacrifices, the prayers, mostly to please my father. But in my heart, I hated it, all of it. I wanted only to acquire more boats so that I could make more money. I wanted to be rich, really rich, so nothing and no one could ever hurt me again."

Hannah stared at David in disbelief. She had never known, never guessed.

"Then He came. Yeshua came down to the dock. He spoke of making us fishermen into fishers of men. He looked straight at me and it was almost as if He were looking into my very soul. But I turned away that day. Not everyone did. Some even left their boats in the care of servants and followed Him that very day. I thought they were lunatics. So did everyone else. We all laughed about them later over a few too many cups of wine. But I could not get Him out of my mind, Hannah. Sometimes, in the middle of the night, I would wake with a start and see His face and hear His words echoing in my ears like distant thunder. I began to hate Him, too, almost as much as I hated the God He said had sent Him."

"David, don't talk that way, not even joking," Hannah interrupted, fearful of a lightning bolt from Heaven striking them both for even speaking of such things.

"Hannah, do not fear, just listen. I was like you. I didn't want anything to do with Him either. Then one of the fishermen--you know of him, Shimon ben Yonah, the big one."

Hannah nodded.

"He was one of those who had followed Yeshua. Then suddenly he was back. He had returned in response to an urgent message that his mother-in-law was ill with a raging fever. Everyone expected her to die, even Shimon, I think. She had been a good friend of my ammah's and had even attended her at her marriage so Abba sent me to deliver salted fish to the family. When I arrived, there was Yeshua! And there she was, too, preparing an evening meal for everyone! I just stared at her with my mouth open and my eyes as big as drachmas. She took the fish from my hands, chuckling at my surprise. She told me Yeshua had prayed for her and the Holy One had restored her health. Just like that! Then she invited me to join them. She sat me just across the table from Him. All through supper, He seemed to speak only to me and all through supper, I wished He had been there when my ammah had been so sick. He talked of a God that loved us all so much that He even cared when we were ill, cared enough to provide healing for our sick bodies, and even cared enough to provide forgiveness for our sick souls.

"Hannah, I saw then how sick my own soul was, hating the Holy One and loving only money. I knew my ammah would not have wanted that for me. I knew I was bringing shame to her memory with the sickness of my soul. Yeshua knew it, too. When dinner was over, He took me aside. He looked at me with such love. Then He spoke to me. I'll never forget His words. He said, 'My son, the One who called your mother to the bosom of the fathers now calls to you. Come, Child.' I wept for the first time since Ammah's death, wept away all the pain and all the anger and all the bitterness as He held me in His arms." David's eyes filled with new tears at the memory.

Hannah almost felt as though she were behind the partition of the women in the synagogue watching as the Torah scroll was lifted from the ark. Something just as awesome, just as solemn had happened to David and for the first time, she wanted to understand it.

"Please go on," she said softly.

"Hannah, somehow Yeshua changed me. Somehow, He changed my heart. Don't ask me how. I don't know. All I know is that I'm not the man I was before I met Him. He's the reason I could work your abba's boats and give the money to your ammah without a second thought. You see, it was Yeshua who taught me that there are some things more important than money, who brought me back to the Holy One, who took away all of my hatred and heartbreak so that I could love Him again. And I can love the Holy One now with all my heart and all my soul just as His Word commands. Only Messiah could do that, Hannah, and He did it for me."

David had moved to Hannah's side. This time she did not move away.

"And what He did for me, Hannah, He can do for you, too. I've seen the same pain, the same hurt, the same heartbreak in you since your abba died. And I've seen the hatred, too. I've seen it all even when others could not see it because they had never known such feelings. But I have known them and I knew them only too well when I saw them in you."

Hannah turned so that David could not see her face. She did not want him to see how close to the truth he had come.

David continued, not accusing, only accepting and caring. "Hannah, the Holy One knows all things. He knew your abba was to be gathered to the fathers. I believe He placed me beside you before it happened so that I could love you and understand you and pray for you. He wants to reach out to you through me just as He reached out to me through Yeshua. You can come, too. He'll heal your heart, Hannah, just as He healed mine."

Tears slid onto Hannah's robe. She knew everything that David had said about her was true. She just didn't know if everything he had said about Yeshua was also true. It was true that she didn't understand why the Holy One had taken her abba; it was also true that a part of her, a part much larger than even she cared to admit, was angry at Him because of it. But she did not wish to displease Him further by accepting what might be total blasphemy.

David sensed her struggle. Some small voice within told him that this was not the moment to press her for an answer. That same small voice assured him that her day of decision was not far off. He knew he could rest in that assurance.

Just then the first rays of dawn climbed above the horizon and lit the sky with a lovely lavender light. David knew in his heart the light would soon dawn for Hannah, too.

THE mingled sounds of happy laughter and bubbling conversation could be heard out in the street and well beyond. The music of the lutes and lyres, the pipes and dulcimer, the cymbals and bells floated on the cool night air and the smells of the most luscious fare available teased the nostrils of all who had assembled. Nearly everyone in the tiny town of Bethany had congregated outside the home of Shimon and Eleazar to see their guests as they arrived for Shabbat dinner. Naqdimon, the revered member of the Sanhedrin had come. Then the Guest of Honor, Yeshua ben Yosef, along with His followers had been cheered wildly as they snaked their way through the crowd from the synagogue and up the stony path to be joyously received by their host.

"May the peace of the Holy One rest upon this house and all who dwell within," Yeshua intoned as He entered and kissed Shimon and Eleazar on each cheek.

Inside, three long tables had been arranged to form a horseshoe in the triclinium style borrowed from the Romans. White linen cloths reached all the way to the floor and the finest silver plates and utensils decorated each place. On the outside of the horseshoe, couches had been arranged so that each guest could recline on an elbow facing the feast.

And quite a feast it was! The air smelled of garlic and mustard and dill. On each table, gleaming bowls of fresh fruit were placed within the reach of each diner along with trays of dried dates and figs. There were platters laden with steaming meats, lamb and veal and beef, and large vegetable bowls holding beans, onions, lentils, leeks, and cucumbers. There were smaller bowls containing olives and almonds and other nuts. Wine mixed with honey flowed into tall stemmed goblets and large loaves of fresh wheat bread rested near bowls of golden honey. Salt imported from the Dead Sea and ground almost to a powder waited near each plate and melons and pastries smelling of sweet cinnamon stood ready to be served for dessert.

Martha and Miriam flitted back and forth from the kitchen to the center of the horseshoe serving their guests, refilling goblets, and replacing empty bowls and platters with a seemingly endless supply of fresh ones. It would have been obvious even to a stranger that this was without doubt the most glittering banquet the little town of Bethany had ever seen. Had one looked more closely though, he would have noted that one guest did not seem at all thrilled to be in attendance.

Rabbi Levi ben Eschol had come only at the urging of his dear friend. He did not wish to be there. The truth was, he did not want to see Yeshua ben Yosef ever again. He absolutely despised the Man. But as much as he loathed the Guest of Honor, he loved his childhood friend. He could not disappoint him, not on this night of all nights.

As was the custom, Rabbi Levi had politely refused the first invitation but he had not done it because of custom. As was also the custom, Shimon had implored him to attend but he had not acted because of custom either. It had been clear to the rabbi that Shimon truly wished him to be present. After so many years, Shimon wanted his oldest and dearest friend to share with him the double blessing Yeshua had brought to his family.

"You must be there with me, my brother," Shimon had begged, "when I gather my friends to celebrate my healing and the restored life of my son. Now that we have found each other again after so many years and so much heartache, it would not be the same without you."

Now Rabbi Levi reclined on a couch at the head table just to the left of Shimon and Eleazar, toying with food he would have relished had it been any other occasion, sipping wine more to dull his senses than to please his palate. He spoke to no one and smiled only at the girls when they served him. It seemed to him as if the evening would never end.

After all had eaten their fill, Shimon struggled to his feet to gain the attention of his guests. When all eyes were focused on him, he spoke, his roaring voice audible even outside in the street.

"My dear friends, I have brought you together this night to honor my Lord, Yeshua." Shimon gestured to his right to where Yeshua reclined with His head modestly down. "As you well know, it was Yeshua who spoke healing into this old body of mine and life into this young man beside me. I am not worthy of the least of His favor and I can never repay Him for His gracious gifts to me and to my son. All I can do is love and worship Him both now and forevermore. And this I do with all my heart. Stand with me now, my friends, and let us thank Him for the blessings He has showered upon this humble home."

To happy cries of "The Lord Yeshua" and "Yeshua be praised," all assembled stood to their feet. Then Yeshua Himself stood, gesturing for the guests to be seated. As He did, Rabbi Levi started for the door, unwilling to hear any more. But someone had preceded him. A small feminine shape had moved from the room into the hallway and now blocked the rabbi's retreat. Much as he did not wish to, Rabbi Levi could not help but hear Yeshua.

"Thank you for your kind words," He began softly, "but you all know that without My Father, I can do nothing. It is He who has healed. It is He who has given life. It is He we must glorify. Let Me join you in lifting our praise to Him and to Him alone."

Cheers of "Praised be the Holy One" and "The Holy One be blessed" resounded through the room.

Rabbi Levi had to give the Imposter one thing: He certainly knew how to make a show of humility and godliness. It only served to disgust the rabbi even more. As the guests resumed their places, Miriam moved past him into the dining chamber. He wanted to leave, to be gone from the presence of the detestable Yeshua but for some reason he seemed paralyzed. It was as though his curiosity required that he remain.

Miriam fell at Yeshua's feet in worship. She held an ornate alabaster box containing precious imported oil of spikenard, an expensive and fragrant perfume and the last gift her mother had given to her before her death. It was to have been saved to delight her husband on her wedding night but before her on this night was One she wanted to delight even more. She broke open the box and allowed its contents to flow onto Yeshua's feet. The intoxicating scent filled the room, the house, even the street outside. Then Miriam removed her veil, unbraided her long dark hair, bent forward, and dried His feet with her tresses.

To most, this was the supreme act of worship. To Rabbi Levi, however, this was just the act of an overly emotional young girl who had uncovered her head and let down her hair before a Man to whom she was not related. The rabbi was scandalized. As he turned to go, he realized that he was not the only one who had taken offense.

One of Yeshua's own followers, the one introduced to him as Yehuda of Kerioth, the treasurer of the group, reached for Miriam's shoulders to stop this display, this waste.

"What on earth are you doing, Girl?" Yehuda demanded gruffly. "Don't you know we could have sold this perfume for a year's wages and fed the poor with the money?"

But before he could go on, Yeshua blocked his hands and in a commanding voice reprimanded His errant disciple. "Let her alone, Yehuda. She does not know it but she has done this to prepare My body for burial. Wherever the story of My burial is spoken of, what she has done this night will be spoken of, too. If it is truly the poor that concern you, you may rest assured that they will always be with you to receive your charity."

The eyes of the two men locked. Yeshua's were firm, sad, yet loving while Yehuda's were angry, enraged, embittered. Rabbi Levi could not believe what he saw yet he knew of a certainty that the relationship between Yeshua and Yehuda was now somehow broken forever. Yehuda stalked from the room and out the door before anyone could speak.

Finally Shimon broke the tense silence. "My friends, let us end this happy evening with a song. Musicians, if you please ... ."

The pipers and players struck up a familiar psalm of praise, the Hallel, and all voices but one harmonized in worship of the Holy One. Instead of singing, Rabbi Levi followed after Yehuda. The young disciple was well down the road to Yerushalayim before the aged rabbi was able to catch him.

"Yehuda, Yehuda," Rabbi Levi called out at last.

Yehuda turned, clearly still irritated. "Who goes and what do you want with me?"

"It is I, Levi. I was also at the dinner tonight. I wish only to speak with you."

Yehuda tapped his toe impatiently, his arms crossed. "Speak on then," he ordered.

"I saw what He did to you, my son. I saw the way He treated you in front of them."

"Then you also saw that I will never let Him do it again. Now what can I do for you?"

By this time, Rabbi Levi had reached Yehuda's side. He smiled up into his face and spoke in a conspiratorial whisper. "Maybe it is I who can do something for you, my son."

"Oh, can you now? And what might that be, Rabbi?"

"Even if your Master would keep you from riches, I know of those who would pay handsomely for just a bit of information about Him." Rabbi Levi baited his hook well.

"Pay handsomely, you say," Yehuda repeated. "And just who might those people be?"

The two men stood together in the moonlight, their heads nearly touching, their words heard only by each other ... and the Holy One. At length they turned toward Yerushalayim and walked down the road side by side. Yehuda had found a new friend and a new source of income for the little leather bag he carried in his sash. Rabbi Levi had found a new friend, too, and perhaps a way to be rid of Yeshua forever.

ଔ 13 ଈ

THE morning had dawned dry and dusty with a hazy sun smiling down upon the thin line of Pesach travelers who made their way along the Yericho Road and up the rugged mountains to Yerushalayim. David led the small donkey along the narrow mountain road that reached higher and higher toward Heaven and toward the Holy City. The magic of the moment had been lost on the anxious little beast who protested each time the wheel of the cart he pulled came too close to the abyss. The animal had no interest in the humans who insisted on taking this road nor did he wish to plummet into the yawning depths with them.

The trek from Yericho up to Yerushalayim was the hardest part of the journey but it was also David's favorite. It seemed to him that he climbed nearly to the sky before Yerushalayim came into view. But what better location for the city of the Holy One Himself?

Dinah chuckled to herself as she walked along beside David, grasping the hand of her youngest so that he would not stray too close to the edge of the road and the precipitous drop below. She was excited with the prospect of reaching the home of her elder sister, Ruth, and her husband, Elihu, who was only the most gifted stonecutter in all of Yerushalayim. It had been a few years since the two had seen each other; indeed it had been since the dedication of the little one whose hand she now held. After the long slow journey and after all that had happened to her, Dinah longed to step under the security of her sister's roof and into the warmth of her embrace.

"I knew we would never make it by Shabbat," she reminded David.

He nodded as he remembered her prediction. Just as she had said, the women, the children, and the elderly had slowed the pace sufficiently that the group from Capernaum had been forced to rest over Shabbat in a mountain pass and continue their journey with the dawn of a new day and a new week.

"Oh, I suppose it really doesn't matter," Dinah continued. "We shall still arrive in plenty of time for Pesach."

David nodded once again. "It's not much farther now, just over that next rise."

As the two looked toward the crest of the mountain, there seemed to be a disturbance up ahead. People were running, waving, shouting. Both David and Dinah wondered if someone had fallen over the edge. Their pace quickened as they hurried to see if they could be of help.

Hannah and Micah had seen the tumult, too. They followed along up the path.

✡   ✡   ✡

Yeshua ben Yosef and His followers had slept at the home of Shimon and Eleazar after the great banquet in His honor the previous night. Then as they made the short trip from Bethany to Yerushalayim, Yeshua was recognized by many in the crowd who were also on their way to the Holy City. Those who had witnessed the raising of Eleazar were relating every detail of the miracle to those who had not. Excitement spread through the masses like fire through a dry field.

Over the years, many had wanted Yeshua to be their King but He had resisted. Now He knew it was time to present Himself to them as the Heir to the throne of King David, not only the political throne but the spiritual one which sat empty in the heart of each mortal until He Himself took possession of it. On a borrowed white donkey colt just like the one King David had once ridden, Yeshua moved toward the crest of the mountain amid cheering throngs.

Yohanan, who had heard Yeshua speak of a coming arrest and trial, a death and a burial, had come to this moment with dread. Yet now his face mirrored the expression of Yeshua's other disciples. After all of the rejection they had experienced during the past three years, they were finally finding acceptance and in a measure none had ever expected. Maybe everything will be well after all, Yohanan reassured himself as the throngs jostled him, swept him along, and carried him to Yeshua's side.

"*Baruch ha ba b'shem Adonai*," the people in the crowd sang to each other in the words of the psalmist, "Blessed is He who comes in the name of the Lord." "Hosanna, hosanna. Save us, save us now," they shouted.

Yeshua knew that it was their nation and not their souls for which they asked salvation. After all He had taught them, they still looked for a Messiah who would chase the hated Romans from their land rather than One who would banish the spiritual darkness from their hearts. They still did not understand. Some never would. But He understood. He knew He had a mission to perform, the greatest mission of His life, the only mission of His life, a mission for them. And He knew that before the week was out, He would complete it. It would be finished.

✡   ✡   ✡

On the edge of the crowd, a group of Pharisees who had come up from Yerushalayim to learn the cause of the commotion now stood with arms folded and faces frozen in disgust.

"Look at them," one shouted to his companions. "They are demented."

Rabbi Levi watched in growing alarm. "See how we just can't seem to win against Him. It looks as though the whole world is following Him."

Rabbi Levi surged forward, anger rising in his bosom like a flame. He pushed his way toward the donkey and the Man who sat upon its back. When he had come as close as he could, he bellowed above the noise of the crowd. "You are only a Man, not a God, Rabbi," Levi shouted at Yeshua. "Tell Your disciples to stop worshipping You."

Yeshua smiled a sad tolerant smile while His eyes spoke of concern and compassion. Finally He answered. "Don't you know that if they were silent, the rocks and the stones would immediately cry out in praise?"

Rabbi Levi stood speechless. *How dare He? How dare He say such a thing? It is nothing but blasphemy,* the rabbi told himself. Then he turned and headed purposefully back toward Yerushalayim, toward the Temple, toward his friends of the Sanhedrin.

The eyes of the Man on the donkey followed him as he disappeared in the throng.

✡   ✡   ✡

Together, David and Dinah approached the top of the mountain just in time to see the figure of a gentle Man rocking gracefully on the back of a young donkey. Around them, people shouted, plucking palm branches from nearby trees and waving them before Him. Others drew off their cloaks and made a path for the small animal.

A look of recognition finally exploded on David's enraptured face. "It's Him," he shouted to Dinah above the tumult. "It's Yeshua."

So that's Him, Dinah said to herself as she observed the procession. Itzak had spoken of Him often. David, too. But she had never before been close enough to see Him. She stood a mute and reluctant witness to an event of which she still had no comprehension.

David ran to join the happy pandemonium. "Yeshua. Hail Yeshua," he cheered.

At the mention of His name by a familiar voice, Yeshua

glanced in David's direction, recognized the young fisherman from Capernaum, and smiled His greeting.

Hannah forced her way through the crowd to David's side. His face told the whole story. She had never seen such a look of adoration, of reverence, of total awe. What power did this Man possess that He could inspire such unreserved and unrestrained worship in one who was usually so calm? Hannah could only wonder. She wondered, too, what her abba would be doing if he were here. She could almost see his face, wide-eyed and worshipful, just like David's. She knew he'd be hailing this seemingly unremarkable Man as his King, too.

Hannah wanted to hate this Yeshua, hate Him because her abba had followed Him, hate Him because her abba had pledged her in marriage to another who followed Him, hate Him because her abba was dead and He had done nothing about it. But somehow she could not look at this Man and find hatred in her heart.

An instant later, Yeshua looked away from David to the young woman at his side. His eyes met hers and for all her trying, she was powerless to look away. There was something about Him, something about His gaze that drew her, welcomed her, embraced her, loved her. Somehow in all of this confusion, He had singled her out and encompassed her in His love.

She had never seen such eyes before, never felt such love. It both enthralled and frightened her. For a moment she thought she was going to faint again. Then she realized that she had forgotten to breathe.

"Did you see Him?" David was saying. "Did you see Him, Hannah? It's Yeshua!"

Hannah gasped for breath. Her words came slowly, softly, as though she had just awakened from a long sleep. "I saw Him. I saw Him." She paused searching for her next word. "And David," she said in a mixture of amazement and awe, "He saw me!"

✿   ✿   ✿

The throng reached the top of the mountain as one. Yeshua, propelled along by the crowd, reached it with them. As they came over the crest of the hill, the city of Yerushalayim lay spread out below them like a jewel in its setting, the sun playing on her rooftops and on the gold of the Beautiful Gate of the Temple like light on the facets of a gem.

This very first view of Yerushalayim was always breathtaking and the crowd gasped in unison. A surge of some unseen power touched the flesh of each traveler and sent shivers along each spine. Most had seen this vista before, some many times. But for some reason, it was different this time. It seemed as if it were a stage set for some magnificent drama and they seemed drawn to witness it. None knew what lay ahead of them. But all of them knew in their hearts that they would never be the same once that drama drew to a close.

AKOV smiled as he watched them weaving their way down the face of the Mount of Olives. Jews from all over the world were gathering in Yerushalayim to celebrate Pesach. They had come to hear again the ancient story of the Holy One's protection of His people so many centuries before, to recall the night the death angel had passed over the land of Egypt claiming the firstborn of every Egyptian household, to remember how the blessed Holy One Himself had hovered above every Hebrew home which bore the blood of an innocent lamb on its doorposts, to praise Him again for the freedom that had come before the morning light.

Perhaps the travelers celebrated all of those things; Yakov simply celebrated his work and the money it brought him. That was all that mattered now that Shoshana was gone. And this was the season when money seemed to flow into his pockets unaided.

It was the week of Pesach and as usual many travelers had already arrived in the Holy City. Some had come early to visit family and friends, some just to engage the best accommodations, some to make special offerings for a newborn child or for a particular sin, and some to undergo rites of purification at the Temple.

Yakov looked forward to this week. He knew his income would increase but he also knew that there would be little of the frantic pace that would mark the actual preparation day, the day before Pesach. Each family would be purchasing a sacrificial lamb and most would be purchasing that lamb from him. He almost chuckled when he thought about all of the unsuspecting families that would be purchasing the same lamb over and over again, making the days even more profitable. As for himself, he no longer made the sacrifices from which he profited. He had seen too much and done too much to put his trust in sacrifices ever again.

Yakov and his father had prepared well. Their pens contained the finest lambs available anywhere in the city. The servants had bathed them, combed their curly coats, washed the discharge from their eyes, cleaned their muddy hooves, all to make each animal appear perfect even if it was not. After that old man had spotted a bruise on one young male a couple of months before, Yakov himself had gotten into the pen with a cosmetic preparation of finely ground white lime and dabbed the bruise until it virtually disappeared. It had soon been purchased by a gullible couple from the south and Yakov had even managed to keep a straight face while they made their selection. It was a talent taught to him by his father, Meshullam, and one on which he prided himself.

For the rest of the morning, Yakov was kept too busy collecting all those tempting little Temple coins to think of much else. That is until the moment Yeshua ben Yosef stood face to face with him.

The court was filled with worshippers whose colorful costumes and headdresses easily identified their places of origin. Yakov hardly looked up when the homespun tunic held at the waist with knotted fisherman's cord and surrounded by a blue robe appeared. When he did, he barely caught the expression of pity in the pale blue eyes of his Customer.

"The blessings of the Holy One be upon You," Yakov began in an effort to sound religious. "How may Your humble servant assist You?"

Yeshua's voice was firm. "These people from all over the world call My house a house of prayer but still you make it a den of thieves." Then Yeshua grasped the edge of the table and with a single quick motion, overturned it sending coins sailing in all directions.

Yakov started to speak, to object, to argue, but the moment his eyes met Yeshua's, he discovered that no words came. He was mute, helpless before this Galilean Lunatic exactly as he had been on the two previous occasions. Those eyes in which he expected to find anger but found only great sorrow and sadness, those eyes reached beyond words down into the depths of his heart and tugged tenaciously at the conscience he kept locked away there.

Yakov turned away and when he had fully recovered himself, shouted at his assistants. "Get this disorder set aright. I shall return later." Then Yakov gave his back to the chaos in the court and retreated from the scene of the conflict. Behind him he heard other tables falling to the ground but he heard not a single protest. The others were just as paralyzed as he, just as powerless before Him. For Yakov, that was at least some small consolation.

✿　　　　✿　　　　✿

Once Yakov was safely under his own roof, he brushed past a surprised Devorah without a single word for her or the crying infant in her arms. He went immediately to his own bedchamber and slammed the door as a warning to any who might wish to intrude on his solitude. He fell to his bed and buried his face in his pillow before he allowed the tears to come, tears of frustration, of fury, of indignation. Again and again his clenched fists pounded the blanket. *How dare He? How dare this Imposter continue to ruin my business during the most profitable days of the entire year? Who does He think He is?*

It was Yakov's long-silenced conscience that finally answered his questions for him. In that instant he knew, just as deep down inside he had always known, just as he had known on that day when Shoshana had asked him about it. He knew all the scheming and swindling, all the cheating and conniving, all the duplicity and dishonesty were wrong. As much as he hated to admit it even to himself, he knew Yeshua had been right all along. What he did was stealing, pure and simple, and it was stealing from sincere souls whose only desire was to be at one with their Lord. Perhaps that made it the worst kind of stealing of all.

Yakov wept again, for himself, for his customers, for the entire corrosive system of which he was now a part. That system couldn't survive without him and the others like him and they couldn't survive without the system. He hadn't originated it and he couldn't change it. He had been born into it just as his father had been born into it before him.

Yakov was now confused. One moment, he couldn't stand the questions in his mind and he wanted Yeshua dead so that the questions would cease; and the next moment, he wanted to follow Yeshua and forever leave behind the awful system that had made of him a thief.

As the shadows heralded the arrival of evening, Yakov returned to the Temple Mount. The tables had been righted, the coins collected, and business went on just as it always had. Simeon was bent over his books and Helah, who was busily cleaning the pens, looked up at Yakov with the same innocent grin his face always bore, oblivious to everything that had taken place. Nothing had changed, nothing except perhaps the heart of Yakov ben Meshullam.

❧ 15 ❧

AS the shadows lengthened and Yakov returned to his business, Naqdimon brushed past him. He had heard that another meeting had been called and he wondered why he had not been summoned to attend it. He found his answer on Solomon's Porch.

"The nerve of the Man!" one exclaimed.

"What Man, Machir?" Naqdimon asked, though in his heart, he knew the answer even before it came.

"That vile Yeshua," Machir answered, spitting the name from between clenched teeth.

Naqdimon spoke in calm and soothing tones. "My brother, what has He done to provoke such rancor?" he asked, placing a steadying hand on his friend's shoulder.

"What hasn't He done? He was here this very day, overturning tables, disrupting the exchange of foreign monies and the sale of Pascal lambs just as He has done before. Now I ask you, Naqdimon, is it possible for our people to obey the Holy One and yet observe Pesach without lambs? Would He have our people violate the commands of the Holy One Himself?"

Naqdimon's weary eyes swept over the scene below where merchants and patrons were engaged in the usual animated activity. "It seems all is well now," he observed.

"You should have been here earlier. You should have seen Him. He turned the court into chaos. Then before He could be arrested, the infirm recognized Him and thronged around Him, praising Him, begging Him to heal them. And what's worse, He did!"

"What's worse for whom?" Naqdimon queried. "Was it worse for the infirm?"

"That rabble!" Machir responded with disgust. "They believe what they want to believe. Do I know if they were really ill in the first place? Do you?"

"Does any but the Holy One know about such things?" Naqdimon replied. "All we do know is that they are not sick now. Is that correct?"

As Machir nodded helplessly, another younger thinner man with fire in his dark brown eyes, interrupted. "It is always the same with you, Naqdimon. Always you take His side against us, against the high priest himself. Are you one of them, too?"

Naqdimon blanched, then blushed. He hoped the approaching dusk covered his obvious embarrassment. "One of what, Baruch? One of those who believes the Holy One is able to heal His people? Yes, I am one of them."

"You know what I mean," Baruch shot back. "Do you, too, follow this ... this ... Healer?"

Again Naqdimon tried to calm the emotions of his friends without revealing his own secret. "Baruch, my son, do you not hear the words which spill from your lips? Is not healing a good thing? Is not a healer a good man?"

Baruch's face contorted in rage. "Not this One," he insisted. "It's hopeless. You're as blind as the poor wretches He claimed to heal today. You refuse to see what He is."

"And what is He, my friend?" Naqdimon asked gently.

"He is the One who would drive us from this place and rule and reign from this very spot if we permitted it. If you value your position, He is no friend to you. Qayafa is right. We must deal with Him and we must deal with Him now. I for one stand with the high priest. Are you with us?"

A chorus of voices answered in the affirmative. Naqdimon shook his head sadly and turned away. He had learned all he needed to know. There was no hope now, no hope at all. And because this was the case, Naqdimon had even more important things to do this evening.

✿   ✿   ✿

Just before the sun settled in the western sky, a little group of people gathered outside the northeastern wall of the city in a small cemetery in the garden there. Hannah held tightly to her mother's hands as David and Elihu entered into an open tomb and placed a small limestone box in its niche.

Ruth put a protective arm around her sister's shaking shoulders.

The boys looked on mutely. The youngest could barely remember Abba and Micah remembered him too well. He remembered everything that had happened on that last day only too clearly.

Itzak's friends and brothers also gathered to participate in the prayer that would close the brief ceremony.

As the box slid into place, Elihu whispered softly to David, "I could have fashioned a nicer one."

David smiled. "I know, I know. Ammah said that very thing. But we had to purchase an ossuary for the journey."

David and Elihu took their places with the family. Then, ten men being present, Rabbi Levi led them in repeating the Kadesh, the simple Hebrew prayer for the dead. The words spilled from his lips in a rhythmic cadence without sentiment or emotion. Rabbi Levi had uttered this same prayer many times and he did so by rote not by feeling. When he was done, he simply turned back toward the city, leaving the family alone with their grief.

Dinah did not want to leave her Itzak in this cold solitary tomb. It was too final, too wrenching. She had loved him, married him, slept beside him, and borne his children. Now she was expected to leave him forever and simply walk away. It was too much to ask of her, too much to ask of the love they had shared.

Hannah, too, made no move to go. Until this day Abba's death hadn't seemed real. She knew it was, of course. She had seen his body and held his cold hand in hers. But even a year later, some part of her was always waiting for him to come through the door, his voice booming, his laughter echoing around her. And in her mind, she was always rehearsing exactly what she would say to him, how she would beg his forgiveness for her outburst of defiance on that last day and how he would take her into his tender embrace and give her that forgiveness freely. Now someone was grasping her shoulders and trying to take her away from him forever. The words she needed to say would never be said; the forgiveness she needed to receive would never be given; the unfinished business between herself and her father would never be concluded. In her fourteenth year, Hannah had suddenly learned that death is very very permanent.

Hannah resisted Micah's gentle tug on her shoulders but only for a moment. There was really no point in remaining. It would change nothing. As she allowed herself to be led away, her tears came in convulsed sobs. Her guilt was still greater than she could bear.

With Elihu on one side of her and Ruth on the other, Dinah, too, was finally able to bid her husband one last goodbye and go from the scene with her head held high but her eyes brimming with tears. She felt no guilt, only an awful sadness that she knew would be with her for as long as she lived.

David shepherded the boys from the scene.

As dusk fell over the bustling city of Yerushalayim, a small group of figures huddled together on a hillside, sharing their strength with each other against the dark night which had fallen in all their lives.

In the city, lamps were lit and lattice-work windows took on a warm glow but there was no light for them, no glow in their hearts. Itzak, husband, father, and fishermen, had been taken to his final resting place and had been left behind forever.

✡   ✡   ✡

Shortly after dark, a thickly built man stumbled through the shadows in the serpentine streets of the little village of Bethany. There was a sharp knock on a heavy wooden door, muffled voices, and the padding of sandaled feet up a stone staircase. The door opened and Naqdimon found himself face to face with Yohanan.

"Peace be to you and all within from the Holy One Himself," Naqdimon began.

"You honor us with your presence," Yohanan whispered as Naqdimon entered and the door closed behind them. "Come, come, you must break bread with us."

"I cannot. Guests await me at my own table and I must not arouse suspicion by being late." Naqdimon struggled to make out forms in the shadows created by several small oil lamps set on shoulder-high shelves to illuminate the room. "Is He here?" he asked finally.

"Yes," Yohanan answered with a smile. "Come. He will be so glad to see you again."

"I fear not," Naqdimon responded, his voice tinged with the sorrow he felt at the awful news he carried. He hesitated. He wanted to be in the presence of Yeshua if only for a moment but he knew Sarah would ask questions. "The news is not good, my son. Yosef ben Qayafa has worked his will with the Sanhedrin. The case has been made, the verdict is already a foregone conclusion, and the sentence as well. There was nothing I could do."

"I always knew this day might come," Yohanan said flatly. "I think He did, too."

"Warn Him, Yohanan. Tell the Master not to come back to Yerushalayim." Naqdimon's voice was pleading now. "Tell Him a reward has been offered to the one who reveals His whereabouts. And if He is arrested, there will be nothing anyone can do for Him. Not even the Holy One Himself can stop them now."

"I think He knows." Yohanan sighed in resignation as he remembered Yeshua's predictions. "But He also knows the Law and I don't think anything can stop Him from celebrating Pesach in Yerushalayim as the Law requires. We can only pray."

"And my prayers will join with yours," Naqdimon assured. But there was an air of inevitability about it all, like a log rolling down a hillside. It seemed fearsome forces were on a collision course and there was nothing anyone could do to stop them.

"We shall see you soon again, my brother," Yohanan called after him.

Neither knew how prophetic those words would be.

✂ 16 ✂

AS Rabbi Levi walked to the Sanctuary for the morning sacrifice, he muttered his morning prayers softly but not silently; he wanted those he passed to be reminded of the duty of prayer most neglected in their rush to be the first at the well or the marketplace. He was at once disdainful of their disregard of their responsibility to their Creator and secure in his own holiness before Him.

Rabbi Levi had said the *Shema* every morning and evening since childhood and he knew it so well that even when his mind wandered to the days he once had walked this path with Yael, the cadence of the ancient words continued. "Hear, O Yisrael, the LORD our God is one LORD. And thou shalt love the LORD thy God with all thy soul and with all thy might. And these words which I command thee this day shall be in thine heart. And thou shalt teach them diligently unto thy children ... children ... ." He could almost feel her hand in his, almost see her smiling face half hidden behind her veil, almost hear her calling him "Saba."

Rabbi Levi went on with his chanting, "And it shall come to pass, if ye shall hearken diligently unto my commandments which I command you this day, to love the LORD your God and to serve him with all your heart and with all your soul, that I will give you ... ."

As he thought of Yael, he couldn't recall her face without recalling another Face, the One that had smiled down upon her on that cold and rainy afternoon on Solomon's

Porch, the Face that had sent her first into dementia and finally into death. He shook his head to rid himself of the memory but he was left sad and lonely when Yael's memory went with it.

Rabbi Levi trudged on. Even in his grief, he meant to bring into the house of the Holy One the sacrifice of praise of which the prophet, Yeremiah, had written so long ago. His prayers continued, " ... Speak unto the children of Yisrael and bid them that they make them fringes in the borders of their garments throughout their generations and that they put upon the fringe of the borders a ribband of blue. And it shall be unto you for a fringe that ye may look upon it and remember all the commandments of the LORD and do them and that ye seek not after your own heart and your own eyes ... ."

As he crossed the bridge from the Upper City to the Temple Mount, Rabbi Levi looked up from his prayers and musings to find that a knot of young men had preceded him, young men who also wore the fringe of which the Shema spoke, young men who also meant to keep the commands of the Lord. He smiled at the very thought that there were others, especially the young, who shared his passion for both the old ways and the old prayers. Then he realized just who these young men were and his face hardened in his hatred and his rage.

✡   ✡   ✡

Rabbi Levi heard nearly nothing of the proceedings that morning. Even the cornets and trumpets which accompanied the singing of the Levites were lost on him though his lips never missed a single word of the prayers which accompanied the sacrifice. He had meant to have a word with the high priest yesterday but another hasty meeting of the Sanhedrin had been called. Now he would not be put off. Rabbi Levi had determined to request a meeting with the high priest just as soon as the sacrifice was concluded.

The priest ended the service by blessing those assembled using the old familiar words of the Torah itself, "May the Lord bless you and take care of you. May the Lord be kind to you. May the Lord look on you with favor and give you peace." At the conclusion, Rabbi Levi leaned into the flow of worshippers leaving the Sanctuary until he was at the young priest's side.

"Would it be possible to speak with his Excellency?" he asked respectfully.

The young priest looked somewhat vexed. "I wish I could be of help," he answered, "but he is busy with the urgent business of the Sanhedrin. Perhaps you would care to wait."

"Wait? I cannot wait," Rabbi Levi replied with some annoyance. "I, too, have urgent business. My own small synagogue will be overflowing with the worshippers who have invaded our city. Please, can you not tell him that I must see him on a matter of the utmost urgency? You see, I have recently had the good fortune to become acquainted with a young man whom I am certain the high priest will want to meet. This young man may hold the key to capturing the elusive Yeshua. You will not forget an old rabbi, will you?" he asked, finishing with a smile.

The priest returned his smile. "My lord," he intoned solemnly, "you may rest assured I will give him your message the moment he is free."

"Good, good," the old rabbi muttered as he made his way toward the great doors of the sanctuary. Outside, Rabbi Levi was surprised to see that the crowd had remained, drawn to a corner of Solomon's Porch. From the midst of the group, Rabbi Levi heard that same voice he had heard once before in this place. After listening for only a few minutes, Rabbi Levi started toward home. As he walked, he muttered to himself, only this time the words which burst forth from his lips were not prayers at all.

Just then, the young priest caught up with him, having obviously received new orders from one in higher authority than himself. After a brief whispered conversation, Rabbi Levi smiled and accompanied the priest in a different direction.

✡   ✡   ✡

The high priest sat in the richly-appointed meeting chamber of the Sanhedrin, surrounded by Pharisees, scribes who were experts in the Law, as well as some of those from his own sect of the Sadducees. As the young priest closed the door behind him, the rabbi moved forward to speak to Qayafa who was already engaged in an animated discussion.

"I understand your differing views but I am telling you that we all want the same thing. And if we are to get it, we will have to put aside our differences and work together. Is that not so?" Qayafa looked from one face to another for silent approval.

"Here is our problem," Qayafa went on. "These are not the old days when we might simply arrest a pestilent fellow such as this, try him according to our Law, and carry out the stoning before the day was over." Heads nodded thoughtfully. "Now the Romans insist that our capital cases be reaffirmed by their own court. This is a troublesome requirement to be sure, but one that may actually work to our advantage."

"Excellency, what do you wish us to do?" an elderly Pharisee asked.

Yosef ben Qayafa smiled. He had them in the palm of his hand and he knew it. He lowered his voice to his most conspiratorial level and spoke. "I am informed by reliable sources that He is indeed in the city. In fact, I understand that He made quite a spectacle of Himself among the animal sellers only yesterday. He will surely make a show of obeying the Law and come here again, counting on His throngs of followers to prevent us from arresting Him in public. And He will be quite right, of course. He knows we cannot risk a riot."

"He is already here," Rabbi Levi volunteered as the high priest paused. "I saw Him not one hour ago. He was present for the morning sacrifice and just before I was brought here, Excellency, I observed Him again in Solomon's Porch spewing forth more of His heresy."

Yosef ben Qayafa only smiled knowingly. This was proceeding even better than he had hoped. The old rabbi's information only proved to everyone that the high priest knew all that was happening and could be relied upon to achieve the desired results.

"Good, good!" Qayafa crowed approvingly. "You see, before we arrest Him, we must carefully prepare a case which will stand up under both our Law and that of the Romans. To do it," Qayafa continued, "will require a carefully executed program of probing and questioning. And that, my brothers, is where you may now serve the Holy One. Before this day is done, we may have all the evidence we will need for both trials and perhaps we can even convince the Romans to conclude this dirty business for us."

There were smiles and nods from all assembled as they leaned closer to learn the details. Yosef ben Qayafa knew his audience well. Each one wanted to have his part to play in the battle before them and each wanted to share in the honor of the victory. *Let them all bask in their own glory as they will,* he thought confidently. *Their own preening will make them perfect tools in my hands.*

✡   ✡   ✡

After those assembled had left, each to execute his part of the plan, only Rabbi Levi remained, shuffling his feet, unsure how to begin. The high priest sensed his difficulty and took the initiative.

"Yes, Rabbi ... Levi, is it?" he began. He vaguely remembered that this was the man who had brought him the news of the alleged resurrection in Bethany a couple of months before.

Rabbi Levi nervously bowed several times before he spoke, "Yes, Excellency."

"So, what is it I can do for you?"

"It is I who may be of service to you once again, Excellency," Rabbi Levi exulted.

"To me? And just how might you be able to be of service to me?" the high priest replied in a tone that was both bored and patronizing.

"Several nights ago, Excellency, I chanced to meet a young man who is one of those who follows Yeshua."

Qayafa had come to despise the little minions, especially the Pharisees, who wanted to draw out every conversation with him by supplying every unnecessary detail just to remain in the presence of the great high priest a moment longer. "Yes, yes. Go on," the high priest prodded hoping to get this particular little minion on his way as soon as possible.

"Ah, but this follower has reason to be unhappy. You see, Yeshua reprimanded him publicly. I heard it. Afterwards the disciple left in a rage and I, Excellency, followed him. I made it my business to speak with him." Rabbi Levi finished with a flourish and a conspiratorial whisper. "It may be, Excellency, that this man would be willing to work with us."

With all the tolerance he could muster on such short notice, Qayafa held his peace to see where the rabbi might be going with his rambling story. "Work with us? How?"

"I know that one of our problems has always been finding Yeshua alone so that He can be arrested without incident," Rabbi Levi confided. "The young man of whom I speak may be willing to let us know when and where Yeshua might be found alone." Rabbi Levi hesitated for a moment but he knew he had to add, "For a small consideration, Excellency."

Suddenly Qayafa hung on every word which fell from

the old rabbi's lips. "He might be willing to sell Him out? Are you certain of this?"

Rabbi Levi fidgeted uncomfortably under the high priest's intense gaze. "Yes, Excellency, I am certain." Then to protect his future credibility, he added, "At least I think so."

Qayafa sat back in a chair resembling a throne and tugged thoughtfully at his beard.

Clearly, the high priest was considering every possibility. After what seemed like an eternity, Rabbi Levi cleared his throat to regain the high priest's attention.

"Yes, yes, forgive me," Qayafa said with a start. "This sounds most promising, most promising indeed."

Rabbi Levi's satisfaction showed in his nearly toothless smile. As a Pharisee, he hated the Sadducees as much as anyone. But he also realized that for the present at least, they held the considerable power of the high priesthood in their grasp. If he wanted to come close to that power and he did, he always had, he would have to deal with Sadducees like the high priest.

Qayafa's eyes narrowed, his mind evidently weighing options. "Rabbi Levi, when may I meet the young man of whom you speak?"

The rabbi was prepared. "I have taken the liberty of arranging to bring him to you this very night, Excellency." Then by way of explanation, he quickly added, "He insists on darkness, Excellency, afraid someone might recognize him, I think."

Qayafa smiled with complete comprehension. If the young man were not really willing to do business, he would not be concerned about being recognized. "Yes, I quite understand. Tonight then. I will be looking forward to it."

As he escorted the rabbi to the door, he whispered, "Now, my brother, you will not let me down, will you?"

"No, Excellency. No. Never," Rabbi Levi assured.

✡   ✡   ✡

Rabbi Levi was late to synagogue that day but he was so pleased with his meeting with the high priest that he hardly noticed. When others did, he simply assumed a most lofty expression and explained seriously, "His Excellency, the high priest, required my assistance following the morning sacrifice." As the men around him exchanged surprised glances, he walked with great dignity to the ark and carefully withdrew the Torah scroll. Never had the diminutive Rabbi Levi stood so tall.

❧ 17 ❧

DAVID ben Asaph had also come early to the Temple with Micah and the twins. David had wanted Micah to observe the stately ritual one last time before his big day and he knew it wasn't too soon for the twins to learn about the beauty of the Sanctuary services. From behind the dark screen which separated the women and children from the men, the boys had watched nearly spellbound as David, clad in turban and fringed robe, participated in the ceremony. Afterwards, as they found each other and turned toward the warm spring sunshine outside, the boys had peppered him with questions.

"Will I really get to touch the Torah?" Micah wanted to know.

"Yes, Child," David answered with a gentle smile. "When you are welcomed into the Sanctuary as a man, you will indeed be allowed to touch it. Only be careful not to touch the actual parchment so that you do not smudge or soil the holy words."

"I will, I promise," Micah responded earnestly.

The twins danced around their brother. "You'll get to touch it, the real Torah," sang Manoah in total awe. "You must tell us just what it feels like," demanded Manasseh.

David laughed at his young charges. "Yes, yes. Now let us be on our way before your mother thinks I have sold you into slavery," he teased.

"Ammah wouldn't care so long as you brought her all the money just like you always do ," said Micah somewhat ruefully.

David was stunned into momentary silence. When he was finally able to speak, his words were fervent and impassioned. "Micah, you must never ever even think such a thing. No matter how many sons the Holy One may give to a mother, each one is precious beyond price. Do you not know this? Do you not know of the love your mother has for you?"

Micah blushed, then hung his head. "I was just joking," he said at last.

But David saw the seriousness in the child's face. Micah had lost his father and a father's special love for his first-born son. Certainly Dinah had been distracted with grief and busy trying to keep her family fed and clothed and cared for all alone but David wondered just when Micah had begun to see these things as evidence that his mother no longer loved him. David wanted to wrap the child in arms of love but he knew his were not the arms the boy really needed.

Just then the crowd rushed past them and toward something on Solomon's Porch. David, numbed by his exchange with Micah, followed along not knowing where he was being drawn. The boys followed, too, wanting to see the cause of the excitement for themselves.

As they approached, David heard the same gentle voice that had welcomed him back into the arms of the Holy One when he, too, was suffering the loss of a parent. It was Yeshua, surrounded by a throng of His followers and teaching all who would take time from the rush of activities to listen. David listened, too. So did Micah. So did the twins.

Yeshua spoke in spellbinding stories. One was of a father who sent his two sons to work in his vineyard. One said he would go but did not. The other resisted but later obeyed. Yeshua asked, "Which of the two sons did the will of their father?" Then His eyes met Micah's and searched for the burning young soul behind them. Micah could feel his blood pulsing in his ears as tears stung his eyes and his breath began to come in short uneven gasps.

David knew he did not understand the message of the story but he carefully wrapped it in his memory and tucked it away in his heart to ponder later. When he looked down, however, David saw young Micah hanging on every word, his small face lit with an understanding David himself did not yet possess. There was something about the father and the sons that spoke to Micah's tormented heart and gave it comfort and direction, something about a task to be done and a father who loved that son who tried to accomplish it.

Micah walked to the home of his mother's family in silence but David could tell that the boy at his side had changed in some inexplicable way. David wanted to inquire of the child, to listen with his whole heart, to offer whatever comfort or guidance he could, but the twins chattered on incessantly. David promised himself that he would find time for Micah as soon as they got home, time to be to him an elder brother even if he could not be to him a father.

As they reached the gate to the courtyard and the twins dashed past, Micah looked up into David's face. It was as if the sun had just risen in the child's eyes. "When we get home, will you teach me to sail Abba's boats?" Micah asked in a small tentative voice.

"Yes, Micah. Oh yes," David answered, enfolding the boy's narrow shoulders in his warmest embrace. "I've been waiting so long to teach you exactly that."

"I think I'm ready now," Micah whispered.

And David knew that Yeshua had conquered yet another heart.

❧ 18 ❧

YAKOV had slept little and when he came early to his place in the Court of the People that morning, it was with reddened eyes that squinted into a pitiless sun and a weary body that longed for rest. That voice, those words had invaded his mind and troubled his dreams. He hadn't been able to get away from the truth of them no matter how hard he had tried.

"Yakov, my son," Meshullam greeted him. "Business will be good today, no?" he queried.

"Yes, Abba, very good, I think." Yakov avoided his father's gaze.

"And no more of what happened yesterday, I should hope."

"No, Abba," Yakov answered dutifully.

"I wish I had been here. I would have told that Pretender a thing in His ear," Meshullam threatened as he raised an angry fist to a peaceful sky.

Yakov said nothing. He knew his father would have been unable to say anything, just like all the others. Perhaps deep down they all knew what Yeshua said was true, perhaps they all knew what they were doing was wrong, completely wrong. *But who can explain this to an old man who knows nothing but his business?* Yakov wondered absently.

The first customers of the day were a middle-aged husband and wife with a flock of little ones clinging to their robes and another in his mother's arms.

"We will be needing a lamb for Pesach," the husband stated in a very business-like tone.

"May the Holy One be blessed," Yakov returned by rote, "Who has given us so many perfect specimens from which to choose."

The husband pretended to know about livestock and Yakov pretended to believe that he did. He finally picked an animal Yakov knew to have rheumy eyes.

"That one," said the husband with a knowing air for the benefit of his family. He held out the Temple coin he had purchased to buy his lamb.

Yakov began to reach for the coin just as he always had. It represented an exorbitant price for such a small lamb even if the animal had been healthy and Yakov knew that it was not. He found himself becoming more and more agitated. He knew most of the travelers to Yerushalayim simply assumed that any animal sold on the Temple premises was perfect. Most were also tired from the journey and anxious to finish their transactions and make their sacrifices. In any event, nearly all were eager to accept whatever animal Yakov placed before them. And over the years he and his father had taken full advantage of those feelings. Could he do it one more time to one more well-meaning worshipper and his family?

Suddenly Yakov covered his face with his hands and groaned loudly, startling the woman and her children. "I'm sorry. This animal is not well and even if it were, it would not be worth so much. Perhaps you would allow me to choose another lamb for you ... ."

"Nonsense, nonsense," Meshullam broke in, grinning broadly. "I think my son has mistaken this beast for another. If I may be of service to you, I'm certain we can conclude our business quickly and to our mutual advantage."

Preferring to be swindled rather than admit he had chosen badly, the man looked askance at Yakov for only a moment before turning to Meshullam. Soon, the sick lamb was gone and the coin was safely tucked away in Meshullam's money box.

Once the couple and their brood had led the small animal away, Meshullam's grin faded into an angry stare. "What has come over you, my son?" he asked accusingly. "Have I not taught you better? The servants could conduct my business better than that."

Yakov blushed in embarrassment. "In that case," he finally answered, "perhaps you should let them conduct it." With that, Yakov walked away not knowing where he was going, not caring. His own torment crowded out his thoughts until he saw another kind of crowd pressing closely together to hear Someone who was evidently speaking.

As Yakov neared, some others approached from the opposite direction. He recognized the five sons of Annas, the old man who had once been high priest. They wore their finest robes, their heads high and haughty, and they were with a group of scribes whose reputations as experts in the intricacies of the Mosaic Law were legendary. As they advanced, the crowd parted like the Red Sea to make way for them and they bowed slightly to acknowledge the courtesy.

When Yakov drew closer, he realized exactly who was speaking. It was none other than the young Rabbi from the north, Yeshua ben Yosef. His ears strained to catch His words.

Then Machir ben Avram interrupted Yeshua with his rude and imperious questioning. "By what authority do You do the things You do," he demanded to know, "and just who gave You such authority?"

Yakov could see the trap just waiting to spring. Everyone knew that Yeshua had no authority from the high priest or the Sanhedrin or even His own local synagogue to teach or to preach. If Yeshua dared to insinuate that His authority came from the Holy One, He would be branded a heretic for even presuming such a thing. But if He claimed that the authority was His own, He would be immediately discredited as just one more pretender with aspirations to greatness.

Yeshua smiled tolerantly. Then with utmost deference, He replied, "May I also ask you a question? And after you have answered Mine, then I will answer yours."

Machir nodded contemptuously.

"It is with regard to the baptism of Yohanan. Was it from Heaven or only of men?"

Machir was momentarily taken aback. He turned to confer with Annas' sons.

"This is clearly political," one offered in a careful whisper.

"This I know," Machir responded sarcastically. "But how can we answer in a way that will not offend this crowd?" Machir realized that both before and after his recent execution by King Herod, the baptist was held in honor among many. Among those who lived in or near Yerushalayim and the Temple, however, Yohanan was viewed as the poor deranged son of one of the priests because he had taken to living in the desert, subsisting on nothing more than locusts and honey, and berating those who failed to follow the Holy One in complete righteousness or to prepare themselves for the coming of His Messiah.

Another of Annas' sons ventured a warning. "Be careful how you answer."

A third began to think aloud. "If we say Yohanan's baptism was from Heaven, He'll want to know why we did not believe and become baptized. But if we tell Him we think Yohanan's baptism was merely of men, this crowd may turn on us in an instant. Many of them think this Yohanan was a true prophet of the Holy One," he sneered.

Machir turned back to Yeshua. After too lengthy a pause, a crafty smile twisted his lips as he thought of the perfect answer. "We cannot tell," he said slyly.

Yeshua only smiled again, knowing He had them but compassionate of the lack of knowledge evidenced by those who had taken upon themselves the mantle of leadership. "If you cannot answer My question, then I cannot answer yours concerning My authority."

Machir's face grew red with fury. The muscles of his jaw contorted as he tried to speak but he found no words. Finally he turned and shoved his way through the crowd. Many were laughing as he passed. Their heads now low, the sons of Annas followed him. They knew their brother-in-law, Yosef ben Qayafa, would not be pleased with their failure.

Yakov could only smile ruefully. They had tried to match wits with Yeshua, a Man of Galilee, whose citizens they considered worthy of nothing more than their disdain. Yet even Yakov had to admit that they had come away the worse for the experience.

As Yeshua resumed teaching, Yakov spied an old man in black robes and recognized him as the one called Rabbi Levi. With him were others of the sect of the Pharisees, easily identifiable to all by their too obvious phylacteries, small black boxes containing a few Scriptures written on a tiny scroll of rolled parchment which they wore on their left arms or their foreheads. Accompanying them were a few powerful leaders Yakov knew to be well placed in the Herodian political party. They followed Herod, the hated Hebrew king who had sold out completely to Roman domination and they had grown rich and mighty for their trouble. They, too, were closing in on the small assembly, slowly insinuating themselves into the gathering, listening, moving, listening again, moving even closer. Finally they pounced.

"Teacher," one of the Herodians began," we know that You are an honest Man, One who isn't swayed by a man's position, One who teaches God's truth fairly."

Yakov nearly choked. He knew the man who spoke had achieved his own station in life by seeking out and attaching himself to others based upon their positions. *Does Yeshua know that He is witnessing a consummate performance by a great actor?* Yakov could only wonder.

"Tell me," the Herodian continued, "is it legal for us to pay taxes to the Romans?"

Yakov knew there was no safe answer. If Yeshua told them to pay the heavy taxes levied upon them by their despised occupiers, this crowd would turn against Him in a moment. But if Yeshua counseled them not to pay, He could be arrested immediately for a serious breach of Roman law.

Yakov also knew that this Man had come south to the city of Yerushalayim to celebrate Pesach. He wasn't privy to all the political machinations of the capital. Yakov thought it most unfair to attempt to embroil Him in them.

Each man in the crowd leaned even nearer to hear Yeshua, each hoping for the answer that would advance his own philosophy.

Rabbi Levi broke the silence. "Shall we pay or not?" he demanded disrespectfully.

Yeshua fixed His eyes gently on the figure of the old rabbi. "Why do you test Me?" He said softly. "Bring a penny to Me so that I can look at it."

It was a strange request and the questioners were obviously puzzled. Did Rabbi Yeshua have no penny of His own?

One of the Herodians fished in the leather purse he carried in his sash and produced a silver denarius. With much ceremony, he handed it to Yeshua.

"Whose picture is this," Yeshua asked innocently, "and what is this writing?"

The Pharisees looked at each other, rolled their eyes, and sneered.

Yakov knew exactly what they were thinking. *This Man purports to be a Rabbi yet He cannot even read or recognize the image of Tiberius Caesar.*

Finally Rabbi Levi answered in an obviously patronizing tone. "It is Caesar's."

Yeshua handed the coin back as though He had no further use for it. "Well then, give Caesar the things that belong to him and give the Holy One the things that are His."

Stifled snickers erupted in the crowd. Rabbi Levi's face became alive with rage as the muscles of his jaw began rippling rhythmically. He turned swiftly for one in advanced years and led the little group of disgraced questioners back toward the Temple gate. *Yosef ben Qayafa will not be at all pleased*, Rabbi Levi thought dejectedly.

Yakov turned away, too, his mind racing at the gravity of the words he had heard. He remembered the old rabbi who had taught him as a child. *What was it he told us?* Yakov struggled to recall the words. *That's it! I remember now! He told us that we were created in the very image of the Holy One so that all the world would know we belonged to Him. That's it! Just as the penny carries the image of Caesar and belongs to him, I was meant to carry the image of the Holy One and to belong to Him forever.*

This sudden realization struck Yakov like a lightning bolt. Other realizations struck just as forcefully. *Look how far I have fallen! There is nothing about me or the life that I now live that bears His precious Image. It's all about money, not about Him at all. Have I lost the Holy One only to have Him replaced by an idol of silver?*

That possibility was more than Yakov could bear. Unbidden tears filled his eyes, spilled over, and were lost in his beard.

Yakov did not know his feet had carried him by habit back to the pens, to the tables, to the business district of the court. When he looked up, it was into the face of his father. Yakov spoke in a voice just above a whisper. "I cannot do this any longer."

"Do what, my son?" Meshullam questioned in his confusion.

"This, Abba. I cannot do this." A wide sweep of Yakov's arm took in all of the business being conducted in the court. As Yakov turned away, his father followed completely baffled.

"Yes, my son. You go home and rest now. The heat of this day has made you ill. Rest, my son. You will feel better tomorrow," Meshullam soothed.

Yakov wondered if his father was right. Was it simply the heat? Would he really feel better tomorrow and be ready to resume business as usual? He could only wonder.

Have I gone mad? he asked himself more than once on the way home. *My father offers me a livelihood that will keep me like a prince for the rest of my days and my children after me. Now I am ready to throw it all away because of Him! How could He possibly know what my rabbi taught me so long ago? He has driven me to the edge of insanity with His accusations and His eyes that look into my very soul and His voice that calls me away from my own father and from the coins with Caesar's image upon them. I will rejoice when they finally get Him. Then perhaps I will find some peace and sanity in this world again.*

Even as he comforted himself with the words, Yakov knew they were not true. He knew that he would never again find peace stealing from poor troubled souls who wanted nothing more than that the smile of the Holy One might rest upon them. And Yakov knew he would find no sanity, no safety for himself so long as the eye of the Holy One was upon him.

❧ 19 ❧

YOSEF ben Qayafa knew the Sadducees well, too well, for he and his father-in-law, Annas, were numbered among them. Like him, most were rich. Those riches had originally purchased the high priesthood for the Sadducees and their well-placed bribes had held it for them all these years.

The common people hated the Sadducees' arrogance and obdurate disbelief in angels or Heaven or a life after death with rewards for the faithful. But the Sadducees did not care. After all, they reasoned, the poor may need to believe in such things as angels and Heaven and rewards after death. They did not. They had riches enough to provide them with a heaven on earth and all the rewards they wanted.

The poor hated their pretentious Greek manners and Greek clothes and Grecian-style homes full of Greek furniture and art. It was joked that if they liked all things Greek so well, they should book passage on one of the many ships which plied the trade route and go there to stay. But the Sadducees didn't care about that either. They could afford the best the world had to offer and the best just happened to come from Greece. They ignored any criticism and went right on ordering imported luxuries from the Greek isles.

Though they were widely despised, Qayafa knew his brother Sadducees had their uses just as he was using them today. He drifted closer to Solomon's Porch, close enough to hear what was being said while remaining as inconspicuous as possible behind one of the columns of the colonnade.

A brother Sadducee had launched into the long tale of a woman who had married seven brothers in turn. Each had died leaving her a childless widow. Since the Pharisees believed in a life after death lived in the presence of God and the Sadducees believed in no life after death at all, the questioner asked Yeshua whose wife the woman would be in the hereafter.

Qayafa rolled his eyes heavenward and smiled. He knew instantly the approach they had chosen. This was one of their favorite old tired trick questions, one they had posed many times and one that usually left their victim scratching his head in puzzlement. They thought Yeshua would easily fall victim to their game and be dishonored before the masses. They delighted in such amusements.

This too may be useful, Qayafa reasoned. *If He says there is no life after this, He will incur the wrath of the Pharisees. And if He says this fanciful woman is in Heaven with her seven husbands, He will be condoning adultery and incest before the very eyes of the Holy One.* Qayafa realized either statement would be beneficial to his case against Yeshua before the Sanhedrin. Qayafa chuckled to himself in undisguised glee.

"You have one flaw in your thinking," Yeshua began gently. "Those found worthy of Heaven are not married and are not given in marriage since they will live forever and not need to bear children. Instead they are like the angels, children of the Holy One."

Yosef ben Qayafa turned away angrily and stomped back toward the council chamber. He did not believe in angels any more than he believed in living forever. Yeshua had presented both as truth and Qayafa was infuriated. *His words leave us no way to accuse Him, not as long as Pharisees occupy so many of the seats in the Sanhedrin.* Qayafa was livid.

✡   ✡   ✡

Another stood in the crowd listening and weeping softly.

Naqdimon thought of his own dear Moshe. Oh, how he longed to believe Moshe was one of those found worthy of Heaven, one of those granted eternal life as a child of the Holy One Himself! But he could not believe that. He had found Messiah but, because of his fear, he had never told Moshe. Now his son was dead, beyond hope, beyond help, beyond Heaven. Moshe, too, would live eternally but in Gehenna, the fires of eternal torment. Naqdimon knew he would ever bear a father's shame both here and in the hereafter.

◖ **20** ◗

DAVID ben Asaph strode across the broad carefully-landscaped courtyard to the home of Elihu and found Hannah giggling with her cousin, Elisheba. It was the first time he had heard her lyric laughter since her father's death and it delighted him. He did not want to interrupt but they had already seen him approach.

Hannah assumed her usual more formal expression immediately. "Yes, David. What is it?" she asked coldly.

"Hannah," he began hopefully, "the evening sacrifice is at hand. The boys are busy at play and your mother is helping with the supper preparations."

At the mention of supper, Hannah sprang to her feet quickly. "I did not realize the lateness of the hour. I, too, am needed," she said as she attempted to brush past David.

"No, no, Hannah," David countered, filling the doorway so that she could not pass. "That is not why I have come. I just thought you might like to accompany me to the Temple for the evening sacrifice."

Hannah hesitated. She had not yet been to the Temple and she most assuredly wanted to go. It was a sight which always caught her breath and filled her with awe. She had last been there with her abba and knew she would feel closer to him there. She hesitated only because she did not want to go with David, to give him any unnecessary encouragement even in this small thing.

As though he sensed what she was thinking, David's eyes softened. "Come with me, Hannah. I promise to be the most gallant of escorts," he said with a flourish and an ostentatious bow.

Elisheba giggled again at the show before her. "Go, Hannah," she encouraged.

Hannah turned to her cousin. "If you will come with me ... ," she began tentatively.

Elisheba interrupted before Hannah could even complete her thought. "I cannot. My ammah will have my head in a basket if I do not set the table for our guests." Elisheba rose from her pillow and crossed the room with long quick strides. She pushed her cousin in David's direction. "Go, go before your ammah catches you and puts you to work, too."

Hannah always felt awkward trying to help out in her aunt's home. Even though her family was not poor by Galilean standards, everything here seemed so much finer than the things she was used to in the homes of Capernaum. This home was a testimony to the gracious art of the stonecutter with mosaics inlaid into every floor, even the courtyard. There were long upholstered couches around this room and the sleeping chambers had high bedsteads made of the finest polished woods and laden with an assortment of cushions and pillows and blankets for the sleeper's comfort. They bore no resemblance to the thin sleeping mats like the one Hannah placed between herself and the cold floor at home. Here there were great seven-branched bronze lampstands with wicks of flax tended by servants instead of the small pinched clay oil lamps with little cotton wicks Hannah and her mother kept filled and trimmed. Instead of the open fire in her mother's courtyard where stews were stirred or the small oven at the hearth where bread was baked on the hot stones next to the flame, this home boasted the latest ceramic oven, divided to separate the food from the fire to prevent burning and vented to the outside to minimize smoking. Instead of simple pottery, here she found glazed plates and cups with designs painted around their rims and serving pieces of solid silver. She was always afraid she would drop something or spill something or even worse break something. She was not lazy but she did avoid getting pressed into service in this grand house. In a moment she had made her decision.

"I will go with you, David," she whispered, still full of misgivings. Then she turned to Elisheba again. "And don't you say a single word about where I've gone, do you hear?"

Elisheba smiled broadly and nodded her agreement. Her cousin was pledged in marriage to David and the wedding would take place in just a few days. Yet she never spoke of David, never joined in the conversation when Elisheba spoke of him. She had never seen a betrothed woman who made more excuses to avoid the man she was to wed. It was almost as if Hannah disliked David. Elisheba was pleased to help bring them together even if only for a short excursion to the Temple.

They said little on their way through the narrow crowded streets of the Lower City south of the Temple. Hannah's breath caught in her throat as the setting sun illuminated with slanting shafts of golden light the high promontory upon which the Temple stood.

"It is beautiful, is it not?" David whispered.

Her eyes wide, Hannah responded. "It must be the most beautiful place on earth!"

Together they went through the southern gate and found themselves in the Court of the People. And quite a number of people there were! Restless lines snaked this way and that. The smells of animals and incense filled the air. But as they turned toward the Beautiful Gate, it was the marble facade of the Sanctuary high above them that captured Hannah's attention. It was there she had gone holding tightly to the hands of her abba and her ammah and the little girl within her was still overwhelmed with the magnificence of it.

"No wonder the Holy One chose this place," she whispered reverently.

David smiled. This was one of the things he most loved about Hannah. After the pain of his own empty childhood, after it had left him broken and jaded, Hannah always gave him a fresh view of the world. Through her trusting eyes, he found he could see beauty and splendor again and, shared with her, his delight was always doubled.

The two approached the twelve steps leading to the Beautiful Gate and to the Court of the Women beyond. But before they could proceed, David's attention was drawn to an argument on Solomon's Porch. "Is it possible?" David ventured. "Is He still here?"

Hannah followed David's eyes toward the sound. "Who is it?" she queried.

"I think it is Yeshua," David answered, his voice trembling. "Come, Hannah."

Hannah took a step back. "No, David, I'm not ready to see Him again. Please take me to the Court of the Women. Then you can return if you wish."

David smiled down hopefully at the young woman by his side. She looked like a frightened deer. He did not want to press her and make her more unwilling. But he did so want her to learn of Yeshua. He responded in a tone that was tender, wooing. "Please?"

Hannah reluctantly allowed herself to be led in the direction of the gathering.

An elderly scribe, a man who was obviously well versed in the scriptures, was speaking, questioning, almost accusing. "Which then is the most important commandment?" he asked in conclusion.

David wondered if this were merely a trap, a deceptive inquiry designed only to embarrass Yeshua and entertain His questioners. This was just the sort of endless debate in which scribes and rabbis seemed to take such pleasure but which could intimidate less stalwart souls. David tensed, fearing that Yeshua would fall into their net and further alienate Hannah.

Yeshua's voice thundered through the porch. "The first commandment is this, 'Hear, O Yisrael, the Lord your God is one Lord: And you must love the Lord your God with all your soul and with all your mind and with all your strength.' This is the first commandment."

Hannah recognized these words as the very ones she had uttered in her final argument with her abba. Her heart broke with the memory of that last terrible day, of what she had done, of what she had caused. She blushed with guilt as she wondered how He knew. She wanted to run from the accusing finger of those words but she could not move.

Yeshua continued a bit more softly. "The second commandment is very similar. 'You must love your neighbor as yourself.' There are no commandments greater than these. All of the Law, all of Scripture is based on these two commands."

Was it Hannah's imagination or were His eyes really directly on her, searching her soul? *My neighbor, my neighbor,* Hannah's mind repeated over and over like the beat of heavy rain. David was her neighbor, just as Yeshua Himself was her Neighbor. Both were residents of Capernaum; both were her neighbors. And Hannah knew she had refused to love either of them.

David stood so close to her that she could feel the warmth of his body and smell the scent of the sun in his hair. She longed to touch him, to hold him close just as he had held her the night he saved her life on the road to Yerushalayim. Her entire being ached for him. Something inside of her seemed to churn and twist at the very thought of him. Though she had denied it, even to herself, Hannah knew in that instant that she loved David ben Asaph, loved him with her whole heart, loved him with a fire and an intensity she hadn't known existed. At long last she knew she wanted nothing more in all the world than to be his wife and the mother of his children.

Still Hannah knew nothing had really changed. She loved David ben Asaph more than her life but not more than her soul. And as much as she loved him, she loved the Holy One even more. This simple Man before her couldn't possibly be Messiah and as long as David believed that He was, she could not become his bride. More than anything else, more even than her love for David, Hannah had to remain true to her Lord. Her eyes fought to hold back tears she could not control.

David's arm slipped around her shoulders to protect her, to comfort her. She pulled away. "We will be late," she said as she ascended the stairs to the Court of the Women ahead of him. David followed, unable to comprehend the storm that was gathering in her soul. She fled to the security of her place behind the screen which separated the women from the men, relieved for the opportunity to regain control of her trembling emotions, glad that David could not see the love and heartache she knew were mingled in her eyes.

✿   ✿   ✿

Below on Solomon's Porch, the questioning old scribe knew he had been defeated. He knew he could not have answered more perfectly had he himself been so interrogated. He could not argue with a single word but merely muttered in wonder, "Well said. You have spoken the truth for there is only one Holy One; there is no other. To love Him with all one's heart and mind and soul and strength and to love one's neighbor as one's self is more than all the burnt offerings and sacrifices in the world."

Yeshua smiled then. "You are not far from entering the Kingdom of God," He said, the invitation implicit.

The scribe knew he would have nothing positive to report to the man who had sent him on his furtive mission, Yosef ben Qayafa. Not anxious to incur the high priest's prodigious wrath, the scribe simply slipped away and melted into the crowd.

✿   ✿   ✿

The afternoon had been a complete waste. Each small contingent Yosef ben Qayafa had sent had been unsuccessful in its assignment. None had been able to trap Yeshua ben Yosef into saying anything that could be witnessed before the Sanhedrin or the Romans in a trial.

When word reached Qayafa, he raised two clenched fists toward the heavens and screamed out in the fury of his rage: "I will yet have the victory. I will yet have the cold corpse of Yeshua ben Yosef hanging on a Roman tree. On my soul I swear it."

✿　　　✿　　　✿

A tense afternoon lengthened into a taut evening. Yeshua ben Yosef and His followers left the Temple and made their way along the Yericho Road toward Bethany for the night. Somewhere on the Mount of Olives overlooking Yerushalayim, they paused in their ascent. Yeshua's eyes swept over the scene before Him. The Temple Mount lay in the distance with all of Yerushalayim stretched out beyond it like a terraced garden; the Kidron Valley and the gentle stream meandering through it which would soon run red with the blood of the Pesach lambs lay in between; and the Garden of Gethsemane was below to His right.

Then Yeshua sat with His disciples for what He knew would be the last time in that place and as they watched the night steal away the sunlight from the city below, He spoke to them of all that would come later. He saw it like a panorama played out on His soul, the nearing destruction and death, the onrushing famines and wars, the coming centuries of division and dispersal. It nearly broke His heart to tell them but He knew they had to know. And through them, He knew others would know as well.

But Yeshua saw something else, too. He saw a distant day when He would rend the skies like lightning, when He would return to this very place, when He would gather to Him every heart that loved Him and bring them all home with Him forever. More than anything, He longed for that day to come.

ABBI Levi hurried through the cool spring night, the hem of his long black robe brushing the Roman paving stones beneath his feet. Beside him, a younger taller man with his mantle pulled over his turban to shield his face from view struggled to keep pace with the crafty determined old rabbi. The beat of their sandals scraped the pavement, then the steps; then they entered into the very palace of the high priest.

When they were alone with Yosef ben Qayafa and a few of his most trusted friends from the council, Rabbi Levi spoke in a scheming whisper. "This is Yehuda of Kerioth." Rabbi Levi emphasized the name of Yehuda's home village to make certain that the high priest knew he was not a Galilean as were the other followers of Yeshua. This detail marked Yehuda as a native Yudean like the high priest himself and established one more point of separation between him and his former friends.

With the introductions made, Yehuda removed his mantle, allowed his eyes to adjust to the light, then surveyed the scene. The palace was larger and grander than he had imagined and the high priest was older than he appeared from a distance. The others present were unknown to him but, from their garb, he was certain they were council members, very rich council members. Yehuda smiled.

"I've heard that you've been badly treated by your Master, my son," Qayafa began sympathetically.

Yehuda looked uncomfortable at the memory of the banquet a few days before. "There were some words between us," was all that he would acknowledge.

"It is a sad thing when we are disillusioned by One we trusted, is it not?"

"Yes, Excellency, very sad," allowed Yehuda.

"I can assure you, my son," Qayafa soothed as he motioned the young man to the chair beside his own, "that you will not be disillusioned here."

Yehuda took the seat offered him but said nothing.

Qayafa smiled. His eyes crinkled giving him the appearance of a favorite uncle. He knew it and he used it well in an attempt to allay any lingering suspicions that Yehuda may still harbor. "Perhaps we can help each other, Yehuda. That would be a good thing, yes?"

"Yes, Excellency. I suppose." Yehuda made a show of his vacillation.

"We must arrange a private meeting with your Master to discuss some matters of mutual concern to all of us." When Yehuda's eyes shifted nervously, Qayafa quickly added, "There has been talk. People have said things, things that have been reported to me, things that I must now investigate." Qayafa's right hand fell reflexively across his chest to indicate his sincerity as he continued. "I hasten to add, my son, the things I have heard may not even be true."

Yehuda nodded.

"But I cannot know of a certainty until I speak with your Master face to face. When my eyes behold His eyes, when my ears hear His explanation, I am sure I shall be satisfied. This may all be nothing but a terrible misunderstanding."

Everyone knew the truth. Yehuda knew it, too, although for the moment he preferred to hear the comforting words of Yosef ben Qayafa. After all, he reasoned within himself cynically, one of such stature as the high priest cannot lie, can he?

Yehuda nodded as his expression softened. The cunning old high priest knew the bird was almost in his grasp. He carefully controlled his countenance so that he would not frighten it from his snare.

"So you see, my son, you can bring the two of us together. You would like that, would you not?"

Yehuda nodded.

"It is just so difficult to see your Master alone since He has become so popular. And we wouldn't wish to create a scene that would cause the Romans to thrust their long aquiline noses into matters best settled between us, now would we? You understand."

Yehuda nodded again.

"So, Yehuda, all we need from you ... and it is such a small thing really ... is a place where we might meet with your Master alone. Now that is not so difficult, is it, my son?"

Yehuda appraised the high priest knowingly. A small sneer twisted one corner of his mouth and a sinister chuckle escaped his lips.

Qayafa looked startled. One eyebrow went up as his glance darted to Rabbi Levi with a silent question, *Have you misinformed me as to this young man's intentions?*

Rabbi Levi read the question in Qayafa's eyes and shrugged, his palms turned upward.

The high priest turned back to face Yehuda. "So, my young friend, may we trust you to help us?"

Yehuda laughed aloud. "Trust? You speak to me of trust? Do you not think I know that you want me to betray Him to you so you can find Him alone and arrest Him?"

Qayafa feigned shock and began to protest his innocence. "My son, I want only to ... ."

Yehuda cut him off. He had taken control of this meeting and he meant to keep it. "Don't bother denying it, Excellency. First of all I wouldn't believe you if you did. And second, I am perfectly willing to do as you request."

Yehuda watched as the high priest went from his affectation of surprise to absolute delight. This time Yehuda had his bird within his grasp and he meant to be certain that it did not get away. "For a price," he added confidently.

Now Qayafa's shock was genuine. He had known his young guest expected some payment and he meant to offer him a small sum for his trouble. But even he could not believe Yehuda's mercenary coldness. He was practically offering to sell his own Rabbi!

Yehuda laughed again. "I have neglected my own business for three years now and will need a few shekels to finance a fresh start," he reasoned using the same soothing tone the high priest had used with him only a few moments before.

Qayafa weighed Yehuda's demeanor in one sidelong glance. "How much?"

"Thirty pieces of silver should be sufficient," Yehuda said flatly.

"My son," Qayafa began, his eyes wide with another display of simulated surprise, "that is a great deal of money." It was indeed much more than Qayafa had planned to offer.

"Do you think you can make a better bargain with one of the others?" Yehuda shot back. "Take it or leave it." When the high priest hesitated, Yehuda added, "Think of it as an investment in the future of your priesthood."

Qayafa didn't want to give this young upstart the satisfaction of besting him in this negotiation, especially in front of others. But what he wanted even more was the capture of Yeshua. After what seemed an eternity to everyone present, he finally spoke. "Thirty pieces of silver it is." But when Yehuda started to extend his hand for the promised payment, Qayafa added, "Payable when you tell us where He can be found."

The two stared at each other for a long moment, neither blinking, neither looking away. They had taken each other's measure and both decided that they had won. Both had gotten what they wanted. With right hands, they grasped each other's right forearms. The deal was done.

A collective sigh of relief erupted from the assembled witnesses. Yeshua was as good as in their hands and they reveled in the anticipation of their triumph.

After Yehuda had disappeared into the darkness, Qayafa and the others congratulated Rabbi Levi. The little rabbi basked in his newfound glory not wanting the moment to end. As he finally departed, Qayafa embraced him and whispered, "I am in your debt, my brother, as is all Yerushalayim this night." Rabbi Levi smiled. Then he kept smiling all the way home.

The others drifted away leaving the high priest alone with his thoughts. A victorious smirk formed on his lips. As he left, he looked up into the starry night sky and whispered to no one in particular, "May the Holy One save us all from our friends." Then he laughed aloud.

ೞ 22 ೧

THE next day, everything was as it had always been. The sun rose, the pink clouds of morning melted away rather than face its heat, and Yerushalayim began to come to life under a springtime sky.

That is ... everything was just as it had always been except in the home of Yakov ben Meshullam. Yakov didn't go to work that day. While Meshullam and Simeon struggled to satisfy the demands of their patrons on one of the busiest days of the year, while Meshullam felt every one of his years in the soreness of his muscles and the aching of his bones, his firstborn son never once came to his side. Meshullam wondered, he grumbled under his breath, he even took it out on the servants and poor hapless Helah. And whenever there was a brief respite from the worshippers thronging his table, his old eyes searched the crowds for that familiar form and face. But Yakov didn't go to work that day.

Instead Yakov lay in the same bed where he had spent a sleepless night pondering the imponderables that had left him with a throbbing headache. Still, he had found no answers to his dilemma, no solutions to the puzzle his life had become.

It wasn't supposed to be this way. From his earliest years he had been reared in the family business and he had been good at it. Meshullam had made sure of that, just as he had made sure of everything. He had even selected the most beautiful woman Yakov had ever laid his eyes upon to be his wife with the hope of many sons to continue and expand the business. Now Meshullam's plans lay in ashes. Shoshana was dead and the only child they would ever have was a worthless girl. She would only grow up to marry and provide sons for some other family's business expansion. And now Yakov had lost all interest in an occupation which promised great rewards but also required great duplicity and deception against the most defenseless of people. Things could not be much worse.

When Yakov had finally tired of torturing himself seeking answers where there were none, he rose from his bed and followed the sounds of his daughter. He found Devorah on her knees before the hearth cleaning the child's soiled bottom and preparing to feed her while the child fingered a small wooden rattle that Devorah had made for her. Mara cooed up at Devorah and Devorah cooed back with soft comforting words that brought dimpled smiles in response. Content in each other, neither had heard Yakov approach.

Yakov stood motionless, watching, observing. There was a softness, a gentleness about Devorah that he had never before noticed and a special bond between the woman and child that had never before been apparent to him. At first he felt almost threatened by it. Then he realized it did not present any peril but was instead a great gift to him. At a time when he had been unable to help himself or his child, this quiet unassuming young woman had come into their lives and helped them both. Little Mara was growing up to be a cheerful child. As Yakov stood there, he realized it was all because of Devorah.

How does she do it? he wondered. *How can she give such love to a baby knowing she will soon have to leave it? I could not do it. I know if I had been aware of the short time Shoshana and I would have together, I could have never given her my heart or loved her so totally. I would have had to protect myself against the coming anguish. Yet Devorah opens her entire being to a child from whom she will soon be separated. How on earth does she do it?*

Just then Devorah started to bare her breast for her young charge. Yakov reddened, looked down at his bare feet, and cleared his throat nervously to let her know he was there.

Devorah was clearly startled. As her eyes focused on Yakov, she covered herself hurriedly. "My lord, forgive me. I did not know you were present," she babbled in her embarrassment.

"There is nothing to forgive," Yakov reassured. "My fault entirely. I should have made my presence known sooner. It is just that ... . I had a very bad night and I suppose ... ." He knew he was rambling. As his tired eyes reached out for hers, he tried again to make some sense. "The two of you were so beautiful together, I simply couldn't look away."

She smiled nervously. "She is a beautiful child, is she not? I never knew her mother but I think she must be very like her."

Yakov still could not speak of Shoshana nor listen to others do so. "I suppose," he said flatly. Tears welled in Yakov's eyes and Devorah looked away rather than embarrass him. "I will take her to my bedchamber to feed her there," Devorah whispered as she moved past him. For only a moment, Yakov felt her warmth and inhaled the fragrance of her hair.

Long after Devorah had left the room, Yakov stood paralyzed in place, feeling feelings he had not known since Shoshana died, thinking thoughts he had not thought except about her. *Now I have truly lost whatever was left of my mind and perhaps my soul in the bargain,* he told himself. *How could I do this to Shoshana? What kind of a man am I that I could even think of another woman with my precious wife lying cold and lifeless just outside the city wall?* A cry of frustration and anguish escaped his lips as he turned toward his sleeping chamber and another day and night alone with his memories and his misery.

✿   ✿   ✿

Yeshua ben Yosef didn't go to the Temple that day either. As a simmering spring sun baked the city of Yerushalayim increasing the tension of those who waited to take Him into their trap, He spent the day in Bethany visiting ones He had loved there, taking leave of some He knew He would see no more. For all of them the hours slipped by slowly as each anticipated the day to come, as each readied himself to assume his role in a drama to be played out all too soon.

ೞ 23 ೞ

NAQDIMON had not come to the palace of the high priest because he wanted to, but only because he had been summoned to yet another meeting on the very same subject.

The setting was just as palatial as the name itself implied for the family of Annas had spared no expense in establishing for themselves a luxurious home away from home. It was built of the finest stone with ornamental iron lattices at each window. The marble floors were polished to a sheen and the lingering scent of cedar paneling hung heavy in the air. The moldings and decorations were of gold and silver and even ivory. The furnishings had been created by the finest Greek artisans and had been brought to Yerushalayim at great cost. Qayafa gloried in these trappings of office and often used them just as he was using them on this night, to awe and intimidate those he considered his inferiors. And that lengthy list included nearly everyone in the Holy City.

After Malluch had ushered him into Qayafa's meeting chamber, Naqdimon sat quietly amidst this breathtaking splendor saying little for he knew it was no use. He listened instead to the shouted comments of speaker after speaker, each louder and more vehement than the one before, each more determined than the last to put to death a Man Naqdimon knew was not worthy of that fate. He also knew there was nothing he could do about it.

Baruch ben Yisroel had raved on and on about the woes Yeshua had pronounced the previous day upon himself and all Pharisees, lumping them together with hypocrites.

They had always despised hypocrites and saw themselves as men of great spiritual superiority to such people. To be labeled with them was more than Baruch could bear.

"He called us fools and blind leaders of the blind. He told us we are not fit to enter the Kingdom of God and accused us of preventing others from entering in as well. Who does He think He is? You should have seen the faces of the Paschal visitors as He held us up to public ridicule. I tell you the Man must be stopped immediately."

Most of those assembled shouted their approval of Baruch's statement.

Naqdimon shook his head. He had known Baruch for most of his life just as he had known his father before him. He knew Baruch was especially vulnerable to such charges.

Baruch had come with clouded countenance to Naqdimon shortly after assuming his father's seat on the Sanhedrin. He had wept before Naqdimon, unsure he could fill his father's place, unsure of his expertise to decide the difficult cases of the Law which came before the Sanhedrin nearly every day. Naqdimon had listened to him, reassured him, and prayed with him. Then he had watched in satisfaction as the young man had grown in both competence and confidence in his new role. But Naqdimon could still see the insecure Baruch of old as he stood among his fellow members and ranted against Yeshua's words.

Ehud ben Haziel, a dedicated scribe who had devoted his life to painstakingly copying the Torah scrolls so that each synagogue might have its own set, was next. He had questioned Yeshua about the greatest commandment and had instantly seen the wisdom of His response. He now tried to calm the members with reason only to be shouted down for his trouble.

Naqdimon was not surprised when Machir, another scribe not nearly so dedicated and never accused of being humble, stood to his feet to angrily recount a conversation between Yeshua and His disciples he had accidently over-heard on the previous day.

"He accused us of loving our distinctive robes, the hom-age some pay to us, and the seats of honor reserved for us on public occasions. Then He accused us of foreclosing on the mortgages of widows while making long ostentatious prayers for mere show. He said we were all damned. And when one such widow dropped her pittance into the trea-sury box, He told His disciples that she was better than any of us who have donated immense sums of money to the treasury. Has this Man ever copied the scrolls until His eyes ached? Has He ever seen to the support of the Temple or of the poor and the needy? How dare He say such things!"

Naqdimon knew the arrow of Yeshua's words had found a ready target in Machir's heart. He wore the finest of ap-parel, most of it imported at great expense. While he was a very wealthy man, he actually donated comparatively little to the treasury and then only when he was certain he could receive public acclaim for his gift. He was never seen at the tiny chamber near the Sanctuary where anonymous contributions might be made for the truly indigent. And no one was as quick to exercise every privilege accorded members of the Sanhedrin.

After everyone had had an opportunity to speak, Yosef ben Qayafa stood and raised his hands for quiet. "My brothers, my brothers," he shouted. "I think it is clear we all seek the same end. And you have my personal assur-ance that we shall achieve it. But we must be both shrewd and patient as we build our case against this Man. His guilt must be made clear to our own people as well as to the Romans or the end of this matter could be worse than the beginning. Do I have your concurrence?"

The chamber erupted with the approval of most of those gathered.

"Good, good," smiled Qayafa, quieting the assembly

again. "I have heard things tonight that may be useful to us. For example, this talk of a kingdom. The Romans might take a dim view of One whose kingdom could be revealed by us to be a challenge to their own. Is that not so?"

Again the gathering rewarded Qayafa with instant endorsement.

"Yes, my brothers. Our victory is in sight. I ask you now to return to your homes and permit me time to consider how we might best proceed. Before we are done, the Romans will be only too glad to rid us of this troublesome Fellow."

The meeting adjourned and every member went to his home secure in the knowledge that his most annoying problem was about to be solved in a way that would leave his own hands clean.

Naqdimon went to his home, too, but with heavy heart. He knew their problems were only beginning and that their hands might never be clean again.

✡   ✡   ✡

In Bethany Yeshua spent His final night in the home of Shimon and Eleazar. It was a bittersweet occasion. His mother had arrived to attend the Pesach celebration with Him and His disciples in just two days. The house was filled with their joyous talk and laughter.

As the evening ended, Yeshua slipped out and sat alone on the stone bench under the little grove of date palms. He could not tell her He would not be able to share the Seder dinner with her, not this year, not ever again. She would know soon enough. As her eldest Son, He had cared for her and her younger children since the death of her husband, Yosef, only a few years before. He could not tell her He would be able to care for them no longer. She would know that soon enough, too. As much as He wanted to confide His innermost feelings to her, to find some solace

177

in the warmth of her embrace one last time, He knew it was kinder to give her these final few hours of peace and happiness.

He had not asked anyone why Yehuda had not joined them. He already knew. A solitary tear escaped His eye and vanished into His beard. He wept, not for Himself but for His lost disciple.

DAVID ben Asaph wandered the marketplace of the Lower City, his eyes alive with the wonder of it all. Hannah, her veil concealing all but her immense blue eyes, and Micah, trying unsuccessfully to appear urbane and sophisticated, walked on either side of him each more excited than the other. For one from Capernaum, from anywhere in Galilee for that matter, there was nothing quite like the marketplace in Yerushalayim with its myriad stalls, each with its own brightly-colored canopy to shield seller and buyer alike from the ravages of a relentless sun. They were often sarcastically described as shambles because of their rather rickety construction and random arrangement but to the eye of an imaginative visitor such as Micah, they seemed like the blazing banners of a desert army.

The marketplace was a must for every visitor to the city. One stall displayed fine fabrics, soft silks and richly embroidered brocades unknown in the north. Here even the colors seemed brighter, the crimson dye coming from the boiled bodies of insects, the vibrant pink from the pomegranate fruit, the sunny yellow from the saffron crocus, and the royal purple from murex shells. Just fingering these luxurious fabrics caused Hannah to catch her breath. The next stall provided a variety of the latest styles in footwear. Micah stood looking longingly at a pair of leather sandals in the Greek fashion. Beautiful baubles of every description with polished gemstones set in silver and gold waited in the stall after that and David thought he would never get Hannah past that one. And all around, the smells of freshly prepared foods and sweet mouth-watering treats teased the palates of each shopper. David and Hannah were nearly drunk with it all and Micah's eyes grew wider with each turn and twist in the path.

Everywhere voices bartered endlessly. It was Yerushalayim. And Pesach, the seven-day Feast of Unleavened Bread which would begin with the Seder dinner, was only a day away. Most people, like David and Hannah and Micah, had come simply to look and compare. They would not do their actual purchasing until the next afternoon, the day of preparation, unless of course they found a particularly good price.

Then David spied a pair of familiar faces. At the baker's stall purchasing a large supply of unleavened bread stood Shimon the fisherman and his friend and partner, Yohanan. Their arms full of parcels, they were obviously getting an early start on their buying. It was so good to see a friendly face from home that David couldn't resist the temptation to greet the two.

David took a position behind Shimon and Yohanan and deliberately deepened his voice as he spoke. "Have the gates of the city now been opened to Samaritans and thieves?" he asked seriously, feigning well the Yerushalayim manner of speech.

Shimon turned with a start clearly ready to argue the point. Instead he was met with David's broadest smile which he promptly rewarded with one of his own. He heaped his share of the parcels into Yohanan's already full arms and happily smothered David in a muscular embrace. "Yohanan, look. It's that scamp from the docks, David ben Asaph!"

Yohanan juggled their packages precariously, trying all the while to greet David. By this time Hannah and Micah had left admiring their latest discoveries, spotted David and his two friends, and had snaked their way through the crowd to join them.

David was quick to share his excitement. "Look,

Hannah. It is Shimon and Yohanan from Galilee. You remember, I spoke to you of them. I met them first at the docks. Then we supped together at the home of Shimon's wife's mother." A note of awe crept into his voice. "It was the same day she was healed, the same day I met Yeshua."

Hannah bowed and kept her eyes downcast in her best maidenly manners. Micah's eyes grew as he struggled to take in the dimensions of the enormous fisherman before him.

David continued. "Shimon, this is Hannah and her brother, Micah. We are to be married the first day of the week."

"And I am certain that you and Micah will make a most unusual couple," Shimon teased, slapping both on their backs. Even Hannah giggled.

"Not Micah ... Hannah," David corrected quickly, his young face reddening perceptibly.

Shimon and Yohanan dissolved in laughter at the thought that David had taken the joke seriously. David reddened even more, then joined in helplessly and laughed until his sides ached.

As Shimon recovered himself and his packages, David asked, "What brings you to the market the day before the preparation?"

Shimon and Yohanan cast dark glances at each other, then looked away. Both became instantly serious. It was Shimon who finally answered. "I wish we knew. This morning, for no good reason either of us can fathom, Yeshua sent us out with instructions to purchase everything we would need for our Seder supper. Since the meat cannot be kept overnight, we can only assume that our Seder dinner is to be eaten tonight rather than tomorrow. We do not even begin to understand it but both of us agree this cannot be a good omen. What is going to happen tomorrow that will prevent us from celebrating along with everyone else?" Shimon wondered aloud.

David was silent. He didn't even know that such a thing

could be done under the Law. It all seemed incomprehensible to him, too.

When Yohanan finally spoke, it was quietly, almost reverently. "I suppose He has His reasons." Yohanan did not really want to think about what those reasons might be.

Heads nodded, agreeing without understanding.

"And whatever they are, I suppose He will tell us tonight," Yohanan continued.

Shimon's face widened into a grin. "Anyway, David, may the Holy One smile upon you and your bride and grant you many fine sons."

He didn't even notice as Hannah's eyes closed reflexively and he couldn't see as the muscles of Hannah's face tightened grimly under her veil.

"And may we meet again soon under less troubling circumstances."

As they parted, none of them knew how impossible that would become.

∽ 25 ∾

YAKOV toyed with a couple of coins oblivious to the incessant jingling of the money. If this was the busiest week of the year for the Temple tradesman, and he knew from experience that it was, then tomorrow would be the busiest day of all. Yakov knew he had to do something. He couldn't just sit here and allow all the work to fall on his father and brothers. He just didn't know what to do that would not involve him in the actual selling.

It finally came to him. After the evening sacrifice, he would go to the court and help ready the stock for the day of preparation when thousands of the devout would storm into the court to select a lamb, have it sacrificed, and take the meat home to their Seder tables. No matter that they probably would never see the meat of the lamb they chose or that they might be given the meat of an animal that was lame, blind, sick, or had only three legs. At least they would have meat to place beside their bitter herbs and unleavened bread as they told their children the timeless story of their people's redemption out of Egyptian slavery. Then Yakov would have no part in the annual deception nor bear any of the responsibility for it.

And so it was that Yakov walked alone through the dusky streets of Yerushalayim toward the Temple at the very time when everyone else was walking away from it.

When he arrived, Meshullam hardly spoke to him. He could make no sense of his firstborn's behavior during this busiest season of the year. Meshullam remained at Simeon's side as the two hovered over their table counting the Temple coins that had come in that day, placing them in leather bags, and closing the top of each bag with a thin leather thong.

Neither they nor Yakov noticed an old rabbi returning to the Temple well after the sun had set. Nor did they see a taller man shrouded in his own mantle as though fearful of discovery who walked with him toward the private chamber of the high priest. They didn't pay any attention when the taller man left a few minutes later with a little leather bag very much like their own suspended from his girdle. And they only barely noticed when a small contingent of Temple guards accompanied by Qayafa's faithful servant, Malluch, marched across the court, exited the northern gate, and turned toward the garden east of the Temple Mount. Neither noticed when Yosef ben Qayafa slipped out of the Temple, crossed the bridge that led from the western gate to the Upper City, and set out for home.

New stock had been brought in just after the evening sacrifice had begun and the court had nearly emptied. Each animal had to be fed, bathed, curried and combed, and treated for any obvious bruises or blemishes. As Helah cleaned each pen, Yakov tossed great armloads of provender into one end of each enclosure. Old ewes bleated and jostled each other to reach their dinner, some dragging their young lambs along on their teats. By tomorrow this time, all of these lambs would be gone, each the main course on someone's Seder table and the dismayed ewes would be sent back to their pastures to produce yet another crop of sacrifices.

Yakov watched the animals sadly. He almost felt like one of them. He, too, had been born to fulfill a role he did not understand, one in which it seemed he also had no choice. He couldn't escape his fate any more than the lambs he watched could escape theirs.

Once the animals were fed, the real work began. With the rush of Pesach, sheep had been brought directly from the fields outside the city, fields owned by the Temple authorities, fields which brought much money into the treasury. There had been no time to examine the stock. Now the soil of the pasture had to be washed and combed from the animals' coats until they were the purest white. Then their hooves had to be inspected and cleaned. Finally their eyes, ears, and mouths were examined and treated.

Yakov was willing to do all of these things. But inevitably some animals would have blemishes of one sort or another. The experienced seller knew many techniques to temporarily cover such marks. Yakov knew them, too, learned at his father's knee from childhood. But these things he would not do, not tonight, perhaps not ever again. Yakov turned each such animal over to his father's knowledgeable hands.

The work took hours. Though father and son labored together, each was silent and alone, alone with his thoughts, alone with the questions of his own heart. Before they were finished, the moon had risen high in the heavens. Wispy clouds scudded across its face as it seemed to come to rest just above the Temple. Then as the clouds skipped away, its light cast an eerie radiance on the activity below.

A long while later, Yakov finally finished, stood, and arched his aching back to relieve the strain of stooping and crouching and bending. He departed the Temple through the west gate, then walked briskly in the direction of the Upper City and home. As he passed the street on which the high priest's family home sprawled on a green hillside, Yakov noticed there was movement, noise, a tumult of some sort approaching from behind. He paused and turned in the direction of the sounds. As the clamor drew closer, Yakov was able to make out the glow of torches, the distinctive clanking of swords against the thighs of soldiers, and the angry voices of a small band of men.

Undoubtedly, there has been another arrest, maybe another thief, Yakov reasoned. He had seen it so often before especially during the various feast days. It seemed the dishonest were as faithful to attend the celebrations as the devout. But why, he wondered, are they coming this way? He stepped back into the shadows to watch and wait for them to pass.

As the approaching mass turned into the street of the high priest, Yakov was shocked to see the cause of the commotion. In the center of a contingent of Temple guards, His hands bound before Him, was Yeshua ben Yosef being led toward the high priest's home.

I knew it was only a matter of time, Yakov thought. *Finally, they have Him. Now perhaps we can all get back to normal.*

Yakov thought he should feel some satisfaction, exultation, elation, at least some relief. After all, his problem had been solved, had it not? But he was stunned to realize that he felt nothing but a twinge of sorrow and for the life of him, he couldn't figure out why.

He stood frozen to the spot watching in surprise as the little parade passed him and continued on to the high priest's home. Yakov had often seen criminals arrested at night taken to the guard barracks to be held until morning. He had never seen one taken before the high priest at such a time. The law forbade trial by night since the accused must have time to consider the charges against him and to produce any witnesses whose testimony might exonerate him. In this case, however, it seemed that the high priest was preparing to try the Culprit immediately.

At the end of the angry group Yakov recognized Malluch, the high priest's young manservant. But Malluch did not appear to be angry at all. Instead his dark eyes were wide, almost transfixed. One hand restlessly rubbed at one ear as though he meant to make certain it was still there. Then Yakov noticed that the side of his face and the shoulder of his mantle were drenched in blood even though there seemed to be no wound.

As Malluch passed, he mumbled incredulously to anyone who cared to listen. "He healed me! Yeshua healed a simple servant like me!"

Yakov could have continued on home but he just couldn't walk away from this scene. He had to know what was happening and he knew he would remain there watching and waiting until he did.

After the guards, their Prisoner, and the bloodied servant passed, Yakov followed. Around the spacious court were the residences of the former high priest, Annas, three of his five sons and their families, and his son-in-law, Yosef ben Qayafa. These men reveled in the honor and respect of their fellow citizens and lived in a manner befitting their station. It was to the home of the family patriarch, Annas, that the guards first led their Prisoner.

As Yakov's eyes adjusted to the flickering of a fire the servants had ignited in the courtyard to fend off the chill of the night, he noticed others, obviously Galileans by their dress, were entering, too. They came one by one or in small groups of two or three. Most stood in the shadows and whispered together; some even wept. One of them, the big one, even warmed his hands over the fire. And when a young servant girl questioned him, he startled her with a few angry words and turned away before she could press him further.

Yakov approached warily. "Are you not one of them?" Yakov questioned. He had not meant it to sound like an accusation; he only wanted information about what was transpiring.

Illuminated in the glow of the fire, the man appeared apprehensive, unsure how to answer. When he spoke, it was to answer a question with a question. "Me? One of whom?"

Yakov pressed. "One of the followers of Yeshua. Are you not one of them?"

"No, not me. I have nothing to do with them," the man answered gruffly.

The man left the warmth of the fire but Yakov could not take his eyes from his huge muscular form. He wandered aimlessly about the court without speaking to any of the other Galileans. Still it was clear from their shared glances that they all knew one another and they were all waiting to know the outcome just as Yakov was. As time marched past with slow and agonizing steps, the big one spoke to another of the servants. This encounter also ended in an argument. From across the court, Yakov heard him shout, "Be damned you child of the devil. I told you I know nothing about Him."

It was at that very moment that the first thin rays of morning light painted the sky pink and purple and the crowing of a rooster could be heard nearby. It was also at that very moment that the guards escorted their Captive from the home of Annas to the nearby home of Yosef ben Qayafa. The long hours of anxiety must have undone the big Galilean for after one look at Yeshua, he burst into tears and fled the scene.

Later others would be led in, then leave after adding their testimony to the proceedings. No one knew what it all meant. All could only wonder ... wonder and wait. Still Yakov stayed. So did all of the others. The tension in the air was almost palpable. And still no verdict came. How much longer could it take? Yakov asked himself. He had no answer but he knew he would remain until the answer came.

∽ 26 ∾

AQDIMON knew the verdict before the trial had even begun but he sat with the other hastily-called members of the Sanhedrin through a parade of witnesses. It would have been apparent to a blind man that most had been well paid for their testimony. It was also apparent they had not been well prepared. All related the tall tales they had been told to tell but when they were questioned, they either had no answer at all or each answered differently. After all his years in the Sanhedrin, Naqdimon found it hard to believe the shabby spectacle being played out before him.

He found it even harder to believe this trial was being held at night, the very same night of the arrest. Yosef ben Qayafa knew the Law better than that. Yet at the same time Naqdimon had to give him grudging respect for what even he had to admit was a brilliant strategy. By conducting the trial at night in his own home, Qayafa guaranteed that it would not be noticed by worshippers passing by the very public chamber of the Sanhedrin on their way to the morning sacrifice. Those who followed Yeshua would never know what had happened to Him until it was too late.

Of course Naqdimon understood why he had done it. More than anything, Qayafa feared a disturbance, even a riot, should all of the believers in Yeshua who were in Yerushalayim that night discover what was being done to Him. He knew that the Romans insisted that their Pax Romanus, their peace of Rome, be respected. Were it to be disrupted, Qayafa knew he would not be the first high priest to be toppled from his position for such a breach. The family had suffered this disgrace before and Qayafa was determined he would not endure it, too.

Finally, when all seemed lost, when Qayafa could not put together the required two witnesses with the same story, he chose to interrogate the Prisoner himself.

Naqdimon marvelled at the serenity of Yeshua. For One from Galilee to stand so calmly before the ruling body of the entire nation, was astounding. He had seen lesser men fall to pieces at the very sight of the council.

"Have You nothing to say in Your own defense?" Qayafa queried brusquely.

Yeshua was silent. It appeared to Naqdimon that He knew His answer would change nothing.

Qayafa looked puzzled. Then he thought of a new line of questioning, a direct frontal attack. "Are You Messiah, the Son of the Holy One?" he asked inviting a reply, insisting on one.

Yeshua smiled compassionately at the man who interrogated Him. "I AM," He said, His voice strong and resolute. Then He added, "The day will come when you will see the Son of man sitting at the right hand of the Holy One and coming in the clouds of heaven."

Qayafa's hand formed a fist in the air as though he had just captured some errant insect. His Prey was finally his and he knew it. Still he was stunned. He had expected some small admission but nothing like this. This was nearly the raving of a madman. But he could not have the assembled council members thinking that this Man was merely insane rather than malicious. He had what he needed. Now he had to cut off Yeshua's reply before his victory vanished.

"What need have we of any further witnesses?" Qayafa asked rhetorically as he ripped his tunic in a dramatic show of his supposed anguish at the reply he had received. "He has condemned Himself out of His own mouth. You have all heard His blasphemy for yourselves. What do you think now? Is He not worthy to be condemned to death?"

Heads nodded all around Naqdimon while he himself moved not a single muscle.

Qayafa calmly resumed his seat and waited for the discussion to die away. They would do exactly what he wanted now. He was certain of it. They would take the matter into their own hands. They might even delude themselves into thinking that it was all their own idea. So much the better. *Let them think what they will,* mused Qayafa, *so long as they do what I wish.*

Some of the members in the chamber became so enraged by Yeshua's declaration that they flew into His face. Some shouted at Him; some spat upon Him; others struck Him. Most merely wanted to make a show of their loyalty to Qayafa for his benefit and perhaps their own future benefit as well.

It was more than Naqdimon could bear for even another moment. He rose wearily and turned away from the scene. Once outside in the cool morning air, he drew in a deep breath as if to cleanse himself from some offending smell. As he traversed the spacious courtyard, he found the face he was seeking. He made no sign of recognition but simply walked past, then paused and spoke softly over his shoulder.

"It is just as I feared, my son."

The young Galilean behind him squeezed his eyes shut against his tears as a look of great torment took possession of his somber face. "I, too, my friend. It is as we all feared."

"Yohanan, please believe me. There was nothing I could do," Naqdimon pleaded. "It had all been arranged. It was an accomplished fact even before He was led into the chamber. Even the Holy One Himself would have been powerless against them."

"I know, I know, my friend," Yohanan soothed.

"Why has the Holy One permitted this travesty?"

Naqdimon agonized. "How could He allow His own Son to suffer such humiliation when He has done nothing more sinister than heal the sick and raise the dead and teach the Holy One's Word? Will He stand by and watch Him die also? Why has He not intervened?"

"You have not asked a single question that I have not asked myself a thousand times this night," Yohanan replied. He said nothing else. He had no answers.

As the slanted rays of morning lit the court and the fire slowly died, the two men drifted apart, each bearing his pain alone.

‹ℰ 27 ℬ›

RABBI Levi was exultant in his triumph. Still he carried his newfound status with great dignity as befitting one who was now so close to the great high priest himself.

After Yeshua ben Yosef had been led from the chamber, Rabbi Levi waited quietly to receive the acclaim of the council. After all, it was he and he alone who had arranged for Yeshua's betrayal and capture. None of the others had been able to do it. Even the high priest had not been able to accomplish it, not without him.

But there were no praises forthcoming. It seemed no one even noticed the old rabbi. He stepped forward. Perhaps they do not realize that I am among them, he reasoned.

"Clear the chamber," Qayafa called out. "I want none but the council to remain."

The guards began escorting guests and witnesses to the door. Still Rabbi Levi remained. Finally the captain of the guard came to him. "This way, Rabbi," he instructed.

"You could not mean me, my son," the rabbi said. "You do not know who I am."

"I know who you are not," the captain menaced. "You are not a member of the council and his Excellency has requested that only the members remain."

The rabbi did not move. He drew himself up to his full height, lifted his chin, and spoke as a king might address a wayward subject. "But I am Rabbi Levi ben Eschol. I am certain that if you will just tell the high priest I am here, he will ... ."

"He will have my hide if you do not move along," the

captain interrupted, his voice rising in both volume and intensity.

"But ... ," the rabbi began, looking helplessly in the direction of the high priest.

Qayafa noticed the disturbance. His eyes locked on Rabbi Levi's. There was no sign of recognition, much less acceptance. The little minion had fulfilled his purpose in Qayafa's grand design; it was now time for him to be on his way and leave the real work to the professionals. He lifted his hand and made the same motion one might use to brush away an annoying insect. The captain nodded and turned back to the rabbi. "That means you, old man," he said as he pushed him from the chamber.

✡   ✡   ✡

Outside, bent under the burden of his dismissal, Rabbi Levi shuffled toward the gate. Did he not call me "brother" only a few days ago? the rabbi asked himself miserably.

"Rabbi," a voice called to him.

He turned, hoping to see the captain of the guard coming to right the great wrong done to him. Instead it was only the boy, the son of Meshullam the animal seller. He could not remember his name and couldn't have cared less at that moment.

"What do you wish?" the rabbi returned curtly.

"Is the trial over?" the young man asked.

"Yes, it is all over," the rabbi answered, walking on.

"Were you there? Can you tell me what happened?"

The irritated rabbi spun around on his heel and faced the young man. "Of course I was there. The trial could never have happened at all without me," he snapped. "And I can tell you exactly what happened. It is death, young man. It is death."

The rabbi turned away and continued toward the street.

Yakov said nothing more. He was stunned at the news when he knew he should be welcoming it. It was the end of his problems, the end of the accusations, the end of those eyes and that voice. Was it not? Suddenly he wasn't sure if it was the end of anything.

✡   ✡   ✡

Inside Qayafa drew together his most trusted advisors, their title a misnomer since Qayafa seldom took advice from anyone. "We have sustained the charge of blasphemy as well as the death sentence it carries. But now, my brothers, we must prepare for trial before a Roman court where blasphemy of the Holy One of Yisrael will not be enough. But I have a plan."

The advisors leaned closer. Qayafa always had a plan and his plans always seemed to succeed. They could not wait to hear this one.

Qayafa continued. "Pontius Pilate, that Roman abomination who calls himself our governor, happens to be in the city this week staying in the palace of his Edomite whore, Herod. Later today he will be no more than a stone's throw from our Temple inspecting the Fortress Antonia."

At this news, groans erupted from all around the chamber. No one was more hated in Yerushalayim than this arrogant infidel who seemed to take pleasure in enforcing his control over helpless Yisrael.

Qayafa chuckled. "Brothers, hear me out. His coming could not be better for us."

Those assembled settled back in their seats, waiting to hear the high priest's logic.

"As you may recall, Pontius Pilate has not always treated us with deference. There was the unfortunate matter of the unspeakable images of the emperor which his soldiers bore upon their standards when he first arrived from his lair in Caesarea. I'm certain you will recall how this man threatened to kill us all rather than remove them and how we all bared our necks to his soldiers' swords rather than have our Holy City desecrated. And I am certain you will recall

195

that after we had thus defeated him, complaint was made to the emperor himself concerning Pilate's actions."

Heads nodded as animated discussion of the event erupted in the chamber.

Qayafa quieted the group with a wave of his hand and continued. "And you no doubt remember when he recently stole money from our own Temple treasury in order to build his new aqueduct. You will recall how easily we aroused the rabble into a riotous mob which he had his men infiltrate wearing Yudean garb. None of us in this chamber will ever forget how his men turned on the crowd in a murderous frenzy, clubbing and stabbing all within their reach. After that awful incident, I personally saw to it that a report was made to the emperor concerning his unconscionable conduct."

Again the men exploded in a rage that had never quite been quenched following the episode cited. Again Qayafa waved them into silence.

"What can we do against him?" someone asked in frustration. "He has imposed the ius gladii, the right of the sword. We cannot even put this Criminal to death without his permission."

"Exactly!" Qayafa intoned triumphantly.

His advisors were taken aback. Pilate possessed all the power; they, by contrast, had none that they could see. They wondered how the high priest could view this situation with such apparent delight.

Qayafa began again in scheming tones. "What you may not remember is that a Roman governor can be recalled to Rome to face the emperor's legendary wrath on the third substantiated complaint of his subjects. They will not even allow their own magistrates to violate their precious Pax Romanus and their precious justice system forever. And, my brothers, we already have two valid complaints against the powerful Pontius Pilate." He spat out the name with contempt.

The beauty of the high priest's plan started to dawn on

those with quicker minds and more political acumen and they were obviously enjoying it. For the benefit of the others, Qayafa continued. "What if we let our esteemed governor know that failure to confirm our death sentence against Yeshua ben Yosef will result in that third complaint?"

"Yes," came the instant reply.

"It's brilliant," said one.

Others were not so sure and quickly voiced their apprehensions.

Qayafa quelled their comments with a single stern look. "But, my brothers, it will not be accomplished with a simple charge of blasphemy which these heathen Romans do not even recognize. Let me tell you how it can be done, how Pontius Pilate can be induced to issue our verdict, how Pontius Pilate can even be convinced to execute it for us so that the people will not later blame us for the death of their precious Messiah."

He had their rapt attention now. He held them in the palm of his hand just as he always did. He could manipulate them as surely as he meant to manipulate Pontius Pilate. He was in his element now and he loved it, loved the excitement of it, loved the exercise of this kind of power over other lesser men.

✿   ✿   ✿

Rabbi Levi had barely arrived home when the sound of rushing feet and a hasty knock on the door caused him to look up from his morning prayers and hurry to open the door. There before him stood one of the high priest's messengers.

At last, he thought. *My contributions are to be recognized at last.*

"Rabbi," the young man gasped, unable to catch his breath. "You are needed at the Temple regarding the matter of Yeshua. Bring all in your congregation who may be trusted." With that he was gone on his way to deliver the same message to other like-minded rabbis with congregations which could also be trusted.

Rabbi Levi had never even had an opportunity to answer. But this was one more opportunity to be of service to the high priest, to come to his attention, to obtain the recognition he so desperately wanted, needed. After years of laboring in relative obscurity and now too near to oblivion for comfort, he hoped his day of glory had at last arrived. He hurried off obediently. *Maybe this time,* he assured himself as he went.

✡   ✡   ✡

"Sir, you cannot do this thing," Malluch insisted in a voice alive with the torment he felt within.

Qayafa's face reddened in rage. "How dare you tell me what I cannot do!" Qayafa shrieked. "You! A nothing! A servant! How dare you speak to me in such a manner!" His arms whipped the air as though he wished to whip his servant in precisely the same way.

Malluch fell to his knees, gripped with fear at what he may have unleashed. "Forgive me, my lord," he pleaded, "but there is so much you do not understand."

Qayafa exploded. "And I need a servant to tell me what I do not understand?"

The boy wanted to cringe, to beg forgiveness for his impudence, to flee the chamber in abject terror. But then he remembered the Man in the garden. He had had every reason to be afraid, yet His eyes had been filled with love instead of fear. His voice had been gentle, not accusing, and His touch had been tender, not harsh. With his remembrance, a wave of peace swept over Malluch's being and gave him the courage to say the words he knew must be spoken.

"Yes, my lord. If I might, I would like to explain those things to you."

Qayafa was startled at the calm of his servant. He stood silent, staring, waiting.

Malluch interpreted this pause as permission to continue and took advantage of it. "My lord, I did only as you commanded. I accompanied the guards to the garden to make their arrest as you instructed. I watched as one of His followers identified Him with the kiss of a friend and the guards surrounded Him. I thought He might run or resist but He did nothing but request that His followers be allowed to go their way."

"Perhaps He is an even greater coward than I imagined," Qayafa interjected, his voice dripping with sarcasm.

Malluch smiled tolerantly. "With all respect, my lord, He is no coward. He is the bravest Man I have ever known." The young servant's voice was almost reverential.

Qayafa looked as though he had been struck. "How much courage is required to surrender?" he asked, his tone cold and scornful.

"He had the courage to stop those who would have willingly defended Him," Malluch replied in awe. "He stopped the very one who took up a sword and struck off my ear." Malluch's hand went almost automatically to the side of his head.

"Your ear?" Qayafa queried. "There is nothing wrong with your ear, boy."

"He restored it, my lord." Malluch's voice became impassioned. "Yeshua cared about me ... me. He healed me ... a humble servant ... and your servant at that. There is not even a scar. There is nothing but this." Malluch pulled his mantle from his shoulders and turned it inside out revealing the dried blood which gave mute testimony to both his injury and his healing.

Qayafa paled. "Take it away," he cried. "My eyes must not look upon such a thing."

"Then look upon the perfection He has wrought upon my ear, my lord," Malluch invited.

"I will not," Qayafa insisted.

"What is it you fear, my lord?" Malluch asked. "You must look. You must see and understand that Yeshua is Messiah for none but Messiah could do such a work. You must understand that you cannot kill Messiah. You cannot kill the Anointed of the Holy One."

Qayafa wheeled around to face his servant, his eyes flaming. "I not only can but I will," he thundered. "Before the Holy One, I swear I will see Him on a Roman cross before the sun sets this day. I will see your precious Messiah dead. I swear it!"

Qayafa shook with rage as his face reddened and his breath deserted him. He stood shaking in his wrath, towering above his young servant, wanting to cower him but seeing he no longer possessed that power. Finally in frustration, Qayafa shouted, "Leave me, boy! Leave me this instant!"

Now fearless but knowing he had failed, Malluch shook his head sadly and complied, leaving Qayafa alone to face his own demons.

❧ 28 ❧

AVID, Dinah, and her children were up with the dawn and on their way to the Temple. The excitement was contagious; even the little ones had caught it. It was all the adults could do to keep them in tow as they walked north from the home of Dinah's sister in the Lower City to the Temple gleaming like the heavenly city of the Holy One in the bright morning sun.

As they approached the southern gate, they heard a cacophony of voices approaching from the west but dismissed it as the general confusion one would expect on the day of preparation for Pesach would begin at sundown. They soon realized, however, that more was afoot than the usual clamoring and conversation in a dozen different languages. Angry shouts could be heard although David and Dinah could not make out exactly what was being said. Inexplicably, when the crowd reached the Temple wall, it turned as one to the north. Before they knew it, Micah, who had run ahead to see what was happening, was swept up in the throng and had disappeared from their view. They had no choice but to follow along if they were to find him.

"Micah, Micah," David shouted, barely able to hear his own voice in the din, knowing there was not a chance that Micah could hear it.

David turned to Dinah. "Please, Ammah, take the children to the Court of the Women. We dare not risk their becoming lost, too."

Dinah hesitated. She did not want to go until her son was found but she could see the wisdom of David's plea.

And she had come to trust implicitly this young man who was to be her son-in-law. She nodded and began herding the younger boys toward the Temple.

Hannah remained behind, her face set in obdurate lines, her blue eyes silently daring David to send her back.

David tried to speak. "Hannah, you should stay and help your ... ."

"He's my brother," Hannah broke in. "I will not leave without him." She added, "And besides, two sets of eyes will be better than one, no?"

David couldn't argue Hannah's logic. "True," he said. "But stay at my side so I do not lose you, too." Hannah nodded and David turned in the direction the crowd had taken.

David barely noticed the tall young man who brushed past him. Had he been paying attention, he would surely have recognized Yehuda of Kerioth. In his hand Yehuda carried a leather bag that jingled with coins but he carried it as though it burned his fingers.

✡   ✡   ✡

Yehuda had not seen David ben Asaph either. He asked directions of first one then another, finally learning that the high priest was closeted with a few others of high rank in his private chamber. Yehuda did not knock and when he entered, he did not wait to be invited to speak. The words of his heart simply would not be stayed. "I have sinned," Yehuda confessed, his anguish evident. "I have betrayed the blood of an innocent Man."

Yehuda did not know what he expected, some small understanding of his plight, some sympathy perhaps. He found neither. Gone was the greeting of only a few days before. The priests and elders were no longer glad to welcome him into their midst, glad to receive the needed information only he could provide. He was now merely an untidy detail in their plot to kill his Master.

The stony visage of one of the chief priests turned toward him. "What is that to us?" he growled at Yehuda coldly. "You see to that."

Others merely laughed. Yehuda had served his purpose. They cared nothing for him nor his remorse.

Yehuda stood stunned and silent, shocked by their dismissal of him when he was in the greatest turmoil of his life. Then he tore at the drawstring of the leather bag he carried until it opened, flung the thirty coins at the feet of his tormentors, and ran from the room.

Yehuda had discovered too late that there really were some things that were more important to him than money. He knew now that there was no compassion in the hearts of the men he had seen, not for him, and certainly not for Yeshua. It was too late to reverse the wheels he had set in motion, too late to rescue the One he had betrayed, too late to save the life of the kindest Man he had ever known.

And Yehuda knew it was too late for him as well. He could not make right what he had made so terribly wrong and he could not live with the guilt of what he had done. They would do it, they would crucify Yeshua; he knew that now and he simply could not live with knowing that they had.

He ran, not knowing where he was going or what he was going to do when he got there. He was running, not thinking, just running. He never thought of the forgiveness Yeshua had offered others or of asking that forgiveness for himself. If he had, he would have thought it was too late and he would have decided he deserved no mercy for he had shown none to Yeshua. Soon Yehuda found himself outside the Temple grounds on the edge of the precipice that led to the Kidron Valley below. A few gnarled trees stood there and it almost seemed as though they were waiting for him. He climbed the highest of the trees at the edge of the hill, removed his sash, and tied one end around a branch and the other around his own throat. But the branch was not as strong as it seemed. When he threw his anguished soul into the empty air, the branch broke beneath his weight. As he fell, another jagged branch cut into his body, eviscerating him in an instant. His last conscious thought was of Yeshua whose end would be even more painful, even more grotesque, and even more prolonged than his own. *I deserve this; He never did,* he thought. Then Yehuda was gone.

✡   ✡   ✡

In the high priest's chamber, uncaring men stepped over the coins as though they were red hot saying, "We will touch no blood money." Instead they decided they would buy a burial ground for strangers and the poor. Then, they reasoned, they could be rid of it while at the same time ingratiating themselves with the masses for their most munificent gift. That done, they left. After all, they had much more important business this day; they had another trial to attend.

✡   ✡   ✡

David was surprised that the rabble seemed to be moving toward the Roman fortress called the Antonia which lay just north of the Temple Mount, adjacent to its northern wall. He ran to catch up, frequently glancing back to be certain that Hannah had not fallen behind.

Up ahead the fortress loomed large, its four towers a forbidding monument to tiny Yisrael's domination by a foreign power. Every citizen hated it, hated the reminder it presented of Roman occupation. Under their breath many quietly cursed it and the Romans inside whenever they passed. David could not imagine why this teeming mass was now demanding entrance.

One of the well-dressed representatives of the Sanhedrin exchanged a few words with the legionnaire guarding the gate. Then all were admitted to the parade ground known simply as the pavement. There an intricate mosaic depicting the victories of Mars, the Roman god of war, fell unnoticed beneath tramping feet. In angry shouts the rabble demanded the presence of Pontius Pilate, demanded he hear at once the case of the Prisoner they had brought with them.

Minutes passed. The shouts grew into a roar. Soldiers took positions around the perimeter, their lances at the ready until the scene could be brought under control. Finally there was movement within the fortress, a gate opened, and an official came forward to placate the dissatisfied citizens before him. He waved the crowd to silence, then spoke.

"His Excellency, Pontius Pilate, Governor of Palestine by the will of Tiberius Caesar, welcomes you," he began officiously. "If you will come with me, his Excellency will hear your petition in the hall of judgment."

"We will not enter under his roof," a member of the Sanhedrin shouted back. "We may not come under the roof of a Gentile on this day of all days when the Holy One Himself commands us not to enter any dwelling where leaven may be present. We cannot thus defile ourselves."

The official looked puzzled. He had absolutely no comprehension of these local superstitions nor did he care to understand them. *Now it is yeast that has become unholy?* he asked himself skeptically. Still there was no point in arguing. "I will present your greetings to his Excellency," he announced. Then he retreated into the peace and quiet of the fortress.

David and Hannah searched the crowd with restless eyes but there was no sign of Micah. Most in the crowd were grown men who were much taller than the boy. It was impossible to see poor little Micah over the heads of such a sea of humanity. They could only wait.

In a few moments, the impatience of the crowd led to renewed demands for Pilate's presence. Soon they were chanting in cadence.

Finally Pontius Pilate appeared clad in a scarlet robe over

a white toga decorated at the throat with laurel leaves embroidered in glittering gold thread. He walked imperiously between four legionnaires, ascended the few steps to a small platform, and took his seat. His guards stood at military attention, their lances at their sides.

"Men of Yisrael, to what do I owe the honor of this visit at such an early hour?" Pilate began sarcastically.

"Excellency, we bring a Man who has transgressed both our Law and yours." It was the strong voice of Ethan ben Esrom, scribe and foremost expert in the Law of Moshe, a respected member of the Sanhedrin and the man Yosef ben Qayafa had personally selected to present the case.

Before he could continue, Pilate interrupted, "If as you say He has broken your Law, then take Him and judge Him according to your Law."

Ethan persisted. "This we have done, Excellency. But it is against your law for us to put any man to death and this Man is indeed worthy of the death penalty. In obedience to your law then we have brought Him to you so that you might pronounce judgment upon Him." Ethan bowed slightly and awaited Pilate's reply.

"Bring Him here," Pilate ordered brusquely.

Temple guards led Yeshua ben Yosef to the platform.

At the sight of Him, David and Hannah gasped in unison. Micah had been all but forgotten in their shock.

David was astounded. "It is Yeshua," he whispered incredulously. "How can this be?" There was no answer.

"What are the charges against Him?" Pilate inquired through clenched teeth. He hated Palestine, hated the climate, hated the people, hated almost everything but his palace overlooking the sea in Caesarea where he wished he was just now. One seditious citizen more or less was of no consequence to him. If he had had his way, he would long ago have crucified every one of them along the roads from here to Rome in the spirit of the empire's legendary retribution following the slave revolt under Spartacus nearly a century before. Then he'd be rid of the entire rebellious passel of them. And, truth be told, he had already crucified as many as he could legally condemn.

Ethan sensed Pilate's irascibility and got immediately to the point. "We found this Man deluding our whole nation and telling people to refuse to pay taxes to the emperor. He claims that He Himself is the anointed One, a King."

Pilate turned toward the Suspect, obviously weary of the nonsense he was hearing. "Are you the King of the Jews?" he questioned in a bored tone.

"You say so," was all that Yeshua replied.

Pilate realized immediately that this was a perfect answer, admitting nothing, accusing no one, providing no evidence for His prosecutors to use against Him.

"I will question this Man privately," Pilate announced. Two of his guards preceded him from the platform. The other pair led Yeshua into the fortress to the hall of judgment.

When Pilate finally reappeared with Yeshua, he was clearly at the end of his patience. "I do not find any fault in this Man ... ." He was just about to free Him when he was shouted down by Ethan and the others who stood with him.

"But He is stirring up the entire populace," Ethan insisted, "teaching among all of our people from Galilee all the way to Yerushalayim."

At the mention of Galilee, Pilate's attention was recaptured. He fixed his gaze on Ethan. "Did you say this Man is from Galilee?" he queried. In answer to their nods, he smiled triumphantly. "Then this is Herod's problem. Let Herod resolve it." He stood to his feet and was gone before anyone could challenge his pronouncement.

In the fortress Pilate chuckled at his good fortune. In one stroke he could show his deference to Rome's puppet

Hebrew ruler and avoid a verdict he knew instinctively was guaranteed to offend someone.

The crowd became ferocious, a writhing snake ready to bite, frustrated in its purpose and ready to unleash its considerable venom on anyone who got in its way. Ethan was finally able to still them. "If it is to Herod we must go then let us be about it," he ordered. As he strode toward them, they made a path for him and turned to follow him across the Upper City to Herod's palace set in the western wall of the city.

Suddenly finding themselves in the front of the mob, David and Hannah were swept along whether or not they wished to go.

Though they had been unable to find Micah, he now found them. There were tears in his solemn young eyes. Over and over he asked, "What does it mean, David? What are they going to do with Him? What is going to happen to Yeshua?"

David placed a brotherly arm around Micah's thin shoulders and reassured him even though there was no assurance in his own heart. "It will be well, my child. He is the Son of the Holy One. No one can hurt Him. You will see." David could only hope that he was right while some dark foreboding deep within his heart told him he was not.

As the mob passed the Temple's western gate, David pulled Hannah and Micah aside and insisted they join Dinah and the boys inside. Hannah's eyes pleaded to be permitted to stay but David refused. "This is no place for a woman," he argued. Micah also begged to remain but he shook his head firmly. "Take care of your sister," he ordered. "See that she gets to the Temple safely." Then David disappeared into the crowd and they had no choice but to obey.

✿   ✿   ✿

Within an hour, the entire scene was about to be replayed in reverse. Herod had taunted Yeshua, tempted Him to perform some miracle to entertain him, and even allowed his soldiers to mock and abuse Him when He would not. The one thing Herod would not do was render a verdict.

Herod knew his subjects hated him and routinely referred to him as the Edomite whore or the emperor's lapdog because of his uncanny ability to remain in Rome's good graces. Most of those over whom he ruled were descendants of the patriarch, Yakov, or Yisrael as he later became known, while he was a descendant of Yakov's brother, Esau. He had never really understood why he should be the hated one. Was it not Yakov who had cheated Esau? It seemed to him that he had a better case for bitterness than they. But centuries of antagonism lay between the two peoples and Herod knew he could not change that. Still he was the consummate politician; he knew the real power lay with Rome, not the Sanhedrin. He also knew that many in his nation saw Yeshua as the Messiah for whom they had been waiting, the One who would cast the Roman infidels from their shores. He had no desire to alienate either side with a decision that could only offend one or the other. No, Herod would live to rule over Yisrael's progeny another day and he would do it by not exercising rule at all.

✿   ✿   ✿

The mob was even more incensed by the time they returned to the Antonia. The delay had done nothing to soothe their tempers; rather it had only served to exacerbate them.

Ethan ben Esrom pushed his way to the front of the throng and waited for Pilate to reappear, crossing his arms over his girdle and tapping a sandaled foot on the mosaic tiles beneath it to indicate his growing impatience. Those nearest him observed his stance and replicated it.

When Pilate returned, his demeanor had clearly changed. Gone was his thinly-veiled annoyance of an hour before; now he seemed tense and uncertain. He immediately took an offensive posture rather than a defensive one. "You have already brought this Man before me saying He is guilty of seducing your people away from obedience to Rome. I have interrogated Him myself and have found no fault with Him," Pilate recounted calmly. "Now your own king has not found Him worthy of death."

Those assembled sensed Pilate might rule against them. A rumble erupted from a thousand throats and quickly grew into a thunderous roar that drowned out Pilate's lone voice.

Roman guards stepped forward menacing the crowd with raised lances. Pilate signaled for quiet and resumed. "Therefore I will have this Man scourged and then release Him."

Pilate could think of nothing else to do even though it made no sense to scourge a Man he himself had already declared innocent. But Pilate knew whipping often left one dead or dying. One would surely be left broken and bleeding, his flesh flayed to ribbons, a sight to tear at the hearts of even the most rabid adversaries. Even this mob will be appeased, he reasoned.

But Pilate had sorely misjudged the determination of those before him. While the soldiers led Yeshua into the fortress, bared His back, and tied His hands to the whipping post in the judgment hall, the crowd waited in stubborn silence. As the Roman whip slashed the air and landed with a resounding crack more times than most could count and with such force it could be heard outside, they maintained their hard callous expressions. David could not bear it. His hands covered his ears to diminish the sound of the whip against tearing flesh. There were no cries of pain. David was glad Hannah and Micah had been spared this horror.

But the soldiers were not finished. One braided a crown

using branches that grew nearby and contained the longest sharpest thorns this Roman legionnaire had ever seen. He jammed it down upon his Victim's head. Immediately blood sprang forth from the many wounds and ran down Yeshua's face into His beard. Another brought an old purple robe and draped it roughly across His wounded back. His eyes betrayed only the merest trace of pain. The soldiers were disappointed with His lack of reaction. They struck and taunted Him, hoping for some greater response but once again their efforts went unrewarded.

After the lash was silent and the soldiers had done their worst, the Prisoner was led back. David gasped at what he saw. If he had not known Yeshua he could not have recognized Him. Indeed he thought it unlikely His own mother would recognize Him now. His back must have resembled the sides of beef which hung suspended at the butcher's stall for the robe the soldiers had placed upon Him was already saturated with blood. Yet He stood straight and tall and slowly turned to face His accusers, His expression revealing both His own agony and His compassion for those who judged Him.

David had never seen such fortitude. "Only Yeshua," David whispered in awe.

In front of him, a man who had heard his remark turned and fixed upon him a look of utter and complete contempt.

David did not care.

Pilate studied the faces in the crowd. "Look at the Man," he demanded. Surely even their bloodlust will be satisfied, he assured himself.

The crowd remained unmoved, waiting for the only verdict acceptable to them.

Pilate sighed in total exasperation. Usually the irascible citizens of Yisrael threatened open revolt at the mere suggestion of the death penalty for one of their own. Now they were not only willing that the death penalty be imposed but stubbornly demanding it.

Pilate had known for many months of Yeshua's growing popularity among His people. *They are just jealous of Him,* he suddenly realized, *jealous of His fame. They want me to end it for them.* And Pontius Pilate did not want to give them the satisfaction of acceding to their will.

Pilate had one last ploy. When he spoke, his tone was almost obsequious while at the same time also imperious and compassionate. "At this festive time of the year, it has always been my custom to release to you one prisoner. I hold Bar Abba whom you know to be guilty of rebellion and murder and I hold this Man whom your own king has found guilty of nothing. Which of the two shall I release?" He reasoned that they could not possibly want a murderer to be released to the same streets where their wives shopped and their children played.

But both Pilate and David were soon bitterly disappointed.

To Pilate's stunned ears, the answer came back almost in unison. "Bar Abba, Bar Abba, we want Bar Abba."

Just then a message was brought to Pilate. As he unrolled the small scroll, he saw the feathery handwriting of his wife. She related the troubling nightmare she had had of this Man the previous night and cautioned her husband, almost pleaded with him, to have nothing to do with His case. Those assembled could not know the great value Romans placed in such omens. Above all Pilate now wanted no part in this decision. But a governor has no choice but to govern. Herod had avoided rendering a judgment. Pilate knew that he could not.

David studied Pilate's face. Even from a distance, it appeared that he was in greater agony than the Prisoner he had just had so severely beaten. David's heart almost went out to him.

"Then what shall I do with Yeshua who is called your Messiah?" Pilate pleaded.

Again the answer came back well-orchestrated and well-directed by the sons of Annas. "Crucify Him, crucify Him."

Somewhere in the crowd, Naqdimon and Yohanan looked at each other and silently shook their heads. What could two do against so many?

Yohanan recalled that Yeshua had predicted everything, His arrest, His trial, even His beating. Yohanan had simply swept such words from his mind because he could not bear to hear them. Now it was all happening just as Yeshua had said. And still Yohanan could not allow his heart to consider the end that Yeshua had also predicted, the end that would come on a cruel Roman cross.

"Why? What evil has He committed?" Pilate questioned, his tone beseeching.

David could not believe what he was seeing. Pontius Pilate, the great governor of Palestine, the emperor's personal representative in this distant corner of his realm, was cowering before a blood-thirsty rabble, begging them to relieve him of the dreadful burden they had placed upon him.

It was clear to David that only one Man present possessed any courage at all and that Man was meant to be the Victim. Instead He stood silent and stalwart, unvanquished and unbowed before all of the cringing cowardice around Him. It was then that David realized the truth. Yeshua alone was in complete command here. David did not understand why He had given His back to be so sorely wounded or why He might even yield Himself to the horror of crucifixion. But David did know that nothing was happening to Yeshua that He was not personally permitting. David stood then in wide-eyed wonder, in unwavering reverential awe of his Messiah, his Lord and his King. He almost felt that he should kneel and worship before the very Son of the Holy One but he found himself paralyzed in the presence of such overwhelming power, unable to move in the face of such magnificent majesty.

"Tell me, what evil has He committed?" Pilate demanded.

"According to our Law He must die because He called Himself the Son of the Holy One," came the answer from the scribes.

Pilate's face became a mask of terror. He knew little of the one Hebrew God but he knew enough of the panoply of Roman gods and goddesses and their capriciousness against mere mortals who defied them. He had no desire to place himself on the wrong side of any god, not even the solitary God these strange people worshipped. He hurriedly withdrew to the security of the fortress, his mind searching for any artifice to remove this terrible dilemma from him. Again he summoned Yeshua for further interrogation.

"Where are You from?" Pilate inquired the moment they were again alone in the fortress. He received only a knowing glance in response. "Talk to me," he demanded. "Don't you know that I have the power to crucify You or release You?"

Yeshua smiled. "You'd have no power at all if it were not given to you from above."

A shiver of fear played over Pilate's spine. He shuddered and Yeshua smiled once more. Pilate almost ran from the chamber. He had never wanted anything so much as he now wanted to be free of this decision and the awful aftermath he feared might follow.

This Man was unlike any of the other Hebrew zealots he had been called upon to judge in the past. He did not exhibit the fiery eyes and the even more fiery words Pilate had found in them. He was gentle, caring, almost compassionate toward the man who would decide His fate. Pilate concluded the Man might well be insane, with all this talk of kingdoms and power from above, but He was certainly no threat to the great Roman empire.

Before the crowd once more, Pilate was greeted with a determined drumbeat growing in both insistence and intensity, "Let Him be crucified, LET HIM BE CRUCIFIED, *LET HIM BE CRUCIFIED!*"

"Shall I crucify your King?" Pilate responded in desperation, hoping against hope that some in the crowd would be willing to claim Him.

"We have no king but Caesar," came the cold reply.

Ethan ben Esrom sensed Pilate was weakening. He turned and caught the eye of Yosef ben Qayafa. The high priest nodded, his pre-arranged signal that it was time to bring this trial to the successful conclusion he had planned. It was time to strengthen Pilate's quaking spine, time to reinforce his shamefully impotent resolve, time to do exactly what Qayafa had ordered should this occur. He came forward and whispered so that only Pilate could hear, "If you let this Man go, you are no friend of Caesar's for whoever calls himself a king speaks against Caesar."

Pilate sagged against the back of his chair as though he had been physically struck. His eyes closed and his face paled. There it was, the terrible threat even he, the great Pontius Pilate, with all of the power of Rome behind him could not resist. Ethan ben Esrom had now made it crystal clear that if the required verdict were not rendered in this case, the third complaint which could end his political career forever would surely be made against him to the emperor. Even though Tiberias Caesar was his friend of many years, Pilate knew the old emperor would be forced to act, not just because of the third complaint, but because this Prisoner threatened his very throne. Pilate was beaten. He knew he had no way out. Still he meant to have the last word.

Pilate called for writing materials. When they had been brought, he scrawled the indictment in his own shaky hand, "THIS IS JESUS OF NAZARETH, THE KING OF THE JEWS."

Ethan protested, preferring it to read, "He said He was King of the Jews."

Pilate would have none of it. He raised a hand to end the debate, glared at Ethan menacingly, and spoke in a tone that dared Ethan to argue, "What I have written, I have written." Then he handed the document to a guard.

Pilate next snapped his fingers and ordered that a basin of water be brought. He stood on trembling legs and ceremoniously washed his hands. As he did, he cried out in an agonized voice, "I am now innocent of the blood of this just Person; you see to it."

As Pilate nearly ran from the platform to take refuge in his fortress, someone shouted after him, "His blood be upon us and upon our children." Others laughed their agreement, never realizing the fearful wrath they brought down upon themselves and their offspring.

Yeshua remained composed as the soldiers led Him away but David's composure failed completely. He covered his contorted face with his hands and wept openly as a little child might weep for a lost parent. How would he tell Hannah who still questioned? How would he explain it to little Micah, so new and fragile a believer? The questions tormented him almost as much as the vile picture forming in his mind of what would come next.

At the back of the crowd, Yosef ben Qayafa only smiled, a smile that quickly twisted itself into a grotesque sneer. He had triumphed at last over his most implacable Foe. And he had done it all without even uttering so much as a single word. No one would even remember that he had been here. If ever there was to be blame, it would belong to others who might be easily offered up on the altar of his all-consuming pride. His power, he assured himself, was now safe.

෬ 29 ෨

THE sun climbed higher in a cloudless sky, its unrelenting gaze illuminating the darkness to be found in the hearts of men. Like a well-lit stage production the tableau taking place below was apparent for all to see.

The morning sacrifice at the Temple had concluded and Dinah had led her children home to her sister's house in the Lower City. Later, as she and Ruth walked to the marketplace to shop for the Seder, they noticed knots of Galileans, their faces streaked with tears. Dinah and Ruth were puzzled but the two could hardly approach men they did not know with questions. Their tension increased in direct proportion to the number of anxious faces they saw among their countrymen. As they neared the stalls, Dinah recognized Yohanna, her neighbor from Capernaum. She waited while Yohanna completed her purchase, then greeted her warmly. She could see Yohanna's round face was tear-stained, too.

Dinah placed a comforting hand on Yohanna's arm. "Tell me, my friend," she began. "What has happened to bring you grief on this happy day of celebration?"

Yohanna leaned closer to whisper as fresh tears came to her warm grey eyes. "You have not heard? It is Yeshua ben Yosef. The wretched Romans and Yudeans have condemned Him to die." Dinah and Ruth gasped in unison at the news as Yohanna continued, "They cannot stand for us to have a Leader, One of our own."

The three had drawn the attention of a young Roman legionnaire whose assignment was to keep peace in the marketplace on this busy morning. As he strode toward them, they separated and he passed them by.

At the stall of the greengrocer, Ruth examined and collected the herbs she would need for the Seder re-enactment of that final night in Egypt, but Dinah seemed distracted. Finally she whispered, "I must let the children know." Ruth nodded as Dinah disappeared into the crowd.

✡   ✡   ✡

"No, it cannot be," was all that Micah could say at the awful news. "There must be some mistake." He paced nervously, angrily, oblivious to his mother's efforts to calm him.

Hannah's face froze. She said nothing of what she was thinking. *I knew all along He couldn't be the One. This would convince even Abba. Maybe now David will see the truth, too.*

Micah clenched and unclenched his small fists. Finally he erupted, "I have to know. I have to see for myself." Then he was out the door before his mother could stop him.

"Hannah, go with him," Dinah ordered. "I do not want him out there all alone. He does not know Yerushalayim that well."

After Hannah had grabbed her robe and veil and slipped out the door, Dinah fretted alone. *This is the day my eldest son is to become a man, the day Itzak and I awaited since the moment of his birth, the day he is to enter into the Sanctuary for the first time with David. Now I do not know where either of them may be or when they may return. What shall I do?*

✡   ✡   ✡

David had followed the angry crowd from the Fortress Antonia, hoping against hope that the Holy One would roll back the heavens and intercede at any moment. As much as he could not bear to see what was happening, neither could he look away. He was drawn like a moth to some terrible flame.

David watched wincing as a heavy roughly-hewn cross was slammed onto Yeshua's bleeding back and He was led with two others along the street leading to the northwest wall of the city. Yeshua struggled valiantly to keep up the pace set by impatient Roman soldiers who reinforced their will with periodic slashes across His bare legs with a Roman riding crop. But His loss of blood combined with His lack of sleep and food and water had clearly weakened Him. Each step was taken with only the greatest effort.

The soldiers hated this duty. More than one witnessing his first crucifixion had been known to wretch violently or collapse in an unconscious heap, much to the amusement of the more experienced who had had the foresight to steady themselves with an extra goblet or two of wine. It was especially trying on a feast day such as this when the city was full of visitors and crowd control and peace-keeping were supposed to be their primary concerns.

But, in the minds of their superiors, this was the perfect time to show the rabble from all over the realm the fate that awaited any who transgressed Roman law. The superiors agreed crucifixions were useful in ridding the empire of those who would threaten it while at the same time providing a dreadful object lesson to any who might contemplate such a threat. The trouble was, it was not those superiors who had to actually conduct the crucifixions they ordered, to drive the nails into living flesh, to hear the agonized cries of the victims. That was left to young legionnaires far from home who were often left sickened and scarred by the experience.

The unfortunate legionnaires who had drawn this day's duty wished only to have it done as soon as possible. They gave no thought to the men who were about to die, to their desire to spend their last minutes with their loved ones or to their families' desire for one more moment to comfort them. Had their minds dwelt on such things, they would have been unable to carry out their awful orders. For these three, though, there seemed to be no family members present, so they did all they could to speed the parade along.

When it became clear that Yeshua ben Yosef could not move as quickly as His Roman tormentors expected, an innocent spectator was pressed into service to carry His last burden for Him. David noticed he was dark-skinned and clad in the garb of the nomads of North Africa. David both pitied him his misfortune and envied his opportunity to provide one final service to Yeshua. David wondered if the man even knew for Whom he labored.

The procession inched forward, ever closer to the city gate and what lay beyond. David moved with it, pushing past taunting jeering bystanders, seeing weeping Galileans who met his eyes with the silent question, *Why?* David still expected the Holy One to intervene. Perhaps a golden staircase would descend out of the clouds and Yeshua would be caught up by the very angels who had come to the patriarch, Yakov, as he slept. Maybe a heavenly chariot would sweep across the skies in a whirlwind and bear Yeshua back to His Father just as it had taken Elijah to the Holy One's side. But still the procession moved on, snaking, squirming, twisting through the narrow street and still there was no salvation in sight.

Unknown to David, Naqdimon and Yohanan allowed themselves to be swept along by the crowd, too. They also anticipated divine rescue, longed for it, prayed for it, believed for it. But it did not come and their hearts pounded faster as the great gate of the city loomed up ahead.

Also in the crowd, a diminutive rabbi in black robes fought his way past unyielding forms. Rabbi Levi was determined to see the end of the hated Yeshua ben Yosef, to rejoice in it, to glory in it. This Man had driven his precious Yael mad; now He would join her in death. For Rabbi

Levi, this was the long-awaited victory, the justice for which he had long been praying.

✡   ✡   ✡

In a grand home not far away, Yosef ben Qayafa sat at his table enjoying an early meal of cheeses and fruits, freshly-baked bread, and wine served by a silent Malluch. Always a stickler for the details of the Law, Qayafa had carefully planned to have his cheese at this time of day because he knew it could not be served alongside the lamb that would be a part of his Seder dinner. He trusted the Holy One would remember his devotion.

Qayafa smiled as he thought of what was taking place outside the city wall. He relished his triumph. There was, however, no need to miss this fine repast, no necessity to expose himself to the horror of the actual event. He would wait until the nails had been driven and the blood had been spilled. Then he would go to see for himself and to celebrate his victory. He smiled once more as he reached for another fig and drew it to his mouth.

Qayafa never even noticed the moist eyes and drawn face of the young man who served him. Malluch, too, knew what was taking place on that hillside and it broke the heart he had already given to Yeshua.

❧ 30 ❧

HANNAH and Micah hurried to the Fortress Antonia and found the once-crowded pavement deserted. Micah approached the fearsome-looking legionnaire on duty and after a brief inquiry, was rewarded with a few words Hannah could not hear and a hand pointing west.

"Come, Hannah," Micah instructed when he returned.

Hannah remained in place. "Why? Why can't we just go home now? Ammah will be furious if you are late to Temple tonight and she will be furious with me if I permit it. Please, my brother, let us return. David will tell us what happened."

Micah started off in the direction in which the Roman had pointed, tossing his words back over his shoulder, "You go back if you wish. I must be there."

Hannah hesitated. She didn't want to go. She didn't want to see whatever waited in the west. But she knew Ammah would be even more furious if she arrived home without Micah. Quickly contemplating her options, she followed her brother, however reluctantly.

✿　　　✿　　　✿

The procession passed the city gate. Outside the formidable stone wall built to resist invasion but unable to repel the hated Romans, David got his first glimpse of the horror that was Golgotha. Before him a treeless rounded hilltop resembling the top of a skull, thus its name, stood out in stark contrast against the clear spring sky. Below it, a sheer rock face dotted with a random arrangement of openings to darkened tombs completed the ominous scene.

The Romans led the way up the back side of Golgotha and reappeared at its top, their prisoners in tow. The prisoners were offered a narcotic drink, a mixture of wine and myrrh to dull their senses and diminish their pain. Two received it gratefully; Yeshua did not, almost as though He felt He must endure the unendurable until the very end. Then the prisoners were stripped of their clothing and forcibly laid upon their crosses.

David's knees buckled. He had been waiting to witness a miracle; now he would witness a murder. He could not watch any longer but neither could he shut out the sound of hammer against metal or the agonized screams of the condemned as the thick nails were driven through their living flesh. He marveled that he had not heard the voice of Yeshua. Perhaps that was the miracle, he thought, and the thought sickened him.

When the hammers fell silent, David looked up only long enough to see Roman soldiers lift the first cross and drop it into the waiting earth. The sound of tearing flesh and an anguished cry were more than he could bear. He turned and vomited. When he turned back he saw that the bright blue sky of morning had suddenly been replaced by slate grey clouds blowing in from the west. Above him three dark crosses stood in stark relief against the threatening sky.

"Have you never seen one before?" a voice behind him questioned.

He swung around to find himself face-to-face with the elderly rabbi who had recited the Kadesh at the grave of Itzak only a few days before. He seemed to be enjoying the event. "No, my lord," he answered, his voice dry and barely audible.

"I have seen many but none so welcome as this one," Rabbi Levi volunteered.

"How could anyone welcome such a calamity visited

upon another human being?" David queried, his voice now strong and filled with emotion.

Rabbi Levi grinned. "When the evil receive the just consequences of their deeds, it is always a welcome sight to those who obey the laws of the Holy One. No?"

"But He is not evil. I know Him. He is a good Man," David defended with passion.

"Ah, you must be one of them, one of the followers of the Galilean Messiah." The way he spat the word out of his mouth told David all he needed to know about where this man's sympathies lay.

David summoned up all his courage. "Yes, I am one of them."

Rabbi Levi laughed. "So what do you think of your precious Messiah now?" he taunted.

David looked back at the horrific scene atop the hill. He found Yeshua's face composed, peaceful, even in the face of this most agonizing pain. Again he stood in awe of his Lord. "I think He has never been more majestic than He is at this very moment when He is lifted up upon the unlikely throne of a cross," David whispered reverently.

The rabbi grew angry. "See what you think as the time passes, my boy. They don't bleed to death, you know. It will not be that easy or that quick for your Messiah. Sometimes it takes weeks, particularly if they have someone to come daily and lift food and drink to their mouths. Without it, they die of thirst in little more than a week. With it, they may die of exposure to the elements. I have even seen them torn to pieces by hungry vultures." Rabbi Levi laughed again as he thought of the hated Yeshua facing such an end. Then he continued. "Usually though, when they can no longer stand the pain of lifting the weight of their bodies against the nails in their feet, they find they cannot breathe with their arms pulled back like that. See if you still think He's Messiah when He's gasping for His last breath." Then the rabbi walked on, seeking a new vantage point from which to get a better view.

David wretched again as another more comforting voice spoke to him. "Fear not, my son," he said. "Remember, Pesach begins with the setting of the sun. They will not permit Him or any of them to remain upon the tree after that. They wouldn't want to be guilty of transgressing the Holy One's Law," he noted sarcastically. "No, they will send the Romans to break their legs so that their breathing will become impossible and their deaths quick."

David looked up into the face of the elderly Naqdimon and found there only compassion for the suffering men above them. Behind him, David saw the face of Yohanan, his eyes red, his cheeks wet with tears. "My brother," Yohanan soothed as he and Naqdimon helped David to his feet and supported him between them. "He's one of us," Yohanan informed Naqdimon.

"I thought so," Naqdimon replied. "None but His own could see His beauty even here."

✡   ✡   ✡

Hannah and Micah pushed against the tide of people returning from Golgotha having satisfied themselves that they were rid of the Infidel Yeshua. They had other more important things to do as Pesach neared. When Hannah and Micah were finally able to elbow their way through the gate, they got their first ghastly view of Golgotha and the awful event taking place there. Hannah gasped as her eyes widened in terror. Micah only groaned in futility. "No, no, no," he wailed again and again. Hannah held her younger brother and he clung to her; both were giving comfort and receiving it, the comfort both had needed for an entire year.

David recognized Micah's voice. Soon he sheltered the two in his long arms, weeping even as he whispered words of solace to them.

Naqdimon and Yohanan waited, unwilling to intrude on so private a moment. Naqdimon finally shook his head sadly and started back toward the city. He could bear no more. Anyway, though he dreaded it, there was something else he knew he must do.

After Naqdimon disappeared from view, Yohanan came to David's side. "I am going up there," he said flatly. "I cannot let Him suffer alone. I must go to Him. I must be there for Him."

"May I come with you?" David asked, his voice soft and reverent.

"No, David," Hannah objected. "Don't go there. I fear what it will do to you. I fear you may never be the same."

David looked lovingly into Hannah's concerned eyes. "Oh, Hannah, don't you see?" David asked gently. "Already I will never be the same, not because He dies but because He lived, not because I see His death but because He touched my life."

"Still you believe then?" Hannah questioned in exasperation.

"Still, Hannah, and always," was David's tender reply. His words conveyed more conviction than his breaking heart held. He, too, questioned. He, too, wondered how the Holy One could allow such a thing to happen to His Anointed, to His Messiah, to His Son. But he could not forget the change that had happened in his own shattered life the day he had met Yeshua. That could not be denied and neither could Yeshua, not here, not now. He could not walk away from Yeshua for Yeshua had never walked away from him.

Once again Hannah grappled with her conscience. She loved David even if she could not tell him so, even if she could never marry him or be to him the wife he wanted her to be. And David was suffering the loss of One he loved just as she had suffered the loss of her beloved Abba.

"Take your sister home now," David suggested to Micah. "I will come soon."

"No," Hannah insisted, her decision made. "If you must go then I must go with you." As she said the words, she did not realize that she was even then assuming the role of wife and helpmeet to the man to whom she did not wish to be joined in marriage.

Together they started up a steep incline made all the worse by the thwarted trees and scraggly shrubs that lined the footpath and reached out for unwary legs and feet and ankles. Yohanan made the ascent quickly in long even strides, but David walked slowly, helping Hannah over the rock-strewn path, making sure Micah was also safe. When they had arrived at the top of the skull-shaped hill, none could speak. There they found Yeshua ben Yosef suspended between Heaven and earth, between life and death, between the inhumanity of man and the love of the Holy One. There they stood face to face with the stark reality of death, the agonizing death of the cross.

༄ 31 ༄

YAKOV knelt in a sheep pen and pulled one of the smallest lambs from its mother's teat. "Come, little one," he murmured, trying to keep his voice calm. "You have been chosen." He knew that even sheep could sense much from the voice of the one who kept them; even they could become skittish if their keeper's voice betrayed tension. The old ewe looked back with frightened knowing eyes as he took her little one from her side forever.

With the lamb held close to his body, he returned to the trading table where Meshullam was receiving a Temple coin from the young couple who had only one small son. The little lamb would provide meat enough for their Seder table.

Yakov did not want to let the little animal go. There was something about it, something about its innocence, its defenselessness, that tugged at his heart. In his troubled mind he could see it being taken to the priest, standing silent and still as the sharp knife was brought to its throat, never understanding the cruelty of man as its life ebbed away in front of its eyes, never knowing why the purity of its soft white coat must be forever stained with its own warm blood.

For some reason, Yakov wanted to hold the little lamb close and run away. He suddenly didn't want to send one more innocent animal to its death. *What is happening to me?* he wondered anew. *What has happened to me since Shoshana died? Why can I no longer even do my work?* All Yakov could do was console himself that this was the purpose for which this lamb had been born, the purpose which gave eternal meaning to its brief life.

The small Temple coin clinked into the box on the table and Meshullam lifted the tiny lamb from his son's arms and handed it to his customer with a smile. "You have chosen well, my friend. The Holy One will be well pleased with the sacrifice He receives this day."

Yakov stood mute and helpless. A perfect innocent lamb was on its way to the slaughter and there was nothing anyone could do about it. The sad fact was no one even seemed to care, no one but Yakov. And Yakov didn't even understand why.

✿   ✿   ✿

Those first to leave Golgotha returned to the Temple with tales enough to fill with dread those who heard them. Most who listened were worshippers from afar, from small towns and villages, from farm lands and sailing ships. None had ever witnessed a crucifixion. Now they hung on every word, their eyes growing wide with shock at what they heard.

Word soon spread like a stain especially when the name of the Man on the center cross was revealed. Many knew Him, most knew of Him, but only a few were known by Him. These wept at the news. The others registered reactions from joy to jubilation.

Yakov watched as they came, one by one, two by two, here a small group, there a little gathering, and all from the direction of the western gate. He watched as heads came together and confidences were exchanged. Again, he knew something was happening and he longed to distract his tormented mind with news of it.

Finally one came to his table to purchase a Paschal lamb. Yakov showed him from pen to pen until he had made his selection. As they led the animal away, Yakov summoned the courage to speak. "I noticed you came from the western gate." When the customer nodded solemnly, Yakov continued. "What is it that captures the attention of everyone coming that way today?"

"Oh, have you not heard?" the customer responded with surprise. "It was the most awful thing these old eyes of mine have ever beheld."

"What was it?" Yakov inquired even more insistently.

"It was Yeshua, the One some thought was Messiah. You know Him?"

"We've met," Yakov replied coolly.

"You will not meet again," the man informed him, a sharp edge of irony creeping into his voice.

"Why? What has happened to Him?" Yakov pressed.

"The Romans crucified Him this very morning."

Yakov felt faint as his breath caught in his throat. He was confused, then even more confused because he was confused. He knew he should be rejoicing but he wasn't and he did not know why. He swallowed hard. He tried to speak but the words would not come. "Is He dead?" he was finally able to croak in a hoarse voice that cracked with emotion.

"Probably not. They say it takes a long time for the end to come. Why do you ask?"

"No reason .... I just .... It's just that I ... ." Yakov handed the young ram to the customer and directed him to the trading table. "Tell my father I will return later," he instructed.

Yakov found himself striding purposefully toward the western gate, toward the western wall, toward ... toward what? he wondered as he walked. *What is it about this Man that draws me so? Why can I not simply walk away?* He didn't know why; he only knew he couldn't. He walked faster, hoping he would not be too late and still wondering why it mattered to him if he was.

◌ 32 ◌

SHIMON and Eleazar had planned to make a leisurely stroll of their trip down the western slope of the Mount of Olives from Bethany. They could make the journey in half the time but this day they would be escorting Miriam, the mother of Yeshua ben Yosef, along with Shimon's Miriam and Martha. All planned to spend the afternoon with Shimon's brother, Reuven, and his family, then attend the evening sacrifice and celebrate the Seder. It was the first Pesach since Shimon had been healed and Eleazar had been raised to new life. They had much for which to thank the Holy One and Shimon was looking forward to doing exactly that.

A sudden knock at the door interrupted Shimon's last-minute preparations. The servants had been given the day to make ready their own Seders so Shimon strode to the door, loosened the latch, and swung it open. A hearty greeting died on his lips when he saw before him a breathless Naqdimon. He had clearly come in a great hurry and his expression was dark with sadness.

"Come in, brother. Tell me what has happened," Shimon murmured. The two disappeared into a small chamber just inside the door. When Shimon reappeared only a few moments later, he was pale, his lips drawn in a straight line, his eyes damp and reddened. He found Miriam in the dining chamber happily exchanging confidences with his daughters, took her aside, seated her in a chair, and drew in a deep breath as he searched for words that did not come. Finally, he began. "Miriam, there is no easy way to say what I must say."

Miriam looked apprehensive. "What is it, Shimon?" Her eyes darted past him to Naqdimon whose face betrayed his distress.

Shimon's eyes fell to his sandals and the marble floor beneath them. "It is about our Yeshua, my dear lady, and it is not good."

Miriam's eyes widened, then closed as she composed herself for whatever might follow. "It will be easier if you say it quickly then," she said softly.

"He has been arrested, Miriam, arrested and tried. I do not know the charge; I only know that He has been found guilty."

Miriam rose from her chair. "I must go to Him. There must be something we can do to help Him?" She searched Shimon's face, then Naqdimon's and read in them all she needed to know. She did not want to believe what her heart told her was true.

"There is nothing anyone can do to help Him now, Miriam," Shimon said, his voice anguished. "They have crucified Him."

Miriam's knees weakened. Shimon supported her as she slumped back into the chair. Her eyes became glassy, staring, distant. When she spoke, her voice was quiet and far too calm. "I knew. I suppose I've always known. The sword which was said would pierce my soul has come just as I always knew it would." She stood then, straight and steady. She looked into Shimon's watery eyes. "And still I must go to Him, Shimon. You do understand."

Shimon exchanged worried glances with Naqdimon before he turned back to Miriam. "You need not put yourself through such pain. He would not want that," Shimon pleaded.

"And what of His pain?" Miriam asked. "Must He endure it all alone? I do not want that," she added with determination.

Naqdimon stepped forward. "I have just come from there, dear lady. I must tell you that the scene is one of the most unimaginable horror. I am certain He would spare you that. And truly there is nothing you can do." Yet even as he said the words, Naqdimon knew in his heart that he would have moved Heaven and earth to be with his own son, Moshe, in his final moments.

Miriam's face took on a calm serenity that astounded both men. "He is my Son, gentlemen. If I can do nothing else, I can be with Him; I can assure Him of my love until the very last moment, until His very last breath. I brought Him into this world and I will see Him out of it." She took a step toward the door. "Now my friends, let us be going. He can never come to me again. I must now go to Him. Come. My Son waits."

Shimon and Naqdimon knew there was no point in arguing. Miriam had summoned strength they had not known she possessed. Truth be told, she had not known that she possessed it either. Perhaps she did not possess it at all. Perhaps it now possessed her. Perhaps it had been given to her for this very moment by the mercy of the Holy One, Himself.

The three left Martha and Miriam and Eleazar behind; there was no time to gather them, no time to explain. In any event, they all thought it best to spare the young ones what they themselves would have to suffer. When they rounded the last bend in the road and Yerushalayim came into view, Miriam raised her eyes ever so slightly. She looked past the Temple, over its stately courts and beyond, to a small hill just outside the city's western wall. Reflected in her eyes, they saw it, too. "My Son waits," she whispered again as she quickened her pace.

☙ 33 ❧

YOSEF ben Qayafa pressed a white linen napkin to his lips, then brushed crumbs from his tunic which had been a gift from his wife, Leah. It was quite the latest fashion, made of the finest silk, and had literally cost its weight in gold. It would not do to have it soiled.

He rose from the table without so much as a word for Malluch, wrapped his robe about him, and walked out to the courtyard and climbed into his litter. He drew the curtains closed around him and leaned back on several plush pillows. He chuckled to himself as he felt the litter rise.

The rhythmic swaying of the conveyance had nearly rocked him to sleep before his servants informed him that they had arrived at the foot of Golgotha. The litter could not negotiate the steep ascent to the crest of the hill. Qayafa grimaced at the inconvenience. Then he alighted from his litter and began the bothersome climb alone.

At the top, Qayafa was met by the sons of Annas, three of whom had previously held his office, all of whom coveted it. With them, stood the same scribes and elders who had recently been outwitted by Yeshua's cleverness, among them Rabbi Levi ben Eschol. All greeted Qayafa with whispered congratulations on his victory. Together they made their way to the foot of the three crosses only minutes after they had been dropped into the earth.

Qayafa looked up into Yeshua's face, feeling nothing but contempt and triumph. "You, who claimed to be able to destroy the Temple and rebuild it in three days," he shouted, "if You are really the Son of the Holy One as You claimed, come down from the cross." Qayafa pretended to wait, keeping up the pretense far longer than necessary to make his point. Then he continued. "He saved others. Why can He not save Himself?" he inquired, deliberately loud enough to be heard by those above him. He and his assembled sycophants laughed at his sly jest.

Yeshua's face contorted with the agony of His body and the humiliation of His soul but He did not answer those who wanted only to persecute Him to the very end. He spoke to the Holy One alone. "My God, My God, why have You forsaken Me, too?"

Qayafa laughed deeply and with satisfaction. The sons of Annas joined in.

At that moment, Qayafa noted the inscription nailed to the top of the center cross. Usually such an inscription carried the indictment listing the charges of which the accused had been convicted and for which he had been condemned to die. In this case, however, there was only one charge and Qayafa feared it might be mistaken for a title rather than an accusation. "THIS IS JESUS OF NAZARETH, THE KING OF THE JEWS," it read in Hebrew, Greek, and Latin so that all who passed by could read and understand and be warned.

Qayafa silently cursed Pontius Pilate for insisting on this sacrilege. He consoled himself by continuing with his tirade. "If He really is the King of Yisrael, let Him come down from the cross right now. Then we will believe Him."

"He trusted in the Holy One," Rabbi Levi chimed in sarcastically. "Let the Holy One free Him now if He will have Him. After all, He said He was His Son."

The men convulsed in sardonic laughter while Rabbi Levi gloried in the approbation of his audience.

Yeshua looked down upon His tormentors, both Roman and Hebrew, with nothing but pity filling his tortured eyes. When He spoke again, it was in prayer, not for Himself, but for them. "Father, forgive all of them for they know not what they do."

The smile fled from the face of Yosef ben Qayafa. He, the high priest of all Yisrael, needed no prayer of forgiveness from this condemned Pretender. He waved a hand of disgust in the direction of the center cross and turned to his friends to bolster his sagging assurance. He read in their faces the same chagrin he also felt though he dared not admit it, not even to himself. They stood back in silence, inwardly writhing under Yeshua's compassionate gaze yet determined to see played out the final act of this drama they had so carefully directed.

One of those dying beside Yeshua took up the diatribe Qayafa had begun, his tone both scornful and supplicating. "If You really are the Messiah, then save Yourself and us."

Yeshua said nothing. How could He expect him to understand? The salvation He provided was not gained by coming down from the cross, only by dying upon it.

On the other side, the second man spoke, "Have you no fear of the Holy One?" he questioned sternly, "especially since we are both condemned, too. And we are judged justly for we receive only the fair reward of our guilty deeds. But this Man is guilty of nothing."

At these words, Hannah lifted her head, wiped the tears from her eyes, and studied the two men who suffered with Yeshua. There was something familiar about the voice of the first, something that both frightened her and reminded her of ... of what? *I know them. At least I think I do.* It was so hard to tell. The soldiers had not been kind to them and their faces were swollen and cut and bleeding. She struggled to remember.

When the light of recognition finally came, it came suddenly and overwhelmingly and far too brightly. "It's them," she cried to David. "Look, David. It's those thieves, the very same thieves who nearly ... ," she paused, not wanting to remember yet reliving every awful detail of that night, " ... who nearly hurt me on the way here. It's them, David. I am certain of it."

They looked smaller to her now, less fearsome, more human, more vulnerable. Her heart broke with the thought that somehow she had placed them upon their crosses, that somehow she was responsible for their plight. She did not yet understand that she had helped to place the other One upon His cross as well.

David searched their faces for only a moment before he knew that Hannah was right. He wondered why he hadn't recognized them before, but of course, on the way here, his eyes had remained upon Yeshua alone. Yet now the fact that they were guilty did nothing to diminish the compassion he felt for them. He wished this fate on no man no matter his crime.

The second thief struggled to take a breath, then spoke again, slowly, painfully, his voice choked with his agony, yet humble, beseeching. This time he spoke to Yeshua alone. "Lord, remember me when You come into Your kingdom."

His words were few but they spoke volumes. They proclaimed belief in Yeshua as Lord, belief in life beyond the endless anguish of these crosses, belief in salvation, even now, even here. And his belief was not in vain.

Yeshua turned toward him and smiled. *Even on this battlefield victory can be won,* He thought and the thought strengthened Him. His voice came strong and full of the life it carried. "Truly I tell you, this very day you will be with Me in Paradise."

As Hannah watched in astonishment, the thief's countenance changed before her eyes. His face relaxed as though a great burden had been lifted from his tormented soul and a great peace had taken its place. His eyes lost their anguish, if only for a moment, and his lips formed a composed smile.

What power does this Man possess that even in this place, His very word can change a man's entire being? she wondered in complete awe of Him. *It is just as David said, just as he described it. Now I have seen it for myself.* Yet even then she could not comprehend it.

❧ 34 ❧

THE sky had grown dark and ominous above him as he made his way through the crowded streets, through the gate, and toward the hill beyond. After the steep climb Yakov was out of breath when he finally reached the top of Golgotha. He paused for a moment and bent forward gasping. He told himself it was to catch his breath but deep within he knew the truth; he knew he wasn't yet ready to face what he knew he was going to see. *Why am I even here?* he kept asking himself. *I've never come for any of the others. Why have I come for this one? And why do I even care when this Man gave me nothing but trouble?* It was all a puzzle to which Yakov ben Meshullam had no solution.

While Yakov waited for his breathing to become rhythmic once again and for his courage to be restored, two well-dressed men and a woman clad in the simple homespun clothing favored in the north brushed by him. For some reason even he did not understand, he followed a few paces behind.

The men remained with the woman, cupping their hands under her elbows to offer her their support. The woman went to the foot of the center cross and looked upward. She swayed slightly, then swallowed hard and steadied herself, all the while gazing up into the face of Yeshua.

Somehow Miriam saw past all of the wounds to find the Child she had once cradled in her arms and put to her breast, the Child she had loved for His entire life. In her eyes He was still whole, still perfect, still beautiful, still her little Boy, and still in need of her succor. When she spoke, her voice was strong yet gentle. "I am here, Son. I am here."

Yeshua's head rolled to the side then forward so that He could look down. Their eyes locked and comforted each other without a word being spoken.

My God, thought Yakov, *she is His mother! How can a mother watch her own Child die like this, the Child she carried under her heart, the Child that came forth from her own womb? How does she stand it?* He thought he could not watch any longer; his very eyes seemed an intrusion, yet he could not look away.

Another younger man also wearing the garb of the Galileans joined the woman and her friends. A smile of recognition formed on her lips. "Yohanan, somehow I knew you would be here. May the Holy One bless you for your faithfulness."

The young man took her small hands in his but he could say nothing; his tears flowed freely, washing across his somber cheeks.

"There, there, my child," the woman said softly as she embraced him. "We will get through this together, you and I. We will get through this together."

Yakov was awed. *How can she bear this? How can she be this strong?* he wondered in astonishment. *Her Son is dying just beyond her grasp and yet she comforts another. Where does she get such strength?*

He thought then of the day Shoshana had been so cruelly and so quickly taken from him. The scene had been even bloodier than this one and to his mind, even more awful. He wondered what he would have done if he had been given the same choice this mother had been given. Would he have remained beside his dying love as she now remained steadfast with hers? Or would he have run away and hid to protect himself from the horror of that moment, the horror of the memories he had never been able to erase from his mind?

And Yakov thought of the way he had dealt with his grief then and since. He had embraced no one, comforted no one, offered no one the solace of his presence, not even his own daughter. When confronted with the selflessness of this mother's love, Yakov ben Meshullam was brought face to face with the selfishness of his own and his eyes stung with bitter tears of regret.

Just then Yeshua looked down upon the two who held each other, sharing each other's burden and giving each other strength. He smiled slightly. Then with great effort, He spoke first to His mother. "Woman, this is now your son." Then to the young man, He said, "Son, this is now your mother." The exertion exhausted Him. He allowed His head to roll backward and rest against the cross which held Him in its death grip.

But Yakov noticed that Yeshua seemed more at peace somehow. Even in His dying, He carried the heavy responsibility of providing for His mother. He did not dismiss it or avoid it. Yeshua accepted it, fully and freely, and even from His cross, He had arranged for her care. It was settled now. His final earthly duty had been discharged and He could rest.

Again Yakov considered the past six months of his own life. He had taken no responsibility for his daughter beyond arranging for the services of her wetnurse. He had dismissed everything else from his mind but his own pain; he had even avoided seeing his child, touching her, and being touched by her in return. In his own life nothing was settled. In his own life he could never find rest.

Before him was a Man nailed to a Roman cross dying slowly and painfully yet He was a Man at peace. Before him was a woman who was watching her Son die the most terrible of deaths yet she was one with Him, a loving parent with her helpless Child. In that instant Yakov would have given everything he had if only he could have found that kind of peace, if only he could have known such a relationship with his own child.

Yakov turned away and permitted the tears to come. He understood at last what he had allowed his life to become. But he also thought that it was too late to do anything about it.

∞ **35** ∞

THE sweet smile of morning sunshine had faded as though it had never been. In its place the dark frown of storm clouds had come, gathering, tumbling, rolling, roiling, chasing each other across the Yerushalayim sky. The tops of the mountains which cradled the city were no longer visible as they lifted their heads above the clouds searching for the sunshine beyond the storm.

Atop Golgotha's hill, Yeshua had requested a drink. Miriam had filled a sponge with the only liquid available even though it happened to be vinegar, and Yohanan had placed the sponge on a reed and lifted it to His lips. Satisfied, He yielded to blessed oblivion.

David and Hannah still stood with young Micah, watching, waiting. *Watching and waiting for what?* Hannah wondered. *I don't want to see Him die,* Hannah anguished, *anymore than I wanted to see my abba dead.* But she knew she could not hide from His death any more than she had been able to hide from her abba's.

Behind them, Yosef ben Qayafa and Rabbi Levi wanted, needed, to see Yeshua's death. Even if the others had hurried away like frightened rabbits in the face of His mother and His friends, they would keep their vigil. They had to know their Enemy would trouble them no more.

The two exchanged angry glances with Naqdimon and Shimon. To Qayafa and the rabbi, they were traitors, pure and simple. Any friend of their Enemy was no friend of theirs. It was now clear to them that these men were indeed His friends and, unbeknownst to them, they had been for some time.

Naqdimon was oblivious to the daggers in their eyes. Instead he saw something else, something he recalled from that blessed night now three years past. He saw his Lord lifted up upon a cross of wood just as the serpent had been lifted up in the wilderness. *Is this what He meant?* Naqdimon asked himself, and with the asking came a thought too overwhelming to even contemplate. *Did He know this would happen all along? Did He allow it anyway?*

Tears burned Naqdimon's eyes as he struggled to remember all that Yeshua had said that night. *Just as the serpent was lifted up in the wilderness to provide salvation, so must the Son of man be lifted up.* A chill swept over Naqdimon, a chill of comprehension, a chill of reverence, a chill of awe. *He knew! And He walked this path anyway. This is the price, the price of my salvation!* Naqdimon buried his face in his hands and convulsed with sobs. *This is the price of my salvation, the price of salvation for all of us. And yet I didn't even care enough to share this most costly of gifts with my own son.*

Yakov stood to one side barely breathing. He thought of the little lamb he had pulled from its mother and held in his arms only a few hours before, its warmth flooding through him, its death a foregone conclusion. *Yeshua is like that lamb,* he thought. *He, too, is taken from a mother's loving care; He, too, will soon die; His blood, too, is shed on this very day when Pesach is about to begin. For the lamb there was a purpose; it was born to die. Is there any purpose to this? Was He born to die, too?* Yakov asked himself.

But these big questions were too much for Yakov's mind to answer. Instead, he wondered if he simply wanted to know that next year this time, there would be no overturning of his table, no scattering of his coins. But in reality he knew that wasn't the truth of it, not any more. For some reason he could not even comprehend, Yakov ben Meshullam now cared about another Human Being more than he cared about himself. He didn't know why but he knew he would remain a while longer, too.

A single Roman centurion and several of the men under his command also remained. They never looked at the crosses above them nor at the men they had nailed to them. Instead they crouched in the dirt and gambled for the clothes they had stripped from their victims. Each carried a flask which seemed to give him the courage to stay, to see the end of the awful spectacle they had created. In the days to come, each one would relive in his nightmares the duty he performed this day.

Hannah drew a startled breath when Yeshua suddenly groaned, then opened His eyes and surveyed the sky above Him. His lips began to move and Hannah strained to hear His voice. She needn't have. When it came, His voice was robust and resolute. His words formed His final prayer. "Father," He appealed so lovingly, "into Your hands I commit My spirit."

Some wept but none moved. None could.

For a moment even the earth seemed to hold its breath. Then all at once lightning breached the blackened sky in a ragged white bolt that sent shivers through all who saw it. Claps of thunder reverberated off the mountains. The rains came, too, as though Heaven itself wished to cleanse the earth of its unspeakable deed. They were heavy rains, angry rains swept by billowing winds. The rain washed across Yeshua's bloodied form and the winds showered His blood upon all who remained at His feet.

Qayafa looked at his once-beautiful tunic, now stained with the blood of the very Man he had so cunningly sent to His death because of his own jealousy, his own desire to secure his hold on political power. He screamed aloud but his cry was lost in the next crash of lightning, the next roll of thunder, the next wave of wind and rain. He fled in terror, stumbling, falling, rising, running. Rocks and small shrubs tore at his feet; branches ripped at his robe and scratched his face. It seemed nature itself was reaching out to exact its vengeance upon him. At the foot of the hill, he hurled himself into his litter but found no safety behind its curtains and no comfort in its pillows.

Rabbi Levi followed Qayafa, spattered with the blood of the hated Yeshua, cursing the Man's final revenge upon him. He fled down the hill, through the rainwashed streets of Yerushalayim to his home, too sickened by what he had seen and done to even care about his Seder dinner.

Yakov, too, found Yeshua's blood washing over him like the atoning blood of the little lamb, of all the little lambs, that would soon wash over the embankment outside the Temple and into the Kidron Brook below. Somehow he found in it a perfect symmetry.

Hannah rubbed her bloodied hands against her spattered robe trying to remove the stain that would not go away.

Little Micah was stunned into silence. He simply stared helplessly at his soiled garment.

As David led them from the hill he, too, saw the blood, His blood, upon his body and his clothes. Yet somehow he found some solace in it, as though he now carried Yeshua with him.

✿   ✿   ✿

Yosef ben Qayafa fled to the security of the Temple. He had touched death this day and death had touched him leaving its fearsome mark upon his body and upon his soul. But the Holy One had ordained that all were to eat the Paschal lamb, even those who for whatever reason would be considered unclean on ordinary days. On this extraordinary day Qayafa pronounced himself clean, clean enough to stand in the Holy Place, clean enough to offer the evening sacrifice, clean enough to begin the Pesach celebration.

In his private chamber where he always clothed himself in his priestly robes, he ordered Malluch to bring a basin of water. Then with a loud shriek, he ripped the bloody tunic from his body and with shaking hands tried to wash away the blood of Yeshua. But the dread which now enveloped him would not be washed away with any amount of water. He thought then of Pontius Pilate, the man he had manipulated into issuing the death sentence, the man who had tried to cleanse himself of Yeshua's blood, just as he was doing now. *Will either of us ever be free of Him, free of His blood?* he wondered. The answer crashed across his mind like the thunder on the hillside. *Never*, it said, but Yosef ben Qayafa did not want to hear it.

Qayafa clothed himself quickly in the ornate garments that only the high priest could wear. During the year these particularly beautiful priestly garments were kept by Pilate, held hostage to his determination to illustrate his control over the Temple. Qayafa hated him for bringing them with him each year at Pesach so that he could make a show of deigning to allow Qayafa to wear them. Yet once he had put them on, Qayafa tried to still his quaking heart with the reflection of himself in all his grandeur in the lookingglass. *Perhaps when I stand in the Holy Place*, he soothed himself. *Perhaps then the smile of the Holy One will rest upon me for what I have done in His behalf this day.*

Yosef ben Qayafa hurried to the Sanctuary where he had always known such pleasure in his position and such peace in his worthiness to hold it. Now, however, both deserted him.

Others came to the Temple for the Pesach service as well. Yakov had changed into his best garment and had taken his place in the Sanctuary alone. Rabbi Levi and his son were there, too. The rabbi was anxious to be in the serenity of the Sanctuary. He needed that tranquility now, perhaps more than he had ever needed it before. Between David and Elihu, Micah had entered wearing his father's robe for his welcome to the Temple as a son of the covenant. Today he was a man. Dinah, her daughter, her younger sons, Ruth and her children looked on proudly from the Gallery of the Women. She had thought they would never arrive in time but the Holy One had smiled upon them and they were here at last.

Out on the hillside, death's deadly work was not quite done. The wind and rain had ceased though an eerie darkness still shrouded the sky. Yeshua looked up steadfastly as though He could see past the dark, past the clouds, and into the very portals of Heaven. His mother and friends watched transfixed. Then in a strong voice, He shouted triumphantly for all the men of all the ages to hear, "It is finished!" Finally, as though He were willing His soul from His tortured body, He exhaled sharply. Messiah Yeshua was dead.

The shofar sounded, calling the people of the Holy One to His Temple. The musicians were in place. The Levites readied themselves to sing their songs of celebration and freedom. Yosef ben Qayafa faced the veil and began to raise his hands in the ancient prayer that would begin this special evening sacrifice as both Shabbat and Pesach began. But the words died on his lips. Suddenly lightning lit the western sky and thunder rolled, beginning as a low rumble and ending like the mighty crash of cymbals. The earth shook violently under his feet. There was a sound above him, a terrible tearing sound. Qayafa looked up and watched in horror as the ponderous veil of the Temple, the veil he himself had commissioned, was torn in half from its very top to its very bottom.

Yakov clutched his breast and wailed aloud. The beautiful veil that had felt the loving touch of Shoshana's gentle hands, was ruined, torn in two like a flimsy rag. But he knew it wasn't flimsy at all. Shoshana had told him. Yakov wondered what power could do that and he found he could not stand before that power. He fell silently to his knees.

Rabbi Levi stood in shocked silence. He did not speak. He did not move. He could not. It seemed the Holy One had already had the last word and Rabbi Levi feared what that word might mean.

David, Elihu, and Micah stood awestruck. Their eyes widened to great round circles, their mouths hung open, their faces paled. They had never seen anything like this; no one had. Elihu and Micah wondered what it could all mean. David didn't know why but he knew intuitively that it must have something to do with the death of Yeshua.

Beyond the veil, in the Holy of Holies, there was nothing, nothing but emptiness and a huge pale rock called the Foundation Stone upon which tradition held that the world had been founded. Though everyone liked to imagine it was still there, the Ark of the Covenant which represented the very presence of the Holy One to every Hebrew heart had long ago been lost when His people had been sent into seventy years of Babylonian captivity because of their idolatry. It had never been recovered. Though no one ever spoke of it, now everyone saw the truth. The Holy of Holies was empty, barren, deserted by the Holy One.

Yosef ben Qayafa stood still, staring, struck dumb. Qayafa now knew what he had never dared admit even to himself--his religion, his position, his very soul were as empty as the Holy of Holies. He thought of the words he had so recently mocked, the words Yeshua had spoken as He hung upon a Roman tree where Qayafa had surely placed Him, "My God, my God, why have You forsaken me?" It was now the silent cry of Qayafa's own heart as well.

✡   ✡   ✡

As the earth continued to shudder, in a lonely little cemetery just outside the walls of the holy city of Yerushalayim, rocks fell from their places and stones sealing some of the tombs were tossed aside. Small ossuaries slid from their niches and crashed to the floor spilling bones into the dirt. Linen-wrapped figures slipped from the stone slabs where they had been resting. But none would know of this until much later. And when they did, they would never be the same again.

Atop Golgotha, a Roman centurion also stood staring, his jaw slack, his mouth agape. He had witnessed the darkness, the lightning, the thunder, the shaking of the earth beneath his feet. He saw the blood which had now been sprinkled upon himself and his men. He had thrust his spear into the side of the One on the center cross to assure himself that He was dead. And he had even ordered the legs of the other two criminals broken in deference to the demand of the local authorities that they die before sundown. Then he had simply turned away, protecting his eyes from their torture, closing his ears to their cries as heavy cudgels shattered their shin bones and shortened their last moments of life. But as another bolt of lightning lit the sky and silhouetted the lifeless Figure on the central cross, the centurion, in a voice that shook with reverence, said to no one in particular, "Truly this Man was the Son of God!"

What the Roman centurion did not see, what he could never have understood even if he had seen it, occurred only a moment later. As the thief who had accepted Yeshua as his Lord gasped out his last breath, the soul of Yeshua Himself, fresh from His victory over the forces of evil in the netherworld, stopped in its upward path for one brief moment. Soul met soul and there was instant recognition. Then, with all the souls of all the righteous dead of all the ages following them, the two made their way beyond the pain, beyond the clouds, beyond the skies, to Paradise, just as Yeshua had promised.

෬ 36 ෨

SHABBAT was a somber day for all Yerushalayim. A chill mist still hung in the air. It
seemed the sun refused to shine upon a
world that had killed the Son of the very One
who had created it.

Word of what had taken place spread like wildfire in a
dry field. Some, particularly the Galileans, wept because
Yeshua now lay dead in the tomb of a wealthy local friend.
They had not even been permitted to take Him home to
Galilee one last time. Their only solace was that Yehuda,
who had betrayed Him for money with the kiss of a friend,
had finally understood the horror of his act and had carried out his own death sentence. Still, that did not bring
Yeshua back to them.

Others who did not know Yeshua wept for the great
desecration of the Temple. The holy veil had been torn
asunder opening the Holy of Holies to the view of mere
mortal men. No such violation of the Holy One's sacred
command had ever happened before. It stunned all who
learned of it and left them with a feeling of impending
doom. The Holy One was saying something but no one
knew what. All they knew of a certainty was that it could
not be good for them or their Temple or their city or their
nation. They cowered under His all-seeing eye.

✿   ✿   ✿

In the home of Benyamin ben Sefa, brother to Elihu the
stonecutter, David ben Asaph sat gazing through a win-

dow at the street outside. The shops were closed for Shabbat, the marketplace was deserted, no business was conducted and no one stirred. Sometimes he leaned back, closed reddened eyes, and seemed to be praying. Sometimes he simply stared into space, his eyes perhaps still fixed on a lonely hill outside the city.

Dinah had come earlier and tried to coax David to eat something, anything, but he would touch nothing. He was to be married to her daughter just before sundown on the morrow yet there was nothing in his aspect that even hinted of a happy bridegroom, nothing at all.

So it was with Hannah. Young Elisheba had been chattering about the wedding plans all morning. Her excitement should have been contagious but her cousin seemed immune. Hannah said nothing but it was clear her heart was not in any of the preparations.

Ruth and Dinah exchanged worried glances over Hannah's head. Neither had ever seen a more unhappy bride. Dinah knew the reason and had shared it with her sister in private whispers but still Dinah felt bound by the contract Itzak had made on the day before his death. She felt bound by love, too, for she had come to love David as her own son. They had never spoken of Yeshua. Religion was, after all, the business of men. But Dinah longed for him to abandon this conviction, especially now, in the face of Yeshua's death, so the two children she loved so much could be happily wed.

Micah was as silent as always. But his was a tender young heart where belief had just sprung up only to be trampled too soon. Now that heart had turned to stone. *I should have known better,* he chastised himself. *Messiah! I don't ever even want to hear the word again.*

Inside David's heart, the same words tried to snatch his faith away as well.

✿   ✿   ✿

Meshullam had slept well and awakened early. He reasoned that while he could not conduct business on Shabbat, nowhere was it written that he could not think about it. This Pesach had been the most profitable ever, leaving him so fatigued that he had not even attended the evening sacrifice. Yakov had been expected to come to his home afterward to share the Seder with the family. Instead Yakov had come to tell them the awful tale of what had happened to the veil his own Shoshana had helped to sew. Yakov had wept as he spoke of it but Meshullam hadn't wept and he wasn't weeping now. He knew people would feel unsettled, bewildered, troubled by it all. And when people felt that way, they made many more than the usual number of sacrifices to get on the good side of the Holy One. He had seen it often before. It seemed everyone got religion in a crisis. Meshullam chuckled, then fled from his bed as though it were on fire and settled into a comfortable chair where he could think about the number of animals he would order in the morning to prepare for the expected increased demand.

On the other side of the courtyard, Yakov hadn't been able to sleep and he hadn't been able to stop crying either. Devorah was becoming increasingly alarmed. After a while she even began to wonder if she and the baby were safe in the same house with Yakov who paced and cried, mumbled and cried, and then cried some more.

"It was all I had left of her," he kept saying. "As long as it was there I could feel close to her for I knew her hands had touched it. Now it, too, is gone. Now what am I to do?"

Devorah had no idea what "it" was. She had no idea of any of the events of the day before. No one had bothered to tell her. She was after all just the hired help and, as such, was not counted worthy of such confidences. She simply cared for Mara just as she always did and each time Yakov paced toward her, she froze, wondering what might come next.

Yakov's eyes found her, looked at her without really seeing, and stared off into space. "All of this has something to do with Yeshua. I know it. It all has something to do with Him."

Yakov paced away and Devorah relaxed. *Yeshua?* she asked herself, recalling another time, another place, another conversation. *Isn't He the One my husband once mentioned?*

✡   ✡   ✡

Naqdimon was exhausted. For the past two nights he had had no sleep. Now everything blended into a long torturous blur. The endless night and half a day of trials, the accusations, the verdicts, the sentence, all seemed like a nightmare where justice was simply a great Leviathan who devoured the innocent. The vision of Yeshua suspended between empty earth and savage sky was before him still. So was the vision of Yeshua's lifeless body being lowered into the waiting arms of himself, Yohanan, and dear Miriam. He had helped to wash away the blood, to cover the ugly wounds with clean white strips of linen, to hold the stench of death at bay with the fragrant spices provided by Yosef, an Arimathean who was both a member of the Sanhedrin and another secret disciple of Yeshua. Then they had all carried the shrouded figure to Yosef's tomb near the Garden of Gethsemane. He wondered if he would ever be able to erase the ghastly pictures from his mind. Then Naqdimon remembered the veil, the shock of hearing that it had been torn in two. At first he had been as terrified as all the others. Now though, as he thought about it, it seemed to be the only thing that had taken place yesterday that made any sense. It was as if the Holy One was so enraged by what had been done to His Son that He simply tore through the Temple as one might tear a flawed leaf from a scroll.

Even as Naqdimon lay in his bed watching through heavily-lidded eyes as the sky lightened outside his window, he still could not help but wonder. *Why did the Holy One permit this travesty? Why, once His Son was lifted up, didn't His powerful hand stop it? Why did it have to end in death? Why could it not have ended in life? If Yeshua really was Messiah and I know that He was, how could this be the end of it all?*

Naqdimon's questions chased each other around his restless brain but he was far too tired to stop them in their endless orbit. Neither did he have any answers for them. He finally placed a wrinkled hand on either side of his pounding head, groaned miserably, and turned from the light that hurt his aching eyes. *What was it Yeshua said about the light? If only I could remember ... .*

✡   ✡   ✡

In the home of Yosef ben Qayafa, the noble high priest remained in his great ivory bed embellished in the Greek key design with the cover pulled tightly around him. He had not closed his eyes all night either. Instead, he had thought of his childhood terrors, when he had been afraid to set a foot on the floor certain that some nameless faceless devil that lurked beneath his bedstead was ready to lunge at his bare ankle and drag him helpless to the fires of Gehenna for that was what the children of the Pharisees had told him would happen to a Sadducee such as himself. Somehow he felt that same terror today. He shivered against the morning chill and drew his cover closer.

I should be happy, he told himself. *I've won the victory for which I long labored! He's dead! Yeshua ben Yosef is dead! And I did it! Me, Yosef ben Qayafa! I hanged Him on that Roman tree as surely as if I had driven the nails myself. Why is there so little satisfaction in my triumph? Why could I not even partake of the Seder? Why have I no appetite even now?*

He knew he had duties to perform, but even more than he had never wanted to leave his bed to face the demons of his youth, he did not now want to walk into the Sanctuary to face the emptiness that lay beyond the veil. In the eye of his troubled mind, he could see it still, torn from top to bottom as though two huge hands had ripped it apart. Whose hands? he wondered. He could think of only One who had such great power. He didn't even want to contemplate what it might mean if His were the hands which had done this terrible thing to the veil and to the Temple and to him.

Then Qayafa thought of his own hands, his arms, his face, his head. *Why do they still feel so ... so ... so marked? Why did the blood of that cursed Man have to splatter me?*

Outside Qayafa's sleeping chamber, Malluch awaited his master's call. The young man's crimson eyes gave mute testimony to a sleepless night spent mourning his Messiah. He could not understand why the Holy One had allowed his master to do this terrible thing. Yet even now, he could only pity his master, not hate him. Malluch knew something that Qayafa was only beginning to comprehend. Only torment awaits the man who would raise his hand against the Holy One's Anointed.

✡   ✡   ✡

Rabbi Levi paced restlessly. Naomi had called him just as she always did, inviting him to share the morning meal with Aaron and the boys but he hadn't gone. He knew he should eat. Though he had sat at the Seder table, while little Ishi asked all the appropriate questions about the first Pesach and smiled as he rattled off the usual replies, he had eaten nothing. It seemed that somehow the blood of that first lamb had mingled in his mind with the blood of the hated Yeshua. He told himself it was only his normal reaction to witnessing the bloody spectacle of crucifixion but he knew it was more than that. When at last he joined the family, his mind was elsewhere.

"Did you see it?" he asked Aaron for perhaps the tenth time since the previous evening.

"Yes, Abba, I saw it," Aaron responded yet again. "It was terrible, Abba, but it will soon be replaced by another veil and all will be well."

Rabbi Levi wondered if all would ever be well again. He wandered away in a daze. He wanted to say the Shema just as he had every morning and evening of his life but suddenly he realized that he couldn't remember the words.

✡   ✡   ✡

The morning mist clung heavily to the Mount of Olives and the tiny town of Bethany. Shimon and Eleazar continually asked themselves the same question. *He saved us. Why could He not save Himself?*

Miriam and Martha cried quietly as they continued their kitchen duties. They wondered why they bothered; no one had any appetite for food anyway.

Sleep had not come to any of them until well after the first light should have brightened the sky. After only a couple of hours of restful forgetfulness, they had awakened again, each wondering if the events of the day before had been nothing more than some horrible bad dream, then reliving the horrible bad dream when they realized that it was all too real.

✡   ✡   ✡

In a small rented chamber above an inn in Yerushalayim, another Miriam finally lay asleep, her eyes still swollen with her weeping. After she had helped Naqdimon and Yohanan bathe and wrap the broken body of her Son, after she had seen it laid lovingly into the princely tomb that belonged to the Arimathean called Yosef, she, too, had kept the long night vigil. Yohanan had stayed with her through the endless dark night. He had taken care of her just as a son would care for a mother, just as Yeshua had asked him to do. But Yohanan was not her son. Yeshua was. Now He was gone forever just as her husband, Yosef, was gone. Now she was truly alone.

Miriam had wept well into the early morning hours while Yohanan cradled her head on his shoulder and whispered words of reassurance she knew he did not feel. All the time, her heart kept screaming, *What will I do without Him? I'm not sure I want to go on. Oh, my Son, my Son, my precious Son, Yeshua! I do not want to live in a world without You.*

⋈ 37 ⋇

BY the next morning, the sunshine had returned, rising languidly in a shimmering Yerushalayim sky. At least the sun was back outside Hannah's window. But there was no sunshine in Hannah's heart. This was the awful day she had hoped would never come, the day she would be forced into marriage with a man whom she loved but with whom she did not share the same beliefs. That was her first conscious thought when she opened her eyes and just as soon as she thought of it, she immediately closed them again to shut out the light of a new day, a day she still could not face. She pretended to be asleep long after she heard the household of her aunt and uncle stirring to life and kept up the pretense until her mother came and gently stroked her hair. Then she stretched and yawned and pretended she had just awakened.

Dinah smiled down at her drowsy daughter. "The Holy One has blessed you with a perfect day," she whispered. "Rise now. There is still much to do."

Hannah turned away in tears. "Ammah, I cannot do it. Please do not force me."

Dinah understood but she knew she had to remain firm. Her husband had sealed the bargain. Now his good name and the reputation of her family required that it be honored. And she knew David was a kind and caring man, just the kind of caring man she wanted for her only daughter. She knew he loved Hannah and would provide well for her. She also knew that he would treat her gently, not as those who considered their wives mere possessions,

259

rather like a prolific cow, and dealt with them in about the same way. But in her heart, Dinah also understood Hannah's feelings; she had felt the same way about this marriage at first. And she did not want to be like so many parents who forced unwilling daughters to marry old men or ugly men or men their daughters simply loathed just to rid themselves of girls with some impediment or to gain some personal or business advantage.

"My daughter, this should be the happiest day of your life, truly the beginning of your life. And David is any mother's dream for her daughter. Tell me why you are so unhappy." Dinah still hoped she might yet be able to settle her daughter's doubts.

Hannah threw herself into her mother's waiting arms. "Oh, Ammah, it is what he believes. He does not worship the Holy One alone. He truly believes Yeshua was Messiah. The great elders have found Yeshua to be false and have executed Him. I do not want to be joined to a heretic who believes in Him still. Please do not force me."

Dinah held her daughter for a long time. Hannah could hear the beating of her mother's heart, strong and steady but faster than usual. When Dinah responded, it was with mixed emotions and anguished soul. "My child, I have no choice. I am bound by your father's contract. There is only one person who can give you the release you seek. That is David himself."

Hannah drew back and searched her mother's face. Was her mother saying all hope was lost or was she offering her daughter a way out? Hannah sprang from the bed and began to bathe and dress quickly.

"Is he here, Ammah?" she demanded. "I will speak to him this very minute. I will tell him this is hopeless. I will prove to him that he should not be joined to me, not now, not ever."

Hannah's words had tripped over one another so rapidly that Dinah had had no opportunity to answer. When Hannah finally took a breath, she did. "Calm yourself,

Child," she began. "He left very early to attend the morning sacrifice. He did not look well. I trust some time in the presence of the Holy One will set all things right."

Hannah made a sour face, then continued with her preparations a bit more slowly. "I want to know as soon as he returns, the very moment. Ammah, promise me you will tell me the moment he returns."

Dinah sighed and her sigh carried a world of feelings in it. *Have we come so far just to have it end like this?* she wondered though she said nothing. *What would Itzak do?* she asked herself though she already knew the answer to that question even though she did not want to know it. "Yes, my child. I will send Elisheba to fetch you as soon as he arrives," she said finally. "But, Hannah, take careful thought about what you do. Do you not realize that even if he were willing to release you, it would mean a divorce? *A divorce*, Hannah! Never has there been a divorce in our family. *Never!*"

Hannah stopped for a moment, then nodded, her young face serious.

"Whatever happens today will change your life forever," Dinah concluded. Her words were serious, too, just as she meant them to be, just as serious as the decisions her only daughter was preparing to make.

"Yes, Ammah, I know it will," Hannah tossed over her shoulder as she brushed her long golden tresses. "I only hope I can make it change my life for the better."

"I pray to the Holy One that it will be so, my child," Dinah said soothingly. "But since the procession is to start just before sundown, we must soon begin to get you dressed."

Hannah blanched. *Dressed for a wedding I have no intention of attending?* Then she smiled a mischievous smile. "But, Ammah, I have no wedding attire. So there cannot possibly be a wedding, now can there?"

Dinah retrieved the bundle Hannah had carried all the way from Capernaum. She removed the remaining clothing until she reached the garment she sought, then lifted it almost reverently. Her hands smoothed the beautiful fabric. "It was mine, Hannah, the very one I wore the day I became your abba's bride. Now it is you who will wear it."

"No," Hannah pouted. "I do not wish to be a bride, not now, and not to David."

"Please, Hannah," Dinah pleaded. "Look at it. I have embroidered it just for you."

Hannah balked. "Ammah, I cannot. I must talk to David as soon as he returns."

Dinah knew any further argument was pointless. Without Itzak to intervene, two stubborn headstrong young people would have to sort things out for themselves. But if David refused to release Hannah from the contract Itzak had made with him, she knew she would have to insist that Hannah abide by it and that knowledge sickened her.

⚝ 38 ⚝

YAKOV tossed and turned restlessly before his eyes opened with a start. At first he did not know where he was. He had been dreaming and somehow in his dream, the veil had been torn in two to reveal Yeshua hanging upon a Roman cross in the Holy of Holies. As soon as he realized he was not in the Temple Sanctuary but safe in his own bed, he rubbed the sleep from his eyes, slid his feet to the floor, and drew his robe around him.

Yakov still did not know what it all meant but it was the first day of the week and he couldn't permit the terrors of the past two days to haunt him forever. He had resolved to try to put them behind him and go on.

The old veil was gone. There would be a new one and, even though Shoshana would never have touched it, even though it would not contain her careful stitches, life would go on and Yakov meant to go on with it.

As soon as he left his bedchamber, he heard Devorah's soft voice singing to Mara, soothing her, enchanting her. It enchanted Yakov, too. She sang a psalm of a little lamb that trusted in its Shepherd and was safe in the Holy One's arms even in the face of death.

Yakov thought of the little lamb he had held only a few days before. *Did it trust me that way?* he wondered. *And when the knife was pressed to its throat, did it feel safe in the arms of the Holy One, too? Or did it just wonder why? Yakov thought again of Yeshua. Did He trust the Holy One at the end? At the last did He feel safe in the Holy One's arms?*

Just as quickly, he thought again of Shoshana. Somehow he could still see the blood and the agony on her beautiful young face. *She trusted me and I planted within her the seed that would kill her. At the end did she feel safe? Were the arms of the Holy One there for her?* He remembered her final words just before she had closed her eyes in death, "I see You. I see Your light. I am coming, Father." Yakov knew her own father still lived. *Was it the outstretched arms of the Holy One she saw in that last moment?* He longed to believe that it was.

Yakov shook his head to clear his mind. He had to get on with his life. He knew if he didn't, if he continued on in his grief and his remembrances, it would ultimately destroy him. It almost had already.

As he entered the dining chamber, Devorah looked up, then smiled when she saw that Yakov's countenance was much improved over the dark aspect of the day before. In her arms Mara responded to her smile and smiled back. "You look well, my lord," Devorah said. "I trust you slept well."

"Yes, yes," he answered almost gruffly. He didn't know what to say. He couldn't share his troubling dreams with a mere employee. Oh, but he so wanted to do exactly that. She seemed so warm, so welcoming. And he was so alone, so needy. It was all that he could do to stop himself from ... from ... from what? From running to her and pouring out all of his frustrations and failures and fears and fantasies? From taking her into his arms just to feel the warmth, the touch of another human being? There was something about her that spoke to his heart but Yakov wouldn't allow his heart to listen, not then, maybe not ever.

He turned and began to assemble the dried fruit, salted fish, and unleavened bread he would take with him to the court of the Temple for his early meal. It was going to be a busy day. He could sense it. He had decided to be early, to make up in some small measure for the way he had neglected his father and his business over the past week. He had to get back to work. For generations, his family had offered an important service to the people of the Holy One from all over the world. Whatever his own unanswered questions might be, he had an obligation, a duty, a responsibility to continue to offer that service. It was his heritage, his birthright. At least so he kept telling himself.

When he had finished packing the same small basket Shoshana had always carried, he noticed his sandals sitting in their usual place beside the door and started to reach for them. In that instant he knew this was not a path he could continue to walk. He did not know where these sandals would take him but he did know they would not take him back to the Temple, back to the deceit and the dishonesty. "Oh, what is the use? What is the use of any of it?" he said aloud to himself more than to anyone else.

Mara began to demand her usual morning feeding, crowding out her father's voice. "My lord?" Devorah questioned. "Did you speak? Forgive me. I could not hear you."

Yakov turned to Devorah and allowed his eyes to rest on her womanly shape. His expression softened. "It is nothing. I guess I was simply thinking aloud. No matter."

He couldn't go. He couldn't stay. He stood still staring at Devorah until she began to wonder if he was as well as she had first believed.

"My lord," she whispered finally, "are you well? Is there something I can do for you?"

Yakov was startled back to reality by her voice. "Yes, yes, Devorah, there is something you can do. If my father comes by looking for me, tell him I am not well and I must keep to my bed. Will you do that for me, Devorah?" His desperate tone made his request sound as if it were the most important one he had ever made of her.

"Yes, my lord, I will do as you ask," Devorah agreed though she was clearly puzzled. "Are you ill? May I call someone to attend you, Ephraim? Rachel perhaps?"

"Just tell him," Yakov repeated more firmly than he had

meant it to sound. "Just tell him," he repeated more softly this time.

"I shall, my lord," Devorah promised.

Yakov left the small basket exactly where it sat, turned, and retreated to the security of his bedchamber leaving Devorah baffled and Mara even more insistent on being fed.

✿   ✿   ✿

Across their common courtyard, Meshullam closed his door behind him, shuffled across the court, through the door of the gate, and disappeared in the direction of the Temple just as he had nearly every day of his life. As he walked, his plans took shape in his mind as an unconscious smile took shape above his beard. He would not be placing the order for stock as he had at first intended. No. Over the long Shabbat he had decided on an even better plan. *Business will be good, good for Yakov,* he promised himself. *Wait until I tell Yakov!* He was certain that his son would be at the stalls to greet him when he arrived. After all, this was the first day of the new week and business must come before anything else.

Meshullam chuckled to himself as he made his way past the familiar landmarks of the Upper City. *Wait until I tell Yakov what I have decided! Wait until I tell him that the press of business is too much for a man of my advanced years! This Pesach tired me far too greatly. Wait until I tell him that I have finally decided to place the entire business in his hands and take my ease! That should restore his former good spirits.* Meshullam chucked again at the very prospect.

✿   ✿   ✿

When Meshullam did not find his son waiting for him at the stalls, he looked dismayed, then concerned. He ordered his servants to see to the few customers who had gathered and returned the way he had come. As he entered his courtyard, he moved purposefully toward the home of his firstborn son. *This has gone far enough,* he thought. *Yakov must assume his responsibilities. He must assume even greater responsibilities now that the business is to be his.*

Devorah admitted the old man to the kitchen, Mara in her arms. Meshullam did not even so much as look at his granddaughter. *So like his son,* Devorah thought.

"Where is he? Where is my son? I must speak with him immediately," Meshullam demanded.

"My lord is not well," Devorah answered as she had been instructed.

But Meshullam would not be refused. He brushed past Devorah startling the child in her arms. Mara's big blue eyes grew even larger with fear and she started to cry as she looked up into Devorah's tense face. "Where is he?" Meshullam interrogated again but did not wait for an answer. Instead he proceeded directly to his son's sleeping chamber and found him pacing nervously.

"My son, are you ill?" Meshullam asked.

Yakov turned toward his father, his young face anguished as he wrestled with the questions that tormented him. At first he did not know what answer to give. In the end, he decided to simply tell the truth. "In my body, Abba, no. I am not sick in body."

Meshullam closed the distance between them and placed a comforting arm around his son's shoulders. "Then what is it that keeps you from your work, from your business, from your family day after day?"

Yakov pulled away and began pacing again. His hands grasped either side of his head. "I do not know," he admitted. "All I know is that I can do it no longer."

"Do what?" Meshullam queried. "What is it that you cannot do any longer?"

"I cannot be a part of it, Abba. I cannot be a part of the deceit and deception."

"But my son," Meshullam countered. "It is not deceit and deception. It is merely good business. It is all a part of being a good salesman."

Yakov stopped and looked appraisingly at his father. "You have not taught me to be a good salesman, Abba. You have taught me to steal."

"Steal?" the old man repeated, shocked at his son's accusation. "Haven't the fathers taught us that he who does not teach his son a trade teaches him to steal? I have simply taught you a trade, a good trade, a very necessary trade, a trade that provides well for you."

Having once begun, Yakov knew that he could not back away from the truth he knew in his heart. "You have taught me to be a thief, Abba. And I cannot be a thief any longer."

The reality of his son's words finally found a resting place in Meshullam's mind. He stammered his reply. "But ... but ... Yakov ... you do not understand. I came here today ... I wanted to tell you ... I have decided ... . Yakov, the business is to be yours."

Yakov gave his father a quizzical stare. Meshullam nodded to assure his son that he had not misunderstood. Yakov turned away in the futility of it all. He had waited for this day for years. Now that it had finally come, it served only to further strengthen his resolve. "If the business is truly to be mine, then I will run it honestly," he said flatly.

"And you will starve," Meshullam responded just as flatly.

"That may be," Yakov agreed. "But better to starve than to steal. Yet I do not believe I will starve, Abba. I believe the Holy One still does not forsake the righteous nor allow his seed to beg for bread. Did the fathers not teach us that as well?"

Meshullam had no answer. He had worked all his life just as his father had before him and always with the same goal, to establish a business he could proudly pass on to his firstborn son. Now it seemed all of his labor had turned to ashes. His son was refusing the greatest gift he had to give, the only gift he had to give. And he couldn't begin to understand why. He left the room, the house, the courtyard, the street, and fled toward the Temple, toward the stalls, toward the only thing he could understand, toward his business. His mind was numb to the people he passed, numb to the landmarks he passed, numb to everything but the words of his son that still rang in his ears.

Yakov remained exactly where he stood. *What have I done?* he asked himself over and over again. And he found that he did not understand it all any better than his father had.

ভ 39 ৶

NAQDIMON woke to the noise of a rather persistent pounding on the door of his home. As he maneuvered his ample girth to the edge of the bed he shared with Sarah, a light tapping on the bedchamber door told him one of their servants sought his attention.

"Enter," Naqdimon instructed sleepily. He knew only some dire crisis would explain such a rude introduction to the new day. After all that had happened, one crisis more or less hardly mattered. He would simply deal with this one just as he had dealt with everything else.

The door opened just a crack. Keturah, a young servant girl, stuck her head into the opening, her eyes downcast. "There is a young man to see you, my lord. He would not give his name but he said you know him and he must see you immediately."

"Is he from the Temple, from the council?" asked Naqdimon, clearly puzzled.

"No, my lord. I think not. At least he is not anyone I recognize."

"Tell him to return later then, please," Naqdimon instructed as he settled back into his bed with the hope of allowing his aged body to fully come awake more slowly just as he usually did.

The girl disappeared. Naqdimon had barely settled down when she began tapping again.

"Enter," Naqdimon repeated, his irritation evident in his voice.

"Forgive me, my lord," the child began. "He says he

will not leave until he speaks to you. He is most insistent." Her voice begged for assistance to remove this unwelcome visitor.

Naqdimon sighed his acceptance of the inevitable. "Tell him I will be along shortly," he directed.

She brightened immediately, relieved that her employer would deal with the mysterious visitor. "Yes, my lord," she returned happily.

Sarah roused long enough to ask, "What is it, my husband?"

"I have no idea who it could be at this early hour," Naqdimon replied. "But I suppose there is no way to rid our home of this impertinent young man except to see what he wants."

He smiled down at his sleepy wife. To his eyes, she was still as beautiful as the day he had first spied her entering the Court of the Women with her mother and asked his father who she was. His father had made a few discreet inquiries and discovered that she was the very marriage-able daughter of a very wealthy landowner east of the river. Then he had done even more; he had arranged for the young woman in question to become his son's bride.

Sarah looked at her husband with a mock frown as her soft brown eyes twinkled with mischief. "Have I still the power to keep you to your bed even when another seeks you?" she teased, anxious to call him back from the deep darkness that had descended over him the past few days.

"Always, my dear wife," he teased tolerantly. "Always. But I suppose I must see to our guest. Then perhaps I can return to you."

"I shall await your pleasure, my lord," she said grandly, pretending seriousness but unmasked by her smile. As he opened the door, he turned, winked at her, and left the chamber.

✿   ✿   ✿

As Naqdimon entered the main chamber of his home, his eyebrows jumped in shock. He had never expected him. He had never come here before, careful to protect Naqdimon's secret. It was Yohanan. And after all that had happened, Yohanan was smiling.

Naqdimon greeted Yohanan warmly. "My son, you honor my house. Come, sit," he said as he motioned toward one of the upholstered couches along the walls. He spied his servant hiding in the shadows. "Keturah, bring something to refresh our guest," he ordered. "Now, Yohanan, tell me what you need of me, my son, and you shall have it."

Yohanan took a seat, beaming. "I need nothing, my friend. I have come to give you news, the best news I could ever bring. He is risen! Yeshua is risen!" Yohanan fairly shouted. "He is alive."

Naqdimon's face revealed the surprise and concern he felt for his young guest. *Has the boy taken leave of his senses? Has it all been too much for him?* he wondered.

Yohanan read his expression and continued. "It is true, dear friend!" Yohanan assured. "I have seen the empty tomb with my own eyes and I know that it is true!"

Naqdimon's mind went through a list of all of the things which might have happened. The list did not include even the suggestion of resurrection. He tried to calm the young man. "Yohanan, get hold of yourself. Let us consider the other possibilities."

"There are no other possibilities. Yeshua is risen," Yohanan insisted. "He once said He would rebuild the Temple in three days but none of us realized He meant the Temple of His own body."

Naqdimon pressed on. "I know that some council members feared His body might be stolen to make it appear as though He had risen. Perhaps that is what has happened. Or perhaps Qayafa had His body moved to prevent its removal. It could even be that some of the Galileans took Him away so that He could be buried at home. It is even possible thieves stole His body away hoping that valuables might be hidden among the wrappings. It happens all to frequently I am told."

Yohanan took the old man's hands in his own as their eyes met. "My friend, there might be many explanations for the empty tomb if that were all. But that is not all. Some of the women, my own mother among them, came early to the sepulchre to complete the preparation of His body which had been interrupted by the beginning of Shabbat. The stone was rolled away, the tomb was empty, and there were angels who told them He is risen. One even saw Him in the little garden surrounding the tombs. There can be only one explanation for all of these things. Our Lord lives!"

Naqdimon could think of no response to such a claim. It was beyond comprehension, beyond all reason. To Naqdimon, it seemed insane. "My son, you must calm yourself and return to reality no matter how difficult that may be just now. We both saw Him hanged upon the tree. We both saw Him die. We even held His lifeless body in our arms. And we bathed Him and wrapped Him and buried Him. This is reality, Yohanan, not angels, not a figure in a garden in the dim light of dawn."

"Please hear me, my friend," Yohanan pressed. "I know what you feel. I felt these same things when I went with Shimon to see for myself the things we had been told. I thought the women who had summoned us were merely hysterical or that the cold grey shadows of dawn had given them false visions. But I was there. I saw it with my own eyes."

"What did you see, my son, that could possibly prove to you that Yeshua lives? Did you see Him?"

"No," Yohanan admitted. "I was too late to see Him. He had already departed by the time I arrived."

"There, you see," Naqdimon asserted confidently. "You saw nothing but an empty tomb, my son. Qayafa may indeed have moved Him to another crypt unknown to us."

Yohanan smiled. He had saved the best for last and he

couldn't wait to tell it. "I saw more than that, my friend. I saw the very wrappings in which we had bound Him. I saw them laying in place, not even disturbed, as though He had simply vanished out of them. And I saw the napkin which had covered His face lying right there beside them, neatly folded as though He had simply removed it, folded it, and laid it down."

Naqdimon's face registered his bewilderment.

Yohanan continued forcefully. "If our exalted high priest had His body moved, if my fellow Galileans had taken it north for burial, if thieves had made off with it in the night, how did they get Him out of the wrappings without disturbing a single strip? And why would they have taken His body without the wrappings in the first place?"

These were questions Naqdimon could not answer, not with any of the rationalizations which had come to his mind. He sat speechless, not knowing what to think, what to trust, what to believe. But somewhere deep within his heart of hearts, Naqdimon allowed a tiny seed of hope to spring to new life.

⚂ 40 ⚃

THE torn veil of the Temple Sanctuary had been drawn together so that the empty interior of the Holy of Holies could not be seen, just as the Holy One had commanded. It would remain there until another could be prepared to take its place. It was before this veil that Yosef ben Qayafa offered his morning prayer, his hands upraised, his head down, his eyes closed. He still could not bear to look at it, to remember what had happened to it, to ponder what it all might mean.

After the morning sacrifice, Malluch summoned Qayafa to his private chamber where the commander of the Temple guard, Gershon ben Benaiah, waited for him, pacing nervously. As Qayafa entered, the muscular young officer removed his helmet and bowed slightly. "My lord, I have brought news, very distressing news I fear," Gershon began.

Qayafa's face stiffened. He did not need to hear any further bad news. The desecration of the Temple veil had been enough. Worse, he knew this officer had been assigned to guard Yeshua's tomb against a robbery by His followers. Qayafa had taken no chances. He had assigned guards to watch the sepulchre day and night lest His body be stolen away. "Tell me," he said curtly.

"It happened early this morning just as the sun started to rise," Gershon began.

"What happened?" Qayafa asked, impatient as ever with endless stories that seemed to go nowhere.

Gershon floundered for words. He knew how what he

was about to say would sound, especially to a Sadducee. Yet there was nothing else to do but tell it just as it had occurred. "My lord, something happened out there, something all of my men and I witnessed, something we can't explain."

"Perhaps I can explain it to you." Qayafa's tone had grown haughty, patronizing.

"It began with the shaking of the earth. You must have felt it." He searched his superior's face for some light of recognition. Finding none, he continued. "There was a bright light and when I looked up, the stone had moved away from the entrance to the tomb and a figure like an angel of the Holy One Himself was sitting upon it. He shone like nothing I have ever seen and his robes shone like ... like the sun itself. Such fear came upon us all that we fell paralyzed to the earth and there we remained until just before I came to you."

"His body. What of His body?" Qayafa interrogated brusquely, grasping the startled officer's robe in both of his hands. "Tell me what happened to His body," he insisted loudly.

Gershon shrunk back, fearful of incurring one of Qayafa's well-known rages. "When I arose from the earth, my lord, it was gone."

"Gone? Gone where? Gone how? Did you see them take it? Have you searched?" The questions tumbled over each other giving Gershon no opportunity to answer. "Tell me, you incompetent fool," Qayafa shouted.

Gershon shrunk back even further into the shadows. "We saw no one but the angel, my lord. He took nothing. We know not what became of the body." When he saw the anger exploding in Qayafa's eyes, he added, "Forgive us, my lord. We simply could do nothing against an angel."

"Angels!" Qayafa shrieked at the speechless officer. "Angels and earthquakes!" He lurched uncontrollably about the chamber, upsetting a table, knocking an inkstand to the floor, breaking the bowl which held his fruit as Malluch followed attempting to set things right.

"You fool!" Qayafa shouted at the speechless officer. "Do you not know what you have done? So there was an earthquake which dislodged the stone from its place and you and your men were so frightened that you took flight like birds thus giving His followers the very chance they needed to steal away His body. Is that not what really happened?" Qayafa now stood toe-to-toe with his terrified officer, redfaced, screaming accusations at him.

"Not so, my lord. It was as I said. We did not once leave our post. We were unable to move even if we had wanted to do so. There was an angel ... ."

Qayafa raised his hands skyward as though he were petitioning for heavenly aid and shrieked at the top of his voice. "An angel ... an angel. You persist in this fantasy, you insolent fool?"

"It is no fantasy, my lord. It is the truth. There was an angel who ... "

"Speak to me no more of angels, you fool," Qayafa interrupted, his rage only increasing. "I believe in no angels. You and your lazy frightened men have allowed them to steal away His body. Now they will claim that He has risen and we will have no way to prove them liars. The end of this matter will be worse than the beginning. Our very nation ... my very priesthood are at stake. Do you not see that, you idiot?"

Gershon said nothing. Any words which came to his mind would only have inflamed the high priest even more and he was not certain he could withstand any further attacks. He had been through enough for one morning.

The man's silence only served to further infuriate Qayafa. "Get out of my sight, you fool. You and your men will face charges for the jeopardy in which you have placed us all. I will do to you exactly what I did to Him. I swear it! I swear it! I will see you all dead for this!"

Gershon could still hear him shouting as he hurried away, fearing for his job, fearing for his freedom, fearing for his very life. He promised himself that he would conduct the most complete search ever undertaken. If there was a body to be found, he and his men would find it. There seemed to be no other way to save them now.

Qayafa raged on, bringing everyone within earshot to attention, frightening the women and children who had not yet left the courts. When his fury was finally spent and his throat hoarse, he slumped into a chair and wept aloud, his hands covering his face as if to shut out the terrible news he had just received.

"Angels!" he whispered to himself. "Angels and earthquakes and disappearing bodies! Of all the nonsense!" He went on and on to no one but himself. "Now they will say He has risen and I will never be able to prove they are wrong."

Suddenly Qayafa grew quiet and still. His hands fell limp in his lap. His eyes widened in response to an idea that was just too shocking even to entertain. "They are wrong, are they not?" he asked himself. The Sadducee within him was not certain that he even wanted to know the answer to that question. *Will I never be free of the blood of that cursed Man?* he asked himself and then he agonized because he did not want to know the answer to that question either.

Malluch had seen and heard everything. His heart swelled with the certain knowledge that his true Lord had indeed risen. His hand flew to his ear. *He is risen, restored,* he assured himself, *just as He restored me.*

cs 41 so

ABBI Levi made his way with slow shuffling gait across the Temple court at the close of the morning sacrifice. Suddenly he stopped and turned in the direction of the most awful shouting he had ever heard in this place, knowing something appalling had surely happened.

Others near the old rabbi stopped what they were doing, too, and stood staring in the direction of the outburst. No one spoke. No one moved. No one knew what to do so no one did anything.

A door swung open making the shouting even louder for one terrifying moment. A tall figure quickly slipped past the door and fled down the steps and across the court. *It is the captain of the guard,* Rabbi Levi said to himself, *the very young man who once ordered me from Qayafa's home.* The rabbi smiled inwardly. *I wonder how he likes being thrust from the high priest's presence?*

Just then the young man swept by him. Rabbi Levi turned and called after him, "My son, stop, stop! I must speak with you."

Gershon hesitated. "What is it, old man? I have business to do this day, the high priest's business."

Rabbi Levi struggled to approach quickly before the young man could get away. "Patience for an old man, my son," he begged breathlessly as he reached the captain's side. "What has happened? What has made our lord so angry? Perhaps I may be of service to him."

"There is nothing you can do," Gershon insisted, his irritation apparent in his voice. "Unless you know what has happened to that body."

"A body? Whose body?" the rabbi demanded.

"The body of the One they crucified. Do you know where it is?" he asked sarcastically.

Rabbi Levi's eyes widened in terror. "Yeshua? Yeshua's body? What has happened to it?"

"Yes, Yeshua's body," Gershon confirmed. "It is gone, missing, and unless I can find it, I may soon be missing, too. So, old man, what can you do to help?"

Rabbi Levi exhaled sharply. He suddenly seemed smaller, shrunken, even more frail than before. "No! That cannot be! It cannot be missing," he anguished. "It cannot be missing."

"Of a certainty, it is missing. I saw the empty tomb myself," Gershon replied ruefully.

"You must find it," Rabbi Levi insisted, clutching the man's arm in desperation. "They must have taken it."

"Who?" Gershon demanded. "Who must have taken it? Do you know something, old man?" Gershon took hold of the rabbi's fragile shoulders, hoping against hope that this prying old man might just have some information that would help him.

"His followers. They must have taken it! Do you not see? Do you not understand? It had to be them. There is no other explanation." Rabbi Levi finished in a whisper, spent, exhausted.

Gershon withdrew his hands angrily. "You know nothing about it, do you, old man?"

Rabbi Levi shook his head helplessly, still numbed by the news he had received.

Gershon vented his annoyance and his fear on the feeble old man. "I know about it. I know that it was no follower, no human being at all, that took that body away. There was an earthquake. Then the stone was moved and an angel was sitting on it and the body was gone." Gershon paused, searching the rabbi's face. Then he continued. "Do you know any angels, old man? Maybe you could introduce me and I could ask them what happened to His body."

Rabbi Levi blanched. This was even worse than he had imagined. Here was the captain of the Temple guard babbling about earthquakes and angels, refusing to support his allegation that Yeshua's followers were to blame. "No, I know no angels," he babbled back weakly. "And you must not speak of angels ever again, not to anyone. Do you hear? It was His followers. You must say that it was His followers. Do you understand?"

Gershon snorted angrily. "Angels or followers, what difference does it make? What matters is that His body is gone and I have to find it." He pushed past the rabbi sending him swirling and almost falling to the pavement. "Get out of my way, old man. I have no time for your demented ravings." Then Gershon was gone, on his way to organize his doomed search.

Rabbi Levi regained his balance and stood staring after the captain unable to move. *This cannot be. Oh, Holy One, please do not let this happen,* he prayed silently. *Please do not allow them to spread the lie that He has risen.*

Then Rabbi Levi, too, was struck dumb by the same thought which held the high priest in the grip of terror. *What if it isn't a lie? No ... that cannot be. I will not even entertain such a thought. No ... that is quite impossible!*

The rabbi continued across the court, moving toward the western gate, toward the bridge, toward home. He appeared as he always had but within his heart a battle raged that he could not halt. *What if it isn't a lie? What if ... .* The terrible thought came again and again to trouble and torment him. And over and over again he tried to silence it with his own thin assurances.

ଓଃ **42** ଃ୦

FOR Yohanan, the news was too good to keep to himself. He wanted everyone to know. He wanted the whole world to know and, if he had anything to say about it, he would get to be the one to tell them.

The sun that lit Yerushalayim could not hold a candle to the light in Yohanan's heart. As he walked along, he hummed a hymn of praise to the Holy One for he simply could not keep silent. He understood now what Yeshua had said about the rocks and the stones crying out. Had that been only a week ago? It seemed longer. So much had happened since. Yohanan knew that if he had been a rock or a stone on this day, he would certainly have cried out his praise to the Lord of life. He simply would not have been able to keep quiet.

After leaving the empty tomb, Yohanan had called at the home of Naqdimon in the northern quarter of the Upper City simply because it was closer and he couldn't wait to tell someone the wonderful news. He was now on his way to the southern quarter, to rented rooms above an inn. It was there that he and Shimon had made ready the Seder. As Yohanan thought of it now, he finally understood why Yeshua had commanded that their celebration of Pesach be held a day early. He had known what would happen all along and now Yohanan knew, too. It had all been a part of Yeshua's plan and even though Yohanan really did not yet completely comprehend the plan, somehow it helped just to know that there was one and Yeshua was in total command of it.

Yohanan wished he could go back to that night, just for a moment, just to rest his head upon Yeshua's breast one last time, just to hear the slow steady pulsing rhythmic beat of His loving heart once again. But Miriam now waited in that upper chamber, waited to know that all that was necessary for her Son's burial had now been accomplished. Yohanan laughed aloud as he thought of the very different news he would soon bring her. A passerby looked at him as though he must certainly be possessed by some demon and that made Yohanan laugh all the louder.

As he passed by the Temple, Yohanan encountered David ben Asaph. David had just left the morning sacrifice and had chosen a circuitous route home just to give himself time to think about all that had happened, about his marriage on this very day to a girl he knew did not love him. The slump of David's shoulders and the lines of anguish clearly evident on his downcast face told Yohanan that he had not yet heard the wonderful news. Yohanan was so glad. It simply gave him one more opportunity to say the words and to savor again the sweetness of them.

Yohanan took only a few moments to tell David, to spread the contagion of his joy to one more follower of Yeshua. When he was done, David's face brightened instantly and his eyes shone. The two clasped hands, then embraced each other, spinning in a circle. Others in the crowd who were also returning from the morning sacrifice parted like the Red Sea clearly wishing to avoid two such crazy men. Yohanan and David eyed them, eyed each other, and burst out laughing in unison.

✿   ✿   ✿

A few minutes later, Yohanan climbed the uneven steps that led to a small upper room in the southern part of the Upper City. There, He found Miriam clutching the very towel her Son had wrapped around Himself when He had bathed the feet of His disciples following the Seder dinner. It was all she had left that He had touched, that had touched Him. The Romans who crucified Him had taken everything else. They had left her nothing, nothing she could hold on to, nothing of the seamless tunic or the soft robe or the linen undergarments that she had made for Him with her own hands.

Miriam looked up as Yohanan entered and when she did, she couldn't believe the expression of joy which enveloped his handsome young face. How could he be so happy? she wondered as she felt uncharacteristic and unwelcome resentment welling up in her heart. *Doesn't he realize what I have lost, what all of us have lost, what the world itself has lost?*

"Ammah Miriam," he said gently, "come sit with me. I have tidings of Yeshua."

Miriam folded the towel. She started to lay it on a nearby table but in the end, she found that she could not let it leave her hands. Instead she clutched it to her bosom as she settled herself upon the same couch on which Yohanan sat. "Tell me, my son. I must know that everything has been done for Him."

Yohanan smiled lovingly. "Ammah Miriam, they went to the tomb but they could do nothing more for Him. You see, He was not there."

Miriam's eyes widened in alarm as she grasped Yohanan's arm. "Not there? Oh, no! What has happened to Him? Where have they taken Him?"

Yohanan took her hands in his. "Ammah, He was not there because He has risen."

"Risen? I do not understand." She struggled to comprehend the incomprehensible.

Yohanan's face burst into a radiant grin he could not suppress and when he spoke, his voice was breathless and ecstatic. "He is alive, Ammah! I know it! I have seen the empty tomb! I have walked in it! And I can tell you of a certainty that He is not there! He is risen!"

"This is not possible. How can you say such a thing? How can such a thing be?"

They were logical questions just as Naqdimon's had been and Yohanan loved telling the story all over again to answer them. Patiently he explained the appearance of the angels and the message of resurrection they had given Miriam's friends who had gone to the tomb in her stead to complete the burial preparations for her Son so that she would be spared that gruesome task. Then Yohanan told her of the empty wrappings which had been placed so lovingly around His body and which had been left behind so neatly. He watched as her face broke into a glorious smile that mirrored his own as she, too, realized that no burial detail, no Galileans, and no graverobbers would have unwrapped the body before removing it. That left only one possible explanation. Yeshua was alive! He really had risen from the dead.

Tears of joy swept across her cheeks. She laughed and cried simultaneously. Then she got up and danced about the room. And the towel which had been her last link to her dead Son, the one she had been unwilling to let leave her hands only moments before, now lay in a rumpled heap on the floor where it had fallen. Miriam no longer needed it.

✿   ✿   ✿

Not more than an hour later, Yohanan climbed the familiar paths of the Mount of Olives to Bethany and turned into the lane where Shimon and Eleazar lived with another Miriam and her sister, Martha. In the next instant their door thundered with his rapping. To his ears it sounded rhythmic, almost musical, but then it seemed that nearly everything sounded like music to him today. He began to chuckle, to chortle, and it was thus Eleazar found him when he swung open the heavy door. And when Eleazar looked startled then fearful at the lunacy before him, Yohanan shook with laughter and held his sides to keep them from bursting with the joy of it all.

Once inside, Yohanan had been unable to sit still to tell the good tidings with expressive face and wildly gesturing hands. He wondered if he would ever tire of telling it but knew he would not. And as soon as Eleazar and his family had heard, they also found it impossible to sit still. Together they whirled about the room, praising the Holy One for His wonderful works among the children of men and for His Son, their risen Lord.

"I knew it!" Eleazar finally exclaimed panting. "I knew He could never remain in that tomb just as He did not permit me to remain in mine." He shuddered as he thought of it. Then his laughter bubbled up within him until it could not be contained.

Shimon clapped his hands in exuberant joy. "What tomb could hold Him? What power on this earth or anywhere else could stay Him?"

The five danced about until they were dizzy with the delight of it all. They still did not understand why it had all been necessary–the terrible trials, the brutal beating, the chilling crucifixion, the terrible tearing of the Temple veil. All they knew was that their Lord Yeshua lived. Suddenly, in all the world and for the rest of their lives, that was all they needed to know.

⊰ **43** ⊱

HANNAH'S eyes ached from watching out the window for David's familiar form to come into view. When he finally appeared at the head of the street, she blinked in surprise at the change in his countenance. Yesterday he had been so sad, so solemn; now it seemed his feet barely touched the paving stones as he almost skipped home. Hannah met him in the courtyard. He swept through the gate and twirled around in the middle of the court. Hannah stared while her heart climbed into the back of her throat where it insisted on pulsing rapidly. When he looked at her with his broad grin, it was clear he hadn't even noticed that the courtyard was being prepared for a wedding, their wedding. But at least he was looking her way. She was finally able to speak.

"David, we must talk," she said soberly.

"Yes, my beautiful Hannah. We must indeed talk. Where shall I begin?"

Hannah was becoming alarmed at David's demented demeanor. "May we begin with our marriage contract?"

"Marriage contract!" David repeated as though he hadn't understood the words. "Yes of course," he shouted, striking the palm of his hand to his forehead as though he had just remembered. "We are to be married, are we not? You and I! This very day just before the sun begins to set as I recall, this very wonderful beautiful glorious day!" David circled one more time. "How could we have possibly been so perceptive to choose this particularly magnificent day for our marriage?"

It seemed to Hannah that David was almost singing his words and he had begun to frighten her. No morning sacrifice she knew of had ever left a single one of its participants behaving in this manner. She wondered if the events of the past few days had been too much for David to endure, if he had completely lost his sanity in the agony of it all. "David, please, this is important. We must discuss our marriage contract like two reasonably rational adults."

"Important!" he echoed. "Yes, there is nothing more important than this day. There may never be anything more important than this day. In the entire history of the entire world, there may never be any day more important than this one, Hannah." He grasped her hands for a moment but returned to dancing when he could not bear to remain in one place.

Hannah blinked several times as the man in front of her became absolutely giddy. She had heard of happy bridegrooms but never one like this. "David, we really must talk."

David stopped in mid-twirl, looked at her, and gauged the seriousness of her expression and of her voice. He came toward her. "Forgive me, Hannah, my own beautiful Hannah." When he reached her, he cupped her face in his hands and continued, "Now tell me, what is this important thing we really must talk about?"

It seemed to Hannah that David was mocking her. She pulled away, crossed her arms, and formed her face into a furious frown.

He simply smiled, a smile that couldn't help itself; it immediately turned into a giggle. He could see she was not pleased so he summoned all his strength to suppress it, gave her his most tender gaze to let her know he was truly trying to be serious, and waited for her next words.

Hannah knew this solemnity might not last long; she determined to take full advantage of it. "David, you must release me from our marriage contract." She could tell from the way his face paled and the muscles of his jaw twitched that she had finally gotten his complete attention. "I must ask you to release me from our marriage contract," Hannah repeated firmly.

"But, my beloved Hannah, why?" he finally asked incredulously.

"From the very beginning, our beliefs have stood between us like a mighty wall, a wall I cannot cross, a wall I cannot pass."

David smiled again. "That wall has just come tumbling down, my love," he exulted.

Hannah could tell she was about to lose control of the conversation again. "David, please listen," she said quickly, then continued immediately. "I cannot believe the way you do. I cannot believe that your Yeshua was Messiah, especially after all that has happened."

"After all that has happened," he echoed as though puzzling over the meaning of the words. "Of course," he responded like the light of dawn had finally come. "You do not yet know all that has happened, do you? I must tell you, Hannah. Then you will surely understand."

"I know what happened," Hannah shot back angrily. "I know that He was tried and found guilty by our own elders. I know that even the Romans concurred. I know that He was crucified, hanged on a Roman tree until He was dead. I know all of this. I was there, David, and so were you. Remember? And I know that the Holy One I worship would never have allowed such things to happen to His Messiah."

David could not match Hannah's anger with his own. There simply was no anger in him on this day of all days. He just grinned tolerantly. "Oh, but Hannah, that is exactly what the Holy One allowed. I do not yet know how or why; all I know is that He did."

Hannah was losing patience. "Oh, David, what has happened to you? You are not even making sense."

"It is not what has happened to me that matters. It is

what has happened to Him, Hannah. That's what matters now."

"David, we both know exactly what happened to Yeshua. He is dead, David. And while it saddens me, that is the end of it. All any of us can do now is accept it. How can you continue to believe in a Messiah who now lies cold and dead and buried in a tomb very near my own abba's? And how can you expect me to marry a man who believes in such nonsense?"

"But it isn't nonsense, Hannah," David began, his eyes glowing, his heart pounding, his face alive with the wonder of it. "You must understand. Yeshua is not cold and dead and buried in that tomb. That tomb is empty, Hannah, empty!" Then his voice grew soft, still marveling at the mighty miracle he now had the blessed privilege of recounting to the woman he loved more than life itself. "He is risen, Hannah! It happened this very morning. Yohanan was there. He saw the tomb and it is empty. He's alive, Hannah! Yeshua is alive!"

Hannah stepped back fearfully. She knew now that David really had gone mad with the pain of the past few days. "David, listen to your words. Do you hear the insanity you are speaking? This is why I can never marry you. This is why you must release me from the marriage contract, David, no matter how much I may love you. Yeshua alive? Yeshua risen from the dead?"

David's blue eyes suddenly glazed. He had forgotten all about Hannah's request to be released from their marriage contract. Instead he had heard only the words he had most wanted to hear from her lips for an entire year. *She loves me! She really loves me! She said it herself! It must be so. Hannah loves me and Yeshua is alive!* David knew that there would never in his lifetime be a day more wonderful than this one.

Before he could speak, Hannah continued. "My dear David," she intoned even more emphatically, "people just do not rise from the dead no matter what Yohanan told you. It is not possible. Do you not see that what he told you cannot be true? David, when people die, that is the end so far as this world is concerned. They may live forever in the bosom of Father Avraham but there is no rising from the dead here. Do you not know that I, above all people, wish that such a thing were possible?" She paused to allow her words to find lodging in David's mind. "David, no one can rise from the dead, not your Yeshua and not my abba."

At that moment their conversation was interrupted as the door of the gate swung open behind them. Hannah and David turned to greet their visitor. "Did I hear my name?" a familiar booming voice called out joyously. In the next instant Itzak, Hannah's abba, strode into the courtyard. Then, after a long moment in which time seemed suspended, Hannah fainted dead away into David's waiting arms once again.

∽ 44 ∾

THE sun was rising toward its zenith in a cloudless azure sky when Yakov's hunger finally forced him from his bedchamber to the dining chamber below. He piled some raisins, a few chunks of cheese, and a piece of unleavened bread on a small plate and took his seat at the table.

Devorah was sitting beside the hearth, her hands busily mending a small white garment he assumed was Mara's. She looked up as he seated himself and smiled a gentle concerned smile. "Are you feeling better, my lord?" she asked softly.

"Better?" Yakov repeated questioning. "I was never ill so how could I feel better?"

Devorah instantly dropped her gaze and blushed in embarrassment, then tactfully changed the subject. "Rachel is at the market and Ephraim is putting your father's home in order from the Seder. The daughter of my late uncle from Capernaum is to be wed late this afternoon. My lord, if it would not be too great an inconvenience for you, I would wish to attend. Rachel has agreed to care for Mara in my absence."

Yakov grunted his acquiescence as he continued eating. From the corner of his eye, he watched as her quick fingers flitted from one neat tiny stitch to the next reminding him of ... of. No, he didn't want to think about that. He forced his attention back to his plate.

"Mara is sleeping, the little dear," Devorah continued. She noticed that Yakov's countenance immediately darkened at the mention of his daughter's name. She struggled within herself. There was much she wanted to say, much she had wanted to say for many months. *Is this the right time?* she asked herself fearfully. *Will there ever be a right time?* was the second question in her mind that seemed to answer the first. *In any event,* she told herself, *I must speak.*

"My lord," she began tentatively.

Yakov looked up and his eyes met hers. It was apparent from her expression that there was something wrong and his own face took on a troubled aspect that matched hers. He laid down his last bite of cheese. "What is it, Devorah?"

Devorah hesitated. She did not know how to begin. She did not even know if she should begin. After all, perhaps it was not her place.

Yakov became alarmed. He rose from his seat and divided the distance between them into two long strides. He knelt at her side and took the mending from her hands. "Devorah, tell me. Has something happened? Is it my father?" Their words of only a few hours before came back to him in dreadful detail. Had he caused something awful to happen to his father?

Devorah's face momentarily broke into a reassuring smile. "No. Oh, no. It is nothing like that. Forgive me. I am so sorry that I frightened you."

Yakov relaxed. He looked up at Devorah. She was so lovely, her face so untouched by the misfortunes he knew she had suffered. And her voice sounded like a song. He had never been this near to her before and he found that he liked the look of her, the warmth of her, the scent of her. He wondered why he had hardly noticed these things before. He decided he had better speak before he made a fool of himself at her feet. "Then what is it? Please tell me. You can tell me anything," he said so tenderly he even surprised himself.

His tenderness surprised Devorah, too. She had seen little of this aspect of him. She knew him only as an icy remote man. She never knew such gentleness existed in him and she found much to her dismay that it pleased her. *Perhaps, this is the time,* she assured herself before she spoke. "It is Mara," she said at last.

Yakov pulled away. "Oh," was his only response.

Devorah had come too far to stop herself. "My lord, she is such a precious child, so beautiful, so good," she said, her words flowing from her lips one after another like water pouring from a burst cistern. "And my lord, she needs you; she needs her father."

"What she really needed, my dear Devorah, was her mother," Yakov countered flatly. "But she killed her." The softness in his eyes had vanished, replaced by the same seething bitterness Devorah had seen so often before. Gone was the guilt he had felt atop Golgotha's hill, gone the instant he had decided that it was too late for him to make any difference in his daughter's life ... or his own. His hostility had returned and he saw it reflected in Devorah's eyes. He looked down into his lap for a moment and returned his gaze to hers only after he had well hidden his anger. "Anyway, she has you," he finished.

"She has me now but whom will she have after she has been weaned and I am no longer here?"

Yakov stood and paced the room. He knew it, of course. He had always known that one day Mara would no longer require the services of a wetnurse. But he had never even considered that this would mean that Devorah would be leaving ... him. He couldn't imagine her not being here when he came home, not sitting by the fire, not smiling when he came into the room. He had never even allowed his mind to entertain the idea of awakening to a silent house, of not hearing her soft voice singing sweet psalms in the morning, of not listening to her laughter as she played with the child. Suddenly Yakov knew he did not want Devorah to leave, not now, not when the child was weaned, not ever. And he also knew that his feelings had nothing to do with his daughter. He did not know or care how she would feel if Devorah left. He wanted, needed Devorah to stay ... for him, just for him.

Yakov returned to her, knelt before her, and took her hands into his own. "Then you must never leave," he said softly.

Devorah started to speak but no words came.

Moments passed. The two searched each other's eyes for some clue to what was happening between them. Yakov moved closer, closer to Devorah, closer to her lovely face. She did not resist. Just as his lips were about to brush hers, the door behind him opened. Devorah looked up quickly expecting to see Rachel, wondering how she could possibly explain their sinful conduct. But a smaller woman's form stepped out of the sunshine and into the doorway.

Yakov turned, his mind racing to find just the right words to allay Rachel's suspicion. His mouth fell open, his eyes widened. *It is ... ! No, it couldn't be! But it is! It's Shoshana!*

Behind Shoshana, a young man came into view, a young man Yakov had never met. *Am I seeing things? Is my mind playing tricks on me?*

Devorah gasped and Yakov realized he was not the only one who saw Shoshana and the man who now accompanied her. Devorah saw them, too, and she knew exactly who the young man was. Devorah knew it was Yonah, her Yonah, her husband.

❧ 45 ❧

NAQDIMON paced Solomon's Porch restlessly. He was waiting to see Yosef ben
Qayafa but hardly knew what he would say
to him when he did. While the two had been
forced by their positions to work together,
as a Pharisee and a Sadducee, they had never really been
close and would never really be friends. Still Naqdimon
knew he had to speak to him now.

It had been several years since he had met Yeshua and
accepted Him as Messiah, several years of hiding, of secrets, of fear, of cowardice. Yes, that was it! As Naqdimon
thought about it now, he knew it was his own cowardice
which had placed him in this untenable position. It was
also his cowardice which had cost his son his eternal soul.
And perhaps his cowardice had even sent Yeshua to the
cross.

*What if I had been honest from the beginning, with Sarah,
with Moshe, with Qayafa? What if I had proclaimed Yeshua as
Messiah, proclaimed it loud and long, proclaimed it from the
housetops from that very first night? Perhaps events would have
transpired differently. Perhaps I could have made them tran-
spire differently.*

Naqdimon finally realized the futility of these thoughts
and groaned inwardly. *Listen to yourself, old man! Are you
in the place of the Holy One? Can you save a soul? Can you
deliver from a death penalty? If the Holy One Himself decreed
that His Son must be lifted up upon a cross just as the serpent
was lifted up in the wilderness, what could you have done to
change it? You probably would have only succeeded in acquir-*

ing for yourself a cross adjoining Yeshua's. He shuddered involuntarily at the very thought. *What good would that have done? And what good do you think you are going to do now?*

Naqdimon continued pacing but each time he found himself near the end of the great colonnaded porch, his old eyes would longingly caress the gate across the court. Each time, he would have to decide anew whether or not to walk through that gate and turn toward home, just as he had done so often before.

It seemed to Naqdimon that he had been pacing ever since Yohanan had left him an hour before. He tried to believe what Yohanan had told him; he wanted to believe it, needed to believe it. But his agitated mind would not rest, constantly searching for another answer, one that was more reasonable, more logical. Yet in his heart of hearts, he knew only resurrection could explain why the Holy One had permitted His Son to suffer and die in the first place. Somehow the Holy One meant to illustrate His complete victory over man's last and most implacable enemy, death. How else could He do that but by a very public death and a very definite resurrection? Yes, that had to be it!

Naqdimon pounded his fist into the palm of his hand. *I must do what I came to do! I must do what I should have done almost three years ago! I must! There is no other way.*

Before his tormented mind could find another route out of his dilemma, the high priest's servant found him. "He will see you now, my lord," Malluch intoned solemnly. "If you will follow me ... ."

"Thank you, my son," Naqdimon replied, his voice more steady than he had expected it to be. He walked confidently behind the young man who led the way to the high priest's private chamber.

Yosef ben Qayafa sat in a lordly chair that might easily have been mistaken for a throne. He eyed Naqdimon suspiciously but never offered his guest a chair or even spoke to him.

At length, Naqdimon cleared his throat and began. "Excellency, may I speak?"

Qayafa ignored his request. Instead he pointed an accusing finger at Naqdimon and spoke in a voice that both interrogated and indicted. "I saw you out there, did I not? I saw you out there."

"Yes, Excellency," Naqdimon finally admitted without shame for the very first time. "I was there."

"I know. I saw you," Qayafa exulted as though he had just solved some great mystery. "And that's not all I saw. I saw that you are one of them. You are one of those that troubles me."

Naqdimon took a deep breath but there was nothing to do, nothing he wanted to do now but to acknowledge the truth at last. "Yes, Excellency, I am one of them." He paused and exhaled deeply. It was good to finally say it aloud, good to finally have it out in the open. Then he added, "But I have no desire to trouble you, Excellency." Somewhere inside himself, Naqdimon felt a cold dark dread that told him it was the Holy One Himself who now troubled Qayafa.

A maniacal satisfaction lit Qayafa's face. "I killed Him, you know," Qayafa asserted. "Me. I killed your so-called Messiah! I killed Yeshua!" Qayafa smiled, obviously pleased with his accomplishment.

"Yes, Excellency," Naqdimon replied sadly. "You killed Him."

Qayafa's eyes smoldered. "And now do you know what they are telling me, Naqdimon?"

"No, Excellency. What are they telling you?" Naqdimon asked quietly, doing his best to humor the clearly crazed man before him.

"They are telling me that His body is gone. They are telling me about angels and earthquakes, Naqdimon." He stopped, struggling to control his anger. When his composure was restored, he continued. "They are telling me that He is risen. They are telling me that Yeshua lives."

"Yes, Excellency," Naqdimon soothed. "They are telling me this as well."

Qayafa's eyes locked on Naqdimon's, searching, prying, probing. "Naqdimon, hear me, it is not true. Do you understand? It cannot be true. We Sadducees know of a certainty that it cannot be true." It was as though by saying it, he believed he could make it so.

Naqdimon measured the man before him with his eyes, then drew a chair close to Qayafa's. He spoke softly yet with great passion. "Excellency, I believe it is true. I believe Yeshua is Messiah. And I believe He has risen from the dead. I believe it with all my heart and with all my soul. And I have come to tell you that perhaps it is time for you to believe it also."

Qayafa's aspect changed in a moment of time. As Naqdimon shrunk back in his seat and blinked with shock, Qayafa leapt from his chair, shouting, his eyes lit with a ferocity that frightened Naqdimon, not for himself, but for the high priest. "No! No! I will never believe it! Never! I killed Him and He is dead now and forevermore. Do you hear me, Naqdimon? I will never believe otherwise and I will never allow anyone else to believe it either."

Naqdimon recoiled as though Qayafa's rage were a physical force that had just struck out at him. He had seen Qayafa many times, in many circumstances. He had seen him cold and calculating, cruel and crafty. He had seen him wild and wily, willful and wrathful. But he had never seen Qayafa like this, careening, crazed and uncontrolled about the chamber.

"Come, Excellency," Naqdimon coaxed, wanting only to calm him somehow. "Come, sit. We will talk. We will make sense of this, you and I."

Qayafa stopped in mid-tirade, returned to his chair, and fixed on Naqdimon a gaze as intense as it was insane. "Yes, you and I, we will make sense of this. I killed Him and He's dead. If He were not, it would mean that He really was the Holy One, would it not? That would mean that I, the high priest of all Yisrael, tried to kill the Holy One. Is that not true? Now Naqdimon, we cannot have people believing that their high priest would do such a thing, can we?"

Qayafa searched Naqdimon's face for some sign of agreement but found only pity and it infuriated him. When he spoke, it was from between clenched teeth and in a tone that implied grave peril. "He's dead! Yeshua is dead! I will never accept anything else. And anyone who does will know my wrath just as He did. Do you understand what I am saying to you, Naqdimon?"

Naqdimon tried to ignore Qayafa's thinly-veiled threat. "Excellency," Naqdimon began softly, "we may have no choice but to accept it. I have heard that Yeshua has already been seen by some. Surely He will be seen by others. We may have no choice but to accept the inevitable ... ."

Qayafa bolted from the chair again, restless, raging, writhing with an inner anger he could not control. "No, Naqdimon! No!" Then he smiled, a darkly ominous smile that sent a shiver along Naqdimon's spine. "I am the high priest, Naqdimon, am I not? If I say that He is dead then He is dead. Is that not so? And I say that He is dead. I say that He is not risen. I say that His followers stole away His body just so they can spread the lie that He is risen. That is it! I, Yosef ben Qayafa, have spoken! Do you understand, Naqdimon? Yeshua is dead and He cannot be risen because there is no resurrection of the dead. That is so, Naqdimon. That is ... ."

The door to the chamber opened. Malluch looked up, gasped, then smiled joyously. Qayafa spun around prepared to banish whoever had dared to interrupt him. Instead Qayafa came face to face with a reality that ruined all of his Sadducean fantasies forever. For in walked his own son, Ami, with Naqdimon's boy, Moshe. They were arm-in-arm and smiling, best friends just as they had always been.

❧ 46 ❧

THE tidings at Temple had undone Rabbi Levi. He paced his chamber, first this way, then that. It had been so carefully planned, so perfectly executed. Everything had gone exactly as he and the high priest had arranged. And he rejoiced that it would never have happened at all if he, Rabbi Levi ben Eshcol had not found the traitor, Yehuda, if he had not brought him to Qayafa at just the right moment. Now it could all be for nothing, worse than nothing, he agonized. Now Yeshua's followers might say that their dead Master has risen. Now they might even be able to convince the gullible.

A soft knock at his door interrupted his troubled musings.

"Enter," he commanded gruffly.

The door opened slightly and Naomi slipped into the room. "Abba, you asked me to remind you when the sun was high. I believe you are expected at a marriage later."

Rabbi Levi slapped his forehead. "Yes, yes, I had nearly forgotten. The daughter of the man I laid to rest just a few days ago. She is to be wed this afternoon. Thank you, my daughter."

Naomi nodded, then started to leave the room.

"How can I go to a wedding now of all times?" Rabbi Levi muttered to himself more than anyone else. His restless pacing began anew.

Naomi turned back toward her father-in-law. "You spoke, Abba?" she queried. "Forgive me, I did not hear."

Rabbi Levi waved her away. "It is nothing, my daughter, nothing at all."

But Naomi knew better. She had never seen him so agitated. "Abba, what troubles you?"

"It is nothing, nothing," he reiterated, his voice rising in volume as well as tension. "Now leave me, girl. I must think of some way out of all this."

Naomi started toward the door again. She knew something was terribly wrong and suddenly she feared for the father-in-law she had come to love. Still, she had no choice but to comply with his wishes. Her hand pulled at the latch of the door.

Rabbi Levi began pacing again and mumbling to himself. "This cannot be happening! This simply cannot be happening! I must do something! I must stop this ... this ... ."

Just as she started through the door, Naomi looked back one last time. What she saw caused her heart to leap into her throat. Rabbi Levi was bent over his chair clutching his breast, his face pale, his lips blue, his mouth moving but making no sound.

"Abba!" she shouted as she rushed to his side. Then she returned to the doorway and screamed for her husband. "Aaron! Come quickly!" She was back to the rabbi's side before the words were out of her mouth. She helped him lower himself into the chair, then patted at his sweating brow with the edge of her robe.

Aaron bolted into the room. He assessed the situation instantly for he had heard of such things before, heard of them happening to others. He knew he might be seeing his father for the last time. He rushed to him and grasped his gnarled hands. "Abba, Abba, please do not leave us," he pleaded, tears streaming down his cheeks, his face lined with concern.

"My son," Rabbi Levi gasped, his eyes floating above his eyelids for a brief moment. "My son."

"Yes, Abba, what is it?" Aaron pleaded.

Rabbi Levi stared into the face of his son, his eyes wide

with the fear of death, his breathing labored from the crushing pain in his breast. "Do not ... let them," he struggled to speak.

"Yes, Abba, anything. I will do anything. What is it? What is it that I must not let them do?" Aaron prayed that his father would be able to finish his plea. If this were to be his dying wish, then Aaron meant to fulfill it.

Rabbi Levi's mouth fought to form the words. "Do not let them ... tell that unspeakable lie." The rabbi could not continue.

"What lie, Abba?" Aaron prompted desperately. "Tell me, Abba. What lie? I will not let anyone tell it."

"Yeshua ... the lie about Yeshua," Rabbi Levi whispered faintly as his visage grew ever darker. "Do not let them say Yeshua has risen. Do not let them say ... Yeshua ... ." His voice trailed off ominously.

Naomi and Aaron looked at each other, the same questions in each of their minds. *Yeshua? What has any of this got to do with Yeshua? I thought He was dead?*

Rabbi Levi summoned his last ounce of strength to grip his son's hands with all his might. "Do not let them. Promise me ... promise me ... promise ... ."

"Yes, Abba," Aaron pledged quickly. He had no idea what it was about the dead Yeshua that so troubled his father but if he must die, Aaron meant for him to die peacefully.

Rabbi Levi's face relaxed with his son's promise. His eyes closed and a faint smile played at the corners of his greying lips.

✿   ✿   ✿

Neither Aaron nor Naomi heard her approach, so intent were they on Rabbi Levi's final moments with them. She came toward them softly, her gaze gentle, her countenance shining, her smile rapturous.

Rabbi Levi opened his eyes for what he thought to be the very last time on this earth. It was then he saw her. Yael. His precious Yael. She was with him once again, with him forever. She was beautiful, happy, smiling, radiant. And ... and ... on her face ... there was no scar!

ভ 47 ৪

ANNAH fought for consciousness and, when she had regained it, she saw the faces of David, her mother, and her brothers swimming above her as though she were seeing them from the bottom of the sea. "Abba," she whispered dreamily. "I thought I saw Abba."

From behind where she lay on one of her aunt's couches, the old familiar voice sounded forth again, this time comforting her. "You did, my child, you did. Your abba is here with you."

Hannah turned. Her eyes opened wide, her jaw slackened. She shook her head to clear away the cobwebs, to find some logical explanation for what had no logical explanation at all. "It is not possible. It is not possible," she repeated over and over.

Itzak smiled. "Oh yes, my child, it is possible. Messiah Yeshua made it possible."

"But I saw your body! You were dead! I attended your burial just a few days ago." Hannah struggled to make sense of what made no sense.

"So I was," Itzak agreed. "So I was. But, my child, I was dead only to this world. In the world beyond, I never died at all. The storm raged and the waters washed over me but in the same instant I closed my eyes on the sea that day, I opened them in the presence of our father, Avraham. Now Yeshua has ushered all of us into the Paradise of the Holy One Himself."

"How can that be, Abba?" Hannah questioned, her puzzlement evident in her young face.

Her abba answered her tenderly, "Because I knew Yeshua as my Messiah, Hannah, I never died and I never shall. I have come to tell you that you also can know Him, Child, and that if you do, you also will never die."

"But I saw Him die, too!" Hannah replied, clearly astounded. "I saw Yeshua die, too."

Abba chuckled. "True again. He died for you, Hannah, for all of us. But like me, He died only to this world. In His Father's world, He was always alive! And now, my child, He has risen just as He said He would. Now He is alive again here as well, alive forevermore. He is the One who gave me new life, too, so that I could be here with you at this very moment."

Hannah's eyes went instantly to David's. "Then it is true? What David told me is true? Yeshua is risen?"

David and Itzak happily nodded in unison. "He truly is Messiah, Hannah, the Son of the Holy One," David reassured.

"Even I now know it," her mother assured. "Even I have now accepted Yeshua as Messiah. How could I doubt it?" she whispered as she took her husband's hand and looked lovingly into his eyes.

To Hannah, this was beyond all reason. It was as if all natural laws had suddenly been repealed and the twin realities of life and death no longer applied. Her mind labored to comprehend the incomprehensible while her eyes told her that the incomprehensible was sitting right beside her in the person of her abba. And that was a fact even she could no longer deny.

"Abba," she cried as she fell into his arms. She could feel the warmth of him, the substance of him. He was real; he was no vision, no dream, and he was with her once more.

In that moment her memory took her back to that terrible day a year before, to the terrible burden of guilt she had carried since, to the terrible need she had always felt to set things right with her father. She pulled away until her eyes locked on his. "Oh, Abba, there is so much I have to say to you, so much you must know." Her words stumbled out. "I am sorry, so sorry for what happened on our last day together. You must forgive me for all the horrible things I said to you ... "

Abba burst forth with the same bellowing laughter she had always known. "Oh, my dear Hannah! Do you not know that you always had my forgiveness? I always understood. And after," he said haltingly, "after I left you, I had the assurance that all would be well with you." He cupped her trembling chin in his palm and looked tenderly into her eyes. He wanted no mistake about what he was going to say. "And, Hannah, all I ever really wanted was to know that all would be well with you."

The accumulated tears of an entire year of grief and guilt poured forth onto Abba's strong shoulder all at once. "Oh, Abba, thank you for understanding, for forgiving me, for loving me anyway," Hannah managed between sobs.

"I will always love you, Hannah," Abba reassured her. "Whether in this world or the next. There is nothing you could ever do to change that." Itzak paused, then spoke again. "And, Hannah, He loves you, too, more than I, more than your ammah, more than David, more than anyone ... more than you could possibly know."

Hannah nodded through her tears. "I think I am just beginning to understand that."

"Then when will you offer Him your love in return?"

"Now, Abba, right now," was all she could say, all she needed to say. She dissolved into new tears, tears for all of the time she had wasted wondering if Yeshua was really who Abba and David said He was, tears for all of the awful things she had thought and said about Him, tears for all of her own rebellion and stubbornness. Her iron reserve had broken. Her questions had finally been answered in a way she never could have imagined. She knew now that Yeshua truly is Messiah, the Lord of life and death, the Lord of earth and Heaven. And as her tears flowed, it seemed they washed away everything, all of her regrets, all of her doubts, all of her misgivings, all of her past. Yeshua was now her Lord as well.

Once she had cried out her heart and dried her swollen eyes, Itzak held her at arm's length and spoke, feigning exasperation just as he had so often before. "Now what is this nonsense I hear about you wanting to be released from your marriage contract?"

Hannah turned and looked sheepishly at David. "I only thought ... . I just wanted ... ." She struggled to find the right words. Finally she stopped struggling and faced the truth.

"I have come to love David more than my life," she said softly. "It was only fear, fear of his beliefs, fear of offending the Holy One, that held me back." She hung her head as she continued. "And it was my own guilt, too, guilt for all of the things I said to you, Abba, guilt that told me that I did not deserve a husband as fine as David after what I had done."

Then Hannah looked up and smiled, a radiant smile that told the story even before her words came. "But now that is gone, all gone. Now there is no more fear, no more guilt. There is just love."

Hannah stood and took David's hands in hers. As she gazed into his gentle eyes pouring all of the love in her heart into that single look, she said, "If he will forgive me, if he will still have me, I want nothing more in this whole world than to be his wife."

David embraced Hannah, holding her closely and tightly as though he never wanted to let her go. At first he was too overwhelmed with emotion to speak. When words finally did come, they were words of praise, praise to the Holy One for giving him all that he had ever wanted, all in the person of the slender young girl in his arms.

"Good!" Itzak declared at last. "I am glad the two of you have finally managed to bring yourselves into one accord for my time is short and I came to attend a wedding."

With that, he withdrew from his sash the betrothal ring David had given him a year before to seal their contract.

Dinah gasped. All this time, no one had known where it was and no one had wanted to admit to David that it had been lost.

Then Itzak placed it on his daughter's waiting hand. "With this ring," he said, "your betrothal is sealed at last. Now, children, shall we get on with the wedding?"

�''48''⋙

YAKOV and Devorah jumped to their feet. Their faces registered their surprise. Their mouths were open yet neither could speak a single word.

Shoshana and Yonah smiled their understanding. It was Shoshana who spoke first. "Yakov," was all she said, all she needed to say. All the love they had known in their brief marriage was carried in the way she caressed his name.

Yakov walked toward her as though he were floating in a dream. "Shoshana? Is it really you?" He touched her hand, her face, and found that they were real enough. Assured that the woman before him was not the product of his own tormented mind, he pulled her to him and clung to her in a desperate embrace. "Oh, Shoshana, I have missed you so much! My Shoshana!"

Shoshana returned his embrace, whispering his name, reassuring him of her love.

As Yakov and Shoshana held each other, Yonah slipped past them and went to Devorah's side. She appeared frightened, unsure of what was happening, unsure of what it meant. He saw the fear in her face. Then he smiled to comfort her. "I am here, Devorah. I am really here. Do not fear. I have come only to love you and to finish a story I started to tell you so long ago."

In the next moment, Devorah found herself in Yonah's arms. Never had they felt so good to her. She willed time to stop so that she would never have to be parted from him again.

As though he could read her thoughts, he spoke softly into her ear. "I have but a brief time, Devorah, and there is much I must tell you."

Shoshana took a single step back from Yakov, their hands still joined, their eyes still feasting on each other.

It was only then that Yakov recovered enough to begin to ask the questions that filled his heart. "How can this be? I saw you die! I was with you when it happened." His mind fought to make the pieces of his ghastly memory of that last awful day fit with the wonderful reality of the present. "What happened, Shoshana? Did you not die? And if you did not, why did you not come back to me? I needed you so much." Yakov clutched Shoshana to him, unwilling to allow her to get away from him ever again.

Shoshana smiled and stroked his hair as though she were soothing a child who had awakened from an awful nightmare. "Yes, Yakov, I did die that day just as you remember. But in a very real way, I never died at all. You see, Yakov, on the very day before my death, I met Someone, Someone for whom death has no finality. He is the One who has given me this moment with you. He is the One I have come to tell you about."

Yakov looked perplexed. *Another man in my Shoshana's life? Another man who can dispel death?* None of it was making sense. He knew Shoshana had loved him, only him. And in any event, there is no man who can triumph over death.

Shoshana laughed, a small laugh, a gentle laugh, the same lyrical laugh he had always known. "Come, my love. Sit and I will tell you everything," she promised. "All of your questions will be answered."

Soon the four were seated at the low table, wives and husbands holding hands and holding each other in the embrace of their eyes. Yonah began. "Devorah, do you recall that night just before my accident when I told you about the Man I had met at the centurion's home? Do you

311

remember how I told you that He had healed the man's servant?"

Devorah nodded, wondering what any of this had to do with Yonah's sudden reappearance.

Yonah continued, "I never got to tell you the end of the story. And I could not rest until I did." He squeezed his wife's hand. "Devorah, it was Yeshua."

"Yeshua!" Yakov interrupted, searching Shoshana's eyes. "Yeshua? Yeshua ben Yosef? The One that ... ."

Shoshana chuckled. "The very One that made a muddle of your business, on more than one occasion as I recall."

Yakov looked back at Yonah. "What do you know of Him?" he asked.

"I know that He healed the servant of the man for whom I worked. I saw it with my own eyes." Yonah returned his gaze to his wife. "Remember, Devorah? Remember when Marcus Lucinius took me with him to his summer home in Capernaum to treat an injured horse?"

Devorah nodded even though she had only the vaguest recollection of his trip. All she recalled was that he had been gone for several weeks and when he came home to her, he was exhausted from the journey. "That was the night you told me about ... about ..."

"About Yeshua," he finished. "But I fell asleep before I finished. And then ...."

Devorah sensed the importance of this to Yonah. "Tell me now," she encouraged.

"I was there, Devorah. When we arrived, we found Marcus' servant ill with palsy. I learned from other servants that this man had been in the family's employ since Marcus was a child. The man was much like a second father to him. No one thought there was any hope he would recover. The death watch had already begun."

"How dreadful!" Devorah exclaimed.

Yonah nodded, then continued, "One of the other servants had heard of this Yeshua, a Rabbi who happened to live in Capernaum."

"He was not a physician then, simply a Rabbi?" Devorah questioned.

"He was a Rabbi, Devorah, but there was absolutely nothing simple about Him," Yonah answered knowingly. "Marcus sent a message begging Him to heal his dear servant. The next thing we knew, Yeshua was on His way to the house. Marcus was mortified! He knew how difficult the Rabbi's life would become if He were to come under the roof of a Gentile, especially a Roman, and he wished to bring no such reproach upon the Man. So he sent another message saying he was not worthy of the honor of having the Rabbi in his home. He also explained that he understood the principle of authority, that he himself was under the authority of another just as his own men were under his authority. Then he pleaded with Yeshua to only speak a word, to say a prayer perhaps, and he knew his servant would be well. I carried that message to Yeshua myself."

"What happened?" Devorah asked. She wanted to hear every detail. Yonah obliged.

"I repeated the message exactly. I knew Marcus wanted no misunderstanding. I needn't tell you that Yeshua was surprised, surprised that a Roman was so sensitive to our religious concerns and surprised that he had such great faith in His ability to heal. He told the throng He hadn't seen faith like that even among His own people. Then He did just as Marcus had requested. He simply spoke. He told Marcus to return home and promised that he would find his servant well."

"And was he?" Yakov interjected.

"Completely!" Yonah exulted. "In truth, he met us at the door concerned that he had caused his master such concern."

"Amazing!" Devorah cried.

"Devorah, from that moment I believed." Yonah's voice was soft but fervent. "I knew He was Messiah. No other could do such a miracle. But the accident happened the day after my return so I never had an opportunity to tell you. He spoke new life into me just so I could tell you now."

Devorah's tone was reverent, incredulous. "Messiah? Messiah has come at last?"

"Yes, Devorah, He has come. Yeshua has come."

Yakov could not let this go on another moment. "Tell her the rest, Yonah. Tell her Yeshua is dead, crucified like a common criminal by some of the very Romans you say He helped."

Devorah looked stricken. She turned to her husband with a question in her eyes.

"It is true, Devorah, Yeshua was crucified. But He is now risen. And because He lives, I live also."

Yakov turned to Shoshana. "You believed in this Yeshua, too?" he asked.

Shoshana's face took on a radiance he had never before seen as she spoke of her faith. "Yes, Yakov, I know He is Messiah. I met Him in the Temple the very day before ... it happened. He touched me with His voice, with His eyes, with His love. Some argued about whether or not He was Messiah. Within me there was no argument. I knew and I believed. I wanted to share the wonderful news with you, but ... you know what happened. I never had the chance. He loves you so much, Yakov, that He gave me one moment more. He allowed me to come just so I could tell you now."

Yakov protested. "If He loves me, why did He disrupt my business every Pesach?"

Shoshana answered confidently. "He loved you enough to stop you, Yakov, to stop you from sinning, to stop you from stealing. He loved you even when He was upsetting your tables and scattering your ill-gotten gains. In fact He may have loved you most just then."

Yakov remembered Yeshua's eyes the last time He had overturned his counting table. They were not angry or accusing eyes; they were sad, caring, loving eyes. They were the eyes that had stopped him in his business pursuits already. But there was so much Yakov did not yet comprehend.

"I don't understand, Shoshana. If He was truly Messiah, why did the Holy One allow Him to die ... like that?" he asked, the horror of the event returning to his tortured memory.

Shoshana's eyes took on an intensity he had never seen in them. "You of all people should understand. Do you not sell lambs that are sacrificed to atone for the sins of our people?"

Yakov nodded miserably.

"Do you not see? Yeshua came to be the last Lamb, the final Sacrifice to atone for the sins of all of us. And He offered that sacrifice; He offered Himself just as Pesach began. It was all a part of the Holy One's plan. It was the Holy One's plan."

Yakov thought of the little lamb he had held in his arms that awful day. He thought of its innocence, its death, its purpose. He thought of all of the questions that had troubled him that day. Now he knew all of the answers. Yeshua had been just as innocent as that lamb. Like it, He had been killed. But now Yakov understood that just like the little lamb he had cradled in his arms, Yeshua's death had had a purpose, too, an even greater purpose. He had given Himself to fulfill the purpose of the Holy One, to make one final blood sacrifice for all the sins of all mankind.

The enormity of this realization swept over Yakov, forever freeing him of his torment of the past week. *Yeshua was the final Lamb! There need be no more lambs sacrificed, no more lambs sold! I need steal no more! I am free, finally free!* Yakov exulted in that knowledge and in the freedom it brought to his heart.

But there was one more thing Yakov did not know. "What of the veil, Shoshana? Do you know what has happened to the veil?"

Shoshana smiled. "Yes, Yakov, I know. And I could never

have hoped the Holy One could have used the labor of my hands in such a marvelous way."

"You think it marvelous that the Temple veil was forever ruined?" Yakov raged.

Shoshana's smile broadened. "Not forever ruined, my love, forever opened, so that all who come to the Father by His Son may enter into the Holy of Holies to commune with Him."

"His Father? You mean the Holy One is indeed His Father?"

"Yes, Yakov. The very same Father who came for me that terrible day, the very same Father who has granted me eternal life just because I believed in His Son."

The four sat silently as the seconds stretched into minutes. There was too much to consider, too much to comprehend, too much to believe. Devorah finally spoke. All of her old logic based on human wisdom had been proven false by her husband's very presence. His testimony demanded belief in a different kind of logic, spiritual logic based on spiritual wisdom. "Yonah, I really think I do believe. Who but Messiah could heal a dying servant? Who but Messiah could restore to me my dead husband?" She then searched Yakov's eyes. "Who could He be but Messiah?"

Before Yakov could speak, the cries of a baby drew them back to the human realm.

"Our daughter?" Shoshana questioned.

"Yes," Yakov replied.

Shoshana rose and moved quickly toward the sound. Yakov followed. He found her beside the cradle, gazing into the face of her child. Normally apprehensive with strangers, the baby smiled up at her mother as though she had always known her. Yakov was transfixed.

"Her name is Mara," Yakov said rather flatly.

Shoshana lifted the baby into her arms. "No ... no, Yakov, her name cannot be Mara. Look at her, Yakov. Look how beautiful she is."

Yakov gazed into the angelic face of his own child and saw her, really saw her, for perhaps the very first time. There were the same round raven curls, the same sapphire blue eyes, the same deeply defined dimples, the same crimson smile. It was as if he were seeing his Shoshana as a babe. In that instant part of him wanted to look away, to flee the pain the circumstances of her birth still aroused. But part of him never wanted to look away again.

"Yes, she is," he murmured softly. "She really is beautiful ... . She is ... just like you."

Shoshana smiled in delight. "Her name cannot be Mara for there is nothing bitter, nothing sad in her little face."

Yakov only nodded helplessly, so captured was he by the beauty of the child, his child, the child he had rejected since the moment of her birth.

"I can stay but a short time and when I am gone, her name must always remind you of the happiness Yeshua has given us to share this day. Every time you speak her name, you must remember me and the joy of this moment." Shoshana paused, considering. At last, she had it. "Her name shall be called Abigail for she shall ever be the joy of her father."

The baby cooed her agreement. Abigail it was.

Yakov laughed. Then his visage darkened as he remembered what Shoshana had just said. "What do you mean you have only a short time? Shoshana, you must stay; you must never leave us again. I need you to be my wife. Mar ... Abigail needs you to be her mother."

Shoshana's expression grew bittersweet. "Indeed my time with you will be brief. But there is one other thing I came to tell you, Yakov. Please hear me. Abigail already has a new mother. And you, my love, will soon have a new wife. This is the blessing of Yeshua and it is marvelous in my eyes. Accept this blessing from His hand for He does all things well. Do you believe this, Yakov?"

Every fiber of Yakov's being struggled against the absurdity of all he had heard and all he had seen this day.

Somewhere deep inside himself, a small voice warned him, *Be careful, Yakov; you may wake up in a moment or two only to discover that all of this has been a dreadful dream.* Yet his own inner voice declared, *If a dream it be, it is a wonderful one and I will live in the beauty of it for the rest of my life.*

Then Yakov recalled Devorah's words, "Who but Messiah?" Now he knew the answer to her question. Now he knew of a certainty. Who indeed? "I believe you, Shoshana, and if you believe in Him, then I believe in Him, too."

"Good, my husband," Shoshana rejoiced. "Now we shall have all eternity together, all five of us. But first, doesn't Devorah have a wedding to attend?"

ℭ 49 ℬ

NAQDIMON and Qayafa stared dumbfounded, first at their sons, then at each other. This simply could not be. But if it were a fantasy, they knew that they were both having the very same one at the very same time.

Qayafa, hardly ever at a loss for words, spoke first. "It is my son, my Ami." In the next moment he was in his son's strong embrace. When he stepped back, he had clearly come to his senses enough to realize what he had just said. He touched his son's arms, his face, even pushed an errant lock of hair back into place. "Ami? It is you, is it not?"

"It is I, Abba," Ami answered.

Qayafa began arguing with himself, arguing with all that he as a Sadducee had always believed. "But it cannot be you. I buried you just a few months past."

Ami grinned. "I know, Abba, but I have been sent to speak to you."

Moshe had moved toward his father who met him halfway across the chamber floor. The two enfolded each other in a long and tender embrace. When at last they parted, Naqdimon's eyes were filled with tears of profound happiness. They were also filled with the reflection of his son.

"My son, my only son!" he began. "Let me look at you." He held Moshe at arm's length and surveyed his form from head to toe. "It is you. It is really you and you are well."

"I am well, my father," Moshe assured.

Then Naqdimon remembered the terrible wrong he had committed against his son. He hoped, he prayed that perhaps it wasn't too late to set it right. "Moshe, there is something I must tell you. I never told you before and I was wrong, so wrong. The Holy One be praised who has given me another chance. Please, my son, forgive a foolish old man for his fear and for his cowardice."

"It is you who must forgive me, Abba. There is a secret I kept from you before and I should not have done so. That is why I am here."

Ami interrupted. "I as well, Abba. There is something Moshe and I never told either of you. We have come to tell you now."

When the four were settled into chairs, the young men looked at each other, unsure how to begin. It was Moshe who finally did.

"I hardly know where to start. It happened one Shabbat. Ami and I had nothing to do. You know, Abba, there really never was much to do in the city on Shabbat," he added in an aside that brought tolerant smiles to the faces of both fathers. "Anyway, in our boredom we did something we should never have done." Moshe looked self-consciously at his father as Ami continued the narrative.

"We went to the pool by the sheep gate, the one called Beit Zata. You know the place, Abba, the cistern with all of those porches and all of those stairs, the one where all those sick people wait for an angel to stir the water so they can get healed, or so they think." Ami rolled his eyes to indicate his opinion of the practice.

Qayafa knew both the place and the superstition well. He had no use for either.

Ami looked down into his lap, embarrassed by the confession he was about to make. "We went there just to make fun of them, the sick people I mean. We were going to toss a pebble into the pool and watch them all come running. Then we were going to have a good laugh. All the boys used to do it."

Naqdimon and Qayafa exchanged glances that asked

the silent question, What is this younger generation coming to? though neither said a word.

"But we didn't do it, Abba," Moshe interjected quickly. "We never had the chance."

Naqdimon appeared relieved.

Moshe continued. "When we arrived He was already there, the One called Yeshua."

Qayafa became agitated at the mere mention of Yeshua's name. "Do not speak to me of that Man," he ordered.

Ami placed a hand on his father's arm. "But we must speak of Him, Abba. He's the One who has sent us to you. He's the One we have come to tell you about."

An irritated wave of Qayafa's hand told his son he would hold his peace.

"He was just walking through. We waited to see what He would do," Ami recounted.

"The truth is we didn't want any witnesses," Moshe admitted.

Ami nodded guiltily then went on. "He stopped by a very old man who looked as if he had been lying there practically forever. Then Yeshua told him to pick up his mat and walk. Moshe and I just looked at each other. We thought His joke was even meaner than ours."

Moshe nodded his agreement. "When we looked back," Moshe said incredulously, "the old man actually did it! He rolled up his mat, put it under his arm, and walked away. We couldn't believe it! He just got up and left like he'd never been sick at all!"

Naqdimon and Qayafa looked at each other with mutual wonderment in their eyes.

"Is that what you came to tell us?" Qayafa asked in an exasperated tone. "We've heard such stories about this Yeshua before. I never placed much faith in them. Maybe it was just as you said. Maybe the man was never really ill at all."

"No, Abba, there is more," Ami answered, "much more."

Moshe was bubbling with the excitement of it even after the passage of so much time and he could not wait to continue. "After He left, we followed Him," Moshe added, sounding every bit the spy. "We followed Him to the Temple. By the time we got close enough to hear, He was talking about people being raised from the dead. Ami and I just stared at each other like the Man must be crazy."

Ami nodded his head rapidly, then continued the tale. "Then He said that whoever heard Him and believed in the One that sent Him could live forever."

"That's not all He said," Moshe interrupted. "He said the time was coming when the dead would hear His voice and live." Moshe turned to his father. "Abba, that's just what happened to us. After seeing Him make that man well, Ami and I decided He really must be Messiah. We believed Him, believed *in* Him, and it was as if something inside of us, something in our spirits, was reborn. That's the reason we are here with you right now."

Qayafa groaned. "My son, my own son!"

At the word, reborn, the light began to dawn for Naqdimon. For all these months he had been grieving because he had thought that his son was lost forever, all because he had never told him about Yeshua, all because he had waited too long. Now he knew Moshe had met Yeshua, too, all on his own. And he was born again, too! "My son, my very own son," he rejoiced as he wrapped Moshe in his arms. "Why did you never tell me, Moshe?" he finally asked.

Shame washed over Moshe's face. "We were afraid. We heard Ami's father talking about Yeshua once and we knew he didn't like Him. We didn't want to start any trouble so we just didn't say anything. We just followed Him around whenever He was in Yerushalayim but we never spoke of Him to anyone but each other."

Naqdimon laughed aloud. *The perfect irony of it!* he thought. *I was afraid to tell Moshe because I knew how close he was to Ami and he was afraid to tell me because he knew how closely I worked with Qayafa.* "And now you have come to share this story with us so we might come to know Him as well?" Naqdimon queried.

"No, Abba." Moshe took his father's hand, his face illuminated by a fervor Naqdimon had never seen in him before. "I already knew you had received Him as Messiah. Yeshua Himself assured me of that. He allowed me to return for just a little while so that I could assure you that I had received Him, too. He said you needed to know."

Naqdimon embraced his son again. "It has been my privilege to believe in Him and to walk with Him for three years now, my son. Yes, He is my Lord and my Messiah, too. But it was the greatest grief of my soul to think that you were lost because of my failure to tell my own beloved son the good news of His coming. It is only the great gift of His grace that He has now permitted me to know the precious peace of your own salvation, Moshe."

"Oh, Abba," Moshe exulted. "Praise be to the Holy One for His goodness to us all."

Naqdimon went on, "All these months, I have been tortured by the thought that I waited too long, that I never told you about Him, that I never gave you a chance to know Him."

Moshe's face broke into a rapturous smile. "He sent me to stop your torment, Abba."

Naqdimon embraced his son, holding him to his breast, bathing him in his tears, wrapping him in his praise to the Holy One.

When they parted, Moshe turned to Qayafa. "Our return must also be for your sake, Excellency," he said as he faced Qayafa, "or the Holy One would not have sent both of us."

"Yes, Abba," Ami agreed. "It must be that the Holy One has sent us to tell you our story, too, just so you can know Yeshua as Messiah."

Naqdimon had never seen Yosef ben Qayafa look more miserable. It was as if his wonderful world of power and position had just come apart in front of him. Naqdimon realized that in a very real way, it had.

Qayafa spoke through teeth clenched in pain, the pain of a soul undone. "You do not understand, Ami. I just had your so-called Messiah crucified. I had Him killed."

Ami's eyes grew tender as he reached out to his father. "I know, Abba. We both know. But just as the lambs were slain for Pesach, He had to die then, too. He had to shed His own blood and give His own life so that we, all of us, could be spared just like the fathers were spared on that first Pesach. Do you not see, Abba? It was all a part of His plan. In your hatred of Him, you did nothing more than carry it out. But He is now risen just as we are risen. And He would not have sent us if there were no hope for you. He still loves you, Abba, and He still wants to give you the same eternal life that He has given us. All you have to do is believe in Him, to accept Him as Messiah just as we have done."

"No ... no ... no," Qayafa cried out. "I cannot. Do you not understand? I have been a Sadducee from my birth. I have staked my life, my priesthood, everything I have, on proving Him a fraud and having Him executed. And I succeeded. He is dead! He is dead, I tell you."

Ami interrupted. "With all respect, Abba, He is no more dead than we are. We are the living proof that He has triumphed over death."

Qayafa thought of the many times in the past few days that he had used that same word, triumph, to speak of his victory over Yeshua. Now his own son was using that very word against him. "No, it is too late for me. What am I to do? Am I to tell everyone that I made a mistake, that I accidently crucified the Messiah we have all been awaiting for centuries? No, this is not possible. If I were to do a thing such as that, I would lose my priesthood anyway. Do you not understand, my son?"

"But, Abba," Ami answered, his tone desperate, pleading. "If you do not accept Yeshua, you will lose your soul. Do you not understand that?"

"No, my son. The Holy One will never permit such a thing," Qayafa reasoned. "Have I not served Him well and for a very long time? Have I not offered up the sacrifices in His name? Has He not even seen fit to set me above all others as the high priest of all Yisrael? No, my son, the Holy One will look upon me with favor in this life and I can never believe in any other life. No, I cannot accept this dead Yeshua as Messiah."

"Abba, please reconsider," Ami begged. "Do you not see? Messiah Yeshua sent us to prove to you that He alone holds the keys of life and death. You made many sacrifices but He made the last one. It is He in whom you must now believe. Please, Abba."

Qayafa brushed away his son's appeal with a quick movement of his hand and a chuckle. "No, my son. It is as I have said. Yeshua is dead. I, the high priest of all Yisrael, have spoken. That means it is so. I do not know what power has brought you here; it may be nothing more than my own tormented mind. But I will never believe it was Yeshua."

Moshe laid a comforting hand on his friend's shoulder. With it came a silent message, *We must trust Him to find your father someday just as He found us.*

The boys stood and Moshe spoke for them. "As we said, our time here is short. We must soon be leaving but before we go, we wish to see our mothers. Then there is one other place here in the city we must go, to the marriage of one of Yeshua's countrymen whom we met as we followed Him about the city. You may come with us if you wish."

"No, no, I will remain here ... at my post," Qayafa replied too quickly. It was clear he wanted to be free of the conviction his son had placed upon him, free of his troubling presence that contradicted everything he had always believed. And he wanted that even more than he wanted to be with his son for whatever time might remain.

Naqdimon shook his head sadly, then turned to Moshe. "I will come with you, my son. I want to be with you for every moment of the time we have left."

Ami gazed at his father one last time. Somehow, he knew he would never see him again, neither in this life nor the next. Still he had the peace of knowing that Yeshua had given his abba this last opportunity. He also knew that everyone must be free to make his own decision just as he had done on that long-ago Shabbat.

"Abba," he began softly. "I never got a chance to say good-bye before. At least this time, I can." Qayafa turned to his son, his self-deception evident in his eyes. "Goodbye, Abba," Ami whispered softly. His words were heavy, weighted, for he knew that this was their final farewell.

When Qayafa replied, it was almost as if Ami would be home in time for supper, as if they would be parted for only a few moments instead of for all eternity. "Goodbye, my son," he said lightly. Then he turned away and stared into space as the three left the chamber together.

Malluch turned away and wept softly for the deadly darkness of soul and spirit that had descended upon his master. As Ami passed by and placed a gentle hand upon his shoulder to comfort him, he spoke. "May I come with you, my lord? I also know Yeshua and I, too, want to be with you for as long as you may have."

Ami embraced his boyhood friend. "Come, my brother."

Naqdimon and the boys stopped in the doorway and turned for one last glimpse of the exalted high priest of all Yisrael. He sat slumped in his lordly chair with his head in his hands. He was a man undone, a man whose entire life had been proven worthless, a man to be feared no longer. Yosef ben Qayafa was now only a man to be pitied.

❧ 50 ❧

ELP Saba," Yael whispered as she rushed to her grandfather's side.

In his memory, Rabbi Levi was transported back in time, back to another day in this very room, back to the day tiny Yael had found her grandfather hunched over his scrolls and offered to "help Saba." He had loved her then; he loved her even more now.

Rabbi Levi's breathing slowed and became less labored, more rhythmic. His eyes were fixed on Yael, on her perfect beauty, her polished grace. He filled his eyes, his mind, his very heart with her. Finally he spoke, "Am I to die, Yael? Have you come to take me into the presence of our fathers?"

Yael smiled and kissed him on the forehead. "No, Saba. You are very much alive and so am I. It is into the presence of Another that I have come to lead you."

"Is it really you, Yael?" Aaron asked.

"Yes, Abba, it is I. Touch me and you will see." She held out her arms to them.

Naomi reached out a tentative hand to touch her daughter's, then fell into her arms. Aaron embraced both his wife and his child in his long arms. Suddenly everyone was crying, weeping with the joy of banished grief.

When they had recovered, Rabbi Levi spoke again. Always as a rabbi, he had sought answers to the great questions of life ... and death. His mind now sought some understanding of the miracle before him. "How can this thing be, my child? I was with you at the instant you were taken from us. I saw you laid in the tomb. I have grieved beside it many days since. How is it that you are here with us again?"

"Saba," she began tenderly, "the Holy One has seen you pouring over your scrolls morning, noon, and night, in daylight and by lamplight. He has led you as you have searched for Him. He knows your heart and He knows the great love for Him that abides there."

Tears formed in the corners of the rabbi's eyes. "Yes, my child. Always the Holy One has been the one great and constant passion of my life. Always it has been my desire to love Him and to serve Him. And ever it shall be so."

"He knows, Saba," she assured Him. "But He also knows that somewhere along the way, you strayed from the path that He wanted you to walk. He had a great and glorious revelation for you. He had prepared you for this revelation by imparting to you a longing for Messiah. To you, it might have been shown the identity of Messiah. You might have received Him. You might have proclaimed Him to His people."

Rabbi Levi became agitated. "Child, you speak of these things as though they were past. Still I long for Messiah. Still I long to know Him. Still I would proclaim Him to His people. Is it too late?"

"But you did know Him, Saba," Yael asserted. "His name was ..."

"Tell me, Child," Rabbi Levi pleaded. "Tell me and I will yet proclaim Him to the whole world."

Yael smiled again. "His name was Yeshua, Saba, Yeshua ben Yosef. Do you not know this Man? Do you not know the Son of the Holy One?"

The rabbi slumped into his chair as if his very life had been sucked out of him. He covered his face with old wrinkled hands. "No ... no ... it cannot be," he sobbed. "The Shema ... the Shema. Do you not remember the blessed words? You yourself heard me repeat them every morning ... every evening ... all the years you lived. The first words of the Shema say the Lord our God is one Lord. It cannot be otherwise, Yael. He cannot have a Son if He is only one."

"Ah, but have you not read in your scrolls of the day that our father, Avraham, sat in his tent door and the Holy One visited Him? Have you not read that the Lord came in the person of three Men? There were three Men, Saba, but our father, Avraham recognized Them and called Them the Lord. He was one Lord but He approached our father as three Men."

Rabbi Levi remembered the passage well. Still his mind puzzled over Yael's interpretation. "Three? How can He be three yet still be one? I do not understand how this is possible."

Yael went on, confident in the perfected knowledge which had been imparted to her. "In the same way you could be a father and a grandfather and a rabbi all at the same time. Are you not one? Yet are you not also three? The Holy One, too, is One yet Three, just like you. He is the Father, the Holy One to whom we have always prayed. But He is also the Spirit of God, the Shekinah glory that once filled the ancient Tabernacle with smoke, the glory before Whom mortal man could not stand. And He is the Son, Messiah Yeshua, the One who walked with our fathers in the fiery furnace. These were the very Three Who met with our father, Avraham. They are the Three that still want to meet with us now. And Messiah Yeshua made that possible."

Yael came to her grandfather's side. She wrapped her arms around him and placed his head on her soft shoulder, comforting him as he wept. When he finally looked up into her face, she spoke to him quietly, soothingly. "Yes, Saba, Yeshua is the Son of the Holy One; He is Messiah. Do you not remember that day on Solomon's Porch, the day I met Him?"

Through his tear-stained face, the light of recognition shown. "I remember. I thought He had harmed you. I thought He had driven you mad. And then when you died ... He had claimed to heal so many. If He was Messiah, why did He not heal you?"

Yael glowed as she answered. "He did, Saba. He healed me inside where it really mattered. He didn't take away my scar on the outside, not then, but He took away all the scars on the inside from all the hurts and unkind words and frightened stares. He didn't heal my body then but He healed my soul. And He did it with a few simple words. He fixed His gaze on me. He saw me, really saw me. Then He told me I was beautiful to Him and He said, 'I love you.' He said it so softly, so gently, yet I knew He meant every word. I could see the love in His eyes, the same kind of love I always saw in yours. I knew my scar didn't matter to Him any more than it mattered to you. In that moment, I knew exactly who He was. He was love and I gave Him my heart. And now, Saba, He has taken away my scar as well. Because you see, Saba, the only scars allowed in Heaven ... are His."

"I thought He had hurt you and I was so angry with Him for hurting such a small wounded child. Then I became even more angry at Him for failing to heal you as He had claimed to heal so many others."

"You were grieving, Saba. You needed to believe what happened to me was someone's fault. But do you not see? It was not. It was meant to be thus. Since the Holy One could reach you no other way, He reached you through me, through my return even after death."

Rabbi Levi was distraught now. He tossed his head as though trying to escape some terrible truth that insisted on remaining right before his eyes. "But if what you say is true ..."

"It is, Saba. I promise you it is."

"Then I am lost forever. I am without hope."

Yael came to his side. "No, Saba. If there were no hope I would not be here."

"But you do not know what I have done," he insisted,

becoming pale and agitated, his eyes revealing the terror in his heart. "I betrayed Him to them, Yael. I was the one who found Yehuda. I was the one who took him to the high priest. If it were not for me He would never have been arrested or tried or found guilty or sentenced to death." Rabbi Levi grasped his granddaughter's hands as though he were reaching for a lifeline. "Yael, if it were not for me He would never even have been crucified. I killed Him! I killed Messiah Yeshua!"

"I know, Saba," Yael said quietly. "I know and the Holy One knows. And, Saba, He loves you anyway. Messiah Yeshua loves you anyway, just as He loves me."

In his anguish at what he had done, Rabbi Levi hardly heard his granddaughter's reassurances. His voice barely a whisper, he concluded. "Yael, if it were not for me He would still be alive."

Yael's face broke into a glorious smile as she knelt at his side. "Oh, but He is, Saba. Yeshua is alive! He has risen from the dead and He is alive forevermore."

Rabbi Levi stared at his granddaughter incredulously.

"Saba, that is what I came to tell you. He is alive and He loves you just as He always has, just as He loved me that day. Don't you see, Saba? Scars on the outside, scars on the inside ... they are all the same to Him. There is no scar He can't heal, no sin He can't forgive."

"He would still forgive me, even now, even after what I have done to Him?" Rabbi Levi asked even more incredulously.

"Especially now, Saba. You see, that is why He died. He didn't die because of your plan; He died because of His plan. He gave Himself to die just so He could offer you the forgiveness you seek."

Rabbi Levi looked baffled. It would have been easy for him to understand Yeshua's anger, even His vengeance. But what he could not understand was His forgiveness.

Yael sensed his inner turmoil. "Saba, you have read your

scrolls for many years. Do they not tell you that the Holy One gave us the sacrifices to atone for our sins?"

"Yes, the sacrifices," Rabbi Levi stammered. "The sacrifices atone for our sins," he repeated almost mechanically as he mentally reached for something he could finally grasp.

"Indeed they do," Yael agreed. "They atone for our sins, they cover our sins, but they could never take away our sins. Is that not what you taught me yourself in this very room when I was but a child and I asked you why all those sweet little lambs had to be killed?"

"Yes," the rabbi said, recalling those halcyon days.

"You told me it was because we human beings kept sinning, didn't you, Saba? We kept sinning and needing to sacrifice more and more innocent animals, didn't we?"

"Yes," Rabbi Levi answered again.

"The sacrifices were never meant to be an end in themselves; they were meant to be only a prediction, a prophecy, of what the Holy One meant to do for us when Messiah came.

"I know you always thought that Messiah would defeat the Romans. You told me about it so many times and I could see the wonder of it mirrored in your eyes. But, Saba, He didn't come to conquer men's armies; He came to conquer their hearts. He didn't come to free us from Rome; He came to free us from sin."

Rabbi Levi was now listening intently, trying to comprehend, trying to put together all the pieces of the puzzle as Yael laid them before him.

"So you see, Saba, it was always the Holy One's plan for Messiah to give His life as a sacrifice for us. When Yeshua died, Saba, He became the last Pesach Lamb we would ever need. He became the final sacrifice for our sin. His blood not only atones for our sin, not only covers our sin, it takes away our sin. And His blood takes that sin away forever."

"But, Yael, my sin is so great ... so terrible ... . First I hated Him. Then I contrived to kill Him. And at the end, Yael, I stood at the foot of His cross and mocked Him. I mocked Him as He was dying ... dying for me. He could never forgive so great a sin as that."

Yael put her small arms around her grandfather. "Saba, there is no sin so great that He cannot forgive it. That's why He came. That's why He sent me back to you ... to tell you He knows all about you, all about what you've done, and He loves you anyway. And, Saba, the best news of all is ... He stands ready to forgive you even now."

"How can He love me, Yael? How can I find His forgiveness?" the old rabbi begged.

The sun rose in Yael's face. That was exactly the question she had been waiting to hear, exactly the question she knew the Holy One was waiting to hear. "All you have to do is ask Him, Saba. Just ask Him. You believed in the sacrifices before; believe in this one. Believe in the sacrifice Messiah Yeshua made and you will be forgiven."

Suddenly it all made sense, all he had studied in all of his scrolls, all he had seen atop Golgotha's hill. Suddenly he could see the omnipotent hand of the Holy One in all of it, from the first animal the Holy One Himself had sacrificed in Eden's paradise to make clothes for sinful man and woman, to the last Sacrifice the Holy One Himself made to provide forgiveness for the sins of all the men and women of all the ages, and for him as well. And suddenly Rabbi Levi wanted that forgiveness more than he had ever wanted anything in all his life.

"I do believe," he whispered softly, his eyes tightly shut against his tears. It was as much a prayer as a declaration. "I do believe in Messiah Yeshua and I do believe in the sacrifice He made for me."

In the next moment, Rabbi Levi came to understand exactly what Yael had felt on that long-ago day on Solomon's Porch. His soul found the same healing she had described. The hatred, the anger, the bitterness, the rage were all gone and in their place Rabbi Levi found the greatest peace he had ever known. The old rabbi was enveloped by the greatest love he had ever felt.

When at last Rabbi Levi opened his eyes, he saw that Aaron and Naomi were kneeling beside him and he knew that they had found that love and peace, too. Above them all, Yael shone with the joy of a family found.

"I love you all but my time with you is short," Yael said finally. "And, Saba, do you not have a wedding to attend?"

ITH Dinah's help, Hannah braided her long yellow hair, put on her blue bridal veil that accented the clear blue of her eyes, and smoothed a wrinkle from the beautiful blue and white wedding garment that had been embellished with the neat stitches of her mother's embroidery.

Hannah wore no cosmetic of any kind and little jewelry for her family owned little, just a few bracelets and necklaces and the headdress composed of ten small coins which would forever tell the world that she was a wife. On her hand there was only the gold ring that sealed her betrothal. Still her beauty was no longer dependent on such superficial things; her beauty now radiated from within.

Hannah examined her reflection in the lookingglass. *This must be what Ammah looked like when she wed Abba,* she thought. *And this must be what the virgin daughters of King David looked like in their blue and white robes.* She suddenly felt at one with all that had gone before and all that would come after.

When Hannah emerged from the bedchamber, Abba was waiting to escort her down the stairs and into her future. He opened his arms and she rushed into them. "Thank you, Abba," she murmured as she buried her face in his shoulder just as she had done on that ghastly day so long ago. "Thank you for bringing me to Messiah Yeshua and thank you for giving me to David."

Itzak laughed that same resounding laugh she had always loved so much and hugged her to him. "Thank you,

my child, for fulfilling every dream of a father's heart."
As they held each other, he looked heavenward and whispered one more word of gratitude. "And thank You, Lord. Even above the raging storm, You heard my final prayer and You have answered it."

In the room below, David was waiting for Hannah, resplendent in a beautiful tunic and robe that Dinah had embroidered with golden palms and fruits and flowers, symbols of the fruitfulness with which she hoped the Holy One would bless their union. Dinah beamed her overwhelming joy at the marriage of the two children she loved so much and at the presence of the husband she had adored all of her life.

Since they were not in Capernaum and David was staying just across the courtyard with her Uncle Elihu's brother, Hannah's procession could not end according to tradition at the home of her husband. Instead it had been arranged that the procession would wind through the narrow streets of the Lower City of Yerushalayim and end back in the broad courtyard between the two houses where the wedding feast had been prepared.

David opened the gate to the street. He touched Hannah's hand and smiled at her, his smile radiating the love for her that had always been in his heart. As she walked through the gate before him, David closed his eyes and with tears of happiness flooding them, he began to pour out words of praise and adoration to the Holy One who had intervened just in time and in a most miraculous way to make this day exactly what he had always longed for it to be, the day he would wed a woman who loved him as much as he loved her. Now she would be his forever. He worshipped before the only One who could have accomplished so great a miracle of love.

As the couple stepped into the street, the music began. Behind them, Dinah and Itzak stepped into the presence of family members and friends of long years past, along with many of their friends and neighbors from Capernaum.

Those assembled gasped almost in unison when they saw Itzak alive and well and attending his only daughter on her wedding day. Stunned faces followed them as they began their march. They knew they were witnessing more than a marriage; they were witnessing a miracle.

Micah, the twins, and the younger boys, who were to go before their sister distributing little gifts of food and sweets to the people along the way, crowded around their father once again, hugging him, kissing him. Even the youngest who had been so small when his father had been taken from him, ran to Itzak and held up his arms to his abba. Itzak's booming laughter welcomed them all into his arms for just a moment. Then he sent them on their way to precede their sister on the most momentous walk of her life.

Elisheba, ready with the flowers she would strew along the route, observed the scene with tears in her eyes. She knew she was seeing a miracle, too, a miracle only the Holy One could have performed. And she believed this miracle had come just to bless the wedding of her cousin. Her young heart swelled with happiness for Hannah and with love for the Holy One.

Itzak's brothers and nephews, along with Ruth and Elihu's sons, carried flaming torches to light the way through the dusky narrow streets. They looked on in wonder as Itzak strode past, their flickering torches reflected in the tears which washed across their happy faces.

The sun was dipping low in the evening sky and the stars would soon begin to show their faces, winking in place, smiling down upon Hannah as she walked happy and resolute toward her destiny. Her fears were gone now and her doubts had disappeared. She more than believed; she knew. She knew the Holy One also smiled upon her and upon her union as well. She knew He had made David just for her and that He had made her just for her David. She knew that they loved each other with their whole hearts and that they both loved the same Messiah. She knew that no matter what the future held, she was secure in the love and protection of both her Lord and her husband. She walked into that future with confidence.

As they moved forward, people gathered to watch them pass. Then, as was the custom, all who could turned in behind the bridal couple and their invited guests to attend their marriage feast. Some clapped in time to the music. Others sang the psalms of praise played by the pipers. Little girls told Hannah how beautiful she looked and little boys stood in awe of her. Men hailed her beauty and her virginity while women tossed flowers and wished her many healthy children.

The scene swam before Hannah in a sea of her own tears of joy. Never before had she felt so completely enveloped by love, the love of her David, the love of her family, the love of her friends, the love of her abba, and the love of her Lord. Except that she couldn't wait to become David's wife, Hannah would never have wanted it all to end.

When the throng of happy celebrants arrived at the courtyard, Rabbi Levi waited to welcome them, standing with a lovely young woman who called him "Saba" and a beaming couple who called him "Abba." David took one appraising look at him and saw that this was not the same angry rabbi he had seen on Golgotha's hill; somehow he was different now and David thought he just might know why.

Others had gathered, too; some Hannah knew, some were new to her. There was an elderly gentleman with a long grey beard who stood with three young men and an older woman. He was introduced to her father as Naqdimon of the Sanhedrin. He presented his wife, Sarah, his son, Moshe, the son of the high priest, Ami ben Qayafa, and Ami's servant, Malluch. Hannah and David were both surprised and honored by their attendance.

Two young couples came toward them to offer their blessings and Hannah wondered if she would remember the names of Yakov and Shoshana, Yonah and Devorah. She knew she would always remember the beautiful little baby girl in Shoshana's arms. Her name was Abigail.

When it was time for the ceremony to begin, David and Hannah stepped under a flowered canopy and took their places before Rabbi Levi. On a small table, an official-looking document, the Keturah, awaited David's signature. Hannah looked at the square angular writing which obligated David to work for her, honor her, keep her, and care for her according to the manner of a man in Yisrael. It was an enormous promise to make and an even more enormous promise to keep all the days of one's life. But David took up the pen without hesitation and signed his name in bold strokes.

Then came the traditional hand-washing for which a shiny silver bowl and pitcher had been provided. David and Hannah held hands above the bowl as the rabbi poured water over them to symbolize washing one's hands of all that had gone before and entering into one's new life in purity of both mind and body. David and Hannah loved each other with their eyes as the old ceremony was performed anew, now truly willing to leave their old lives behind forever, to come together as one for the new life the Holy One and His Son, Yeshua, had before them.

Rabbi Levi lifted a silver goblet containing new wine high above the bridal couple. Then he began his benediction, his prayer for the blessing of the Holy One to rest upon Hannah and David. He seemed nearly overwhelmed as he started to pray, almost as though he found himself in the presence of the Lord the moment he closed his eyes, for indeed he did.

Soon Hannah and David would take their first sip from the same cup representing the cup of life in which they were now united for all time. Whatever came, they knew they would face it together.

As Micah watched, he thought about the wedding feast. It would begin as soon as the rabbi said "Amen." The tables were filled with more delicacies than he had ever imagined. His Aunt Ruth had made most of them with the help of his mother and cousin. Their joint labors had been filling the house with wonderful scents and smells for days. His mouth watered in anticipation. He wondered if the rabbi would drone on endlessly.

As the benediction ended, the rabbi raised his frail hand high above the happy couple and intoned the familiar words that would unite them forever, "Take her according to the Law of Moshe and of Yisrael." With that, Hannah and David were officially wed.

At that moment, Elisheba, Hannah's only attendant, and Micah, the little brother in the Lord David had chosen to be his friend of the groom, stepped behind them and crowned them with garlands of fresh, fragrant flowers.

Suddenly the air in the courtyard came alive with a power, a presence that everyone felt though none could explain. A vapor, a smoke settled over the entire gathering but particularly around the bridegroom and his beautiful young bride. Then the light of the processional torches faded in the face of a translucent brilliance that stood just behind Rabbi Levi. People gasped, their eyes wide with wonder, as the light seemed to fuse itself into the form of a Man clad in glistening white, a Man with scars in His hands, His feet, and just above His brow. His hands were extended as if He, too, wished to bless the young couple before Him. His voice thundered through the courtyard. "My children, I, Yeshua, now join your hearts as one in My love. Go in peace and My peace shall go with you." David and Hannah looked up into His gentle face, His loving eyes, and immediately fell to their knees in worship.

Rabbi Levi turned, recognized the risen Yeshua, and bowed before Him, too. "My Lord and my God, my Messiah," was all he could say.

Yeshua placed His right hand on the rabbi's head, smiled, and spoke. "I knew we would meet again, you and

I, and I knew you would believe. I love you and I forgive you all. Welcome, My son."

Rabbi Levi wept at His feet for the joy of his salvation. He recalled that day so many years before when he and Shimon had confessed their sin before the old rabbi and known the peace of sins forgiven. That was as nothing when compared with this.

Throughout the courtyard and the street beyond not one of the five hundred present remained standing. There was not one who doubted that they were all in the presence of the Lord. Each one had fallen before His power and now knelt in His presence. Most were praying, praising, weeping before their Messiah.

In the front of the crowd, Yael wept, too. Her time was almost over but it had been even more wonderful than she had expected. Now she was ready to go home. She wrapped her parents in a final farewell. Then she leaned close enough to her grandfather to whisper, "I love you, Saba, and I will see you soon."

Itzak drew his sons around him and wrapped them all in the warmth of his love, whispering words of encouragement and love to each of them. Then he bid them farewell as he had not been able to do on that awful day so long ago. Somehow they understood. There were no tears because he was leaving them, only smiles of joy that he had come. He cupped Dinah's face in his palm, held her one last time with his eyes, and kissed her gently. For a long moment, there were no words spoken between them. After all their years, no words were needed. Just before he left, he promised, "I will wait for you, my love."

"And I will come to you ... and to Him," Dinah promised.

Moshe drew Naqdimon into his arms. "It won't be long, Abba. Then we shall be together for all eternity. I'll be waiting for you."

Naqdimon nodded, too filled with emotion to speak.

He turned to Ami, kneeling all alone. "Maybe in time ..." Naqdimon tried to encourage.

Ami shook his head sadly. He knew better. His earthly father would never be coming to meet him but he knew that his heavenly Father would. Somehow that was enough.

Shoshana turned to Yakov and held him for a long moment with their child between them. She tried to put all the love of a lifetime into one final embrace. Yonah clasped Devorah to him, then held her at arm's length as though memorizing the moment.

Finally Shoshana took Yakov's hand as Yonah took Devorah's. They placed the two together. "Love each other well. Love each other for us," Shoshana whispered. "Then we will all meet once more and we will never be separated again, not from Him and not from each other."

Shoshana placed her daughter in Devorah's arms, then turned back to her husband. "And, Yakov, be sure and tell our daughter of Him."

He nodded his promise.

At the motion of Yeshua's outstretched hands, Shoshana and Yonah, Moshe and Ami, Itzak and Yael stood and moved toward Him. In an instant they were gone, beyond the crowded courtyard, beyond the gate, beyond the street, beyond the wall of the city.

As they made their way toward the same cemetery near the Garden of Gethsemane from which they had all come, others joined them, others who had known both the pain of death and the joy of resurrection, others who had come for just a little while to attend to matters that had been left unfinished at their deaths.

When all had gathered, Messiah Yeshua smiled down upon them and extended His nail-scarred hands. "You have all done well. Now come, My children," He beckoned, "and I will lead you home."

EPILOGUE

OD'S Word tells us that on the day of His resurrection, Messiah Yeshua, Jesus, brought others with Him, others who went into the Holy City of Jerusalem and appeared to many. We can only wonder what took place then, who they were, who they may have seen and whose lives they may have touched by their coming. This book is nothing more than one imagining, one pale possibility of what might have occurred then. No one knows of a certainty.

We do know of a certainty that this will never happen again. We do not have the luxury of waiting until one returns from the grave to be convinced of our sin or to believe in Jesus for our salvation. The next time the dead in Christ rise it will be at the sound of the last trumpet of God. Because this is so, there are some lessons we might take from this story.

Itzak and Hannah would have us understand that one never knows when he will spend a last moment with a loved one. They would tell us to resolve our conflicts quickly so that if death should come before we meet again, we would carry no guilt, we would feel no remorse, we would not be left to wish for one more "Goodbye," one more "I'm sorry," one more "I love you." Christ came to bring reconciliation, to reconcile us to God and to reconcile us to each other. Accept that reconciliation. Let it flow into your heart, into your life, and into your relationships.

Yakov and Shoshana, Yonah and Devorah want us to know that even when death ends relationships here in this world, the Lord has planned new relationships to encourage and sustain us along the way. There truly is life after loss, no matter how great that loss may be. Reach out for it and embrace it. Those who loved you would want you to know love again and when you join them in eternity, you will all meet together joyously as children of the heavenly King.

Naqdimon, or Nicodemus as some call him, would tell us not to wait to share Messiah with another. No reason will be important enough, no excuse good enough should we lose that precious one to death before we summon the courage to speak. The years of regret that stretch ahead of us can be long and anguished. Tell them the Good News now.

Rabbi Levi and Yael want to tell you that it is never too late. No matter how old or how young you are, no matter what you have done, no matter how scarred your life, no matter how great your sin, Jesus still loves you, He still died for you, and He still stands ready to forgive you. If you don't know Him yet, the rabbi would be happy to make the introductions. Just do what he did; accept Jesus, accept His sacrifice, accept His forgiveness and it will be yours. He waits, His arms open wide, to welcome you.

And what about Qayafa, or Caiaphas as he is better known to history? What would he say to us if he could? He would no doubt tell us that there is nothing more important in this life or the next than knowing Jesus Christ as Saviour and Lord. What would he do with Jesus who is called the Christ if he had one more opportunity?

What will you do with Christ today? He waits just now for your answer.

If you enjoyed this book by Susan Smith,
you will want to order:

Coming to Maturity
How to Grow Up in God

by
Stelman and Susan Smith

Coming to Maturity tells you how to grow up in
God. It takes you from coming out of bondage in
Exodus, through claiming your inheritance in
Joshua, to sitting down in heavenly places as a sol-
der of Christ in Ephesians. As you make this journey you will learn the secrets of spiritual growth
and maturity. But watch out! You might never be
the same again. This is the book that Judson
Cornwall said should be in every Christian's library.

Ask for it in your favorite bookstore or order directly from McDougal Publishing.